PRAISE FOR THE WRITING OF MICHAEL ROWE

Wild Fell

Finalist for the Shirley Jackson Award

"The mysteries of love and time haunt the beautifully wrought pages of Michael's Rowe's superb ghost story. . . . *Wild Fell* is supernatural fiction of the highest order." —Clive Barker

"An atmospheric ghost story that grips from the first page." —Tim Lebbon

Enter, Night

"Skillfully brings to mind the classic works of Stephen King and Robert McCammon. But the novel's breathtaking, wholly unexpected and surprisingly moving conclusion heralds the arrival of a major new talent." —Christopher Rice, author of *Burning Girl*

"With *Enter, Night,* Michael Rowe does the near impossible and rescues the modern vampire novel from its current state of mediocrity with his dead-on portrayal of the gothic small town, rich characters, and deeply frightening story." —Susie Moloney, bestselling author of *The Dwelling*

October

"Michael Rowe's talent shines through in this terrifying story of social persecution [and] black magic." —Lee Thomas, Lambda Literary and Bram Stoker Award–winning author

ENTER,
NIGHT

ENTER, NIGHT

A NOVEL

MICHAEL ROWE

OPEN ROAD

INTEGRATED MEDIA

NEW YORK

Copyright © 2011 by Michael Rowe

Cover design by Ian Koviak

ISBN: 978-1-5040-6395-1

This edition published in 2020 by Open Road Integrated Media, Inc.
180 Maiden Lane
New York, NY 10038
www.openroadmedia.com

For Brian McDermid, With all my love, now and always

And for Kate Davis Gyles and Michael Edward Gyles,
My two favourite things that go bump in the night

ENTER, NIGHT

But first on earth, as Vampyre sent, Thy corpse shall from its tomb be rent; Then ghastly haunt thy native place, And suck the blood of all thy race.

—Byron, "The Giaour"

In the general belief, however, there was but one land of shades for all alike. The spirits, in form and feature, as they had been in life, wended their way through dark forests to the villages of the dead, subsisting on bark and rotten wood. On arriving, they sat all day in the crouching position of the sick, and, when night came, hunted the shades of animals, with the shades of bows and arrows, among the shades of trees and rocks; for all things, animate and inanimate, were alike immortal, and all passed together to the gloomy country of the dead.

—Francis Parkman,
The Jesuits in North America in the Seventeenth Century

The past is never dead. It's not even past.

—William Faulkner, *Requiem for a Nun*

NIGHT DRIVING

CHAPTER ONE

Friday, September 22, 1972

The vampire in the dirty green army surplus jacket and cowboy hat boarded the Canada Northern Star Charter Lines bus from Ottawa to Sault Ste. Marie at noon.

Jim Marks, who had been driving for Northern Star for twenty-five years and would retire early at the end of October, looked sourly at this late arrival. He was tired of waiting and wanted to get the trip underway. It was a long one, and boring. The total driving time would be nearly eighteen hours. There would be a refuelling and dinner stop in Toronto at five p.m. and another in Sudbury later that night. He wished he'd joined one of the majors years ago, bus lines like Greyhound or Voyageur Colonial, with normal, civilized hours and routes instead of old charter dinosaurs like Northern. He was too old for this job. He felt every one of his forty-eight years tonight, and his ass in the driver's seat felt ninety.

"Ticket," Jim grunted, extending his hand. The vampire gave him the ticket. Jim tore off the driver's half and handed the remaining portion back.

Jim, of course, didn't see a vampire. He saw a filthy hippie.

In fairness to the vampire, any man with hair below his collar looked like a filthy hippie to Jim Marks. The world was crazy.

Between the hippies down in the States and that commie Jane Fonda carrying on over in Viet Nam and all the drugs and weird music— never mind the fact that you couldn't tell the boys from the girls anymore—the planet was going to hell in a handbasket. If Jim Marks was the Prime Minister of Canada, the first thing he'd institute was mandatory haircuts for every male over the age of five.

The vampire took the ticket and moved down the aisle. His hockey bag banged against the metal armrests a couple of times. Jim resisted the urge to tell him to be careful. There was nothing to be careful of, but the metallic noise was annoying and Jim already had a headache and a long night drive ahead of him.

None of the other passengers noticed the vampire as he passed. No one notices anyone on buses unless they are exceptionally beautiful or handsome, or dangerous-looking, or extremely fat—in which case the potential seatmate can look forward to a very long, very uncomfortable ride. The vampire was none of these things. He was entirely nondescript—a bit more dishevelled-looking than the average bus passenger, maybe a little dirty, but not remarkably so for a passenger on a night bus through the mining towns of northern Ontario. He seeped into his seat near the back of the bus like cigarette smoke and settled in for the ride north. For all intents and purposes, he might have been a ghost—felt rather than seen, whose passage might have been marked at most by a momentary waft of air. Or, marked by nothing at all. He wasn't sure what people felt as he passed, but he did like to imagine the worst.

In his seat near the back, the vampire covered his eyes with the brim of his cowboy hat and laid his head against the window. He closed his eyes and tried to sleep. If he slept, he would dream. If he dreamed—as he now could again, since he'd stopped taking the pills that flattened out his thoughts, rendering his movements turgid and his dreams uneventful and quiet—the voice would come to him and tell him what to do next. The voice did come to him, and he smiled in his sleep as he listened.

In Toronto five hours later, the vampire got out and stretched his legs. It was raining.

He ordered a hamburger, fries, and a Coke at a greasy spoon on Edward Street, not far from the bus depot, so he could keep his eye on it. He left his hockey bag on the seat, knowing that no one would look inside. He looked through the windows of the diner and watched the cold sluice down, dirty waterfalls of greasy urban soot against the glass. His gaze flickered up to the darkening argentite sky. The rain was intensifying. By his calculations—and he was nothing if not obsessively fastidious about facts—the moon had been ninety-seven percent full last night and would be entirely full when it rose tonight, and remain so through Saturday as he completed his voyage north. While the rain and clouds might try to hide it, the full moon would still be there. The vampire would know. He'd feel it rise and he would grow stronger and stronger.

When the vampire was finished eating his hamburger, he took out the paperback novel he always carried in the side pocket of his army surplus coat with the intention of reading it to pass the forty-five minutes until it was time to re-board the bus.

He patted his pocket, feeling an unfamiliar bulge there, and frowned. He'd forgotten he still had the fucking things. He looked around to make sure no one was watching, and then he took the grimy, nearly full bottle of pills out of his pocket, squinting to read the label. With a ragged thumbnail, he scratched off his name. Then he carried the Thorazine to the garbage can near the door of the diner and tossed it in. He glanced about again to make sure no one had noticed him. Of course no one had noticed him. They never did.

CHAPTER TWO

The coach was less than half full as it pulled out of Toronto at 6:15 p.m. Jordan Lefebvre was glad of it. He had his choice of seats. He chose two on the left-hand side of the bus, towards the back. He placed his guitar and his rucksack on the seat next to the aisle and leaned his bruised face against the window. The cool glass felt good against his swollen skin. The sun left the sky early in mid-September and the coming night rode alongside it beneath a shroud of rain as the driver navigated his way out of the city, turning north onto Highway 400.

Jordan was seventeen, almost eighteen, and today he had run out of both money and luck. He'd heard the term "rock bottom" before, but he never expected to have reached it before he was old enough to legally drink and vote. On the other hand, today he was finally a man. He'd grown up hearing older boys talk about how great it felt to finally "lose it." It didn't feel great to Jordan. He touched his swollen bottom lip, probing it gently. He winced when he found the split skin and his finger came away wet and red.

Jordan had arrived in Toronto three months earlier from Lake Hepburn, a small mining town in northern Ontario that no one in Toronto seemed to have heard of—a fact few people he met there had ever allowed him to forget. He'd brought his guitar, a few changes of clothes—a couple of pairs of Lee Riders, some underwear, some faded flannel bush shirts, a spare pair of boots.

Lake Hepburn was one of the thousands of ubiquitous northern hockey towns where boys became drinking, fighting, hockey-playing men by their mid-teens, if not earlier. Men for whom two options existed: working down the mine, or joining the army. Neither appealed to Jordan. He had the bruises to show for it—those you could see and those you couldn't. Towns like Lake Hepburn tended to scar their sons in the same way the mines scarred their fathers, a cycle of mutual exploitation that had gone unquestioned, generation after generation.

Jordan had always been his mother's favourite. She'd bought him a secondhand guitar when he was fourteen and would listen to him practise for hours. She encouraged his dreams and told him he sounded like Jim Croce. Jordan loved her the way he loved no one else. His father called it beatnik crap. Jordan was a mystery to his father, a man with neither the time nor the inclination for mysteries, especially under his own roof.

Late at night, Jordan sometimes heard his parents arguing through the wall of his bedroom. His father's voice would rise and Jordan would catch words like *normal* and *wrong* and *dreamer* and *other boys* in between his father's raw profanity. Those were the times he knew they were discussing him. His mother's voice would rise in answer. Jordan heard words like *be someone* and *out of this town* and *success*. And *dreams*, which sounded like a completely different word when his mother said it. Then the furniture would crash. Things would break.

One night when he was twelve, during one of their increasingly frequent arguments, Jordan heard the brutal smack of flesh meeting flesh. He'd jumped out of bed and opened his parents' bedroom door to find his mother bleeding from the mouth and his father standing over her, trying to pull her to her feet. Jordan smelled the liquor from the doorway. His father stank of it. It seemed to be coming out of his pores.

"She's fine," his father was muttering. "She fell. It's all right. Go to bed. Go on, get out of here." His mother was trembling.

Her eyes were wide open and she shook her head imperceptibly, silently imploring him to do what his father asked.

"Mom? Mom, are you OK? What's happening? What happened?"

"I'm fine, Jordie. Your Dad and I were just talking and I tripped on the carpet and fell. I'm all right. I just bumped myself. It's OK. Go to bed, Jordan. Don't make a fuss."

Jordan hadn't moved. He'd looked his father full in the face, holding his gaze for a long, defiant moment, refusing to drop his eyes. His father's flat, open hand began to rise, but it stopped in mid-air. That one time he thought better of it and lowered it to his side. As he looked down at his bleeding wife, Jordan could have sworn he saw a flicker of shame.

It would be the last time his father exercised that restraint, however. Jordan never saw shame again. It was as though seeing his own brutality reflected in Jordan's eyes extracted too high a cost, one his father bitterly resented having to pay.

The beatings began a week later. They began as random slaps across the back of Jordan's head for clumsiness or for "acting smart." They evolved into whippings with a leather belt for chores not done to specification, or any other occasion when Jordan failed to live up to his father's variegated standards of acceptable behaviour.

Jordan learned to stay out of his father's way as much as possible, which, in a small house, wasn't much at all. He learned to dress in layers, so the bruises wouldn't show; not that he was likely to get much more than *pro forma* sympathy from the adults around him. In Lake Hepburn, the disciplining of children, especially boys, was a family matter and one best dealt with inside the family. There was one consolation: when his father's belt came down across his body, raising welts and cuts on his ass and legs, he knew that his mother was being spared.

"Why don't you ever fight back, you fucking little pissant?" his father had asked once during one of the beatings. He'd even managed to make the question sound reasonable. "Why don't you try to take me? Why don't you try to make me stop?"

But Jordan never fought back. He sensed on some primal level that he was paying for his mother's safety by acting as the object of his father's rage. Unfortunately, Jordan's capacity to endure pain was remarkable. The beatings lasted from the time Jordan was twelve until he was seventeen.

The last time his father beat him was the night before got on the bus to Toronto three months ago. His father had come home drunk from the Legion Hall and tripped over a kitchen chair on his way to the fridge. He'd stormed up the stairs and woken Jordan with slaps and punches, screaming about his irresponsibility. The belt had come out remarkably quickly considering how drunk his father was. Jordan got the worst of it across his naked back and shoulders before his father, exhausted from his exertions, stumbled to his own bedroom and passed out.

Jordan's one regret, that pre-dawn morning when he'd snuck out of the house with his rucksack and guitar and hitchhiked to the next town over, was that his mother would be frantic. He'd left a note in her sewing basket telling her he was going to be all right and that she shouldn't worry. He had two hundred dollars he'd been saving for two years, plus fifty he'd taken from his father's wallet.

When he'd arrived in Toronto late that first night, Jordan had checked into a dirt-cheap hotel on Jarvis Street frequented by hookers and their johns that stank of industrial cleaner and cockroach spray, and underneath that, pussy and dried semen. After a week in the hotel, his chest and legs were covered with bedbug bites. He'd found a "roommates wanted" notice tacked on the bulletin board of a bookstore on Spadina, not far from the university. Two men in their early twenties shared the apartment with a girl who was pregnant by one of them, though she was unsure of which one. None of the three seemed to find anything unusual in the arrangement.

"It's all beautiful," she said. "We're all, like, one, you know?"

At that first meeting, the older of the two men, Mack, had been pleasant enough towards Jordan. The younger, Don, had regarded him with distrust. The girl, who said her name was Fleur, seemed entirely ambivalent, if friendly enough. After she'd introduced herself, she went into the kitchen and made herbal tea. She'd asked Jordan if he wanted some. He politely told her no. He couldn't bring himself to tell her he had no idea what herbal tea was.

Mack told him, "There's a mat on the floor near the kitchen. It ain't much, but it's clean. First and last month's rent would be great if you have it. First is OK, I guess, if you don't. You got a sleeping bag?"

"No, afraid not," Jordan had said. "But I can buy one, I guess. Still cheaper than a bed."

"No problem," Mack said. He'd gestured towards the closet. "Brian left one, I think. He OD'd. Bad trip. He don't live here no more. You can have it if you want it."

Don, who was sitting on the floor stroking Fleur's hair, suddenly looked up. He glared at Jordan. Then he turned to Mack. "Why don't you just give the place away for free, for fuck's sake?"

"What's your problem?" Mack said mildly. "He don't got a sleeping bag. We got an extra one. What's the issue?" Fleur leaned her head back on Don's chest. She closed her eyes and sighed as though this were a conversation she'd heard before, and it bored her.

Don said, "How old is this fucking kid?" He pivoted his head and glared at Jordan. "Seriously how old are you?

"I'm seventeen," Jordan said. He smiled tentatively. Don's sudden aggression had momentarily driven away any thoughts of the intrinsic creepiness of sleeping in a dead man's sleeping bag. "But it's OK. I have money for the rent. I brought it from home." He patted his jacket pocket. "Right here."

Don said again, "For fuck's sake. Do we need a kid here? Are we that fucking broke?"

"Jesus, what's your problem? He's fine. In case you haven't noticed," Mack said, looking pointedly at Fleur's swollen belly, "we need some bread right about now."

Jordan said, "Hey, if this isn't going to work out, you guys—I mean, I don't want to get in the way, you know what I mean?" His voice cracked. He sounded like a kid now, even to himself.

Fleur giggled and, for the first time, gave Jordan her full attention. She smiled widely. "Relax, man. It's beautiful. Don, relax, baby. It's cool. The kid's all right. Aren't you, kid?"

"Yeah, sure. I mean, yes. I'm all right."

She laughed. "You're cute, kid. What was your name again?"

"Jordan. Jordan Lefebvre."

"Nice."

Don flushed a deep red. The cords on his neck suddenly stood out in sharp relief. He scowled and looked away while Jordan and Mack shook hands awkwardly.

"Welcome, man," Mack said. "Don't worry about the sleeping bag. We washed it. It's clean."

That afternoon, Jordan had returned to the hotel on Jarvis. He'd packed his rucksack and put his guitar back in its case. He paid the bill, and checked out. He sniffed the sleeves of his flannel shirt, catching a whiff of roach spray. His nose wrinkled in distaste.

As he set out across downtown towards the apartment, Jordan had allowed himself to believe, for the first time since he'd arrived in the city, that he might have some sort of future here, free of his father's shadow. The July sunlight had been hot and bright. Jordan felt sweat gathering under his armpits and along the line of his back. He stopped and shrugged off the strap of his guitar, placing it gently on the sidewalk. He took his flannel shirt off and tied it around his waist. *Yes, better.* Jordan squinted, shielding his eyes with his left hand. He scanned the still-unfamiliar cityscape and assessed the quickest route to his new apartment and the beginning of what he believed was to be his real life.

He'd found a job washing dishes and occasionally busing tables at a restaurant on King Street that paid him just enough to cover his rent and keep from starving. His roommates, by and large, ignored him, though Fleur and Mack seemed to like him, which made him feel like an adult. Occasionally Fleur brought him a cup of herbal tea when she was making some for herself.

He sometimes caught her staring at him when she thought he wasn't looking. Once, when she'd been looking, he'd turned to smile at her. She'd smiled back, but it wasn't the sort of smile she used when Don and Mack were present. It seemed somehow private, somehow inviting, though Jordan would have been at a loss to identify exactly what sort of invitation was being extended.

On one of those occasions, he'd become aware of Don standing in the doorway. Don looked from Fleur to Jordan, and then back again. His eyes had been cold as two chips of black ice. Jordan had felt a territorial menace coming off Don in waves. Unlike Mack, who was always amiable, even if he seemed perpetually stoned, Don had never relaxed around Jordan. And he watched Fleur the way a wary dog watches a piece of meat—covetously and on guard for challenges to his primacy.

In the three months that he'd lived with them, Fleur's belly had grown round and full. Jordan occasionally wondered what it would be like to be born in this apartment, not knowing which of the two men was your father.

He'd asked Fleur once, when they were alone, if she knew. She smiled at him and pressed her index finger against her lips.

And then, that afternoon, after three months of silence, he'd called his mother in Lake Hepburn to tell her he was OK. He called from a payphone in the early afternoon when he knew his father was at work. She finally picked up after six or seven rings. When she came on the line, Jordan knew there was something terribly, terribly wrong. Her voice was small, and her words sounded like she was speaking them through a mouthful of meat.

"I'm fine, Jordan. Are you all right, honey? I've been so worried."

"Mom, what's going on? What's happening?" Jordan squeezed his eyes together against the images that rose in his mind: his mother's careworn face bruised purple and swollen, her body crisscrossed with belt marks. Broken glass, broken doors, holes in the walls. *I should never have left*, he thought. *I should have tried to take her with me, at the very least.* On her end, he heard his mother begin to sob and he damned himself with guilt. *I should have known that if I left, he'd start hitting her instead of me.*

"Mom, I'm coming home. Right now. I'll be there by tomorrow."

"Jordie, listen to me. I want you to stay where you are. Don't come home. I don't know what he'll do. He was real mad when you left."

"Can you go stay at Aunt Lee's?"

"I'll be all right. Please don't come back here, at least not now. I'm all right, I promise."

"I'll be there as soon as I can, Mom. I'm coming home soon. Then, I'm going to kill him."

Jordan had walked back to the apartment in the rain. When he arrived, Fleur was sitting at the kitchen table writing in her journal. She raised her head and pushed her long hair out of her eyes. When she saw that he'd been crying, she stood up, her face softening into an expression of concern.

"Hey baby, what's the matter?"

The simple kindness of her question had threatened what little self control Jordan had still been able to exert.

"Ah. Nothing. Rough day. Lost my job," he lied. "I don't think this is for me after all. I should never have left Hepburn."

She stood up and reached out her arms. He allowed himself to be enfolded, welcoming the tenderness. Then, Fleur was kissing him and unbuttoning his shirt. He kissed her back, at first with a virgin's tentativeness and then with an entirely unfamiliar, instinctive aggression. He smelled patchouli and Halo shampoo as he pressed himself against her awkwardly, feeling the rise of her belly wedging them apart.

"Are you sure we should—"

Fleur slipped her tongue into this mouth, cutting him off. She ran one hand through his hair, still damp from the rain. She slipped the other down the front of his jeans, taking his cock— which felt harder to Jordan than it had ever been—between her fingers and squeezing it with an exquisite, expert skill. She undid the button and pulled his jeans and his boxer shorts down across his naked hips. He pushed them the rest of the way down till they were tangled at his feet and kicked them away, naked, for the first time, in the presence of a woman. If his nakedness shamed him at all, it was transitory. Jordan had three thoughts simultaneously. The first, that he was going to get laid—seriously and thoroughly laid— for the first time in his life. The second was that the first woman he was ever going to fuck was pregnant with another man's child. The third, that he didn't give a good god damn because he was going to get laid— seriously and thoroughly laid—for the first time in his life.

A fourth thought—that this was as dangerous as anything he'd ever done in his life, knowing that Don could come home at any moment— came and went in another wave of lust.

When Fleur shrugged off the bathrobe she wore, Jordan saw she was completely nude. Her belly arched gently outwards from a body that was more slender than he would have expected, freed of the smocks and baggy shirts she'd worn during the time he lived there. Jordan marvelled at the pale curves of her body, the swollen breasts and the soft delta between her legs, almost hidden by the press of her belly. When she knelt down and took his cock in her mouth, he thrilled at the unfamiliar sensation of her mouth and tongue on a part of his body that only he had ever touched.

She's beautiful, Jordan thought, surprised. He realized that he had expected her body to look grotesque and distended in its fecund state, but he'd never seen anything as desirable in all of his seventeen years. He put his hands on her upper arms and awkwardly raised her to her feet, leaning forward to kiss her. The feeling of his cock against her flesh made him light headed. He reached out tentatively and touched her breasts. She moaned softly in response and arched her back, offering herself further. Her nipples were moist with fluid lactate that tasted sweet against his tongue.

He allowed himself to be led to the bedroom she shared with Mack and Don. Fleur lay down on the bed. Jordan spread her legs with his knees and pressed himself between her legs.

"No," she whispered, as he started to grind. "Slow down. Not like that." She climbed on top of him and gently lowered herself on him. Jordan gasped as he slipped inside her. "Like this. Slow. Yes, slow down. Good. Yeah."

"I love you," he blurted out, realizing, even as he said it, how ridiculous he sounded. But at that moment, he was telling the truth. He loved her. He'd never loved anyone so much in his life. He laid his hands over her belly.

"Hush," Fleur said. "Don't talk. Just fuck me."

"This is my first—I mean, I never—" Jordan wasn't sure if he was apologizing to her or warning her, but it was suddenly very important that she know he was a virgin.

Fleur whispered in his ear, "Oh baby, I know. That's all right." She put her hands on his ass and guided him into her. "Like this. Now, just go with it."

When he came, Jordan cried out, a sound from deep in the back of his throat, one that sounded foreign even to him. He felt himself dissolving, as though everything from his waist down had become insubstantial. He shouted again, this time as his body shook with erotic aftershock.

He was drenched in sweat. Rivulets of it ran from his hair into his eyes, making them sting. He was suddenly terribly thirsty.

"I need a glass of water," he said, inclining his head towards Fleur. "Do you want one?"

"Yeah, please." Her voice sounded very small. She gathered the sheets and blanket around her body and rolled away from him, staring at the wall.

"Are you all right?"

"Yeah. You'd better get dressed. Don will be coming home soon."

"Yeah, you're right." Jordan looked at her again. "Are you sure you're OK? You don't sound it. I mean, you wanted to, right?"

"Yeah, I wanted to. Hurry up, now. Get our water, and get dressed."

Jordan was halfway back across the kitchen floor with two glasses of water, still naked, when he heard the sound of a key in the lock. He looked back over his shoulder into the bedroom. Fleur was sitting upright on the bed, her mouth a perfect oval of terror.

The door swung open and Don stepped across the threshold. Jordan smelled the whiskey even before Don looked up and saw him standing there, frozen in place. Don took in Jordan's nakedness, the two glasses of water, and Fleur on the bed with the covers gathered around her.

"What the *fuck*? You *whore*! And with this fucking *kid*?" He whirled to face Jordan. "You little piece of shit, I'm going to fucking kill you."

Don drew his arm back and slapped Jordan across the face. Jordan's vision went white, and the two glasses of water shattered on the floor. When Jordan stumbled backwards, pain singing through his head, Don punched him, knocking him to the floor. Jordan felt the broken glass cut into his palms as he tried to stand. Don clenched his fists and turned, stumbling, towards the bedroom.

Fleur screamed. "Don, it didn't mean anything! Don't hit me! The baby! Don't hurt the baby!"

Don leaned down so his face was inches from Fleur's. "Who's fucking baby is it, you whore? Is it mine? Is it even Mack's? How many other guys have you been fucking while we've been out busting our asses trying to keep a roof over your head? You slut!"

Jordan stood up. His nose was bleeding and his left eye and bottom lip were swelling shut. "Leave her alone," he said thickly. "Get away from her, you asshole." Don turned towards Jordan, his face contorted with rage. A line of snot ran from Don's left nostril. Jordan was again assailed by the familiar smack of sour whiskey on his breath.

"What did you say, you little—"

Jordan hit Don as hard as he could with his closed fist. It was a perfect punch, an instinctive punch, the sort of punch he'd seen his father throw back home. It took them both by surprise. Don fell backwards and crashed into the bedroom closet. To Jordan, the splintering sound of the cheap plywood slats as they snapped beneath Don's weight was deeply satisfying. He grabbed Don by the hair and pulled him to his feet. Then he hit him again, and again.

He hit him the way he'd always wanted to hit his father—not only for what he'd done to Jordan, but for what he'd done to Jordan's mother.

He beat Don until his face was a pulpy mash of red, and until he thought he felt the bones of his face about to yield.

Fleur screamed. "Oh my God, Don! *Don!*" She took a step towards Don, still clutching the sheets against her body. "Jesus, baby! Are you all right? Jesus!" She reached for him. He slapped her hand away.

"Don't fucking touch me." He got to his feet and wiped the blood from his mouth. He pointed a finger at her. "I'm going for a walk. If this fucking kid isn't gone when I get back, I will be. You and Mack can raise the baby on your own, whoever's baby it is. And you," he said, turning to Jordan, "go back to whatever shithole you came from. You don't belong here."

Jordan heard the front door shut and the sound of Don's feet on the stairs, then the fainter slam of the door to the street.

"You need to get out of here," Fleur said, staring past him to the door. Her face was ashen and there was an edge of hysteria in her voice. "He can't leave me. He just can't. You have to go."

"Go? Where?" Jordan screamed. "Where am I supposed to go?"

Fleur was moaning now. "It's his baby. I need him. You have to leave. Get dressed, for God's sake, and get out of here."

"I thought you said it was everybody's baby?" He reached for his jeans and pulled them on. "He's going to hit you again, you know. You and this kid you're about to have."

"Oh, God, I'm sorry. Look, it was a mistake. It was nice, you're a great guy, but . . . look, get dressed. You have to leave. He'll be back in half an hour, I know him. If you're here, he'll leave me and the baby."

"What about Mack?"

"What *about* Mack? It's not his baby. He won't be able to help me take care of it!"

"What, you fuck me, then when I save you from that asshole, you throw me out? That was my first time, you crazy bitch! Jesus. Where am *I* supposed to go? I don't know anyone else in this shitty fucking city. I don't have any money, and I don't have any-place to go! What's wrong with you?"

"I don't know, go back home. Go back to your hometown. You said yourself it wasn't working out here for you here. You said you lost your job, right? You can go back to that town you're from. What's it called? Lake Huron? You can go there, can't you?"

"I can't even afford a bus ticket home," Jordan said dully.

Fleur spoke quickly. "There's a hundred dollars in the bottom drawer." She gestured frantically towards the dresser. "It's inside the peanuts can, under my clothes. Go look. It's under those sweaters."

It took Jordan less than fifteen minutes to pack what little he'd brought to the city, and since he'd accomplished nothing, been nowhere, and done nothing, he had nothing to take back with him except what he'd brought. When Fleur left the room, Jordan lifted a half-full bottle of rye from the nightstand beside the bed that he hoped was Don's and quickly tucked it into his bag.

In the bathroom, he gingerly washed his face with cold water. He winced, marvelling at how quickly the wounds from Don's fists had bloomed under his cheek and beneath his eye. The blood had stopped, but he looked rough as hell. There was a bottle of prescription painkillers on the upper shelf in the medicine cabinet. The prescription was made out to "Benson, Don," he noted with grim pleasure as he put the bottle in his knapsack. Jordan would need it later, he was sure. His nose probably wasn't broken, but Don had hit him pretty hard. It was starting to hurt like hell. He hoped Don felt worse than he did and that he'd go looking for these pills as soon as he came home from his round-the-block sulk.

Piece of shit, Jordan thought. *These people are crazy. Especially Fleur. Crazy bitch. They're all crazy bitches. They marry men that hurt them and kick the ones who don't hurt them out the door. And when the kid is born, he'll be next. Just like I was.*

He heard her knocking on the bathroom door as he turned off the faucet and dried his face on the dirty towel hanging over the bathroom curtain.

"Are you OK in there? Come on, Jordan, you've got to leave. He'll be home any minute." She was dressed in her smock again, and it looked like she'd run a comb through her hair. Her eyes were puffy from crying, but she was visibly calmer, more like the flower power "it's all beautiful" freak chick he'd met three months ago.

"One question," he said in the doorway. "Why? Why me? Why now?"

She shrugged. "I liked you. You're cute. Don and Mack, you know . . . Well, we're all going to be together once the baby is born, and I thought—"

He cut her off. "He's going to hurt you. And he'll hurt the baby. He's not going to stop."

Fleur shook her head. She smiled blankly and said, "No, he's not like that. I just made him jealous. He's never like that. He'd never hit me."

Half an hour later at the bus depot, Jordan asked the ticket vendor when the first bus for Lake Hepburn was leaving. He told Jordan there was a Greyhound departing for Sault Ste. Marie at midnight with a stop in Lake Hepburn just after 5:00 a.m.

At some point between the apartment and the bus depot, it occurred to Jordan that he had very likely committed a crime by beating Don as badly as he had. A crime that Don could report to the police, one that could land Jordan in jail. And if he was in jail, he could kiss off any chance of saving his mother from his bastard father. He looked around the station guiltily, half-expecting to see police officers coming through the doors, pointing at him and drawing their guns.

"Anything before that?"

The ticket vendor looked up and raised his eyebrows when he saw Jordan's bruises. "Not a fan of our great city, I see. Okie-dokie, just a minute." He checked the schedule again. "Well, lookie here. There's a Northern Star bus leaving in an hour. Ticket's almost half the price." He leaned closer to Jordan. "It's sort of an old bus, kid. Not real comfortable. If you wait for the Greyhound, you'll have a smoother ride. You look like you could use it."

Jordan said, "I'll take the Northern ticket, please."

The vendor sighed. "Round trip or one way?"

"One way, please," Jordan said. He paid for the ticket and went to wait on one of the benches near the platform.

CHAPTER THREE

Jordan boarded the bus at six p.m., making his way to the back where, as fate would have it, he met the vampire, who was sitting in the opposite row of seats.

He smiled sympathetically at Jordan and said, "I hope you made the other guy look worse, at least?"

Jordan turned his head. "Excuse me?"

"Your face. It looks like you were in a fight." Jordan thought the man might be in his late thirties, certainly no older than forty. He was darkhaired and clean-shaven, but his face had a thick five o'clock shadow. "Was it over a girl?"

"Yeah, it was a bad fight," Jordan said. "And it was over a girl. And the other guy did look worse. A lot worse."

"My name's Richard," the man said, extending his hand across the aisle. "Richard Weal. My friends call me Rich."

"Hi, I'm Jordan." He shook Weal's hand warily. He wasn't used to talking to strangers, but since the ride was going to be a long one, he figured it was better to be friendly than not, if only to ensure a peaceful trip.

Weal smiled. "Where're you headed?"

"Lake Hepburn," Jordan said. "Just before Sault Ste. Marie." He shrugged off his jacket and put it on the seat next to him. Feeling obligated, he asked. "How about you? Going far?"

"A town called Parr's Landing," Weal said. "It's been a long ride for me. I've been riding this bus since Ottawa. That's five hours already. I can't feel where my back ends and this seat begins."

"Never heard of it," Jordan said. He shrugged. "I mean Parr's Landing, not Ottawa. You have family there, in Parr's Landing?"

"It's near Marathon." Weal smiled again, revealing a mouthful of yellowish teeth that looked like they hadn't been brushed in days. "On Lake Superior. In the bush. In the middle of *nowhere*, truth to be told." Weal laughed, an abrupt high giggling screech of hilarity entirely out of sync with the rest of his delivery. "I used to live there a long time ago. I'm an archaeologist. I'm doing a PhD at the University of Ottawa on the history of the Jesuit settlements in northern Ontario during the seventeenth century. Or rather, I was. I took a bit of a sabbatical, for health reasons. But I'm going back to complete some of my research." He patted his hockey bag. Jordan saw that his nails were filthy, the cuticles crusted with what looked like dried mustard and ketchup.

"So . . . you got family there?" Jordan repeated, more out of politeness than anything else. He'd not finished high school by the time he escaped his family tumult in Lake Hepburn and he had no idea what a PhD was. He was having a hard time following the conversation. He wondered if he'd taken more of a hit than he'd thought when he landed on the floor. His head was beginning to pulse in earnest. "I mean, in Parr's Landing."

Weal smiled at that. "Blood family." He covered his mouth with his hands and giggled again. "The best kind."

"Sorry, what?"

"Never mind." Weal held up a thick sheaf of papers bound with a heavy clip. "I've been re-reading the manuscript of this book I'm writing. I've been editing it. It's going to come true soon."

"It's going to *what*?"

Weal leaned close enough to Jordan's face for Jordan to smell his breath, which was quite foul. "I said, it's going to be published soon." His eyes narrowed. "Why, what did you think I said? Are you hard of hearing?"

Jordan pulled back, nauseated by the odour of Weal's breath. "Sorry," he said. "My head hurts pretty bad. You know, the fight."

He decided then to bring the conversation to a close. He wouldn't have felt like talking, even to someone less unkempt and, frankly, weird. He wanted to sleep. He felt like shit and he wondered if maybe Don hadn't actually managed to break his nose after all. He looked up the aisle, but all the free seats were in the back, where he already was. He couldn't easily move without calling attention to his desire to distance himself from Weal and he had no desire to antagonize him, or otherwise engage his attention beyond what he still hoped was just small talk. "I think I'm going to close my eyes, Rich." He yawned in an obvious way he hoped didn't look too fake. "I'll talk to you in a bit, OK? You can tell me more about your book."

"Oh, of course, young sir," Weal replied. He had removed the clip and was turning the pages. His nose was pressed so close it was almost touching the paper. "I do apologize for rambling a bit. It's been a long day. I'm a bit knackered myself." He smiled. "That said, I've got my book. And my tools." He patted the hockey bag again. "Would you like me to wake you up when the driver stops in Sudbury for dinner? I imagine we'll all be quite famished by then."

"Sure," Jordan lied. "Please do." He leaned his bruised face against the cool glass of the bus window and closed his eyes. He promised himself that when the bus stopped in Sudbury, he was going to change his seat as unobtrusively as possible.

There was a crest on the first page the freak had waved at me, Jordan thought aimlessly. *And it said University of Toronto. Not University of Ottawa.* And then he chastised himself. *Stupid thing of you to notice. Like you'd ever wind up in either of those places, you big dummy. What do you know about any of that shit?*

His face hurt like hell. Then he remembered the painkillers he'd stolen from Don's bathroom. He reached into his knapsack and took out two of the pills. He swallowed them dry, trying in vain to work up a mouthful of spit to ease their passage down his throat. He gagged at the acrid dry taste. He remembered the whiskey in his bag and took a long pull straight from the bottle. He shivered, his eyes watering. His face *really* hurt. He took another pill out of the bottle, considered it for a moment.

He knew nothing at all about drugs, or what might constitute an overdose, and was flying blind. *What the hell,* he thought, and popped it in his mouth. He took another swig of the whiskey, and another. The amber liquid seared his throat, the heat travelling down through his body to his empty stomach, radiating outward towards his extremities, leaving him light-headed and warm.

The pills had an immediate effect. A slide show of mental images flickered across the screen of his mind—his mother, his father, Fleur, their lovemaking, and, of course, Richard Weal. Jordan's lips and jaw felt numb, and he was utterly relaxed.

Outside, the city was consumed by the night and vanished entirely, leaving an eternity of highway stretching north as far as he could see. Only distant neon stars, rendered opalescent by the rain, broke the blackness. Lulled by the motion of the bus beneath him, Jordan yielded to the barbiturate admixture of painkillers and whiskey coursing through his system. He closed his eyes again, and slept.

CHAPTER FOUR

The bus travelled a north-northwest route along the Trans Canada Highway towards Georgian Bay, exiting onto Highway 69, continuing north around Georgian Bay towards Parry Sound. The rain stopped, giving way to thick fog that drifted in from the rolling farmlands on either side of the highway, which then gave way to tracks of young pine forest.

The moon, which had begun its ascent hours before in the rain, came out from behind the scudding black rain clouds, frosting the road on either side of the bus with silvery light.

In Barrie, a mother and her five-year-old daughter boarded, and in Parry Sound, four passengers who'd boarded in Toronto disembarked. But no one from Parry Sound boarded. After five hours, the bus pulled into Sudbury for a half-hour refuelling stop.

Jordan slept through Jim Marks's announcement that all passengers could step out, stretch their legs, and get something to eat at the diner next to the terminal.

No one boarded after the break, Jim noted sourly. His mouth tasted like bad coffee and cigarettes and his back ached. He felt his jacket pocket for the Dexies he kept there. He hated using the amphetamines, mostly because of what they did to his stomach. Though at his last physical, Doc Abelard had warned him that the Dexies, in conjunction with his hours, the cigarettes, and the forty extra pounds he was carrying around his waist wasn't doing his ticker any favours. *Just as a last resort,* Jim told himself. *Don't want to fall asleep and crash this old bitch before I get a chance to collect my pension.*

He looked back. He counted five passengers in the back of the bus as he pulled out of the lot: an old lady sitting two rows behind him who had asked him three times already "just to be sure" that he was stopping in Whitefish; the teenage boy sleeping against the window halfway to the back who hadn't gotten out at the Sudbury stop; the tired young mother with her little girl—Missy, he'd heard the woman call her back at the dinette; and the guy in the very back row reading a book. *Come to think of it,* Jim thought, *that guy didn't get off the bus in Sudbury to stretch his legs, either.* One of them—the kid, he thought—was getting off in Lake Hepburn. The other guy had bought a ticket all the way to Sault Ste. Marie.

There were fewer and fewer passengers on the northern routes, Jim realized, and he wondered how long Northern Star would be able to hold out. His retirement wouldn't come a moment too soon.

Jim turned the bus west on Highway 17 and repeated the name of the coming towns like a mantra: Whitefish, Spanish, Serpent River, Thessalon, Garden River, Lake Hepburn, Sault Ste. Marie.

It would be hours yet before dawn. It was going to be a long fucking night.

At 4:15 a.m., Jim Marks pulled the bus over to the side of the road to investigate what he feared might be a flat tire on the right side. He took his parka down from the overhead compartment, put it on, and stepped outside.

Overhead, the full moon shone down like a headlight. The thought came to him—as it happened, one of the last thoughts he would ever have—that he'd never seen a night this bright and clear up north. The radius of the moon's light aureole was such that while the larger sky was as blackest black, the area around the moon itself was indigo blue.

He shone his flashlight along the undercarriage of the bus. The tires were all intact and none were damaged. He shrugged.

Whatever he had heard and felt, at least it wasn't a flat. He'd include the incident in his report and the mechanics could check it out when they pulled into Sault Ste. Marie. He checked his watch. They'd only lost fifteen minutes. He stepped back onto the bus and looked down the aisle. The passengers seemed to have slept through the stop, which, given that most bus passengers on long routes were light sleepers, was itself a miracle.

Jim settled himself into his seat. He fastened his seat belt and started the engine.

In his peripheral vision, he caught an abrupt flurry of motion in the rearview mirror and looked up.

The man in the army surplus jacket from the back of the bus wasn't asleep at all. He was wide awake. He was running along the aisle of the bus with spider like agility, past the sleeping teenager, past the woman and her little girl, towards the driver's seat.

Jim opened his mouth to tell the man to go back to his seat and sit down, but nothing came out. Then, suddenly, the man was directly behind Jim and drawing back his arm. In his hand, he held something long that gleamed in the overhead light of the cabin. The last thing Jim Marks saw was a flash of silver in the gloom as the man's arm came down viciously in a wide arc.

Jim threw his arms up to protect his face, but it was too late. There was a short, blinding sheet of white-hot pain and sharp pressure as the chisel end of the archaeological rock hammer split open his skull, but his conscious mind barely had time to register it as pain. He was dead before he hit the floor.

Jordan was jolted awake as the bus swerved on the highway. For a moment he didn't know where he was. He'd been dreaming that he was caught in a thunderstorm, or an earthquake. There had been the sound of thunder and of a woman singing some sort of high-pitched, screaming lament. It had been a harsh, unpleasant sound—one that, even asleep, had filled Jordan with dread.

He blinked and looked around him. Then he felt his face begin to throb, and he remembered that he was on a bus.

Jordan looked down at his watch. It was five a.m. His mouth was parched. He half-stood in his seat and looked around. The darkness inside the bus was complete except for the green glow coming from the dashboard. Squinting, he could make out the shape of the bus driver hunched over the steering wheel, but nothing else. He tried to remember what time they'd left Toronto—six? Six-thirty? It was now five in the morning. They weren't due to reach Lake Hepburn till after six. And had the bus been full? He tried to remember—half full? A quarter full? He switched on the overhead light above his seat. The weak bulb illuminated nothing besides his seat and the seat next to his.

The bus was moving very slowly and he heard gravel under the wheels. *Gravel? We're supposed to be on a highway.* Jordan pressed his face against the window. Beyond the thick fog, there was nothing but blackness. He saw no other cars, no gas stations, and no highway lights of any kind. It was as though the outside world had simply been swallowed up. The rows of seats ahead of him were tombstone-shaped in the gloom. He shook his head, trying to shake off the thick, gauzy haze left by the painkillers and the whiskey.

Something's not right here. Something's not right at all.

Jordan stood up and was assailed by an unfamiliar odour that made his stomach clench. For a moment, he was sure he was going to puke. It reminded him of iodine and rust, or the rotten smell of sulphur, or stagnant pond water, or shit, or some foul combination of all four.

He stepped out into the aisle of the bus and felt his way along the rows in the darkness. The smell grew thicker as he advanced. The bus was unbearably hot, as though the driver had turned up the heat as high as he could. Again, his head throbbed and he felt his stomach contract in protest against the thick smell in the air.

How can the driver not smell this? It's disgusting! How can he keep driving and not wonder if anyone is sick back here? For that matter, how could any of the other passengers stand it?

Jordan took another step up the aisle and slipped in a slick patch on the floor. The forward motion of his foot and his own weight carried him backwards. He lost his balance and fell, landing on his tailbone and elbows. Bolts of sharp pain shot up his arms and spine. Wincing, he rose to his feet and flicked the switch above the nearest empty seat. In the watery halo of lamp light, Jordan held his hands out in front of him and stared. His first thought was that perhaps he'd cut himself when he fell. Then he looked at the legs of his jeans. They were smeared and wet, and as red as his hands. Jordan knew what the smell was. He was covered in blood—not his blood, someone else's. Someone very close by. He stifled the scream that threatened to erupt from his throat, and turned on the light above the seat in front of him.

Then, Jordan did scream. There was no way *not* to.

He was looking at the body of a woman with her throat torn out. The blood from her wounds—there seemed to be at least two, apart from her torn throat, including a deep gash in the top of her skull from which a thick paste of brain, bone fragments, and hair, was leaking like red oatmeal. It had all but obliterated her face. Her left ear looked as if it had been half-bitten off and lay raggedly against the side of her skull. Jordan looked at the seat next to the woman's body. Amidst the rags—no, not rags, a little girl's fluffy pink coat marbled with great whorls of crimson— Jordan was just able to make out a tiny red hand and a dangling green rubber boot.

Up ahead, at the front of the bus, the slumped shape behind the wheel drove erratically forward, apparently oblivious to Jordan's screams. In the driver's window, thick tentacles of fog beckoned and recoiled in the yellow headlights. Jordan thought he could make out clumps of trees crowding in on either side of the road. They were definitely not on a highway. Jordan had spent his entire—if brief— life in the country and he recognized a country road when he saw it, even at five a.m. in a blind terror at the scene of some sort of grue- some bloodbath through which he'd apparently slept like the dead in a haze of painkillers and whiskey. But he was awake now—com- pletely, horribly awake. Either that, or his nightmare had some- how followed him out of his dream and into real life.

He screamed, "Stop! Stop the bus! Stop the bus! She's dead! Somebody killed a lady!"

Calmly, the driver turned the wheel of the bus and pulled over to the side of the highway. There appeared to be no haste, no urgency in the sequence of movements.

Still not right, Jordan's mind gibbered. He shook his head frantically. *Am I still asleep, or is this really happening?*

Another wave of slaughterhouse stink rose from the woman's body and Jordan vomited. Then, smelling his own puke, he vomited again.

When he stopped retching and stood up, he saw Richard Weal standing there beside the steering wheel. In his left hand, he held a pickaxe. The blade of the axe was clotted with clumps of flesh and hair. In the right hand, he held a red-spattered butcher's knife with an eight inch blade. To Jordan, he looked like a monster out of a horror movie. The entire bottom half of his face was caked with blood. The front of his shirt and army surplus jacket were soaked with it and shone wetly under the dim overhead lights of the driver's cabin.

As Jordan's terrified mind shook off the last remaining shred of torpor and his eyes grew accustomed to the gloom, he saw the bus driver's mutilated body crumpled at Weal's feet. Half his skull was missing and his throat had been torn out.

"The blood is the life," Weal said thickly, licking his lips. He waved the pickaxe idly in Jordan's general direction. "I told you, I brought my tools. He tells me how," Weal said reverently. "He speaks to me. They told me, in that . . . *place,* to take the pills. But when I did, I couldn't hear him anymore. He showed me how to do this. He sends dreams into my brain. He wants me to find him so I can live forever. I'll be like him. I'll be able to fly."

"You're crazy," Jordan whispered. "You're fucking crazy."

Weal smiled, his teeth red. "No, no, I'm not crazy. He wants me to wake him. He wants me to find him where he sleeps and wake him. He loves me." Weal cocked his head like a dog listening for a supersonic whistle. "He's speaking right now. I can't believe you can't hear it. He says I should kill you, because if I let you live, you'll tell everyone about him. About us."

Weal wiped the knife on his pants and began swinging it lazily in front of him like a pendulum. Jordan heard the hiss as it cut the air. Weal took a step towards him, still swinging. Jordan jumped back, slipping again on the gore-slick floor. Weal took a compensatory step forward as though he were leading in some ghastly tango.

"No, I won't tell! I swear! Please, please, let me go! Please! I have to get home." Weal swung the knife in wider arcs and feinting half-jabs at Jordan. He grinned, advancing. Jordan backed up farther. "My mom needs me! My dad's hurting her. Please, if you kill me, she won't have anyone to protect her. Please, don't. Oh God. I'm begging you."

"The blood is the life," Weal whispered. "And I'm going to live forever."

He struck hard with the knife, slashing Jordan across the chest. The blade shredded Jordan's shirt, and bit deep into flesh and muscle. He screamed as the blood rose from the wound. Jordan clutched his chest and backed away. Weal kept advancing, driving Jordan backward, slashing with each step, cutting Jordan's hands when he tried to ward off the swinging blade, slashing his neck and face when Jordan's bleeding hands were elsewhere.

When finally Jordan staggered and fell, dizzy from shock and pain, Weal turned him onto his back, almost lovingly. He kissed Jordan on the lips. Then he drew the knife across his throat, severing his carotid artery. The last thing Jordan felt were Weal's lips against his throat, lapping at the blood that gushed from the wound.

Through dying eyes, Jordan looked up and tried to focus on his murderer.

Weal's face became his own father's face, full of deadened, murderous rage. Then it was Weal's face again. Then his father's. Then it was Weal's again.

Directly behind Weal, a tenebrous, mist-like column was forming, vaguely human-shaped, but seemingly made entirely of darkness. Its head (or whatever part of it looked to Jordan most like a human head) was inclined towards Weal's ear, and it was indeed whispering to him but, now dying, Jordan heard the whispering, too.

It said, *Wake me.*

In the end, dying proved different than anything Jordan had ever imagined it might be.

For one thing, it seemed to go on forever, long past the point where the pain had stopped. Past even the point where his heart stopped pumping and his brain died. As Jordan drifted above his body, he looked down at himself, bleeding out on the dirty floor of the bus, and felt the truest compassion he'd known. He saw himself as he'd never seen himself in any mirror while he'd been alive. He saw the fragility of his body and he realized how tenuously human life was contained by such brittle shells of flesh and bone under the best of circumstances.

Dimensions of brilliance exploded outward as he continued to rise.

Past, present, and future fused together in a continuum. There were no more secrets. Every truth of the world was laid bare to the dead.

Jordan knew, for instance—and not without satisfaction—that his father would die of pancreatic cancer two years from now, in 1974. He would go quickly, but not without terrible pain. He knew that his mother would remarry, this time to a man who would cherish and care for her. He also knew that, late at night, as she lay in bed with her gentle, loving husband sleeping beside her, she'd think of Jordan's father and his cruelty and wonder if that wasn't, in its own way, real love. In those moments, she'd glance over at her sleeping husband and hate herself for wishing he wasn't just a bit harder, just a bit rougher, the way a man ought to be. Then she'd remember the terror, and she'd forgive herself for those treacherous thoughts. She'd lay her head on his chest while he gathered her in his arms till she, too, slept, dreaming of Jordan, telling herself over and over again that he was somewhere safe, living his life, and knowing in her mother's heart that he was gone.

He drew comfort from the knowledge that Fleur would leave Don before the baby was born and that the violence that had marked Jordan's life would never mark that of Fleur's son.

Jordan continued to rise.

He saw that the dead were everywhere, masses of them, like a vast eldritch ocean that stretched in every direction. Men, women, children— even animals. He laughed with revenant delight. The sound of his laughter fell in a shower of ectoplasmic blue sparks in the ether of this strange new in-between dimension where everything and nothing was the same as it was in life.

When Jordan was alive he'd once asked a priest about whether or not dogs had souls. His own dog, Prince, had died from eating poisoned bait in the woods the previous week, and Jordan had been inconsolable. The priest assured him that animals had no immortal souls and reprimanded him for being stupid enough to believe they did. Jordan had cried, but he suspected the priest was wrong—or lying. For years afterwards, he'd felt Prince's presence constantly when he was alone, especially at night in his room where the dog had always slept.

Here the dead crowded the desolate country road where Weal had awkwardly parked the bus, peering curiously through the windows, tapping noiselessly on the glass in an endless, one-sided attempted dialogue with the living. Finding none inside the bus, they scampered along the roof and launched themselves into the night like spectral fireflies in search of living receivers who could hear their voices. They looked as they did in life, and in death seemed neither overjoyed to be free of their mortal bodies nor particularly tormented. No wings, no harps, no robes. They just . . . *were.*

Jordan felt the warm press of millions of souls caressing his own as they passed through him. He realized now, as he never had when he was alive, how *not alone* he had always been. *What a comfort it might have been to know that,* he thought as he reached out to receive them.

As Jordan was absorbed into the massive vortex of spiralling black light, he looked down one last time.

Below him, in the road, Richard Weal had stepped out of the bus with his hockey bag full of bloodstained picks and hammers and saws. He withdrew a bottle wrapped in a dirty towel. Stuffed into the bottle's opening and held in place by the stopper was a wick made of cloth. Weal took a lighter out of his jacket pocket and lit the wick. The flame glowed brilliant blue. He hurled the bottle through the door of the bus. It shattered on impact, igniting a fireball that engulfed the interior of the bus in a matter of seconds. Even before the gas tank blew, Jordan knew his body was burning, and that when the authorities found the scorched out hulk hours later, there would be nothing left of him to identify.

Riding Weal's shoulders, the great black shape that only the dead could see pressed close to him, whispering to him, rippling and undulating with malignant purpose as Weal picked up his hockey bag and began to walk.

Jordan knew—as he knew *everything* now, including the terrible end of Weal's story—that there would be unlocked houses along the route to Parr's Landing. There would be trusting people. There would be cars driving north with passengers who felt sympathy for a lone man hitchhiking home to a northern mining town to be with his sick daughter or his dying wife. Weal's bag of hammers and knives and picks would do the rest. All the while, the great black shape folded its wings around Weal and urged him forward.

And then, the part of Jordan Lefebvre that was still tethered to his experience of dying flickered out entirely, his essence becoming one with the souls around him, passing completely from the world of the living into the gloomy country of the dead.

CHAPTER FIVE

Monday, October 23, 1972

That morning at the Blue Heron Motel—thirty miles outside of Sault Ste. Marie on the edge of the northern Ontario bush country, near the village of Batchawana Bay—Christina Parr woke just after sunrise from a dream of her dead husband, Jack. It was a widow's dream—an inchoate dream of the deepest and profoundest longing. She woke from it with her arms outstretched as though to receive an embrace.

Christina knew that if either of the other two occupants of the motel room had asked her to relate the dream's narrative to them, she would have been at a loss. The language of her grief was private and even now, after almost a year, Christina was still painfully learning its vocabulary and orthography.

She raised herself on her elbow and looked down at her daughter, Morgan, lying next to her. Asleep, buried in the blankets with her black hair (*Jack's hair*) half-covering her face, Morgan looked younger than fifteen. Lightly and tenderly, Christina smoothed it out of Morgan's face without waking her. Across the room, in the other bed, her brother-in law, Jeremy Parr, snored softly, his bare arm outside the blanket, pulling it in to his body as though he were a cold, small child.

Christina had been dreaming of Jack almost nightly in the nine months since the accident. The dreams varied in scale and intensity like music, from the highest soprano pitch of remembered fragments of joy, to the deepest, lowest *basso profundo* of grief and loss. From the latter, she would wake up sobbing, her throat dry and raw as though she had been swallowing graveyard dirt, feeling as if she were buried alive, and the darkness of her bedroom a sealed, airless coffin. On those nights, when she switched on her bedside lamp to try to read the book she always kept on her night table for this exact purpose, knowing full well that she wouldn't be able to forget the yawning, empty space next to her on the bed, she wondered whether the pain would ever end, or if this was what she had to look forward to every night for the rest of her life.

Last night was different, though. Last night she dreamed she and Jack were together, walking in a vast green pine forest shot through with gold sunlight. Jack was leading her by the hand. She could still feel the imprint of his palm in hers. She looked at the inside of her hand, half expecting to see his fingerprints. With the insight peculiar to dreamers, particularly dreamers of love, she knew it was one of the forests near Jack's family's house in Parr's Landing, where they'd both grown up. It was a dream of comfort and security, a dream that drew on emotional subtitles that stretched back over the course of eighteen years, including the two years they'd spent together in high school in Parr's Landing before Morgan had been born. The dream felt like an augury, but of what she wasn't yet sure. The now familiar ache was there, of course. But this morning it was tinged with something she couldn't quite identify.

Christina looked at her watch. It was 7:25 a.m. The light leaking through the motel curtains was deep orange, a pellucid autumnal hue that was unique to northern regions where the snow came fast and early and winter ruled for seemingly endless months. The light spoke of stars in the violet-blue early morning sky, of columns of Canada geese streaking south across the vastness of Lake Superior and Lake Huron, while below them, the forests turned the colour of fire and rust and blood.

Then she realized what the dream had been tinged with and the thought came, unbidden and profoundly bittersweet: *I'm almost home. My God. I never, ever thought I would come back here.*

Christina dressed as quickly and quietly as she could so as not to wake Morgan and Jeremy. She donned a pair of jeans and pulled a bulky sweater over the thin T-shirt she'd slept in. In the bathroom, she splashed cold water on her face and ran a damp comb through her thick blonde hair. There were faint purple smudges under her eyes, but all in all, she thought, she looked pretty good for a woman who had just driven ten hours across the country from Toronto to Sault Ste. Marie, with a heartbroken and anxious teenage girl and a twenty-five year old gay man at the end of an affair he claimed was the love of his life—and for whom this was as reluctant a homecoming as it was for her.

There was a diner across the street from the motel. Christina sat at a booth near the window and ordered scrambled eggs and home fries. From where she sat, she could watch for Morgan in case her daughter woke up and came looking for her. It seemed unlikely, given how deeply she was sleeping when Christina had left the motel room. Sleep was nature's best balm. Morgan and Jack had been exceptionally close, perhaps closer than most fathers and daughters, and his death had devastated her.

That, coupled with the sudden uprooting from the only home she'd ever known—in the only city she'd ever known—to move to a town she'd only ever heard discussed in the most negative terms by her parents, had taken a visible emotional toll.

What sort of a mother packs up her grieving teenage daughter and loads her into the back seat of a rusted-out 1969 Chevy Chevelle and drives her to the ends of the earth to start a new life, you ask? She took a sip of the fresh coffee, wincing at the bitterness and adding more sugar. *A broke one, that's who. A broke widow whose freewheeling, romantic, carefree late husband hadn't taken out life insurance because he thought it was bourgeois, but took out a second mortgage on their house without telling her—one she found out about when the bank foreclosed on it. A woman with no job and no savings, but who had a rich mother-in-law, one who might despise her, personally, but might still feel a sense of dynastic responsibility for her granddaughter out of love for her eldest son, if nothing else.*

At least, she thought, *I hope she will.*

As she ate her breakfast in blessed silence, Christina watched as the light advanced. She'd forgotten how clear that light was, especially in the fall. The mist on the lake was burning off as the sun climbed higher. On the other side of the lake, she could make out a scattering of white buildings underlined by a dirt road at the foot of the sloping, mountainous hills stretching against the blue sky. Alone in the booth at the diner with her thoughts, accountable to no one, and with nothing around her at that moment that had any bearing on her life, she gazed out the window as the sunlight touched the burnished leaves of the line of maple trees framing the motel where her daughter slept.

When she was sure she could see the beauty, she allowed herself to feel hope.

Christina felt a sudden crashing wave of terrible longing for Jack, one that stunned her once again with its ferocity. Tears blurred her vision, but this time she didn't wipe them away. She rode the pain like a wave, not fighting it, cresting with it instead, allowed it to deposit her, gently and safely, in a rational place.

She paid her bill and left the diner to wake up Morgan and Jeremy. They still had a four- to five-hour drive ahead of them to Parr's Landing and whatever waited for them there.

They were on the road within an hour and a half. Morgan and Jeremy were awake, showered, and packed up by the time she got back to the motel. Christina was surprised but pleased. Getting Morgan ready in the morning had been an ordeal more or less from the day she'd turned thirteen. The waitress at the diner smiled at her when the three of them trooped over and sat down at the booth she'd left twenty minutes before.

Christina said, "A couple more hungry customers for you before we get back on the road this morning."

"Couldn't get enough of our good country cooking, eh?" The waitress beamed at Morgan and Jeremy. "Is this your hubby and your little girl? She looks just like her handsome daddy. You want some hot chocolate, honey?"

Christina felt Morgan flinch beside her. She opened her mouth to tell the waitress that Jeremy wasn't her father but her uncle, but before she could say a word, Morgan smiled at the waitress and politely replied, "Just some orange juice, please."

When the waitress returned to the kitchen with their order, Christina turned to Morgan and said, "That was very nice of you, sweetheart. It was very considerate."

Morgan shrugged. "It's not her fault. She didn't know. And I *do* look like daddy and so does Uncle Jeremy, so she wasn't all wrong."

Jeremy said, "Your father had all the looks in the family. Ask your mother. He was so handsome when he was your age that everyone was in love with him. Your mom was the only girl in Parr's Landing who'd ever caught his eye. It was like *Romeo and Juliet* with those two."

"*Romeo and Juliet* was a tragedy," Morgan said. The previous year, her class at Jarvis Collegiate had studied Shakespeare's play in English Lit. The teacher, Mr. Niven, had run the Franco Zeffirelli version of the film on the reel-to-reel projector in the classroom and Morgan had fallen in love with Leonard Whiting. "Mom and Dad weren't a tragedy. They ran off and got married. They had me. They got out of Parr's Landing. Romeo and Juliet never got out of Verona."

"You're right, they did get out of Parr's Landing." Jeremy's eyes met Christina's over the table. "They did. They got away and they met their destiny. And the best part of their destiny was having you." He reached over and put his hand over Morgan's. "I'm so very, very glad they did."

Morgan allowed Jeremy to hold her hand for a brief moment, and then pulled it gently away as though to avoid hurting his feelings. Her love for her uncle was unquestioned. The question for Morgan seemed to be how much of that love she could show without feeling disloyal to her father, at least for now. Christina observed their interaction and saw that Jeremy understood. She sent a silent prayer of thanksgiving for Jeremy's presence to whichever divinity took under its wing the families of fatherless girls and husbandless wives.

When the food arrived, Morgan took a bite of her toast and asked Jeremy, "Isn't it weird having a town named after you? I mean, I'm going to see my name everywhere, aren't I? That's going to be weird. Wasn't it weird for you and Daddy?"

"It *was* weird," Jeremy admitted. "But you get used to it. Your dad and I never thought twice about it. You won't either, after a while. And the town wasn't named after *us,* it was named after our great-grandfather— your great great-grandfather. He founded the town in the late nineteenth century. That was a long time ago, and nobody thinks about it anymore. We're just like anybody else."

"Then why did you leave? Why did you move to the city? If it's so great, why didn't you stay?"

Jeremy glanced around the diner, which was slowly filling with people. He lowered his voice slightly. "Morgan, you know why I had to leave. There were . . . problems. I know you know what those problems were. Your dad and mom and I have told you about them. We don't need to discuss it again here, do we?"

Morgan looked chastened. "I'm sorry, Uncle Jeremy," she said. "I didn't mean to make you feel bad."

"It's fine, Morgan. But we have to remember that we're not in the city anymore. Things are a lot different out here. There are things we can talk about in public and things we can't talk about."

Time to nip this one in the bud, Christina thought. "Sweetheart, I know you're nervous about today. I know you're nervous about meeting your grandma for the first time, especially after everything we've told you about her. Try to remember that the bad things we told you about happened a long time ago. Your dad and I were very young and your grandma and grandpa were very mad at us for running away together and having you."

"They didn't want you to have me?"

"Morgan, we've talked about this before. They didn't think it was right for us to have you since we weren't married."

"But you *did* get married. You *are* married."

"They wanted your daddy to stay in Parr's Landing, go to university, and take over the mine. When the mine shut down, they blamed him for not being there to help save it. They were mad at both of us, honey. But they weren't mad at you."

"I don't think we should go there. I think we should go home."

"That's all in the past," Christina said, ignoring Morgan's last comment. "Your grandma Parr was very nice to invite us to come and stay with her for a while." Christina saw Jeremy wince. She pursed her lips to signal to him to keep quiet. "We need to get back on our feet."

"Why couldn't we get back on our feet in Toronto?" Morgan's bottom lip began to tremble. "Why did we have to come here? Daddy didn't want us to come back here. He *hated* it here. He told me so. And now you're making us move here. It's not fair."

"I know, Morgan. But we have to make the best of it when there's no alternative. And believe me, there's no alternative. It'll be what we make of it."

"It'll be fine," Jeremy said. "It's a beautiful part of the country, Morgan. And your grandma's house is very old and very big. There are wonderful log beams on the ceiling and lots of paintings on the walls. It's on the top of a hill with a great view of the town and the river below it."

She brightened. "So, are we rich? I'd like to be rich."

Christina and Jack had never been the beneficiaries of any part of the Parr fortune after they'd left the Landing together, so there had been no reason to inculcate Morgan with any illusions of wealth. As a result, it had simply never occurred to Morgan that her new life in Parr's Landing would be any less hand-to-mouth than her old life in their house in the Cabbagetown district of Toronto.

"Morgan—" There was a warning edge to Christina's voice.

"Your *grandmother* is rich," Jeremy corrected. "Well, she's not as rich as the family used to be before the thirties. But yeah, she's rich." Jeremy looked across the table at Christina. This time, she was the one who winced. "But she's very stingy, so it doesn't matter if she's rich or not. It doesn't matter to *us*, anyway. But you'll get to stay in a beautiful house, one that's so big you won't hardly have to see the rest of us unless you want to."

"Beautiful, beautiful," Morgan said sullenly. "I always know when you're lying because you say things like 'beautiful' instead of describing them properly. It's not beautiful at all, is it? It sounds like an old witch's castle or something. Daddy said she was an ogress. He said she ate her young. I bet it's a horrible house."

Jeremy smiled. "I think your father was speaking metaphorically, sweetheart. Did he really say that she ate her children?" He laughed. "Did he actually use that phrase—that exact phrase?"

"Yeah, he did. Why?"

"Because that was my line. That was something I said to him once about your grandma. I was kidding, of course. I don't think she literally eats her young. Although, she might want to eat her granddaughter. You never know. You're delicious." Across the table, Christina felt Morgan relaxing. Jeremy had succeeded in distracting her from her fretfulness. She'd started to giggle. Jeremy continued, his voice ominous. "The winters are very long up here and Parr's Landing is in Wendigo country."

"What's a Windiggy?"

"Not 'Windiggy,' *Wendigo*. It's an Indian legend. The Wendigo was a cannibal spirit that possessed men and made them eat human flesh."

"That's disgusting," Morgan said, her nose wrinkled in distaste. "I bet it's fake anyway. There's no such thing."

"When we're settled in, I'll take you up to Spirit Rock," Jeremy said. "I'll show you the Indian paintings on the cliffs above Bradley Lake. You can see for yourself. They're supposed to be paintings of a real Wendigo. Your dad and I used to swim there when we were kids. Everyone in town has seen them."

"For real?" Morgan's blasé façade of adolescent disinterest slipped momentarily. She'd loved legends and stories ever since she was a little girl, something Jeremy had clearly remembered and was now using to his advantage. Christina again met his eyes but this time she smiled. He smiled back.

"Well, the paintings are three hundred or so years old," Jeremy said seriously. "And they're pretty faded. But yeah, that's what they're supposed to be. There was a Jesuit missionary settlement on the site of the town sometime in the seventeenth century.

There are lots of stories about it. Parr's Landing is a pretty inter-esting place if you know what to look for."

"Mom, why didn't you tell me any of this stuff when I was growing up?"

"Oh," Christina said, affecting nonchalance. "I don't know. It's something you really need to see for yourself." *I didn't tell you any of this stuff because I didn't want to think about any of it. I wanted to forget it all. And I never wanted you to be curious enough about it to go find out about it on your own. You were supposed to be my city girl. And instead, here we are.* "It's really a beautiful town in its own way, Morgan. I think you're going to like it a lot. At least let's try to give it a chance, shall we?" She looked hopefully at Morgan. She laid her hand on top of her daughter's, much as Jeremy had done earlier, but this time Morgan didn't pull her hand away.

She squeezed her mother's hand. "OK, mom, I promise. It'll be OK, you'll see."

The waitress came back to the table. "All done? Can I get you folks anything else?" She looked at Morgan's plate. "Honey, you didn't eat very much. Not a big eater, eh? Would you like some-thing else? Some pancakes or something?"

"No, thank you," she replied. "I wasn't very hungry. I'm not much of a morning person. But the food was great."

"Just the bill please," Christina said, reaching for her purse. "We have to get on the road. We still have a long way to go."

They took Highway 17 north along Lake Superior towards Mon-tréal River.

Christina drove steadily, her eyes on the road. After half an hour, the silence in the car became oppressive and she turned on the radio, hoping that music would, at the very least, act as some sort of mental bridge by which the three of them could come out of their private thoughts and meet each other half-way. The reception was terrible. She'd forgotten the degree to which the igneous granite of the Precambrian Shield, covered with the thinnest layer of soil, interfered with radio transmis-sion in this part of the country. She turned the radio off and pushed an America eight-track into the deck, humming along to "Horse With No Name" until Morgan asked her to stop so she could enjoy the music. Christina smiled at that, but she stopped humming. At the very least, it meant that Morgan's mind was temporarily occupied by something other than how much she missed her father, or her dread at the thought of starting a new life in as alien a place as a teenager from Toronto could imagine.

Through the windows of the car, the landscape grew wilder. The original Trans-Canada route had been Highway 11, called "The King's Highway" in a colonial forelock-tug to His Majesty King George V. The unforgiving terrain of the two-billion-year-old Precambrian Shield had been so resistant to taming when it was being built in 1923 that the Algoma Central Railway, which had connected Sault Ste. Marie to various northern Ontario mining towns, including Parr's Landing, bypassed the 165-mile gap between Sault Ste. Marie and the Agawa River. The "Big Gap," as it was called, had been a treasure trove of virgin timber surrounded by deep gorges and rivers bracketed by steep-walled granite canyons. In 1960, the newly completed Highway 17 made the route shorter and simpler, but no less dramatic than its antecedent highway, along which Christina remembered driving with Jack—and with Morgan slumbering in her womb—nearly sixteen years ago. Of course, sixteen years ago they had been driving in the opposite direction, towards a new life. Perversely, she reasoned that she was still driving towards a new life, but in a completely different sense.

Ironic, she thought. *Ugly, tragic, but ironic nonetheless.*

On either side of the car, the highway rose and fell, bracketed here and there by soaring granite cliffs of rose and grey stone. Forests of maple and birch planed off from the highway into the distant badlands like great wings of red and gold. Christina saw the edges of algae-encrusted swamps laced with dead logs and slippery rock, and deep pine everywhere. As they approached the town of Wawa, the maple and birch gave way to a mélange of birch and various other deciduous trees, as well as conifers, adding the blessed rigour of dark green to a palette from which Christina felt nearly drunk with colour. Through the window,

Morgan squealed with delight and pointed to a moose standing back from the road beside a tamarack swamp. As the car swept past, the moose ambled back into the deeper brush, either cautious or indifferent to their passing.

In Wawa, Morgan made Christina stop the car so she could look at the twenty-eight-foot tall metal statue of the Canada goose that had been built twelve years before, in 1960, and dedicated to the town that had taken its name from the Ojibwa word for "wild goose." After Morgan had taken a few pictures with the ancient secondhand Kodak Brownie 127 Jack had bought her for her thirteenth birthday, she said she was hungry. They drove through the town and stopped at a roadside chip stand run by a taciturn old man and his wife, the two of them virtually indistinguishable one from the other, with short-clipped grey hair, ruddy skin, and wrapped in denim and lumberjack flannel.

Jeremy bought beer-battered fish and salted chips wrapped in newspaper. Morgan fetched blankets from the car and they sat down to eat at one of the nearby picnic tables.

As they devoured the surprisingly delicious fish and chips, Christina mentally calculated how much money she had spent, including moving out of their rented house on Sumach Street, plus gas, food, and lodging since they'd left Toronto, and realized she was dangerously close to depleting what funds remained.

She looked up at the sky, less bright and blue at two in the afternoon than it had been when they left Batchawana Bay that morning. They were still about three hours away from Parr's Landing, off the main highway and deep into the northern Ontario badlands at that. Christina felt another flare of anxiety as she realized they would need to fill up the Chevelle's gas tank. She hoped they didn't run out of gas or break down before they got to Parr's Landing. She calculated that they would arrive near five p.m. when it was beginning to get dark.

There would be nothing for miles if anything happened. Christina had no desire to spend the night on the side of the road, miles from nowhere in Ontario bush country while the forest came alive around them in the impenetrable blackness she remembered well from her childhood.

* * *

Beside her, Jeremy Parr, lost in his own thoughts, remembered the blackness, too, though his blackness, while different from Christina's, was no less implacable.

Jeremy didn't regret accompanying his sister-in-law back to Parr's Landing—not because he was ambivalent about returning to the locus of the worst emotional pain of his life, but because he knew there had been nothing else to do. He'd been fired from his bartending job the previous week, and even if he hadn't been, there was no way—at least in the short term—that he would have been able to support the three of them. Christina had no job skills, and Morgan's mourning had been such that there was no question Christina had to be there for her daughter.

Jack and Christina had saved his life. He felt he owed it, especially to his dead brother, to try to keep Christina and Morgan safe. And right now that meant going home with his sister-in-law and his niece and watching over them while they were in his mother's house.

Jack and Christina had taken him in without question after his mother had sent him to the private clinic in North Bay to get help for his "problem" after he tried to kill himself in his seventeenth year. Adeline Parr had signed all the requisite papers, and Jeremy had been loaded into a limousine in the middle of the night and told not to resist, or he'd be restrained.

"This is for the best, my darling," Adeline had told him, standing back, delicate and ladylike, as he fought with the two burly orderlies who were holding him by either arm and pushing him towards the car. "This is all for your own good, you'll see. You'll be safer there, too. The town is too small, and you've made it too dangerous for yourself to live here with the things you've done. When you come back, you'll be cured. Things will be different—you'll see."

A sympathetic maternal smile never touched her eyes. They were cold and practical, the eyes of a widow used to issuing orders to inferiors—orders she expected to be obeyed. Adeline had been entirely unmoved by Jeremy's tears and his pleading to be allowed to stay, that he would be good, that there would be no more trouble with other boys, that what happened hadn't been his fault. Adeline had stood in the hallway of Parr House, immaculate in a black wool suit and pearls and watched her younger son dragged out of his home in the middle of the night and shoved into the back seat of a black Cadillac Fleetwood with blacked-out windows.

Turning to the driver, who had obviously been summoned to wait by the front door in case Jeremy put up too much resistance, she pointed a manicured index finger towards the drawing room off the main hallway and said, "His bags are in the other room. Please see to it that they're loaded immediately. Tell Dr. Janek at the clinic to telephone me if there's anything else."

And with that, she'd turned away, her high heels clicking on the black-and-white marble entryway, without ever turning back.

At the Doucette Institute, the psychiatrists set about attempting to cure him of his affliction. For six months, Jeremy endured icy baths, and electric shocks applied to his hands and genitals while being forced to watch black-and-white films of naked, oiled, muscular men. He was strapped to chairs in darkened rooms for hours, and injected with apomorphine, after which he was forced to drink two-ounce shots of brandy to induce nausea. When the nausea became nearly unendurable, the room was heated and bright lights were shone on large photographs of male nudes, and he was told to select the one he desired the most. At that point, Dr. Janek played a tape describing his "illness" in graphic, sickening detail until Jeremy vomited out the drugs, and was given more. The tape was played every hour. After thirty hours, detecting dangerous levels of acetone in Jeremy's urine, he was sent back to his room to recover.

But the treatments always began again. Other nights, he was awakened every two hours by congratulatory messages about how different his life would be once he'd conquered his "inversion" and been rendered "normal." Every morning he was injected with testosterone propionate and made to listen to records of women's voices, lush and frankly sexual voices that, to Jeremy, merely sounded whorish and insectile through the scratchy speakers of a turntable.

In sessions, Dr. Janek—who, Jeremy noted with fresh disgust at every session, had terrible pitted acne scars on his face, and eyes that were even colder and more censorious than his mother's, and breath that made Jeremy think of an open grave—forced him, over and over again, to repeat every graphic aspect of every sexual fantasy he'd ever had. In the end, Elliot made them up, which seemed to satisfy Dr. Janek, who seemed unable to distinguish between fact and fantasy when it came to what Jeremy told him.

Worse still, he forced Jeremy to reveal every intimate detail of his discovered friendship with Elliot McKitrick. He made him describe Elliot's body—every part of it, what he'd done with it, and what Elliot had done to him by way of reciprocation.

That implacable, dry voice, impatient, professorial and peremptory: *What did you do with that boy, Jeremy? Tell me again.*

Weeping in reply: *He's just a friend. We're friends. It only happened once. We didn't mean to do anything wrong. I'm sorry. It only happened once. I'll never do it again. I'm cured now. Please, please, please let me go home. I want my mother. No more tests. They hurt too much.*

And, coming full circle, Dr. Janek's oily, coercive compassion again: *How are you going to be better, Jeremy, if you don't trust me? You do want to be normal, don't you? Don't you want to be cured?*

At night, locked in his cell-like room, he'd cry himself to sleep, wondering what he'd ever done to be sent to this place.

On the nights he was allowed to sleep through till dawn instead of being woken every two hours by the recording, he dreamed a mosaic of familiar images—Parr's Landing itself, swimming with Jack in the cold black water of Bradley Lake beneath the centuries-old Indian paintings of the legendary Wendigo of the St. Barthélemy settlement etched into the granite cliffs that stood sentinel around the lake. He dreamed of his mother's house. In those dreams, he explored the vast dim rooms on the upper floors of the house. They were dreams of secrecy, as though he were hiding, though in the dreams it was unclear what he might be hiding from. He dreamed of his mother—dreams of guilt and chastisement and shame, dreams from which he sometimes awoke gasping for breath, feeling as though he'd been caught *in flagrante delicto* committing some terrible crime for which the punishment was being sent away forever.

The worst dreams were those of Elliot McKitrick, because Elliot berated him as Jeremy wept, telling him that Jeremy had ruined Elliot's life forever by being so *weak* and *sick* and such an *invert* and leading him astray, destroying Elliot's chances for a respectable life among decent people. And in those dreams, Elliot's voice wasn't Elliot's voice at all—it was the voice on the tape.

After six months, Jeremy lost twenty-five pounds he could barely afford to lose. He had dark circles under his eyes and almost-healed burns on the most private parts of his body. But Dr. Janek had pronounced him cured and he'd been allowed to return home.

Adeline welcomed him home as though he'd been away visiting relatives which, as it turned out, was what she'd told everyone in Parr's Landing who'd asked where Jeremy was.

On his first night home, Jeremy and Adeline ate dinner in the mahogany-panelled dining room at Parr House. Although it was just the two of them, Adeline ordered the table to be set formally with Viennese damask and Georgian silver, as though Jeremy were a visiting dignitary instead of her seventeen-year-old son who had just returned under the cover of darkness from a private psychiatric hospital.

"I expect things to be different now, Jeremy," Adeline said. "With the boys, and your . . . incident. They will be, won't they? I missed you so much while you were away. It was hard enough when your brother got that slut in the family way and ran off without a word. The detectives said he was in Toronto, living openly with her. Openly. Can you imagine?"

This line of lament—her abandonment by Jack five years before; the "slut"; Morgan, the "bastard granddaughter," whose existence Adeline had discovered when she hired a private detective in Toronto to find Jack— was one Jeremy had heard many times before from his mother. He'd long since learned to let his mother's invective run its course, especially on this one topic of family betrayal.

"And apparently they have a five-year-old. My only grand-daughter, born *illegitimate*. But still, never even a photograph!" Adeline looked pained. "Can you imagine? Your old mother hates to be left alone, darling." Adeline paused delicately as though she were waiting for him to hold a door open for her, or pull her chair out. She laid the sterling silver fork in her hand elegantly against the gold rim of the plate. "You won't disappoint me, will you, Jeremy? You *are* cured, aren't you? Dr. Janek assures me that you are, and that we won't have any more trouble. Because if we do," she added, "he has also assured me that there will always be a place waiting for you at the Doucette."

Jeremy ran away that night.

He hitched a ride with the driver of a supply truck returning to Wawa from a round-trip delivery. From Wawa, he'd hitchhiked to Toronto over the course of four days of near-starvation and beneath a thick coating of accumulated highway grime. Most of his rides assumed he was a runaway of some kind, but because he was frail and small, his rides took pity on him, especially those men who were travelling with their wives.

After two days, he became aware of a solidarity of sorts among night drivers. Night drivers seemed more inclined to understand, even sympathize, with the notion of escape, or flight, or adventure in a way that those who travelled openly and respectably in the propriety of daylight might question. Jeremy answered as few questions as he possibly could without being rude—easier at night, somehow—though he willingly participated, as best he could, in any conversations his benefactors chose to initiate, seeing it as the least he could do under the circumstances.

But Jeremy still held back as much personal information as he could. He knew his mother would find him eventually, if she chose to, but he was determined to leave as sparse a trail as he could. In his mind, he entertained cinematic, paranoid fantasies of police interrogations of the drivers who moved him farther and farther away from Parr's Landing. At seventeen, those inter-rogations seemed entirely feasible in a world where a seemingly omnipotent *magna mater* like Adeline Parr could lift a telephone from its cradle and, with one call, condemn her own son to six months of torture and sadistic psychological experimentation— all with no more effort than it took her to order a freshly killed animal from the butcher shop on Martin Street in Parr's Landing.

The last eight-hour leg of his journey from the town of Thunder Mouth was in the back of the red Volkswagen bus driven by the lead singer of a folk quartet from Saskatchewan—three men, John, Wolf, and David, and their "girl singer," Annie—who were moving east to follow the burgeoning music scene that was in full flower in the coffeehouses of the run-down Yorkville section of Toronto. They told Jeremy about a club called The Purple Onion where they had been invited to perform. Annie told him he reminded her of her baby brother, Victor, back in Estevan.

When they stopped at a Red Barn on the side of the road just before Durrant, Annie bought him a Big Barney and fries, and a chocolate milkshake. Jeremy was certain that nothing he'd ever eaten before in his life had tasted as good as that hamburger. She watched him devour it as though he'd never seen food before and quietly ordered him another one. He ate that one slower, but only marginally.

Back in the van, he fell asleep in the back seat to the sound of them singing "Jimmy Crack Corn" in four-part harmony. When he woke up, it was early evening. They had arrived in Toronto and were driving down Yonge Street. Looking out the window at the shops and the people, he touched the breast pocket of his jean jacket where the carefully folded piece of paper with Jack and Christina's address was, and breathed a deep sigh of relief. If he'd believed in God, he would have said a prayer. He felt entirely safe for the first time since he was a small child.

At Bloor Street, the musicians let him out. Annie tucked a five-dollar bill into his pocket and told him to come see them play sometime.

"I'm sorry we can't take you right to your brother's, but we're running behind schedule as it is," said Wolf, squinting down at the map in his hands. "The neighbourhood you're looking for is called Cabbagetown. According to this, it isn't far. Just walk east till you get to Parliament, and then turn right. You should be able to find Sumach Street real easy. If you can't, just ask."

"Thank you guys so much," Jeremy said. "And thanks for the burger, Annie." Impulsively and clumsily he reached out and hugged her. Inhaling in the caramel scent of her hair and skin, taking the soft, warm, nurturing femaleness of her, he marvelled at the difference between her hug and the agate-hard brittleness of his own mother's hibernal embrace. Jeremy held tightly to Annie for a moment, and then let go.

"Be safe, little man," Annie said, ruffling his hair. "Have a big life." Then she climbed back in to the waiting van and the door slid shut.

The red Volkswagen turned right on Bloor, towards Yorkville; Jeremy turned left on foot towards Cabbagetown, each in the direction of their respective destinies.

Arriving at the house on Sumach Street, Jeremy rang the doorbell. Jack answered the door. Before Jeremy even had a chance to speak, Jack pulled him into the house and hugged him as though he would never let him go. Behind him came Christina and five-year-old Morgan. When she saw that everyone else was crying, Morgan companionably burst into tears, which made all of them laugh.

Late that night, in front of the fireplace, he and Jack talked while Christina and Morgan slept upstairs. Jack wept when Jeremy told him about what they'd done to him at the Doucette Institute with the express permission of their mother. He, in turn, explained to Jeremy that his mother had tried to pay Christina's parents to force her to get an abortion. When they refused, Adeline Parr had warned them to be careful, because a mining town was fraught with potentially fatal accidents. Christina's parents told Christina what Adeline had said, and Christina, in turn, told Jack.

Jack confided to Jeremy that they believed that Christina's life—and the life of the baby she was carrying—would be in danger if they remained in Parr's Landing. So they'd escaped that night much like Jeremy had.

"I'm so sorry I left you," Jack said. "Forget our mother. Forget everything you knew before. You can be yourself here. If you want to be . . . well, you know, if you want to be with . . . men, that's OK with me. It'll be fine with Christina, too. We've known . . . homosexuals before, you know. There are some right here in this neighbourhood. They're nice fellas, run the antique shop on Parliament. We'll make our own family here. A new family. You don't have to go back."

"What if she comes looking for me? What if she tries to force me to come home?"

"You're turning eighteen in a couple of days, Jeremy. Remember, last year they lowered the age of consent from twenty-one to eighteen. She can't touch you even if she wanted to, from a legal standpoint. She can't *make* you go back."

"You know she hired detectives to find you and Christina," Jeremy said fretfully. "She knows where you live and everything. She'll know I'm here."

"Let her," Jack said defiantly. "I don't care. Also, she didn't try to get me to come home, remember? She just wanted to know where I was. She wants to be in control. That's always been the most important thing for her, our whole lives. Besides," he added, "I don't think she'll come looking for you. She's probably happy to have you out of the way. You can't embarrass her here."

"She sent me away. She can do it again. If we get any hints that she's after me, I'll have to leave. I just can't go through that again. I'd rather be dead."

"Don't worry, Jeremy. I won't let her."

Then Jack held him as Jeremy wept against his shoulder. When Jeremy's sobs had subsided, Jack took his brother's hands in his own.

"Stay here, Jeremy. Be an uncle to Morgan. Be Christina's brother-in-law. Love whomever you want. I don't care, and neither does Christina. I'll protect all of you. I'm never, ever letting you go again."

It was a promise Jack kept faithfully for the next ten years. He kept it right up to that night in February, nine months ago. Driving home from an out-of-town sales call in Guelph in a sudden snowstorm, he hit a patch of black ice on an eastbound highway while trying to avoid an oncoming snowplow. The car fishtailed, then spun into a three-sixty, crashing into the guardrail. He hadn't been wearing a seat belt. The outward trajectory of his body was stopped only by the steering wheel, which crushed his chest and lungs in a fraction of a second.

Jack Parr died of thoracic trauma and internal bleeding while waiting for an ambulance from Guelph that finally arrived twenty minutes later. By that time, Christina had been rendered a destitute widow, Morgan had been rendered a half-orphan, and Jeremy had been rendered the only son of Adeline Parr, the long-abandoned ogress of Parr's Landing.

CHAPTER SIX

What?" Jeremy was startled out of his reverie. He turned to Christina. "Sorry, Chris, I didn't hear you. What did you say?"

"I asked you what you were thinking about. And keep your voice down," Christina whispered. "I think Morgan's asleep." She checked her rearview mirror and saw that her daughter was, in fact, sleeping in the back seat of the Chevelle, with her head leaning against the wadded-up sweater she was using as a makeshift pillow.

"Oh, I don't know. I was remembering things. I was thinking about Jack."

Christina was silent, her eyes on the road. Then she said, "I know. I've been thinking about him all day myself. This is the one thing he never wanted to happen. But what can you do? Life is what happens when you're busy making other plans, right?"

"You know, it could be all right. She might have changed, you know."

"I don't see her forgiving any of us for leaving—especially me, since she blamed me for—" Christina looked into the rearview mirror again. "Well, for the way I changed her plans for the family. I also have a feeling she blames me for Jack's death, too. She didn't directly say it in the letter, but it was there all the same."

"Having the surviving son be someone like me wasn't part of her plan for the glories of the Parr family, either, Chris. Don't take all of this on yourself. She never forgave me for being queer, let alone for failing her loving attempts to cure me. I still have nightmares about that sadist. Dr. Janek, I mean," he said wryly. "Not Adeline. Though she's been known to haunt a dream or two, as well."

"Well, I have nightmares about Adeline all the time."

Jeremy peered into the darkness through the windshield. There was no light anywhere except what was provided by the Chevelle's headlights bouncing off the gnarled logging road. "It's pitch black out here. I guess I forgot what it's like at night. Jesus, it's Saturday. If I were home I'd be dancing with handsome men at the Parkside or the St. Charles right now, with my shirt off and a bottle of poppers in my nose. Ah, memories. They're all we'll have to sustain us out here in God's country. Where the hell *are* we, anyway?"

Christina said, "We're just south of Marathon and about five miles to Hattie Cove. After that, about half an hour."

"That was my attempt at humour, by the way," Jeremy said. "I'm hurt that you didn't laugh. I mean, about the poppers and the dancing."

"I just doubt that it's much of an exaggeration," Christina replied tartly. "And besides, right about now it sounds pretty amazing. Have you thought about it, by the way? I mean, what it's going to be like for you back home being openly hom . . . sorry, *gay*," she corrected herself, using the word that Jeremy and his friends applied to themselves.

"You said 'home' to refer to that place," Jeremy said. He shuddered. "It's not my home. Toronto is my home."

"You know what I mean."

"Yes, I do." He sighed. "Sorry, I didn't mean to bite your head off. And yes, I've thought about it a lot. Of course I'm not going to be 'openly gay' there. You don't get to be 'openly gay' way up north. I don't think they've even heard the word 'gay.' It's 'faggot,' 'fruit,' or 'queer.' Or, something worse. Aside from the fact that I'd get killed—scion of the great Parr name or not—who on earth would I 'be gay' *with*?"

"Have you thought about that guy you used to know? What was his name—Elliot? Elliot McCormack?"

"McKitrick. Elliot McKitrick. And no," Jeremy lied, "I haven't. I haven't thought about him in years."

"I wonder what happened to him?"

"I do know that his father beat him up pretty badly when he found out about us. I heard about it from my mother. Used a whip on him, apparently. My mother said I should be grateful that she loved me enough to send me to the Doucette instead of doing to me what Elliot's father did to him." He was silent for a moment. "I don't know what happened in the end."

Softly, Christina asked, "Did you love him? I mean, 'love-love'?"

Jeremy sighed again. "Oh, what's love? I fell in 'love' a lot in Toronto. I certainly thought it was 'love-love.' With Elliot, we were both young." He paused. "Yes, I did love him, I guess. He was so handsome, almost as handsome as Jack."

"I sort of remember him. I went to school with his sister. She was pretty, too."

"Elliot's probably fat and bald now and married to some water buffalo with seven kids. That is if my mother didn't have him killed." Jeremy laughed mirthlessly. "Jesus, *why* are we doing this? Remind me?"

"*I'm* doing what I have to do," Christina said. "I have no money and no place to go. We couldn't keep staying on people's couches, and I couldn't support Morgan by working as a waitress, let alone help her through this grieving period, if I was away every night. Not yet, anyway. That's why I wrote to her. No, Jack didn't want me to ever have to do this, but it's something we should have thought about when he was alive. And frankly, Adeline owes me for what she did. And she especially owes Morgan. She's her granddaughter, for Christ's sake." Christina reached over and touched Jeremy's knee lightly with her fingers. "You, on the other hand, are being a saint on this earth for coming with us to protect us. Jack would have been so proud of you."

"How much do you think she"—Jeremy indicated Morgan with a nod of his head, not wanting to say her name in case it woke her—"has figured out about what happened back here before she was born?"

"I don't know. We've always been very careful when we spoke about the family, as neutral as we could possibly be. We didn't want to plant monsters in her head."

"Maybe it'll be different this time," Jeremy said. "Maybe things will have changed and it won't be . . . well, the way it was."

"What was that Faulkner quote from *Requiem for a Nun* that Jack loved so much?"

Jeremy closed his eyes. "'The past is never dead. It's not even past.'"

They drove in silence for half an hour, the car interred in the northern Ontario darkness as effectively as if it was a mine cart travelling a mile and a half beneath the earth. Then the road abruptly widened and Christina gasped.

"Look," she said.

Jeremy looked. He drew in a sharp intake of breath.

It was as though the night sky had begun bleeding muddy orange light from a rip in the clouds, threaded now with skeletal fingers of luminous red and yellow. And the clouds now parted like stage curtains, revealed the low full moon, vast and sovereign, and seemingly large enough to touch the edge of the earth.

Beneath the moon, the town of Parr's Landing rose out of the blackness, stretching to meet it. Beyond the town, the vast forests and the cliffs above Bradley Lake held Parr's Landing in the same stony centuries-old embrace.

This was the same view the Indians had for a thousand years before the arrival of the French and English. It was the same view the French Jesuits first saw when they arrived on the shores of New France, travelling by canoe and overland to build the doomed mission of St. Barthélemy to the Ojibwa in the seventeenth century.

It was the same view Christina Parr had seen every night for the first seventeen years of her life, and the last vista of Parr's Landing she'd seen when she turned her head, like Lot's wife, that night almost sixteen years in the past when she'd fled the town with Jack Parr.

Unlike Lot's wife, however, Christina hadn't been turned into a pillar of salt as punishment for looking back. But for its part,

Parr's Landing might as well have been petrified by her backward glance for all it had changed.

Faulkner was right, she thought.

"Wake up, Morgan." Christina called gently over her shoulder. And before she could stop herself: "We're home." Then she turned the Chevelle left on Main Street, onto Martin Street, and began the steep uphill climb towards Parr House.

PARR'S LANDING

CHAPTER SEVEN

Adeline Parr heard the sound of wheels on the gravel below her bedroom window and thought: *Now it begins*. She sighed. *I hope it's not all too awfully unpleasant.*

She stared intently into the bevelled mirror of the nineteenth century Biedermeier burlwood dressing table at which she sat and took her own measure in the glass. The result was pleasing, if slightly severe, and it suited her purposes admirably. She adjusted her pearls, and then took a piece of tissue paper from the enamelled box and expertly blotted the lipstick on her bottom lip till it, too, was flawless. By habit, she glanced at the silver-framed photograph of her dead husband and smiled at it as though waiting for Augustus Parr to tell her how beautiful she still was.

Her gold Piaget watch read eleven-thirty. She sighed again. Adeline stood up and smoothed her dark grey skirt, crossed the floor of the bedroom, and closed the door behind her. Then she went downstairs to greet the adventuress who had stolen and murdered her favourite son; her bastard granddaughter; and her great mistake of a second son.

The smile Adeline had been practising froze on her face when she first laid eyes on Morgan, hanging shyly behind her common slut of a mother, in the doorway of Parr House.

Adeline barely registered Christina, but she felt her heart might stop when she saw Jack's face staring back at her. Jack's face, except it was the open and trusting face of a young girl, with none of the rage Jack had shown Adeline before he left. The girl's hair was the same as Jack's— thick and dark brown, with caramel highlights when the light hit it just so. Her eyes were the same as Jack's, too: dark brown, almost-black irises with pupils like dark pools.

"Welcome, Morgan," she said. "I'm your grandmother, Adeline Parr. It's nice to meet you."

Adeline extended her hand and Morgan shook it politely. Under other circumstances, she would have been delighted to see that the girl had been inculcated with some measure of good manners, but she was still privately reeling from the shock of meeting the ghost of her eldest son. The girl's skin was lighter than Jack's but more like Adeline's own, which she knew would please her when she recovered.

"It's nice to meet you, too . . . Grandmother."

For Morgan, there was an edge of a question in the way she said it, as though she were uncertain—not about who Adeline was, but what to call her. Certainly nothing in Adeline's severe elegance inspired cuddly appellatives like "granny" or "grandma," nor had stories about Adeline been any significant part of Morgan's childhood mythology, apart from the odd cryptic reference by one of her parents.

"Yes, you may call me Grandmother," Adeline said, smiling graciously as though she were bestowing a great favour on Morgan. "I dislike diminutives, especially when addressing one's elders."

"Yes, ma'am. I mean, yes, Grandmother."

Adeline smiled down at Morgan again, then looked past Christina, whom she still hadn't greeted, to where Jeremy hung back behind them in the doorway.

"Hello, Mother."

"Behold the prodigal son returns," Adeline said. Her expression was neutral. "That's Luke 15:11-32, son. I trust that, even given your lifestyle, you haven't entirely forgotten the word of God?"

"Have you been rehearsing that for the last ten years, Mother? Or did it just spring to mind when you saw me?" Adeline's eyes shifted quickly to Morgan, then back at her son. "I wouldn't expect you to say something as simple as 'welcome home,' but still—The Bible? Luke? My 'lifestyle'? Before I even cross the threshold?"

"Don't be insolent, Jeremy. I won't have it. You're not back in *Toronto*."

She spat out the word Toronto as though it were foulness— the way a religious fanatic might have said *Babylon* or *Sodom*. "You're in my house, in the town founded by your ancestors on a site made holy with the blood of Catholic martyrs. You can behave and show me respect, otherwise you needn't cross the threshold at all."

"I'm not seventeen anymore, Mother," Jeremy said. "I'm almost thirty. It's been a while since I've been susceptible to that tone of voice, or those phrases." He met his mother's eyes evenly. "It's been a very long drive and we're very tired, especially Morgan. Shall I bring our bags in from the car, or should we drive down to the village and see if the Gold Nugget motel is open at this hour? I'd rather not start the talk in town about us being back by signing my name—the Parr name—in a motel register at this hour, especially not for three of us. But I will if that's what you'd prefer we do. It's your call, Mother."

Thwarted fury passed across Adeline's face like summer lightning, but too quickly for anyone but Jeremy to have seen it, and he only noticed because he'd seen it before and recognized it for what it was. Jeremy had played the one card he always had at his disposal—Adeline's particular personal horror of scandal. The threat of exposing their clandestine return—the slut who'd gotten knocked up by Jack Parr, then married him; the faggot; the illegitimate daughter—to public discourse was a powerful one. Adeline's face was very pale, and two spots of colour had appeared high on the ridge of her cheekbones. But the neutrality of her expression hadn't changed.

"Quite," Adeline said, calmly. "Welcome home. You're most welcome, all of you."

"Mrs. Parr—" Christina began.

"Morgan?" Adeline said, cutting Christina off in mid-sentence, turning instead to her granddaughter. "Why don't you help your Uncle Jeremy with the suitcases? I have a nice room prepared for you upstairs. It's very pretty. I think you'll like it. And you must be tired. It has a canopy bed. Do you know what that is?"

"Yes, Grandmother." There was an unfamiliar impressed awe in Morgan's voice that chilled Christina to the core. "I've seen pictures of one. They're beautiful."

Adeline laughed, a silvery hostess laugh. "Well, hurry up and get your bags out of your car and you can see your bed, darling. Uncle Jeremy can show you the way." She turned to her son. "Morgan will be in the east wing. In the yellow room, Jeremy. You'll have your old room, of course. We'll put dear Christina next to Morgan. Everything has been prepared." When Jeremy and Morgan had gone out to the car, Christina turned to Adeline. "Mrs. Parr, thank you so much for taking us in. As you can imagine, it's been a very difficult time for all of us, especially Morgan."

"Christina, please listen carefully to what I am about to tell you," Adeline said coldly. "I will only say it once, and then we will never have this conversation again. Let me be perfectly plain: taking you and Morgan into my home is an act of charity, one I'm very happy to extend. She is, after all, my granddaughter—my eldest son's child, and very likely the end of our family line. What you and Jack did was unforgivable, and I do not—and will never—forgive either of you for it. You took my son away from me, and now he's dead." Adeline paused, composing herself.

"That said," she continued implacably, "as my son *is* dead, I can only do one thing—the right thing. And that is to take you into my home and extend to you all the privileges of a daughter-in-law, if only for Morgan's sake. You will live here at Parr House as long as you need to. Morgan has already been enrolled in the town high school, and instructions have been given to the administration that any harassment of her based on any . . . past questionable history involving her birth, Jack's death, or Jeremy's perversion, is to be dealt with immediately and harshly. When she has graduated, I shall see to it that her university tuition is paid for and that she is properly prepared for life in the way that you ensured my son, Jack, would never be when you got pregnant and ruined his life."

"Mrs. Parr—"

Adeline raised her finger to silence her daughter-in-law. "I'm not finished. In return, you will conduct yourself respectfully and respectably in and out of this house. You will stay out of my sight except for mealtimes, at which time we will all be together. You will defer to my wishes at all times, especially with regard to Morgan's upbringing while she is under my roof. Unlike you, she is a Parr by blood rather than by convenience."

"By *convenience*?" Christina practically shouted the word. "I ~~was pregnant! We were in love! You forced us to leave here! You~~ threatened my family! I never saw my father again because of what you did to us. He died while I was in Toronto, and he'd been dead for six months before I even found out he was gone! And for what? Jack and I loved each other. We have a beautiful daughter—your granddaughter—and we were happy. We had everything before he died. And when he did, I had nowhere else to come except back to the Landing."

"Don't raise your voice to me, Christina. You and Jack made your own choices. If you find my conditions too arduous, *Mrs. Parr*," Adeline added, putting a vicious accent on the marital title she clearly felt Christina was unworthy to bear, "you may leave my house and fend for yourself. You will be entirely on your own, as will your daughter."

From outside, Christina heard the Chevelle's doors slam shut, and the sound of Jeremy and Morgan's feet on the gravel of the circular driveway in front of Parr House.

"Do we understand each other, Christina? Be quick. I hear Jeremy and Morgan coming back in from the car. I warn you—be very, very careful in case you're thinking of making a scene in front of your daughter and my son. I can make life even more difficult and painful for you than it is right now. Believe me. You have no idea the scope of my influence."

Oh, but I do, Christina thought, feeling fresh hate and fresh desperation in equal measure. *I do. I felt it fifteen years ago, and now I'm feeling it again tonight. Nothing has changed. Nothing.* Her vision blurred. Adeline's pale, hard face swam. Christina brushed the tears away with the back of her hand, realizing suddenly that this particular die had been cast the moment she'd first heard that Jack had been killed on that highway back in February. The rest of this drama was a matter of everyone playing their assigned parts, particularly Christina, at least until she could figure a way out, back to the city. Any city. Anywhere but here.

"Yes," she replied.

"Yes *what*, Christina?"

"Yes, Mrs. Parr. We understand each other."

"Good. Oh, and Christina . . . ?"

"What?"

"You may call me Adeline. After all," she added, the mockery in her voice both cruel and unmistakable, "we're *family* now."

When Morgan and Jeremy came through the door, laden with suitcases, the sight of Adeline smiling beatifically with her arm around Christina's shoulders greeted them.

To Morgan it looked as though her mother had been crying. With the trusting innocence of her inexperience and tender age, she assumed that her mother and grandmother had been discussing her father. It was either that, or the reunion was an emotional one for her mother, given that it was her first time back home since Morgan had been born. She looked at her smiling grandmother and saw only sweetness and an implied offer of safety and security. In that moment, her heart overflowed with relief, and with gratitude towards Adeline.

Morgan put down the two suitcases she was carrying and walked over to where the two women stood and took her mother's hand. She squeezed it gently, wordlessly assuring her that she was all right, that everything was going to be all right, that she loved her.

For his part, Jeremy merely stared, his mouth open. The tension in the air may have been beyond Morgan's experience to understand, but Jeremy recognized it immediately and it carried the whiff of sulphur. Unlike his niece, he had an excellent idea of what had transpired while they had been fetching the suitcases and wondered, not for the first time, what had possessed them to return to this awful place and willingly put themselves at the mercy of this horrendous woman. He was suddenly wracked with the guilt of not having been enough of a man, enough of a brother to Jack, to find some way to support his niece and his sister-in-law. He'd been an idiot to think Adeline might have changed in the ten years he'd been away, let alone the fifteen Christina had. And now they were trapped in this monstrous house, in this town that had always seemed to him to be a blight on the edge of nowhere.

For now, he swore to himself. *Just for now. I'm going to figure out how to get us the fuck out of here. I will. I have to.*

Adeline stepped in between Christina and Morgan, edging Christina almost imperceptibly to the side with her elbow. She put her arms around Morgan's shoulders and hugged her tight.

"My family is restored to me," Adeline said. "Especially my long-lost granddaughter. How very, very wonderful."

Jeremy shuddered. "Come on, ladies," he said. "I'll show you where your rooms are. I think I still know my way around this dump."

Jeremy took them upstairs, then excused himself and continued up the staircase to his own room after bidding them goodnight.

"I'll be on the next floor up, second door to the left of the corridor," he said. He and Christina exchanged a long, meaningful look. "Wake me up if you need anything at all. *Anything,*" he repeated.

She smiled gratefully and squeezed his hand. "We're fine. I'm just going to get Morgan to bed, and then hit the sack myself. I'm worn out. Are you going to be all right up there?"

"Right as rain," Jeremy said wryly. "I'll see you in the morning. Unless something has changed in the last ten years, breakfast is at seven in the dining room. Sleep well."

Once Christina had settled Morgan in the opulent "yellow room" and put her to bed (with Morgan gushing all the while about how *beautiful* the room with its canopy bed was, and how *great* it was for Grandmother Adeline to let them stay there, and why didn't she or Uncle Jeremy *ever* tell her *how nice* she was—until Christina felt she would surely scream), she unpacked her own suitcases in the room that had been assigned to her across the hallway from Morgan's.

Her room was a fraction of the size of Morgan's and very simply furnished by comparison. She knew that Adeline was making yet another point about Christina's dubious standing in the family, but she didn't care. She hadn't come back to Parr's Landing in search of any status Adeline Parr might extend or withhold. She'd come back for exactly what she'd been given downstairs, however cruelly Adeline had presented the goods—some security for Morgan and a roof over their heads while she figured out what to do next. She hadn't sold her soul to Adeline, though she may have put it in escrow for the short term.

So be it, she thought. *Whatever it takes. It's not forever.*

She looked out the window and saw that the moon was going down. Her watch read three a.m. Christina suddenly felt more tired than she could ever remember feeling.

She undressed quickly, not even bothering to wash her face or brush her teeth, and pulled on the red flannel nightgown she'd brought with her. She climbed into bed and pulled the covers up around her neck. The room may have been spare, but the mattress was welcoming. As she closed her eyes, she thought briefly of Jack and wondered if she'd dream of him tonight, here in the house in which he'd grown up, and what shape the dreams would take, if and when they came. She hoped they would.

Christina was fast asleep within minutes of laying her head against the pillow, and for the first time in months, her dreams were entirely uneventful.

At the exact moment Christina was falling asleep and the moon was completing its descent, Richard Weal was butchering a sixty-year-old widower named Alan Carstairs in his bed, in a remote fishing cabin just outside the town of Gyles Point, twenty-five miles south of Parr's Landing, on the shore of Lake Superior.

Weal had broken in soundlessly—the door had been

unlocked, of course—and surprised Carstairs, who was dreaming of his late wife, Edith.

He hadn't been able to bring himself to come up to the cabin at all during the three years since her lingering death from cancer. Today, finally, he had. He'd driven to the cabin, arriving just as the sun was setting over Lake Superior and the waves were high and wild. Inside, he'd lit the kerosene lamps and eaten supper by lamplight.

Carstairs felt the vast emptiness of the cabin all around him and he knew he'd made a terrible mistake coming back up here today.

Edith had been a real Canadian girl. She'd loved the cabin when she was alive and he'd felt her presence *everywhere*, even on the weekends he'd come up on his own to fish, leaving her back in the city with their son and daughter. He saw her blue earthenware pitcher on a shelf by the sink. When she was alive it had always been full of wildflowers—masses of goldenrod, bouquets of Pink Lady's Slipper, wild purple harebell.

Her watercolours of the hard granite shoreline were hanging throughout the cabin. Carstairs knew that if he brought one of the kerosene lamps over to the pine walls outside the ring of yellow light, he'd see them there, under three year's worth of dust. But he realized he didn't want to see them. She was gone, and no alchemy between his own loss and memory and the wild forest magic of this rocky coastline was going to render vivid something that had forever left his life.

Carstairs wept at that realization which, to him, was like watching her die all over again. His sobs made his shoulders ache. Around him, the silence and the darkness seemed to swell and expand till it was vast and huge, and he filled it with a loud keening that came from a deep and terrible empty place inside. He had never felt older or weaker—or more alone—in his life.

When Carstairs felt he had no more tears to shed, he splashed water on his face and pressed a cold washcloth to his eyes. He briefly thought of leaving the cabin that night, but he was a practical man—it was late and he was too tired to drive. It would be dangerous. Before he went to bed, he set his alarm clock for five a.m. He intended to get an early start back to the city, then telephone a realtor from home and put the place on the market. He mounted the stairs to the upper floor, holding the kerosene lantern in front of him, looking straight ahead. Then he undressed and climbed into the cold double bed.

Asleep, his Edith had come to him like an angel of mercy and comfort.

In the dream, Edith was a still just a girl from Trout Creek he'd fallen head over heels for as a student at Wesley College in Winnipeg in 1929. She was young like she had been on their wedding day. In the dream, there was no cancer—and in fact, never would be any cancer. Edith opened her plump, tanned arms to him and said, *Where have you been, Alan? I've been waiting for you. I've missed you so, my darling. It's so beautiful here.*

When he woke in the darkness, it was a grinning Richard Weal he was holding in his arms and the foetor of spoiled meat, body waste, and decay was everywhere.

Carstairs didn't see the knives at first, but he felt them immediately.

In the end, his death had come much more quickly than Edith's had—though, like hers, it was not without pain. Weal had been leisurely with his tools this time, and he'd enjoyed himself very much.

After he was finished, Weal re-lit the kerosene lamp on the dining room table and washed his knives and hammers in the kitchen sink, enjoying the cozy *thump-thump-thump* as the water from the copper bottom of the sink sluiced away hair and flesh and blood from the various blades. He dried them carefully so they wouldn't rust.

Upstairs, he wrapped the various segments of Carstairs's body in bloodied sheets and tied them with baling twine. Then he carried them downstairs and buried them on the property, deep enough so the animals wouldn't dig them up for food when the winter freeze made their hunger savage.

In the darkness, he bathed naked in the icy waters of the inlet, screaming when the cold burned his skin. Then he dried himself with a rough towel, rubbing hard to bring the warmth back to his limbs. He found clean clothes hanging in the bedroom closets of the cabin. They smelled a bit musty and were slightly big for him, but he dressed quickly. Weal packed the remaining clothes he'd found in the closet into the duffel bag Carstairs had brought for this trip to the lake.

Rifling through Carstairs's wallet, Weal found five hundred dollars and several credit cards. He left the credit cards, knowing they could be used to track him if it should come to that. But he doubted it would. It wouldn't be long now till his life changed.

The voice had grown stronger and clearer, and more urgent, like a radio signal in his brain. It faded in and out as he drew closer, or veered away, from its source.

But tonight the voice had been very, very clear. Clearer than it had ever been.

Weal could picture his Friend—for that is indeed how he had come to think of the voice in his head, as a loving Friend, one who'd been his closest companion since the night he'd first heard it five years before—suffocating beneath mounds of flinty soil and shield rock, choking on clods of cold earth, struggling to be free, screaming in the suffocating darkness of the centuries.

And when he'd lapped the blood from Alan Carstairs's slashed throat, his holiest of personal communion rituals, an image of the place had seared itself into his brain. It had appeared entirely unbidden, but it was clear as an Ektachrome slide.

Wake me, his Friend pleaded. *You are close, very close, to the place you seek. Find me. Wake me. I will repay you with rewards beyond your wildest imaginings. I will raise you up to a god.*

CHAPTER EIGHT

Twelve-year-old Finnegan Miller liked to get up when the house was still quiet, while his parents were still fast asleep in their room upstairs, and take his black Labrador, Sadie, for a long walk around Bradley Lake. In October, he woke before sunrise. His routine was unvaried: he dressed in his room, fed Sadie in the kitchen, found her favourite red rubber ball, then put on a jacket and slipped out the back door of the house with Sadie at his heels.

In short order, she'd run ahead, tail wagging, nose to the ground and he'd be the one following her instead of the other way around.

Bradley Lake was half a mile from his house on Childs Drive. To call it a "lake" would flatter it, especially given the proximity of Parr's Landing to the shore of Lake Superior, which always seemed to Finn to be more like an ocean. According to legend, Lake Superior never gave up its dead, and in school, Finn had learned about the terrible history of shipwrecks during storms of almost supernatural ferocity there—the wreck of the *Mataafa Storm* in 1905, the *Cyprus* in 1907, the *Inkerman* and *Cerisoles* minesweepers in 1918. Surely, Finn thought, no body of water that carnivorous, with that much of a taste for human flesh should rightly be called a lake.

But Bradley Lake was a lake—vast, serene, with water so deep and cold it often looked black. Rising directly above it were a tiered grouping of rocky outcrops of Canadian Shield granite cliffs surrounded by a rich taiga forest of black spruce, jack pine, and Ontario balsam poplar.

Once at the lake, the path Finn took was a mile and a half around and lined with paper birch and balsam fir. When he was younger, he'd heard stories of coming upon bush animals in the darkness, but he'd only ever seen one—a buck, last fall—and it had run off when Sadie started to bark and chase it. He'd tried to restrain her but in the end he realized that not only would she never catch the buck, she would have turned tail immediately if it had ever stopped and turned towards her with its antlers lowered.

Finn's father had for a time urged him to let him train Sadie for hunting, but Finn despised the idea of hunting, and his father, who had learned which battles to pick with his son, decided to let it drop. Sadie's status as Finn's best friend—indeed, his only friend—was thus enshrined. This morning ritual hike, with Sadie bounding ahead of him through the bush, was sacrosanct. It was a ritual that was only ever interrupted if Finn was sick or injured, which he rarely was. On those mornings, Sadie would lie beside his bed in his room and whine pitifully until she realized he wasn't ignoring her, but wasn't able to take her out. Then she would lay her head on her front paws and look up at him with reproachful amber eyes.

Sometimes she brought the red rubber ball to him and dropped it at the foot of the bed, as though it were the most marvellous idea ever.

Finn enjoyed the darkness and the silence of this last hour of night best in the late autumn, when the air coming in off Superior was damp and raw, and the yellow and red leaves on the trees lining the path showered water down on him when he accidentally knocked them as he passed by.

While most boys his age might have preferred to stay under the covers for as long as possible in the morning, Finn wasn't most twelve-year-olds. He'd never been like "most" boys his age, no matter what age. This seemed to cause the adults around him more consternation than it caused him. Finn may not have had friends, other than Sadie, but he couldn't miss something he had neither had, nor ever felt he needed.

Besides, Finn was in love. Completely, utterly, and irrevocably in love for the first time in his life. It was a secret he worked hard to hide from his parents, who were already worried about his inability to connect with his peers. No point in making it worse.

He was in love with Dracula.

Specifically, he was in love with *The Tomb of Dracula,* a comic book series, the first issue of which he'd found in early summer of that year on the lowest rung of the spiral comic rack at Harper's Drugs. Like all true loves, no matter the age at which they occur, it was a blinding, all consuming passion that left little room for reason.

Finn thrilled to the cover: a luridly inked four-colour depiction of the fanged Lord of the Undead carrying the limp body of a curvy blonde in a green mini-dress. Dracula's cape was edged in orange satin. Mist swirled in the foreground. In the background loomed a castle framed by a full moon. The banner read NIGHT OF THE VAMPIRE! With his heart in his mouth, he'd paid his twenty cents and pedalled his five-speed Huffy Dragster with the metallic gold banana seat as fast as he could back to his house on Mission Street.

Back home, in his room, with the door closed, he'd read it from cover to cover, memorizing the names of the characters— Frank Drake, Clifton Graves, Jeanie and, of course, Count Dracula himself—as well as the storyline, until he could recite the script.

In the first issue, the skeptical hero, Frank Drake, discovers that he's a descendant of Count Dracula and has inherited a castle in Transylvania. With the intention of turning the castle into a vampire-themed tourist resort, he travels to Romania with his best friend, Clifton Graves, and Frank's fiancée, Jeanie (*she doesn't need a last name,* Finn noted, with an unfamiliar flush, *not with boobs like those*). Clifton discovers the skeleton of Count Dracula in the castle's dungeon and pulls the stake out, bringing the vampire back to life. Dracula attacks a village barmaid and kills her. The vampire returns to his castle and overpowers Frank

Drake, who tries to prevent Dracula from turning Jeanie into a vampire. He drives the Count away with Jeanie's silver compact mirror. But before he vanishes, Dracula issues a cryptic warning: *"Know this, Frank Drake—you've won but a battle . . . in the final analysis, the game is mine—as it always has been—will always be—mine—forever mine!"* And indeed the game turned out to be Dracula's—Jeanie had been transformed into a vampire.

Finn sighed in ecstasy. Then he read it again, from start to finish. Then he read it once more. It was perfect.

Harper's Drugs always seemed to carry comic books later than the date on the cover, something that had never bothered him before his first issue of *The Tomb of Dracula*. The following week he asked Mr. Harper about it and he'd told Finn that they'd already travelled a long way by the time they got to Parr's Landing. He haunted the drugstore for a week, then two, then three, but there was no sign of issue two.

In desperation, Finn sat down at the desk in his bedroom and wrote a letter to Marvel Comics in New York City, using the address he'd found on the bottom of the first page, and taped a twenty-five cent coin to it.

Dear Marvel Comics, he wrote. *I am a recent reader of your Comic Book Series,* Tomb of Dracula. *I live in Parr's Landing, Ontario, Canada where it is sometimes very hard to buy your products. Can you send me Issue #2? I have enclosed 25 cents (in Canadian money) for the comic plus postage to my country. My address is c/o Gen. Delivery, Parr's Landing, Ont. Thank you very much. Sincerely, Finnegan Miller.*

As it happened, the fates elected to smile on young Finn Miller— some kind soul at Marvel returned his twenty-five cent coin along with a manila envelope containing a copy of issue number two.

Dear Finnegan Miller, came the reply. *Here is a copy of the second issue of* T.O.D. *We hope you enjoy it. We are returning your twenty-five-cent coin. May we suggest you put it towards a subscription? We don't send out mags from our office as a rule, but are happy to help you out this one time. Sincerely, your friends at Mighty Marvel.*

Finn's joy knew no bounds. Issue number two was even more lurid than its predecessor. This cover featured Dracula turning into a bat in front of a huddled clutch of terrified Londoners cowering in an archway as a woman in a miniskirt lay crumpled at the Count's feet, obviously dead. The lining of Dracula's cape this time was a glorious blood-red. The issue's tagline shrieked, A SHRILL *SCREAM* SPLITS THE AIR IN *LONDON AT MID-NIGHT—WHO STOLE MY COFFIN?*

Well, obviously Frank Drake did, Finn gloated. Now all hell was going to break loose. He flung himself across his bed, rummaging in the paper bag of candy from Harper's Drugs till he found what he was looking for. He bit the tip off one of the grape-flavoured Pixy Stix straws, and then poured the sweet-and-sour powder onto his tongue, letting it luxuriate there for a moment before he swallowed it. Then he started reading, picking up the story as though it were a letter from an old friend, or rather what he imagined reading a letter from an old friend would be like.

Afterwards, he thought briefly of asking his parents if they'd buy him a subscription for his birthday, but he knew they didn't trust American companies with their money, even the relative pittance it would cost for a subscription to *The Tomb of Dracula*. Besides, the day after he received issue number two from the kind soul at Marvel, the shipment of new comics—including *The Tomb of Dracula*—arrived at Harper's Drugs like rain after a long drought. Issue number three had arrived on the spiral rack in a relatively timely fashion, considering how far away Parr's Landing was from New York City.

Finn was coming up to the highest point of land around Bradley Lake. He looked around for Sadie, but she was nowhere to be seen. The sky was lightening, streaked with broad shards of dark pumpkin and deep purple, and the water reflected the advancing dawn, colours running slick as oil paint.

Finn called out to the Labrador. "Here, Sadie! Here, girl!" His voice ricocheted off the rock face. He called out again. "Sadie, come! Come! Here, girl!"

He frowned. This was unlike her. While she liked to bound ahead at her own pace, exploring, she always remained within earshot and usually scampered back several times as if to check that her master was following her. Finn listened for the sound of barking or rustling in the underbrush, but heard nothing. He looked backwards, squinting into the dimness of the path but saw nothing.

The tops of the trees shook in a sudden burst of cold wind, releasing a cloud of dead autumn leaves that cascaded down before being hijacked by the sudden shift in the air currents and tattering off across the lake. The sky was reddening in advance of the sunrise, the light shadow dappled and obscure.

For the first time ever, Finn was aware of his isolation. He was a mile and a half from home and his dog was nowhere to be seen. He looked around uneasily. The familiar landscape of rough-hewn cliffs rising out of black water looked suddenly barbaric and vaguely lunar.

"*Sadie!*" Finn called again. This time there was an edge of panic in his voice. Hearing nothing, he screamed, "*Here, girl! Sadie, COME!*" He whipped his head wildly from side to side. "*SADIE! COME!*"

And then from high above him he heard the sound of screaming—a high-pitched, rending lament that tore through the early morning air and shattered into echoes against the shield rock of the cliffs. It came again, then again. And this time, Finn recognized the voice as belonging to his dog.

"Sadie! Sadie! Where are you?" He tried to orient himself to what he now realized was a high-pitched howling that had never been part of Sadie's vocal repertoire. If pure animal terror or pain could be distilled, this is what it would sound like.

Oh my God, what if she's hurt? What if she has her foot caught in some sort of leg trap left by one of these assholes who hunts up here in the fall? What if she's broken her leg or something? Please God, let her be all right.

He crashed through the bush in the general direction of Sadie's screams, first left, then right, then doubling back and stopping to check if he was in the right place, or at least headed in the right direction. The acoustics of Bradley Lake played tricks with the sound of Sadie's howls, seemingly sending it in every direction but its true source.

And then, dead silence. *Oh my God,* he thought again. *Please, no.* Finn came around the bend of a copse of trees and an outcropping of lichen-covered granite and saw Sadie cowering against a boulder thirty feet away—teeth bared, lips drawn back from her gums. She was growling low in her throat, her eyes wild and fixed on a point three feet from where she crouched. Her ears lay flat against her skull. The line of hackle fur along her backbone stood up in an arch and her entire body was contorted away from the spot. The Labrador's fluffy tail was straight as an eel, and tucked up far between her hind legs.

At his approach, Sadie's eyes rolled towards Finn. She growled again but didn't move. When he took a step closer, her body seemed to draw itself in tighter, and for one crazy minute Finn was afraid she might attack him.

"Sadie?" he called softly. "Come here, girl. What's the matter? Come here, Sadie." He held out his hand. The Labrador looked at him, and then back to whatever she had been staring at. Whining softly, she lowered her head and looked imploringly at Finn.

"Good girl," he crooned in his most soothing voice. "Come, Sadie. Good girl. Come here."

Slowly, she stepped backwards, then turned and skirted the area, giving it a wide berth, trotting over to where he was standing and burrowing between his legs as though pleading for sanctuary. He reached down and stroked her head. The dog shivered violently, panting harshly. As he continued to caress her, the shaking subsided slightly.

What the hell is going on here? Finn wondered. He looked at the spot again. There was nothing unusual about it, certainly nothing he hadn't seen before on any number of hikes out here by the lake, or indeed anywhere in the vicinity of Parr's Landing. Curiosity overtook him and he took a step away from Sadie, towards the rocks.

Immediately, behind him, Sadie began to whine. He looked back over his shoulder and said, "Shhhh, Sadie."

The dog was unconvinced and continued to whimper piteously as though begging him to stay with her, to not walk any farther in that direction, to take her home and away from here.

For Finn's part, curiosity had overtaken caution. He glanced around him—it was flat land; there nowhere for anything dangerous to be slumbering or hiding. Immediately, he discounted a very short mental checklist of wild animals he might risk provoking into violence by surprising them.

So what the hell was she so scared by?

He stopped abruptly, struck by a sound. Actually, it was not a sound at all, but rather a complete *absence* of sound. He heard Sadie whining; he heard his own feet crunching in the dead leaves and twigs at his feet. But all around him, there were no dawn sounds of birds twittering, no fluttering of wings above him. Even the wind seemed to have stopped abruptly. It was as though a cone had descended on this area, trapping Finn and his dog but shutting everything else out.

He took three more steps. He realized he was standing directly below the ledged rock wall upon which the Indian paintings thought to be of the Wendigo of St. Barthélemy were etched.

He looked down at the overgrowth between the rock formations. There was a crack of some sort, a hollow-looking fissure in the earth that looked like it might have been the opening to a cave mouth at some point, perhaps hundreds, or even thousands, of years ago. It looked too narrow to be an animal burrow, and he doubted Sadie would have had the reaction she did to a snake.

Finn stamped gingerly on the ground and, finding it solid, stamped again.

He knew that Parr's Landing, like many former nineteenth-century mining towns, was honeycombed with underground tunnels. Some of the tunnels were so old they could no longer be located on modern surveyor's maps, and there had always been tales in town of children wandering into the bush, falling through overgrown mine shaft covers. Finn had long suspected the stories were apocryphal, the primary intention being to keep small children close to home. No one he knew could recall a specific instance of it happening to anyone *they* knew, but it never hurt to be careful.

He leaned down to pull away some of the smaller rocks and fallen detritus of dead leaves and fallen branches, and the curious and entirely illogical thought came to him that he was disturbing a grave.

Reaching out with his right hand to lift away the first branch, he heard a piercing shriek of terror that was almost human erupt directly behind him.

He screamed involuntarily and turned around to see Sadie launching herself in the air, her black body twisting as though trying to catch something in her jaws, something hovering above her head, something that Finn could not see, however wildly he whipped his head back and forth. Again and again Sadie leaped and snapped, twisting her body into an epileptic funnel of black fur and sharp white teeth.

Then she lay prostrate on the ground and howled, peal after banshee peal, till Finn—now badly frightened himself, though still not sure of what—bolted past Sadie towards the trail, shouting at the top of the lungs for her to *COME!*

The Labrador was on her feet like a gunshot, galloping behind Finn as though pursued. Neither looked back—not until Finn's lungs felt like they were burning, not until both boy and dog were well within sight of the familiar path that led around the lake, and not until they'd taken the turn that led towards the safety of home.

CHAPTER NINE

Through the windshield of his blue Ford Ranger XLT pickup, Billy Lightning saw the dark-haired boy with the black dog close at his heels tearing out of the woods as though they were being chased by the Devil himself. From the direction the boy was running, Billy knew he'd come from the vicinity of Bradley Lake. Billy felt a snake-strike of sharp dread, but immediately dismissed it as unwarranted.

The boy was probably late for school or something, or for breakfast. He chided himself for living so much in his head that he automatically assumed the worst. On the other hand, if one were going to automatically imagine the worst about anything, especially right about now, Parr's Landing would be the place.

Billy turned left onto Main Street, then, thinking better of it, took the network of rural roads that allowed him to circle the town at a more leisurely pace. His eyes restlessly scanned the tree line behind the houses he just passed, seeking out the omnipresent boreal forest beyond it that always seemed to be waiting hungrily to grow wild again, perpetually on the verge of reclaiming the land from the settlers who'd forced something never meant to be domestic into subjugation.

Billy couldn't decide if this restless cruising in the truck was some inherited hunter's instinct, or if he was just delaying the inevitable, which was walking through the front doors of the police station in Parr's Landing and telling the constable in charge that something terrible had woken up and was, even now, slouching towards his town.

Police Constable Elliot McKitrick looked up from his paperwork when the tall, broad-shouldered Indian, wearing a leather jacket over a lumberjack shirt tucked into old blue jeans, came through the door. The man's thick black hair was tied back in a neat ponytail. His features were refined and vaguely ascetic, and the horn-rimmed glasses he wore lent him a scholarly air. He looked anywhere on either side of forty-five. The leather jacket looked expensive and was certainly not from around here.

For Elliot McKitrick, who was not without certain ingrained cultural prejudices when it came to Indians, the authoritative demeanour of the man coming towards him struck him immediately. The man carried himself as though he were accustomed to going where he pleased and being listened to when he spoke. Elliot disliked him instantly.

"Help you, sir?" Elliot asked politely, betraying none of his private assessments.

"Yes," Billy said. "I'd like to see the officer in charge, please. My name is William Lightning."

"That would be Sergeant Thomson, Mr. Lightning. He's currently away from his desk. Is there something I might help you with?"

Billy sighed. "When will he be back? It's rather important."

"Couldn't say, sir. He was on an out-of-town call early this morning in Gyles Point. I suspect he'll be in later on today. I'd suggest you wait—" Elliot shrugged, indicating the hard-looking wooden bench near the doorway of the station. "—but it might be a while. Perhaps you'd like to tell me what this is all about, or else come back later on today when the sergeant is back at his desk?"

Billy hesitated, as if unsure of how much information to share. "May I ask, have you had any unusual occurrences in the area lately?"

"Unusual, how?" Elliot replied warily. "What do you mean?"

"Oh, I don't know," Billy said in a neutral voice. "Prowlers, break-ins, anything like that?"

Elliot stiffened. "Sir, that's not the sort of information we randomly share with just anyone who walks in off the street. Is there a specific reason you're asking? If there is, I recommend that you tell me right away. This isn't sounding very good for you from my point of view right now."

Now it was Billy's turn to bristle. "I beg your pardon, constable? What do you mean by that, please?"

"Sir," Elliot said, putting a slight patronizing emphasis on the word "sir" that made Billy seethe inside, "an Indian comes into this detachment office and asks me if we've had any break-ins, but won't tell me why. If there had been any break-ins, I'd have to wonder why you knew about them, and why you were asking about them. As it happens, there haven't been any, but I'd still like to know why you're asking."

"I'll leave my name," Billy said coldly. "Please ask Sergeant Thomson to call me when he's back." He wrote *William Lightning* on a pad of blotter paper and handed it to McKitrick.

"Where are you staying?"

Billy noted that the policeman had omitted the word "sir" this time. "I'm going to check into the Golden Nugget motel," he said. "On the edge of town, near the road in."

"I know where the Golden Nugget is, Mr. Lightning. I live in this town."

"*Dr.* Lightning, Constable—" Billy squinted at Elliot's nametag. "—McKitrick. Please have Sergeant Thomson call me. I drove all night to get here, so I'm going to rest for a few hours. Please have him call sometime after twelve noon."

When he reached the door, Billy turned back. The look he caught in Elliot McKitrick's eyes before he quickly glanced back down at his paperwork was like a slap across the face. It had been decades since he'd seen that look, or felt the way it was intended to make him feel.

For one vertiginous moment the present fell away and Billy saw himself reflected in the cop's eyes: a small bronze boy with a crude bowl haircut cut and fearful eyes—one child among fifty other children marching in two flanks through the streets of Sault Ste. Marie, all with the same bowl haircut, dressed in identical woollen jackets the colour of cardinal's wings flashing crimson in the winter sun.

He let the door of the police station slam behind him as he stepped into the street and crossed over to where his truck was parked. Only when he opened the driver's side door and stepped up into the seat did he realize he was shaking.

Morgan Parr had awakened at six a.m. in her canopy bed in her new room at Parr House feeling entirely rested for the first time in months. She stretched languorously and wiggled her toes under the yellow silk duvet. She'd glanced out the window and seen that it was still dark outside. Unlike the neon-spackled darkness at home in the city, this northern darkness was absolute and unyielding. She thought perhaps she detected a band of lighter black, not quite yet grey, in the eastern window.

So tired had Morgan been the night before, after the final leg of their journey north, that she'd barely registered her surroundings before falling into a thick sleep. Now, she took the room's measure slowly, one luxurious detail at a time.

There was a delicate scent of lavender and violet wafting from the eighteenth-century yellow-rose-flowered Meissen hard-paste porcelain bowl of potpourri sitting on the mirrored dresser on the wall adjacent to the bed. Morgan had never seen or smelled potpourri before and was charmed by the mix of dried flowers and lavender seeds. The walls themselves were smoky cream, the windows framed with heavy yellow velvet curtains. On the walls hung a variety of oil paintings— some Canadian wilderness scenes that featured Lake Superior and the surrounding shield, a scattering of English watercolours of gardens and seascapes. There was also an oil portrait of a young girl who, even then, had the features of the adult Adeline Parr, but without the hardness Morgan had seen in her grandmother's face last night. The portrait, she realized, was of Adeline at roughly the same age Morgan was now.

Morgan discovered that the room had an adjoining bathroom. (*My own bathroom!* she'd thought delightedly, stamping her feet on the thick cream carpet of the bedroom in a little dance of girlish euphoria.) She'd splashed her face with cold water in the sink, and then turned on the shower. Under the hot spray, she'd washed her hair, sluicing away the grime and sweat of the long car ride.

After towelling off and dabbing some Johnson's baby lotion on her face, Morgan combed her damp hair with a wide-toothed comb and dressed in a clean pair of jeans and a soft blue sweater. She looked at her Timex. It was seven o'clock.

Checking her image in the mirror over her dresser one last time, she smiled at her reflection, well pleased with what she saw there. She took a deep breath, then headed downstairs for breakfast with her grandmother.

When Morgan entered the dining room, her mother and Jeremy were already seated. They were looking down at their plates. Jeremy's face was red and Morgan's mother was furiously buttering a piece of toast. The tension in the air lay like a miasma over the table. The only person who seemed unaffected by it was Adeline, who looked up from her gold-rimmed breakfast plate and smiled pleasantly at her granddaughter.

"Good morning, dear," Adeline said. "Did you sleep well?"

"Yes, Grandmother." Morgan looked inquisitively at her mother and her uncle, then back to Adeline. "Thank you."

"You'll find breakfast laid out on the sideboard over there," Adeline said, indicating the gleaming silver-domed platters on the sideboard's surface. "Beatrice will be removing them and clearing the table promptly at seven forty-five, so I advise you to select what you wish to eat and begin. You don't want to be late for your first day in your new school."

Morgan looked around. "Who's Beatrice?"

"Beatrice has been with this family for most of her working life. Her husband, James, is our driver, and he will be driving you to school this morning shortly after you're finished with breakfast. There will be forms to fill out, I'm sure. You don't want to start off on the wrong foot."

Christina looked sharply at Adeline. "I'll drive Morgan to school this morning, Adeline. I was sure I made that clear earlier."

"Out of the question," Adeline replied. Her tone was peremptory and dismissive. "Morgan will be fine on her own. She's fifteen. She doesn't need mollycoddling, and frankly I'd like her to have the advantage of starting school with a minimum of gossip to deal with about—well, about recent life events."

"Jesus, Mother." Jeremy looked disgusted.

"Are you referring to her father's death?" Christina said, hearing a certain shrillness in her own tone that was entirely alien to her. "Or are you referring to the fact that her uncle doesn't love women? Or that her mother has brought her back to this town she swore she'd never even think of again because she had no other way of providing for her? Which 'recent events' are you referring to, Adeline? Which 'recent events' should stop me from driving my daughter to school this morning?"

"How you—"

"Mom, maybe Grandmother is right," Morgan interrupted. She looked beseechingly at her mother, as though imploring her to concede, if only just this once, for the sake of peace. "I'll be fine. I'll tell you all about it this afternoon when I get home."

Christina recognized at once that her daughter was trying to avert a scene between herself and Adeline, and she was momentarily chagrined that she'd allowed Adeline to draw her into yet another power struggle so soon. She was particularly struck by Adeline's willingness to fight in front of Morgan, consequences be damned. This was not going to be easy, living here with this woman. She took no prisoners. No wonder both her sons had fled as soon as they were possibly able.

"All right, Morgan. If you're sure."

"Of *course* she's sure, Christina," Adeline interrupted, her voice once again the creamy matriarch's voice, the one that brooked no dissent from staff or other inferiors. "For heaven's sake. She's fifteen years old. Morgan will do very well. She can meet her teachers and make some new friends without her mother hanging off her like an old secondhand winter coat." Adeline laughed softly at her own joke. "Besides, Christina, you and I have a great deal to do this morning, a great deal to discuss. You also, Jeremy."

"I don't know what you think we have to discuss, Mother. I'm going out for a drive today. I don't intend to be back until dinnertime. I've been away a long while, and I'm going to explore some old haunts. It's going to be a beautiful day, according to the radio, and I'm going to look at the leaves."

"Yes, and why don't you go visit some of your old friends from school, son," Adeline said cruelly. "You have so many. I'm sure they'd be happy to see you back in town."

Jeremy's laugh was forced, but defiant. "Maybe I will at that, Mother. Maybe I will."

"I think I'll join you, Jeremy," Christina said, surprising herself with her own defiance. She guessed that Adeline was unlikely to be able to retaliate against both her and Jeremy's defiance, at least not right away— and frankly the notion of being trapped in Parr House all day with this woman was more than she could bear right now. "I'd like to look at the leaves, too. Shall we pack a lunch and make a day of it, Jeremy?"

"Young woman, you are not on holiday," Adeline snapped at Christina. "I'll have you remember that while you are under my roof."

Adeline looked across the table at her granddaughter, pale and staring at her plate, not eating her breakfast. Her mouth tightened in frustration, realizing she'd been outmanoeuvred into choosing between causing a disruptive scene in front of Morgan, or letting it go. Adeline had no compunctions about chastising either the common strumpet who had killed her eldest son, or her youngest son, the depraved invert disgrace to his name, but she was intent on winning Morgan to her side. She was shrewd enough to realize that this was not the way to do it.

"Very well, Christina," Adeline said, her voice as sweet as frozen sugar water. "You two go out and reacquaint yourselves with the town. Perhaps it's a good idea after your drive. It won't hurt you to see how far you are from Toronto, both geographically and otherwise. It would be a mistake to think otherwise, as I'm sure you'll remember after a day out driving around. And Jeremy is quite correct. I also heard on the radio how lovely the weather is going to be today. Just be back by dinner. It gets dark very quickly out here and the night comes down fast. You don't want to get lost."

"Your concern is touching, Mother," Jeremy said. The sarcasm in his tone was a facsimile of his mother's own. "Considering that both Christina and I grew up here, it hardly seems likely that we'd get lost, but I promise you we'll be careful."

"Good," Adeline said briskly. "Now, since everyone's plans for the day have been arranged, I believe I'll take my coffee in my sitting room." She rang the bell beside her plate, and Beatrice appeared in the doorway.

"Yes, ma'am?"

"Beatrice, Mr. Jeremy and Miss Christina won't be here for lunch, and I believe Miss Morgan has eaten all she's going to eat of your delicious breakfast. Would you please bring my coffee into the sitting room? And the newspapers? And tell James that Miss Morgan will be ready to leave for school in five minutes. Have him bring the car around to the front of the house."

"Yes, ma'am." Beatrice poured Adeline a fresh cup of coffee from the silver coffeepot, adding a small splash of cream. She placed it on a silver tray and carried it out of the dining room without a word.

In spite of themselves, Christina and Jeremy watched her performance, spellbound. The time between Adeline Parr deciding something would happen and it happening was minuscule, whether ordering a cup of coffee from the housekeeper, or ordering her younger son to spend six months incarcerated in a mental hospital.

For her part, Morgan read the subtitles in the room. They were not yet entirely clear, but she had the first serious inklings that they were not as welcome in this house as her mother and uncle had initially led her to believe. Her eyes travelled to the far wall of the dining room. She noticed two more formal oil portraits, this time two boys: her father, immediately recognizable, and her uncle, fairer and frailer, more delicate even then. She tried to read the expression in their eyes, looking for some clue to help her understand better what was going on, but she was too far away. She promised herself that she would examine them when she had more time, perhaps after school.

Adeline laid her napkin on the table. She pushed herself away from the dining room table and rose to her feet in one languorous, elegant movement. "How nice to have our first meal under this roof as a family," she said. "I shall expect to see you all at dinner. Six-thirty on the dot, mind." And just like that, she was gone, leaving a faint trace of Bulgarian rose perfume in her wake like a contrail.

Elliot McKitrick was in the back office of the station looking for a file when he heard the bell above the door tinkle again. He grimaced. If it was that goddamn pushy Indian again, he swore he wasn't going to be as nice this time. He closed the file cabinet with an audible bang and marched into the main room of the station expecting to see Billy Lightning looking down at him from his fancy-mouthed height, but it was Dave Thomson, his sergeant, looking none too pleased, and paler than a goddamn albino underneath his permanent ruddy windburn.

"Hey, Sarge, you're back," Elliot said. "How were things in Gyles Point?"

"Not good," Thomson replied. "Get me a glass of water, would you? Make sure it's cold."

Elliot went into the back room again and took a glass from the cupboard above the sink. Then he let the tap run until the water was like ice before filling the glass. He brought it back into the main office. Thomson sat at his desk looking through some papers. Elliot handed him the glass. He took it without a word and drank it down in one long, deep draught.

"What's going on, Sarge? What happened over in Gyles? You look . . . well, what's up?"

"Murder, maybe. Fella by the name of Carstairs, from out by North Bay. Has a fishing cabin outside of Gyles. A neighbour saw lights on in there last night and went over this morning early, thinking the man might've come up. First time in years, apparently, since his wife died. The neighbour found the place empty but said it smelled like something had turned. There's blood all over the upstairs bedroom, but no body anywhere, and no car. He called the RCMP, and Gill Styles called me in as local backup.

The neighbour was right. It smelled like a meat locker. Styles's men are trying to locate Mr. Carstairs, but so far no luck."

Thomson paused, his eyes dark-rimmed. "Not the sort of thing we're used to up here at all. No, not one bit."

"Jesus," Elliot said. He cleared his throat. "Sarge?"

"What is it, McKitrick?"

"Sarge, we had a visitor earlier. Sort of weird, really. An Indian. Came by asking all sorts of strange questions about whether or not we'd hand any break-ins or anything weird in the last few days. It didn't seem like he was, you know . . . right in the head. Also, he was real uppity. Pushy. Not like the ones we have around here."

"What'd he look like?"

"Fancy leather jacket. Jeans. Shirt. Had a real snooty way about him, like he was looking down on us. On me." Elliot looked outraged. Thomson raised his eyebrows and smiled faintly at Elliot's entirely out-of-place indignation, considering the circumstances. Insecurity had never been one of Elliot McKitrick's problems. Thomson had known him since he was a kid—he hadn't been lacking in self-esteem, or female attention—since he first sprouted pubes, maybe even before. Every town had its golden boy, and in Parr's Landing, Elliot was it. In high school, he'd been a big, strong, handsome kid, star forward on the Parr's Landing Predators hockey team, and star teenage swordsman in private, if the gossip down at the Legion hall—enthusiastically confirmed by Bill McKitrick, Elliot's father—was to be believed.

This Indian must have really gotten under the kid's skin, Thomson thought. If he hadn't just visited what was very likely a murder scene before breakfast, and if the stink of copper wasn't clinging to the inside of his nostrils and, he imagined, his clothes, he might smile. He might even take a bit of piss out of the kid. But he didn't feel like smiling, and he didn't feel like teasing.

"Did he give a name?"

"Yeah, let me see. He wrote it down." Elliot went to his desk and retrieved the piece of paper. "William Lightning," he read. Elliot omitted the title "Dr." out of spite, then thought better of it, just in case it might be important. "*Dr.* William Lightning, if you can dig that. Medicine man, more likely."

Thomson sat upright. "What did you say? William Lightning? *Billy* Lightning?"

"You know him, Sarge?" Elliot frowned. This wasn't the reaction he'd been counting on.

Thomson paused. "Not sure. There was a Billy Lightning here some years ago. This guy was a young fella, though. He was here with his father—some sort of archaeologist from a university down in the States or something. They were here doing some kind of dig out by Bradley. Something to do with the Indian village from the olden days that used to be here. They got old lady Parr's permission to dig and everything, I heard. They had to leave. Something to do with one of the students they had with them. He got sick or something. They had to shut the whole thing down."

"And this Lightning was there? You sure? What happened?"

"I don't remember," Thomson said. "It was just before I transferred out here from Sault Ste. Marie and I never got all the details. It was all finished and done with by the time I took over in '58." Thomson paused.

"I wonder what he's doing back here? And why he'd show up right about now?"

"You think he might've done it, Sarge? Those questions he was asking seemed really, really strange."

"Did he say where he was staying?"

"He's at the Nugget. He said to phone him after twelve noon." Now Thomson *did* laugh. "Did he, indeed? Well, that's interesting. I'm thinking it might be worth a drive out to see Mr.—excuse me, *Dr.* Lightning. Maybe we won't phone him first. Maybe we'll just pay him a surprise visit and see who's who and what's what. What do you say, Elliot?"

"Sounds good to me, Sarge," Elliot replied. Privately he hoped that the Indian would put up a fight. He was itching to use his nightstick on him, and this seemed like it might be as good a time as any to break some bones.

CHAPTER TEN

It is a curious paradox about small towns: although there is less distance to traverse, from one end to another, than in cities, almost no one walks anywhere. Unlike cities, where there are never any shortage of cars and trucks belting exhaust, people all seem to be from somewhere else. In cities, pedestrians walk to their destinations. In small towns like Parr's Landing, on the other hand, the average citizen would be as unlikely to walk to the store around the corner to get a quart of milk as they would be to do without altogether.

It was therefore entirely in keeping with small town tradition—even poetic, though perhaps only to Jeremy Parr himself—that he and Elliot McKitrick should each get the first glimpse of each other in ten years through the windows of two cars going in opposite directions down a wet country road littered with fallen leaves in deepest October.

Jeremy, who had been expecting something of this sort today, was still taken aback to see Elliot, much less behind the wheel of a cop car. He recognized him immediately, even though Elliot was wearing aviator shades. The square jaw, the perfectly formed brow, and the close-cropped dark crew cut was unmistakably that of Elliot McKitrick, as were the powerful shoulders and arms beneath the blue uniform jacket.

Yes, it was Elliot—his Elliot. Changed, but still somehow exactly the same.

Something flared somewhere in the region of his chest. Not pain exactly, definitely not joy, and certainly nothing as clichéd as his "heart stopping." But he was suddenly acutely aware of a profound absence and loss, the sharpness of which shocked him.

"Was that him?" Christina asked as the cars passed each other. "It was, wasn't it?"

"Yes," Jeremy said, not trusting himself to say anything further, or perhaps simply incapable of it. "Just *drive*, Christina." He hunched down in his seat, eyes straight ahead. "Move it, for God's sake."

For his part, Elliot's well-honed policeman's instinct for danger set off warning bells in his head in the same instant he experienced a similar emotional reaction to Jeremy Parr's, minus Jeremy's internal poetry about absence and loss. Elliot's life had thus far been divided between pleasure and pain, hunger and satiation, success and failure, desire and repulsion, safety and danger. It had been a jock's life, a warrior's life. Now it was a cop's life, or at least the way Elliot imagined a cop's life to be, an extension of his physicality and prowess elsewhere.

The sight of Jeremy Parr—whom he recognized as effortlessly as Jeremy had recognized him—inspired both desire and danger. The first impulse went directly to his groin, briefly slapping his heart the way a buddy might slap his shoulder. The second, more dominant, impulse was awareness of acute danger, in a robotic Lost in Space sort of way.

Danger, Elliot McKitrick! warned the metallic voice in his head. *Danger, Elliot McKitrick!*

"Who's that, do you suppose?" Thomson grunted, turning around to follow the retreating Chevy Chevelle as it headed in the direction of Bradley Lake.

"Dunno," Elliot said noncommittally, looking straight ahead, exactly the way Jeremy Parr had seconds before. "Didn't get a good look. If you want me to find out, I can track 'em down after we catch up with that Indian at the Nugget. Those two were probably just lost tourists, coming up here to check out the goddamn leaves."

* * *

Billy Lightning was sleeping when the knock came on the door of his motel room. It was not a friendly, managerial knock. It was as sharp and definitive as brass knuckles. He hadn't realized he had a splitting headache until he'd woken to that rapping sound.

God, he thought. *It's that stupid young cop. Idiotic of me to think they'd use the phone like I asked.* He squinted down at his watch. It was ten forty five. *Or, for that matter, wait until after twelve noon like I very politely asked.*

"Just a minute," Billy called out. "I'll be right there." The knock came again, harder. "I'm coming!" he shouted. "Jesus *Christ!*"

He opened the door of the motel room. There were two of them this time. The young one from the station, and an older one with a more seasoned and rational mien.

The older one spoke first. "Mr. Lightning?"

Billy sighed. "*Dr.* Lightning, but yes, that's me. And you're Mr. Thomson?

"*Sergeant* Dave Thomson, Dr. Lightning." Thomson smiled dryly and Billy relaxed somewhat. The younger one stood behind Thomson at attention, like a plastic G.I. Joe doll, his face impassive.

"Come in, gentlemen," Billy said. "I've just checked in." He gestured to the two chairs on either side of the Formica kitchen table on the far side of the room. "Would you like to sit down?"

"No, thank you, Dr. Lightning," Thomson said politely. The younger one—McKitrick—just shook his head and continued to stare at Billy.

"Dr. Lightning, I wonder if you'd mind if I asked you a few questions? Constable McKitrick told me you stopped by the station today with some of your own. Perhaps we can sort this out and answer each other's questions. How about that?"

"As you wish, Sergeant Thomson." Billy sat down on the edge of the bed and stretched his legs. "You'll forgive me, but it's been a long drive. I'd rather not stand. I'm a little sleep deprived and I hadn't expected you before twelve noon."

"Absolutely." Thomson smiled. "According to Constable

McKitrick, you were curious about any break-ins that we may have had in the area. May I ask why?"

"I recently lost my father, Sergeant Thomson."

"I'm sorry to hear that, Dr. Lightning." Thomson made a sympathetic face, and waited for Billy to elaborate.

"He was murdered. In his home. In Toronto. About six weeks ago."

"I see. Again, I'm very sorry to hear that. It's a terrible tragedy to befall any family. But surely, Dr. Lightning, you didn't drive all this way on the matter of your father's death? What could break-ins in Parr's Landing have to do with that very sad event?"

Billy took a deep breath, realizing in advance how what he was about to tell the two police constables was going to sound to them. He wished they were sitting in the police station, as he'd originally planned, or at the very least that Thomson had phoned, as Billy had made clear was his preference.

You're not in the university now, Dr. Lightning, he reminded himself. *You're back up north. Remember that, for your own good.*

"Sergeant Thomson, my father spent some time here in Parr's Landing twenty years ago, in 1952. He was an archaeologist at the University of Toronto."

"Yes, I know."

Billy raised his eyebrows. "You *know*? How do you know?"

"I joined the Parr's Landing detachment as a constable shortly after his crew left town, but I remember hearing about it from my predecessor, Sergeant Bowles. He told me all about the excavation. He spoke very highly of your dad."

"Thank you," Billy said. "Did Sergeant Bowles tell you what happened? I mean, why my father had to terminate the excavation?"

"No, sir, he didn't. Forgive me again, Dr. Lightning, but I have to ask—what does this have to do with why you're here, and what does it have anything to do with possible crimes in Parr's Landing?"

Billy gestured again at the chairs on either side of the table. "It's a rather involved story, gentlemen. I'm happy to explain, but you really should sit down."

Thomson sighed and pulled out a chair. He sat down. He nodded to Elliot, indicating that he should sit down, as well. The younger man rolled his eyes, but sat nonetheless. He pulled a note pad from his jacket pocket and began writing.

Thomson asked him, "What was your father's name, Dr. Lightning? For the sake of clarity in our report?"

"His name was Professor Phenius Osborne." Billy said, and then spelled it out.

Elliot raised his eyebrows. "Sorry, what? He was your father, I think you said? Why do you have a different last name than him? Wasn't his name Lightning, too? Or did he change it? Was he an Indian, too?"

"I was adopted when I was twelve years old, constable. From the St. Rita's residential school in Sault Ste. Marie," Billy said coolly, ignoring the second part of Elliot's question. "I was William Osborne for six years. I took back my name legally when I turned eighteen, with both of my parents' blessing."

"You mean the Osbornes' blessings, don't you?" Elliot persisted. "Did your Indian parents influence you in some way?"

"My birth father had died by the time I was able to look for him—my search for him was also with my parents' blessing. The Osbornes were my legal parents, and were—and are—the only parents I have ever had. My mother—Margaret Osborne—passed away five years ago." He turned to Thomson. "Is this really relevant? I fail to see how the details of my adoption are relevant at this point, and I'm finding Constable McKitrick's questions intrusive and crude. Do you mind?"

"I think we have enough information for right now, constable," Thomson said evenly. "No need for you to take any more notes. If we need a formal statement from Dr. Lightning at some point, I'm sure he'll oblige us. Right, doctor?"

Billy nodded impatiently. "Yes, of course."

"Please tell us your story, Dr. Lightning. The sooner we get all of this cleared up, the better we may be able to sort it all out."

And then Billy braced himself and told the two policemen his story.

CHAPTER ELEVEN

"In the summer of 1952, we came to Parr's Landing to excavate the site of the St. Barthélemy mission to the Ojibwa," Billy Lightning began. "My father was writing a book about the history of the Jesuit settlements and the long-term effects of Christianization on the native population since the seventeenth century. My father brought two graduate students and me. It was my first trip with him.

"I hadn't yet decided on either archaeology or anthropology as a career, but my father felt it was important that I be part of this particular project because of my native ancestry. When my parents adopted me, they took me to Toronto and placed me in an expensive, progressive private school, one that was respectful of my heritage. Money can buy you almost anything," Billy said, the trace of bitterness not entirely disguised by his professorial delivery. "Even respect from other people. At St. Rita's in the Soo, the priests had done everything possible to beat the Indian out of me. My father and mother wanted to try to heal some of that, and they believed that an excellent education was the best way to undo some of the damage.

"One of my father's students on the dig was a young man named Richard Weal. Dad described him as the most brilliant student he'd ever had. His IQ was in the highest percentile, and he had an academic history that was stellar, as well. I think Dad saw him as second son."

"How did that make you feel?" Thomson asked.

"It didn't make me 'feel' one way or another, Sergeant Thomson. My parents took a twelve-year-old orphan boy out of a church-run hellhole and into their homes and their hearts. They gave me the best education money could buy. Their love for me wasn't a question in my mind. My father's pride in Richard wasn't a threat to me at all. It wasn't that sort of relationship. I was Dad's son, not Richard."

"Just establishing the facts, Dr. Lightning. Please go on."

"The second student was a young man named Emory Greer. He and Richard barely knew each other at the time they agreed to join my father on this dig. They were both students of his, but from very different backgrounds. Emory was very quiet and self-effacing. He was deeply studious, even by post-graduate standards. Richard, on the other hand, was a star in and out of the classroom. As an undergraduate, he'd been on the varsity track team—as I recall, his event was the decathlon. He was popular with everyone.

"The dig had been intended as a three-month project. We'd made two teams—I was assisting my father, and Emory and Richard were the second team. My father had arranged with the Parr family for us to work in and around the region of Bradley Lake between June and August. Everything had been going relatively smoothly. Even the black flies were manageable that spring, which, the locals told us, was unusual. It had been cold, so maybe that's what kept them at bay.

"In any case, we were making a bit of progress—some arrowheads, bits of utensils. Some coins. Nothing particularly remarkable, at first. We also found what we thought might have been an altar chalice of some sort. That was a banner day. As I recall, Richard found that particular item.

"After about the second week, we noticed that Richard was acting strangely. He would go silent for hours on end, almost like he couldn't hear us. I remember on one occasion, early on, we were five miles into the bush from Bradley Lake, and Richard was on his knees brushing something—a patch of rock, or something—to clean it. He suddenly looked up and said, 'What?' No one had spoken to him, or said anything for that matter. It was a completely quiet day."

Elliot asked, "Echoes, maybe? From in town? Sound plays funny tricks up there on that escarpment sometimes."

"No, not that day," Billy replied. "There wasn't even any wind. Richard got very angry with us. It was completely out of character for him to get angry like that, especially with my father. Richard actually *cursed*—again, very odd. He was quite a Christer, you understand. He was never pushy about his religion. He kept it to himself most of the time, but I know he was a fairly devout churchgoer, and I never heard him swear. He stormed off into the bush and said he needed to clear his head. He took off in the direction of the cliff where the Ojibwa pictographs are located."

"I'm sorry—the what?"

"The Indian paintings," Thomson explained without turning to look at Elliot. "Go on, Dr. Lightning. We're listening."

"When Richard didn't come back for lunch, Dad went out to look for him. Dad spent about two hours, and then came back without him. He said he couldn't find him anywhere. He was pretty worried—like I said, he was very fond of Richard. At five, we were just about to drive into town and report him missing when he came wandering back to the site. His face was scratched and dirty. There were bits of branches in his hair. His clothes were filthy.

"My father's first thought was that he'd been hurt in some way. Richard stumbled a bit, like he was drunk. He tripped and fell, then lay there for a moment. We rushed over to help him up. He seemed disoriented."

Thomson said, "Was he drunk? Did he have a bottle back out there in the bush?"

"No, he wasn't. In fact, the first thing he did when we picked him up off the ground was down an entire canteen full of water. He drank it like he was trying to put out a fire in his throat. Dad told him to slow down and take it easy, but Richard just brushed him away and kept drinking till he'd drained the entire canteen dry.

"My father asked him where he'd been. Richard seemed confused by the question. He believed it was just before lunchtime.

My father told him it was close to five p.m. and he'd been gone the entire afternoon. He thought we were joking until Emory showed Richard his watch. Richard said he'd gone for a walk—he'd been very angry, he said. He was convinced that we were playing tricks on him before.

"He said he heard a man say his name, practically right beside his ear. My father told him he must have imagined it, but Richard said he hadn't imagined it. He said he heard it clearly. Then he'd heard it a second time, fainter, but no less clearly. When he'd looked up, there had been no one there except us. He hadn't believed us when we said we hadn't heard anything, which was why he stormed off."

"Did he say where he'd gone?" Thomson asked.

"He said he'd gone for a walk. He said he didn't remember anything else."

"But you say he was gone for—what, five hours? And he didn't know where he'd gone?"

"As I said, he thought he was only away for about twenty minutes. He said he'd walked in the general direction of the cliffs where the pictographs are located. He said he didn't know why he'd left the site, or how far he'd walked."

Thomson said, "You say he was scratched up? Dirty? Did you ask him how he got that way?"

"Yes, sergeant, of course we did." Billy said. "Richard looked down at himself like it was the first time he'd seen the dirt and the scratches. He actually seemed surprised. He said he must have fallen. My father asked him if he'd maybe hit his head and had been unconscious the whole time, but Richard said, 'No, I'd have remembered that.' He didn't remember anything, but he said he would have remembered the pain of falling down. Dad checked his head—no bumps, no cuts, nothing. He was drenched in dried sweat, Dad said, which was odd considering that it was a cool day and he hadn't really done much work that morning. But my father said his clothes were stiff with it."

"What happened then?" Elliot had abandoned any pretence of disinterest in Billy's story at this point. He leaned forward in his chair, elbow on a knee, chin cradled in his knuckles.

"We drove him to the one doctor in town. On the way, he drank a second canteen of water, more slowly this time, but again—all the way down. I don't remember the doctor's name."

"Probably Doc Oliver," Thomson said, more by reflex than anything else. "He died in '69. Good man. Smart fella, even for a doctor."

"As I said, I don't remember. It was more than twenty years ago. In any case, the doctor checked Richard over and said he couldn't find anything wrong with him. Nothing broken, obviously, no evidence of any concussion. The doctor actually suggested that it might have been a mild form of heat stroke, but that it would be hard to tell because of all the water he'd drunk as soon as he came back to the site. He told us to take Richard back to the motel and put him to bed so he could sleep it off.

"Richard was sharing a room here at the Nugget with Emory. That night, Emory woke up to find the door to the motel wide open. It was a bright night. There were a lot of stars. Richard's bed was empty. Emory put on his bathrobe and his shoes and went to the doorway. Emory saw Richard kneeling in the middle of the road leading to the motel. He was completely naked. According to Emory, although Richard's back was to him, he looked like he was praying. His hands were folded in front of his chest and he was staring off towards the edge of town, looking in the general direction of Bradley Lake with his head slightly bowed.

"Emory pulled a blanket off his bed and ran over to Richard. As he got closer, he could tell that Richard was fast asleep. He'd obviously been sleepwalking. Emory said it was a miracle he hadn't been hit by a car or a truck down there in the road. He put the blanket around his shoulders and tried to get him to stand. He told my dad that Richard struggled at first but that he eventually came along with him. Emory said Richard was muttering in his sleep."

"What was he saying?" Elliot asked.

"Emory said he couldn't really make it out, but that it sounded like Latin."

"Latin? You mean, the language?"

"More specifically, Ecclesiastical Latin."

"What's the difference?"

"Ecclesiastical Latin is a form of Latin that deviates from classic Latin in that it's marked by certain lexical variations. It's also the form of Latin used in the Latin Rite of the Catholic Church. It can be found primarily in theological works and liturgical rites."

Thomson looked doubtful. "All of that from some muttering in the middle of the night? In the middle of the road outside this motel?"

"Emory's undergraduate and Master's degrees encompassed religion, history, and ancient languages, sergeant. His PhD work with my father was an extension of the work he was doing on his studies of the early Church in Canada and its cultural impact. Also, he was a devout Catholic."

"Assuming it really was Latin—and I'm sort of doubting it, to be honest—did this fella know what Richard was saying? Could he make anything out?"

"Oddly," Billy said, "he did think he caught one phrase—he thought Richard said '*Abyssus abyssum invocat.*'"

"Which means what, exactly?"

"It's from Psalm forty-two, verse seven. It means 'Deep calleth unto deep.'"

"You said he was a regular 'Christer,'" Elliot said. "Maybe it was something he heard in church sometime?"

"Richard was a Methodist, constable. His undergraduate degree was in English Literature. He didn't speak Latin at all." Billy paused. "He said something else, according to Emory. It sounded like '*Suscito me.*'"

"Sorry, Dr. Lightning—this means what?"

"Roughly translated, it means 'Wake me.'"

"He wanted Emory to wake him up?" Elliot said. "So he asks in *Latin*?"

"It didn't appear that he was speaking to Emory, based on what Emory said about it the next day, when he told my father and me what had happened."

"All right, never mind all that," Thomson said impatiently. "It doesn't signify one way or another, does it? Did he remember anything about the sleepwalking the next day?"

"No. He said he'd had some peculiar dreams, but he had no memory whatsoever of the sleepwalking. He also laughed when Emory asked him if he knew Latin. He said the only Latin he knew was Pig Latin. He said he felt a lot better than he had the day before. So we went to the site and went back to work. It was a good day—bright, sunny. Not hot, but pleasantly warm. Richard seemed to be in a terrific mood, at least to start with.

"As the day progressed, though, Richard became a bit listless and irritable. He snapped at Emory a couple of times for no good reason and, at one point, threw a shovel. It didn't hit anyone, of course, but it was so out of character for Richard that we all noticed it. I think at one point my father may have wondered if Richard had been malingering the previous day—you know, storming off and pretending to have gotten lost because he was angry about something he wasn't being honest about—but he was mostly concerned about Richard's behaviour being so out of character for such a good-natured young man."

"Drugs? Could it have been that he was doing drugs? It sounds to me like he might have been on some kind of dope," Thomson said.

"I already told you, sergeant," Billy said, "Richard was a straight arrow."

"OK, this is all very interesting, Dr. Lightning, but I'm going to have to ask you to get to the point. Why are you telling us about something that happened twenty years ago to some graduate student who doesn't live here in Parr's Landing? And what in the name of sweet biscuits does any of this have to do with why you're here? Or with your father?"

"Let me finish the rest of my story, sergeant, and I'll tell you."

Thomson sighed deeply. "Very well," he said. "Go on. But please, get to the point soon, Dr. Lightning."

"Do you know why we had to leave Parr's Landing, sergeant—I mean, we, the crew?"

"Some sort of medical problem, I recall hearing. Some sort of accident?"

Billy said, "There was indeed an accident, but it wasn't the sort of accident one normally associates with a dig. Richard attacked and nearly killed Emory a week later."

Elliot glanced at Thomson as if to say, *Do you believe this?* But Thomson's expression was neutral, and his eyes on Billy betrayed nothing.

"After the sleepwalking incident," Billy said, "Richard became more and more withdrawn. Emory told my father that he slept badly. He tossed and turned all night, and occasionally spoke in his sleep."

"What did he say?" Thomson asked. "Do you remember?"

"Emory said that not much of it made any sense. Except one night, Richard woke up screaming that he was buried alive. Emory said he was drenched in sweat. He had apparently thrown his covers all over the floor of the motel room and was flailing his arms like he was trying to dig himself out of a hole.

"The next morning—again—Richard had no memory of the event at all. He got very angry with Emory. Richard accused Emory of lying just to confuse him. By that time Emory had started to be afraid of sharing the motel room with him. He told my father he wanted his own room. My father was initially reluctant to accede to Emory's wishes, not only because it wasn't in the budget, but also because he was afraid that such a drastic action would just make it worse. Richard, you see, didn't believe any of this was happening. I think on some level, he believed we'd all been playing a joke on him since that first day he wandered off."

"So, what finally happened?" Elliot asked. "You said he almost killed the other fella, this Emory?"

"We'd been out on the site all day, that last day," Billy said. "Richard had apparently had another bad night and not a lot of sleep. He was sullen and withdrawn. It was a hot day, too, that day—really hot, very humid. There were a lot of bugs, black flies and the like, that we hadn't had to deal with over the course of the dig up till that point. The sort of weather that makes people jump out of their skin at a moment's notice when someone looks at you the wrong way. Everyone's shirts were plastered to their backs before noon, but there was no wind and the bugs were a nightmare, so we kept them on and just . . . well, endured.

"When my father announced that we were breaking for lunch, Richard gathered up his things, as he had been doing since the first day since his bizarre experience with the quasi-amnesia, and prepared to go off and eat his lunch alone. My father objected. He insisted we all eat together as a group."

"Why?" asked Thomson. "After all that had gone on? Why would he antagonize him like that?"

"Dad might have been trying to see what sort of a reaction it would provoke in Richard. I know my father was growing increasingly concerned about Richard and had spoken to both Emory and me privately about sending Richard back home to Toronto to get some help, and finishing up the dig as a trio."

"What was Richard's reaction?"

"He became furious. He accused my father of overstepping his bounds and taking advantage of his status as Richard's professor in order to 'control' him. His rage was completely out of sync with either my father's request, or anything else, including how irritable we all felt in that heat. My father insisted again, and for a moment Richard looked at my father as though he wanted to murder him. It looked to me as though Richard would attack him. Emory and I both stood up at the same time. Richard looked at all three of us, and then stalked away into the bush, towards the cliffs, without looking back.

"Emory said, 'I'll go after him. Let me see if I can talk to him.' My father said, 'No, I'll do it. It's my responsibility.' But Emory insisted, saying that it was obvious that Richard was furious about my father taking a paternalistic role in this situation, and that perhaps talking to someone closer to his own age would be less threatening. So he took off into the bush looking for Richard."

"What happened when he found him?" Elliot asked. "I mean, I'm assuming he did?"

Billy took a deep breath, and then exhaled slowly. "Yes, he definitely found him. But first, we found Emory. When he wasn't back in half an hour, both my Dad and I had a bad feeling about it, so we went to find him. We did, about half a mile from the camp. It wasn't hard—we just followed the sound of his screaming."

Again, Elliot found himself asking, "What happened?" But this time, he sounded less like an interrogating policeman than he did a young boy listening to a ghoulish campfire story. Dave Thomson caught the subtle tonal shift and glanced at the younger officer. Elliot didn't notice. Billy held his full attention.

"We found him," Billy continued. "Emory had collapsed against a boulder about a hundred yards away from where the path veered sharply upward to the hill that led to the cliffs. At first, we thought he had fallen and maybe broken his arm, but his screaming was too obviously the sound of someone in terrible, terrible pain. His knees were pulled up and he was clutching his shoulder and writhing in agony in the dirt. My father ran to him. Emory kept screaming. Dad gently pulled his hand away from his shoulder to see what had happened. His shirt was soaked in blood that was gushing out of a severe, deep wound in his shoulder. Emory's face was paper-white—he was obviously in the early stages of shock. My father asked him what had happened, and he was able to say just one word before he passed out. He said, *Richard*.

"Dad tore off his own shirt and tied it around Emory's shoulder in a clumsy tourniquet. He said, 'We need to get Emory to the hospital right away.' We picked him up as gently as we could, then carried him, half running, all the way back to the camp. Once there, we lay him across the back seat of the van and drove down the hill as fast as possible to the doctor's office. Thank God he was in. The doctor said it looked like Emory had been hit with an axe, or some sort of ice pick, in the shoulder.

"By that time, Emory had regained consciousness, though he was in terrible pain. The doctor gave him a shot of something strong— morphine, maybe? My father asked him what had happened, and Emory said that Elliot had been hiding behind one of the rock walls, and had jumped out and attacked him with the chisel end of an archaeological hammer. Emory said something else before the drug knocked him out cold. He said that Richard drank his blood."

"Drank his *blood*?"

"Yes, that he'd attacked him with the hammer, and drank the blood from the wound. That he'd pressed his mouth against it and sucked it. He also said that Richard had told him that 'the voice' had told him to do it, and that the voice was coming from 'the caves.'"

"The caves?" Thomson said. "What caves?"

"He claimed there were caves in the cliffs," Billy replied. "Are there?"

"Well, yes. There are caves. Parr's Landing is a mining town. The ground underneath it is full of tunnels. Some came about when the mine opened a hundred years ago, but one of the reasons the mine opened was that there were caves and gorges there in the first place. Combined with the gold they found, it made for ideal conditions. But that's something that Richard could have discovered all on his own, without a 'voice' guiding him. So—he was plain crazy the whole time? Some kind of breakdown?"

"Emory was picked up by an ambulance plane and taken to hospital in Sault Ste. Marie. In addition to the blood loss, he'd suffered severe nerve damage from the wound. The RCMP caught Richard a couple of days later. He'd been living outdoors in the area around Bradley Lake. I saw him when the cops brought him in. He looked like a monster out of a horror movie. His clothes were torn and filthy. His face and hands were scratched, and his face was smeared with Emory's dried blood. His eyes looked like an animal's eyes, but even wilder. He didn't seem to recognize either my father or me. He claimed he didn't know who Emory was."

Billy stood up and walked across the room to where his suitcase lay open at the end of his bed. He rummaged through his clothes, and then withdrew a thick manila file folder encircled with a plastic band. He brought it over to where the two policemen sat and put it down on the table between them.

"What's this, then?" Thomson said. He looked down at the file and read the handwritten label. It said *Richard Weal case: Clippings and Notes* in faded blue ink.

"It's the story," Billy said simply. "It's what happened. They arrested Richard and charged him with assault and attempted murder. He was still raving about voices in the rocks when they took him away under police guard. He was declared unfit to stand trial and was incarcerated in a mental institution outside of Montréal for fifteen years." Billy tapped the folder. "It's all here—everything. My father's notes. Newspaper clippings. The arrest, the trial, everything. My father made a copy of this before he died, and mailed it to me. He said he was working on a book about what happened—and what had happened before."

"What do you mean, what had happened before? Before *what*? You mean, with Richard?"

"Not just with Richard," Billy said. "There's a history of violent incidents associated with this place. That history stretches back almost two hundred and fifty years. What happened with Richard and Emory has happened before, and right around here."

"Again, Dr. Lightning," Thomson said in a pained voice, this time not even trying to cover up his impatience, "this is all very interesting. I'm sure your father's book would have been fascinating. Forgive me for repeating myself again, but you still haven't answered my question about why you're in Parr's Landing *now*."

"Because I think Richard Weal murdered my father in Toronto six weeks ago, Sergeant Thomson."

"Do you have any evidence of that, Dr. Lightning?"

"Nothing that would likely convince you, Sergeant." Billy sighed. "It didn't convince the police in Toronto."

"Humour me," Thomson said. "Why do you think he killed your father?"

"My father was killed with a hammer blow to the head. The police say he may have known his killer, because there was no sign of forced entry, but the house had been ransacked, from top to bottom. Nothing of any apparent value was taken—things like my mother's Georgian tea service and some fairly expensive art was left where it was. Given that the vast majority of valuable objects were left behind, the police concluded that it was likely some sort of drug-related break-in."

"You said 'the vast majority of valuable objects' were left behind. Were the police able to ascertain what *was* taken, if anything?"

"The originals of these notes," Billy said, picking up the folder, "were missing from his study. What was also missing was a translation from the French he'd been working on. An obscure document from the *Jesuit Relations*—the letters written by the Jesuit missionaries to New France and sent to the Society of Jesus in Rome in the seventeenth century."

Thomson looked dubious. "These papers were 'missing,' you said? I doubt they considered that a motive for murder. Was any money taken?"

"My father had always kept some emergency money locked in his desk," Billy said. "The desk was unlocked when the police went over the place, but the money was still there. He might have kept some money elsewhere, but I couldn't confirm or deny that to their satisfaction. The case is still open, technically, but they seem to have made up their minds. They said that there's no evidence that it was anything other than what they said it was."

"It sounds like a tragedy, Dr. Lightning," Thomson said. "But the police were likely correct. Had Richard Weal been in touch with your father? Had he made any threats?"

"No," Billy admitted. "Nothing he shared with me. But the missing documents—"

"Dr. Lightning," Thomson said, rising, "we're sorry to have bothered you at this difficult time. You're, of course, welcome to travel anywhere and do anything. I don't think I would have chosen Parr's Landing as a place to recover from the death of my father, personally, but to each his own. Constable McKitrick and I will be on our way. Thank you for your time, sir."

"I'm telling you, Richard Weal killed my father. And he's coming here. I know it. He has my father's papers. He believes something is speaking to him in the rocks."

"Afternoon, Dr. Lightning," Elliot said. He opened the motel door and held it open. Before stepping through, Thomson turned to Billy again.

"Dr. Lightning," Thomson said. "You never told us what happened to Richard Weal. Did the police ever find him to question him?"

"No," Billy replied. "They didn't. He'd been released from the institution a few years back, according to the information I was able to acquire on my own. If he was getting outpatient treatment somewhere, there weren't any records immediately available, and since he wasn't seriously considered a suspect, no one looked very hard to find him."

"I see. Well, that settles it, as far as we're concerned, I think. Thank you again for your time, Dr. Lightning. We'll be on our way now, I think."

And they were on their way. Billy Lightning closed the motel room door behind them. The silence of the motel room embraced him. He sighed, as much in relief as in frustration. Eventually the relief overtook the frustration. He hadn't expected them to believe him, but he realized that he'd bought himself a bit of time, if nothing else.

Billy picked up the file folder of his father's notes and went back to the bed. He sat down, opened the file, and began to read what he'd already read hundreds of times before. Maybe this time, it would say something new. He felt a pang of sharp longing at the sight of his father's handwriting on the smudged carbon. The unfathomable sense of his loss returned to him like a plaintive, restless ghost.

Elliot McKitrick and Dave Thomson rode in silence for the first few minutes of the ride back to the police station. Then Elliot spoke.

"What did you make of that?" he asked. "That was some story. Do you think he's telling the truth?"

"Easy enough to check it out," Thomson said. "At least the part about his father's murder. The rest of it happened more or less the way he said it did, but I think it was pretty much an open and shut case back then of a guy who had a nervous breakdown and got locked up for it."

"What about the Doc? Do you think this Lightning might have had anything to do with it?"

"I'll run his name by the RCMP and see if anything comes up," Thomson replied. "But I don't think it's going to add up. I think what we're looking at is a series of tragedies, starting with this poor Weal kid going off his rocker and being packed off to the bughouse. Then the old man gets murdered years later, and his son connects the two worst events of his life and comes up with an answer he can live with. No more, no less."

"What about the rest of it? The spirit voices and the weird stuff?"

Thomson shrugged. "You grew up here. You know how many stories there are. Those Wendigo stories, for one. Local legends. Every town has some. As for the rest of it, well, life was tough here a couple of hundred years ago. Winters were long. Things happened. People probably did go crazy, as much from the isolation as anything else. If this Weal fella read about this stuff in some history textbook in school, it'd be *in* his head already when he went *off* his head."

Elliot looked doubtful. "So, you don't think Weal might have anything to do with what happened up in Gyles?"

"On the say-so of *Dr. William Lightning,* he of the crazy story we just heard? I don't think so. As far as anyone knows, Weal could be dead." Thomson snorted. "I think Chief Bill's headdress is on a bit tight. He's a bit cocked-up about his father's death, that's all. That's got to be hard for anybody. But do I think some possessed crazy hobgoblin has driven thousands of miles from God knows where just to come back here to live out of doors by Bradley Lake and eat people?" This time, Thomson laughed out loud. "No, I don't think so."

"It'll be Halloween in a couple of weeks," Elliot said. If he were an older man, and more seasoned, let alone more secure in himself, he likely would have been readier to admit to being more relieved than disappointed to hear Thomson dismiss the Indian's story. "Maybe we're due for a new spook tale to add to all that Wendigo bullshit we've been hearing for years up here in God's country since forever."

"God's country," Jeremy Parr said wistfully to Christina. He closed his eyes and breathed deeply. The air was wonderfully cool, but not too cold for comfort. It smelled of autumn—fallen leaves, the scent of cooling earth and the flowering of benign rot, the sleepy prelude to winter. The morning had started out cold, but the day had warmed again. They had parked the car a few miles out of town, past Bradley Lake, on the old logging road. They sat on a red flannel blanket. Above them, the sunlight streamed down through the cathedral of orange-leafed trees, turning everything around it the colour of caramel apple glaze. "Elliot always called it 'God's country,'" he said by way of clarification. "Today I can see what he meant."

Christina's eyes were closed, her face in the sun. She sighed. "What are you going to do, now that you've seen him? And he probably saw you, too. If he didn't see you, he's heard that you're back. Are you going to go see him?"

"What would be the point? It was ten years ago, and the way it ended, it was like a bad dream that we had ten years ago. He's probably married, probably has kids. It was one of those things that was never meant to happen at all."

"But it did happen," Christina said kindly. "He was your first love. And it didn't end the way it was supposed to end."

"Maybe it *did* end the way it was supposed to end. Have you noticed that love doesn't flourish in this town? You have to leave it in order to keep it. Especially," he added bitterly, "my kind of love."

Christina started to say something conciliatory in reply, something to suggest that Jeremy was being melodramatic or unnecessarily dour, but she didn't. It occurred to her that her own story more or less proved his point, and she couldn't think of any love stories off the top of her head that had blossomed and flourished in Parr's Landing. Her own parents more or less tolerated each other, focusing the love they'd obviously once had for each other on their children. The house where Christina grew up was full of pictures—her jubilant parents on their wedding day, photos of the two of them on picnics, her mother sitting on the back of her father's motorcycle, the two of them on a Ferris wheel at a country fair.

In those pictures, their love for each other had been nearly tangible, but once Christina and her brother entered the montage of images on the walls, a certain steeliness had set in. In later photographs, her mother seemed detached, her father more stoic than loving. It was as though the diffusion of that young love, its dispersal into the larger world of children, mortgages, church, work for subsistence wages in a northern mining town—survival, really—had damaged the love in transit, alchemically transforming it at a cellular level into something else, something greyer. Christina tried to remember her parents ever embracing, but nothing came to her.

The cancer had taken her mother when Christina was fourteen. Christina tried to remember her parents ever embracing before her mother got sick, but nothing came to her. She wondered if that gradual distancing would have eventually happened to her and Jack, and even as she wondered it, she had her answer: *No, of course not.* Because, as Jeremy said, they'd gotten away.

To change the subject from her own memories, as well as to distract Jeremy from his, she asked, "How do you think it's going with your mother?"

Jeremy shrugged. "So far so good, I guess. I don't think she's all that happy to see either of us, but she seems happy to see Morgan, at least. Did you see her last night? She couldn't keep her eyes off her. And this morning, she was quite testy when you said you wanted to drive her to school yourself."

Christina laughed. It was not a happy laugh. "I think that had everything to do with her not wanting me to be seen around town with Jack Parr's daughter—even if she is my daughter, too—more than it did any great grandmotherly love, don't you?"

"Not sure," he said. "I hadn't realized how much Morgan actually looks like Jack—I mean *really* looks like Jack—until I saw all the pictures of him as a kid that Adeline has around the house. For her, it must be like having his ghost come back to haunt her. I think that's why she's trying too hard to make friends with her. The rest of us are just an inconvenience to be dealt with."

"I don't know," Christina said. "I have a bad feeling about it somehow. Then again, when it comes to your mother, I've only ever had bad feelings. So this is nothing new."

"I wonder how Morgan is doing in school today? First day in a new school—hell, and not just any new school. Our old school."

Christina sighed. "I've been trying very hard not to think about it, Jeremy. Thanks so much for bringing it up."

"Sorry."

"No, it's all right." She picked up a yellow leaf beside her and held it between her fingers, examined it, and then flicked it away. "This is probably the hardest part. I can protect her from almost anything else but this. In Toronto, at Jarvis Collegiate, she had her friends and her routine. She wasn't anything special. Here, God only knows."

"Hey, she'll be fine," Jeremy said in a soothing voice. "This is Morgan you're talking about. Also, besides being our wonderful girl in her own right, she's Jack's daughter."

"Everyone used to worship Jack, but it wasn't because he was a Parr, it was because he was—well, Jack. Morgan isn't Jack. She doesn't have the experience of growing up here with that name and getting used to what it means. She doesn't have the . . . the . . ."

"The antibodies?" Jeremy said, suppressing a smile. "Is that what you mean? She hasn't been inoculated against being a Parr in Parr's Landing? She doesn't have the antibodies to the virus?"

Christina threw a pile of the yellow leaves at Jeremy. He laughed, covering his head. He threw a handful of the leaves at Christina, provoking answering laughter in return.

"Yes," she said, brushing the leaves out of her hair. "That's what I mean. Exactly. She doesn't have the antibodies for this town. Morgan is a city girl." She grew serious again. "These kids can probably smell it on her. They always could smell *difference*. They're terrible when they find it, too. You know that better than anyone."

"Yep," he said quietly. "I do."

"See, that's what I'm worried about. We don't belong here—either of us. And Morgan *really* doesn't belong here. She belongs at home in the city, with me there for her every afternoon when she gets home from school and wants to cry over her dead father, or talk about how she feels about it." She began to cry, at the same time thinking, *Jesus, enough with these waterworks, already. I can't keep doing this.* "I'm failing her. This isn't what Jack would have wanted. I just know it."

Jeremy rolled towards Christina. His expression was so sad that she instinctively reached for his hand and squeezed his fingers before he even had a chance to speak. When he did, his own voice was thick. "Christina, I'm so, so sorry,"

She wiped her eyes with her sleeve. "About what?"

"About—all of this," he said. "About not being to be able to take care of you both. About letting things get to the point where we had to come back here. I was so busy making my own life that I didn't have a contingency plan. I've been beating myself up about it since we arrived here. I'm so sorry."

"Hey," she said softly. "Shut up. OK? It wasn't your job to take care of us. Jack didn't expect it from you, and neither did I. All three of us moved away from here to get on with our lives, and to get away from all the . . . the bad *shit* here." Christina propped herself on one elbow and looked Jeremy in the eye. "Jack always took care of *everything*. I guess, in a way, we were still kids in our own minds. Not smart of us, I know. But he would have hated to hear you blame yourself for this. If he were around, he'd be busy blaming himself for not taking out insurance because somewhere in the back of his mind he still thought of himself as a rich boy. And I'd be busy blaming myself for not making it a priority myself, and for not reminding him that he lost that 'rich boy' status when he married me."

Jeremy said dryly, "You two were always ideally matched."

"You know what? There's no one to blame, and it's a waste of time. It's nobody's fault. We couldn't have predicted what happened. And," she added, "nothing would have stopped Adeline from simply offering to help me out when I called to tell her about Jack's accident. All she had to do was say, 'What do you need, Christina? What does my granddaughter need? It's yours.' But she didn't. She let me *beg*, like some sort of sharecropper instead of the mother of her son's only child. Then she condescended that I could come back here with Morgan and live off her charity.

"*You* on the other hand," she said, squeezing his hand, "offered to come back here to this place in spite of all the terrible memories it holds for you. You did it for Morgan and me. Which makes you the one person in this whole sad story who offered to step up to the plate. We'll never forget it, either of us. So let's not hear any more about blame, OK?"

Jeremy squeezed back. "OK," he said. "Thanks, love."

"Now, what are you going to do about Elliot McKitrick? You're going to meet up with him sooner or later. It's a matter of time. How's that going to be for you?"

Jeremy was silent for a moment. The he spoke. "It's going to hurt like hell," he said. "One way or another, it's going to be a killer."

Morgan's new homeroom at Matthew Browning Memorial High School smelled like chalk, wet wool, some sort of disinfectant, and old wood to her. It didn't smell like Jarvis Collegiate back home. It wasn't that it smelled bad, it just smelled foreign and fundamentally inhospitable. It wasn't just that the ceilings seemed too high, or that the architecture of the place made her think of the 1950s—an era she didn't know, but had read about in magazines, and could picture. It wasn't that the contrast between the wild autumn northern light coming through the arched windows contrasted sharply with the fluorescent lights hanging from the ceiling threw an industrial pall over the scene.

It wasn't just that everything looked even older than it was, or that the Queen looked preternaturally girlish in the yellowed picture hanging in the wooden frame on the wall adjacent to the blackboard (as opposed to the more matronly representation of Her Majesty on the wall of her homeroom at Jarvis), or that in the brand new black-and-white picture next to it, Prime Minister Pierre Elliot Trudeau looked like a French movie star.

It was all of these things and none of them, rolled into a tight ball of dislocation. She was an alien in an alien place, where none of her markers of familiarity lined up.

Being an intelligent girl, Morgan was able to recognize that her response was an emotional one. Being a confident girl, it didn't throw her as much as it might have thrown someone less sure of herself. Her mother would have been surprised at just how much of her father's daughter Morgan Parr actually was.

Some of the boys had looked at her with frank interest. A

smaller number of the girls had assessed her as a sexual threat, and she felt a chill drift of hostility coming from them. But the majority of the students, both male and female, regarded her with the curiosity reserved for the interjection of something brand new, even foreign, into their social ecosystem.

When the teacher, Mr. Churchill, had introduced her as "Morgan Parr who has transferred to our school from far-away Toronto," she wasn't sure what had caused them to raise their eyebrows more—the fact that she was from someplace as far away as Toronto and therefore, by definition, exotic, or her last name, which was as familiar to them as their own.

But if she'd had any real doubts or fears about fitting into a new school, they'd been dramatically allayed by her visit to the principal's office when she had arrived at the school that morning before the start of classes. She'd opened the door to the outer office and found that she was expected. The sixtyish woman with a mauve-rinsed marcel wave and the kindly face sitting at the desk had smiled warmly at Morgan.

"Welcome to Matthew Browning Memorial, dear," she'd said. "We're so glad you've made it here safely. Your grandma told us you were coming. We've been expecting you. We've all been looking forward to it."

"Thank you, ma'am," Morgan said shyly. Privately she tried to picture the adamantine Adeline Parr as anyone's "grandma," least of all her, and suppressed a fit of spontaneous giggling with effort.

"My name is Miss Quinn. I'm the secretary," the older woman said, beaming. "Why, you look just like your father, dear. He was one of my favourite students. He was always so polite, with a smile for everybody. I knew him ever since he was a little boy." A pained look crossed her face. "We were all so sorry to hear that he'd passed. So very sad."

"Thank you, ma'am," Morgan said again, charmed by the older woman's familiar and loving evocation of her father. She was unused to the feeling. Usually, mentions of her father by strangers distressed her. But there was something soothing and motherly about Miss Quinn, and Morgan was surprised at the sense of comfort she experienced in hearing her father mentioned by the older woman. She caught a whiff of Evening in Paris as Miss Quinn crossed the floor to knock on the door marked *Mr. R. Murphy, Principal.*

"I'll just let Mr. Murphy know that you're here," Miss Quinn said.

She opened the door and stepped inside. A few minutes later she came out and said, "Go on in, dear. Mr. Murphy wants a few words with you. I'll get your papers all filled out for you in the meantime."

Morgan stepped into the office. The principal rose from his chair when she entered. He gestured to the chair in front of his desk. "Hello, Morgan, I'm Mr. Murphy, the principal. Please sit down. We're all very glad to have you joining us here at Matthew Browning, even this late in the season. We all wish it could have been under different circumstances, of course. But still, we're delighted to have you."

"Thank you, sir," she replied.

She waited for Mr. Murphy to continue. "I don't need to tell you that I don't usually invite the new students in here for a chat before they start school. Heck," he added with a good natured, avuncular chuckle. "I've known most of them, one way or another, since they were boys and girls. But your grandmother, Mrs. Parr, met with me and discussed your . . . ah . . . specific circumstances."

"You mean the fact that my dad is dead?"

"Yes," he said. "That, in addition to the fact that you've come to us from Toronto, although both your parents were originally from here. Your father was one of the star pupils of this school, in addition to being from our finest family—your family, now."

"Yes," Morgan said sweetly. "Mine and my mother's. My mother drove us here. She and my Uncle Jeremy, of course. We all came back to town together. Well, *they* 'came back.' I've never lived here. Did you know my mom when she lived here? Her last name used to be Monroe. Christina Monroe. Before she married my father and became Christina Parr."

Mr. Murphy flushed deep scarlet. "Yes, of course, your mother is also from here," he said. "I remember her well. Your grandmother told me that she was coming back. I'm sorry about her loss, as well." Morgan waited silently for Mr. Murphy to get to the point, which he promptly did. "Morgan, your grandmother wanted me to make sure that you understand that whatever . . . uh . . . choices your parents made sixteen years ago about how to . . . uh . . . comport themselves . . ."

"Sir," Morgan said, politely. "If you mean that my parents were in love and ran off to Toronto to have me, they both told me the story. I grew up knowing it."

"Well, you're a very self-possessed and liberal-minded young lady, Morgan, aren't you?" He chuckled again. "You sounded just like your father there, for a minute. That's the sort of thing he would have said, and he would have said it just like that, too."

"Thank you."

"Anyway, to get to the point, Morgan, you grandmother wanted me to make sure that you felt welcome here at Matthew Browning, and that you knew that we were behind you one hundred percent. If you have any problems with any of the kids, you just come and let me know."

"What sort of problems, sir?"

"Well," he said. "Some of them are . . . well, not as liberal-minded or as modern as you and your mother. And your father, obviously. They might . . . say things. Things that aren't necessarily very nice."

This time Morgan's puzzlement was genuine. "Things like what?"

"There are some . . . unfortunate names for children whose parents haven't gone the conventional route to . . . uh, matrimony. Names that aren't used by polite people, and while we're very proud of our student body, occasionally, in the heat of the moment, people say things they . . . ah, regret later. Parr's Landing can be conservative in some ways. You do know what 'conservative' means, don't you?"

The flush had returned to Mr. Murphy's face, and now

Morgan felt sorry for him. She had a vague idea that he was trying to allude to illegitimacy, but since he wouldn't come out and say it, there was no way for her to address it directly. The notion caused her no particular distress. There had been children of hippies at Jarvis, and some of their parents weren't formally married. As non-churchgoers and *de facto* nonconformists in their own right, Jack and Christina Parr had been very careful when it came to inculcating their daughter with the sort of prejudices that would be taken for granted in a town like Parr's Landing. Also, growing up with Uncle Jeremy, those prejudices would have been hard for her parents to reinforce, even if they'd wanted to.

"Mr. Murphy," she said, gently, "my parents were married before they had me. My mother was pregnant when she was married, but she was married when I was born. They've talked about this with me since I was a little girl. I don't know what my grandmother told you, but we were a pretty normal family. My mom and dad loved each other very much. And names aren't going to bother me, anyway. I've been called names before. But thanks for worrying about it. It's nice of you."

Mr. Murphy sighed with obvious relief. "Well, that's good," he said. "But, as I said, your grandmother asked me to speak with you, and to make sure you understood that she . . . that is to say Matthew Browning Memorial won't tolerate any shenanigans from other students when it comes to you. Mrs. Parr is a very valuable member of our school board, and her . . . your family has very deep, very valuable roots in our community. We want you to feel welcome here. And," he added, almost hesitantly, "I'd very much appreciate it if you'd share with your grandmother that we had this little chat, and that you understand that my door will always be open if you have any problems at all. Anything. Just let her know I said that."

My God, Morgan marvelled. *He's afraid of me. He's afraid of my grandmother, so he's afraid of me, too. He wants me to make sure she knows he did what she wanted him to do. He wants her to know he did her bidding. What sort of family is this that I'm a part of? What, am I royalty all of a sudden?*

"Yes, sir," she said aloud. "I'll make sure to tell Grandmother we talked, and how nice and helpful you were about all of this. I'm sure everything's going to be just fine."

"Well," he said, puffing up his chest. "Good, good. Very fine indeed. All right, Morgan, Miss Quinn will give you your class schedule and show you where to go. And you have a good day, Morgan!"

"Thank you, Mr. Murphy." She stood up and shook his hand. This time, he did not rise in his chair, and Morgan was relieved to have the balance of power restored to a more traditional paradigm, with the principal acting like a principal again instead of acting like her grandmother's lackey. In the same way Morgan was fascinated by her apparent newfound—and entirely alien—importance by virtue of her last name, it also disoriented her and made her uncomfortable.

She thought briefly of taking it up with her mother later tonight when she got home, but instinctively understood that it would only cause more tension. Her grandmother, she already knew, would be the wrong person to speak to about this for reasons she couldn't articulate, but understood clearly nonetheless. *Maybe Uncle Jeremy would be able to shed some light on it,* Morgan thought. Uncle Jeremy always seemed to know what was going on, even when no one else did. She realized suddenly that Uncle Jeremy was, like Morgan herself, a Parr by blood. It was something that had never occurred to her at home in Toronto, but out here in this wilderness, it seemed to count for something. What, exactly, it counted for, she wasn't sure. But she was sure she would find out sooner or later.

She left the principal's office. Miss Quinn handed her a sheaf of papers, including her class list.

"Follow me, dear," she said. "I'll show you where your homeroom is." When they got to the classroom door, Miss Quinn offered to introduce her to her homeroom teacher, Mr. Churchill, but Morgan politely declined. She already felt like she was dancing on the surface of Saturn and it wasn't even nine o'clock yet. Miss Quinn patted her hand, understanding that Morgan had already had enough of standing out. The first bell of the day rang.

She took a deep breath and walked into the classroom, smelling chalk, wet wool, disinfectant, and old wood.

At lunchtime, playing truant from the grounds of Parr's Landing Public School with his dog-eared copy of *Tomb of Dracula* issue #3 placed carefully in his durable orange canvas book bag, Finn caught sight of the girl with the long dark hair sitting by herself under the elm tree in front of the high school down the street. He promptly fell in love the way that only a twelve-year-old boy can.

Not since Finn laid his eyes on *Tomb of Dracula* issue #1 had he seen anything as beautiful as Morgan Parr—whose name was still a mystery, and would remain so for a time yet.

She ate alone, which puzzled him. How could admirers not surround anyone that beautiful? Parr's Landing's population was 1,528 (give or take) so new faces were easy to spot, and he'd never seen this girl before. His eyes reverenced the way the sunlight brought out the bands of honey and cinnamon-red in her dark hair. She ate her sandwich with a lack of self-consciousness that he'd never seen before in a girl of her age.

His short life to date had been spent entirely within the precincts of his hometown. While he'd dreamed of what life must be like outside of its boundaries, certainly he'd never seen any evidence of it other than what he'd gleaned from television, magazines, movies, or, of course, his beloved comic books. The girl across the street was clearly not a local, so she became the screen upon which he projected his vision.

She looked up suddenly, as though she realized he was watching her. Her eyes scanned the street across from the school where he was standing. Instinctively, he ducked behind another elm tree and prayed she hadn't spotted him and found him creepy.

He didn't care a whit about being caught off the school grounds— he never had been caught before. Finn had learned to close his eyes and pretend to transform into mist, like Dracula did when Rachel Van Helsing, the glamourous blonde vampire huntress from *The Tomb of Dracula,* shot an arrow at the Lord of the Undead with her crossbow. Finn wasn't crazy; he knew he didn't turn into mist. But he also knew that whenever he pretended he turned into mist, he was somehow never caught doing anything he didn't want to be caught doing. And right now, what he wanted was for the girl not to catch him staring at her. He closed his eyes and . . . transformed into mist.

Her eyes passed over where he stood behind the tree without registering him at all, as far as he could tell.

He breathed a sigh of relief and stepped back out from behind the tree. He took one more longing look at her eating her sandwich. He imprinted the image on his memory like a photograph, promising himself he'd see her again—soon.

Then he turned and jogged back to school, all thoughts of both lunch and his comic book momentarily forgotten, as old loves so often are when a rival first appears.

At two in the afternoon, Elliot McKitrick realized that he needed desperately to be alone to think, so he told Thomson that he was going to take the cruiser and do a loop of the town and the area around Bradley Lake. He told the sergeant that he'd be on radio if he needed him and that he wouldn't go far, but he wanted to patrol the town line in light of what had happened in Gyles Point the previous night.

"Good idea," Thomson said without looking up. "I think the tank is a bit low, so fill her up on the way back, would you, McKitrick? I'm going to stay here and make some calls. I want to check out a couple of points of Dr. Lightning's story."

"Sounded fishy to you, too, Sarge?"

"Not necessarily," Thomson said, not looking at the younger man. "Just . . . well, there are some things I want to check out."

Elliot stood in the doorway for another moment, waiting for more. When it was not forthcoming, he opened the door and went to where the cruiser was parked. He turned the key in the ignition and headed towards the road that led out of town.

He smoked as he drove. He wasn't supposed to, but he realized he had been in a state of suppressed anxiety ever since he'd seen Jeremy Parr on the road earlier that morning. His heart was beating like a triphammer and his mind was cloudy with memories he'd been suppressing for a decade—memories that were sharper than he'd ever dreamed possible, given the time that had elapsed since that last terrible night before Jeremy had been sent away and Elliot's father had beaten him till he bled.

Through the windshield, the town looked as it always did, except for the fact that someone had ripped a hole in the airtight zone of security and comfort he had come to rely on over the last ten years. Suddenly his world, usually as well ordered as a soldier's sock drawer, seemed dangerously askew.

What Elliot wanted to know was *how* askew, and why. He had learned as a very young boy that self-examination was called "navel gazing" and that real men didn't do it. And Elliot was a real man. His entire life— with one notable deviation from the straight and narrow—had been dedicated to being a real man. He had spilled a great deal of sweat and blood to assure that end.

But until Elliot was sure in his own mind that the only thing that was fucking him up about Jeremy Parr's return to Parr's Landing was the possibility of bad gossip being stirred up again, he wasn't going to be at peace in his own mind.

Suddenly Elliot felt as though he were suffocating, as though he were buried alive. The car felt like a coffin with metal sides and no air. He pulled over to the side of the road and half-stepped, half-fell out the door into the cold fall air. He drew in great gasping breaths, filling his lungs with oxygen as though he had just broken the surface of a pit full of quicksand, his lungs full of mud and silt and filthy water.

For a moment, he felt as though he might vomit, but he closed his eyes and concentrated on his breathing until the nausea passed and his mind cleared.

Goddamn you, Jeremy, why the fuck did you have to come back here? Why didn't you stay away?

Of course there was no answer except for the sound of the wind and the distant squawk of crows circling somewhere high above Spirit Rock. Elliot shaded his eyes and followed the sound of the crows, but he couldn't see them. He scanned the cliff, looking for the birds, but to no avail. A cloud passed over the sun, shattering the rock face into a diorama of light and shadow. And then something *did* move up there on the ledge. Even before his eyes caught the blur of motion, his brain *registered* motion. Something upright, pacing carefully. And then it was gone.

Elliot stared at the spot where he'd seen the shape, then shouted out, "Hello? Is someone up there?" His voice sounded abnormally loud to him in the late-afternoon sunlight. The echo mocked him and, of course, there was no answer. But he had seen it. Something that ought not to have been up there, something entirely out of place, something out of the natural order.

He thought of Thomson's description of the murder scene at Gyles Point. *There's blood all over the upstairs bedroom, but no body anywhere.* He thought of the Indian, Billy Lightning, who had just arrived in town the morning after the murder with (in Elliot's opinion) a preposterous story and no good reason for being in Parr's Landing at all. By his own account, madness and death seemed to follow the Indian around.

Elliot privately flattered himself that he had natural-born police instincts, even when he knew he was only burnishing his self-image for the sake of his own ego, but he still felt the hair rise on the back of his neck, and he instinctively reached for the holster of his gun and withdrew it.

And yet there was nothing to see now. No movement, not even a shadow, which is probably what it was to begin with. He shook his head to clear it and rubbed his eyes, then looked again. There was nothing but the cliff's edge and the daubed smudges of the Indian paintings of the mythical Wendigo of St. Barthélemy. What the fuck had that been up there? And why did he reach for his gun? Elliot McKitrick had rarely been spooked by anything in his life, and never by Bradley Lake or Spirit Rock. Everyone in Parr's Landing had heard the stories. Those stories were for scaring children and for getting chicks to cuddle up closer. He thought of the years he'd spent out here, swimming, whiling away his summer nights on blankets, in front of bonfires. He'd lost his virginity here when he was fourteen, and yes—he'd even brought Jeremy Parr here that first night when they'd gotten drunk and had . . . well, what had happened, happened.

He pushed *that* memory down brutally. His head throbbed with the beginnings of a headache that he knew was going to be one for the record books.

Elliot sighed. He re-holstered his gun and walked slowly back to the car. He needed a drink in the worst way. He'd always felt that Parr's Landing was the beginning and the end of his world, that everything he ever needed was here and his for the asking, but as he turned the ignition, he wondered for the very first time whether Jeremy had been the smart one, the one to leave Parr's Landing and make a life for himself somewhere where no one knew him, and no one cared who—or what— he was.

He turned the cruiser around and headed for the road back to town, kicking up gravel in the car's wake that smacked against the metal like the sound of caps exploding. Elliot automatically checked his rearview mirror as he tapped the accelerator. In the mirror, he saw the lake, occluded by dust devils and exhaust from the car.

What he could *not* see was the shadow moving again, high up on the ridge where he had stared, so long and so hard, trying to identify the source of his sudden and unaccountable sense of dislocation and— though Elliot would never have admitted it, even to himself—fear.

From his perch high up on the ledge, Richard Weal watched the police cruiser drive away towards town. He'd briefly considered killing this one if he'd come too close, but he'd decided to allow him to live—for now. Instead, Weal had remained completely motionless, willing himself into invisibility, not moving a muscle until the policeman had left of his own accord. *Lucky for him,* Weal thought. *Cops are so stupid.*

Still, he reasoned, the policeman's blood might have been useful, and it would certainly have spared Weal the pain he knew was coming. But another killing, now, when he was so close to his destination, would only serve as a dangerous distraction. After leaving a string of bodies between Toronto and Parr's Landing, it would be a cruel and pathetic ending for him to be caught killing some small-town yokel of a cop at this point.

He'd consulted the sheaf of papers in his hockey bag a thousand time or more. He could practically recite the text by heart. This was the place. *This* place—here, now. His friend's voice had never been this clear, this compelling and demanding. And when he closed his eyes, he saw visions of blood and bones and smoke. He saw the path through the caves of rock and stone as though it were lit by torchlight.

Weal's heart soared with love and pride and yearning. He laid his face reverently against the wall of rock and said, "I'm coming, Father. I'm coming for you now. Tonight, we'll be together. I swear."

CHAPTER TWELVE

When the final bell rang, Finn bolted from his seat and ran for the door of the classroom as quickly as he could without looking like a total jackass. He didn't hear Mrs. Morris tell him to slow down, and he moved too quickly through the halls of the school for either the teachers or the hall monitors to tell him to stop running. Through the swinging front doors he flew, taking the steps three at a time till he hit the pavement, still running.

He had to get to the high school. He had to see the girl. If he didn't, he would die. It was that simple. She'd been all he was able to think of all afternoon, and he was now sure that he was in love with her. And he didn't even know her name.

Finn, out of breath, found the girl standing under the same elm tree where she'd sat having lunch an eternity of hours ago. Though out of breath, he still managed to come to a relatively inconspicuous stop not far from where the girl stood. In his mind, he pictured himself as a cartoon figure caught doing whatever he was not supposed to be doing, and whistling innocently with his head in the air. *What? Who, me? Not a thing, officer. I just happened to be barrelling down this street at a hundred and fifty miles an hour. Girl? What girl? I'm not following a GIRL!*

Finn prayed she hadn't noticed him, and his prayers were answered again: she clearly hadn't noticed him. She hadn't looked up from the sheet of paper she was staring at.

A group of noisily shouting children from the primary school ran past on the other side of the street. Startled by the sound, the girl looked up and saw Finn staring at her.

Here it comes, Finn thought. *This is where she looks at me with disgust and says, "Eeew, what do you want, you creepy little kid? Get lost! Stop staring at me, or my boyfriend will put your head through a wall!"*

Instead, the girl smiled, and said, "Hi there." She stood expectantly until Finn realized she was waiting for him to say "hi" back to her.

"Hi," Finn said. "You new in town?" Feeling stupid, he added, "You must be new in town. I've never seen you before." Then he felt even more stupid, because it made him sound like he knew every girl in town, which he didn't. *Moron, Finn raged to himself. You're such a goddamn MORON.*

"Yeah," she said. Finn thought she had a beautiful voice. Her cadence was unlike any other he'd heard. He thought this was what Rachel van Helsing might sound like—sophisticated, vaguely foreign. Totally sexy. "I'm new," she added. "Really new. I just arrived last night. It's my first day in town." She walked over to where Finn was standing and put out her hand. "My name is Morgan. Morgan Parr."

"Wow," he said. "Parr, just like the town. You sure moved to the right place! Ha ha!"

"Well, I'm staying with my grandmother. Up on the hill. My family sort of named the town, or something, so maybe it's not so weird?" The girl sounded embarrassed, instead of snooty, maybe even apologetic. Finn was immediately mortified by what he'd said.

"Sorry, I didn't know. I mean . . . I'm sorry I laughed. I'm not sorry that your last name is Parr. Like I said, everyone in town knows everyone else here, so when someone new comes to town— which they never do— everyone notices. Especially if they're kids. Which they never are. So . . . welcome, I guess. Where you from?" *Stupid, stupid, stupid. You sound like a babbling idiot.*

"Toronto," Morgan said. "My dad . . . well, my dad died a while back, and this is where my mom and dad were from. So we came back. Well, my mother and my uncle came back. I've never been here before." She paused. "You never told me your name."

"Finnegan," he said, and then added before she could, "like the dog puppet on Mr. Dressup, on TV."

"We didn't have a TV at home," she said wistfully. "My parents didn't think it was good for me. I never saw that show. Nice name, though."

"I hate it."

"Why? It's beautiful. It sounds Irish or something."

"You're just being nice," he said. "It sounds like the name of a dog on a television show. Nobody is named 'Finnegan.'"

"Well, it doesn't sound like the name of a dog on television to me," she said. "Besides, try living with a name like 'Morgan.' My dad called me 'Sprite,' but that just sounded like a soft drink to most people, so we just kept it between us. No one else is allowed to call me anything but 'Morgan.'" She looked at her watch. "Gee, I have to get home. My grandmother seems to be pretty tough about being on time." She looked at him quizzically. "Hey, Finn, do you live far from here? Do you want to walk for a bit? I don't know anyone in town. I could use the company."

"Sure," Finn said. Then, daringly, "Can I carry your books for you?"

She laughed. "No, I'm OK with the books. They're not heavy. But thanks, anyway. I'll be happy for the company."

They walked through the streets of Parr's Landing, with Finn guiding Morgan. Her directional recall, honed by years of living in a busy city led her to suspect that Finn was taking her the long way home, but she didn't mind. She was less worried about her grandmother's schedule than she'd let on, since there was an hour and a half yet till dinner and she had no desire to see Adeline before then. Finn seemed interested in her life, and what she had to say. He pointed out local landmarks—the Church of St. Barthélemy and the Martyrs, the Parr's Landing Library, Harper's where he got his comic books. Finn never stopped talking. After months in close quarters with only her mother, and occasionally Uncle Jeremy for company, she was happy for the proximity of another young person, especially as she'd been more or less ignored by everyone in her class that day. It was as though she had been marked not only as an outsider, but also as an off-limits outsider. There had been no overt hostility that she could detect, but no warmth, either.

She wondered if this had been some of her grandmother's doing, though how—or why, for that matter—was a mystery. It would be one thing for Adeline to be able to order her mother and uncle around, but if her scope of influence included not just the administrators of her school, but even her fellow students, her grandmother was in a league of her own.

Finn, on the other hand, seemed eager for her company. Morgan hadn't had a great deal of experience with boys, but as a life-long pretty girl, she had been the recipient of crushes before, and was adept at recognizing them. Unlike other girls, however, she didn't cherish crushes, or collect them as tributes. What she felt for the boys who brought their adoration to her was compassion and empathy. Even at fifteen, she knew that the boys who were drawn to her were putting themselves out on a limb. And here was Finnegan Miller of Parr's Landing, Ontario walking her home. She *had* seen Mr. Dressup—of course she had, everyone had—though she would never have admitted this to a boy who was that sensitive about sharing a name with a dog puppet.

He was cute, Morgan thought. It was too bad he was so young. He was going to be a very handsome boy when he was a little older. "So, how old are you, Finn?" Morgan asked as casually as possible. Her fingers trailed along a hedge as she passed, and she didn't look at him when she asked the question.

"Twelve," Finn replied. He looked down and kicked a pebble off the sidewalk with the tip of his sneaker. "You?"

"I'm fifteen," Morgan said lightly. "Just turned." In spite of her casual tone, she realized how stating her age, and their age difference, had set the parameters of their friendship in a way that disappointed Finn. Morgan hoped that they could still be friends, because so far he'd been the one friendly face in Parr's Landing, and she could use a friend right about now.

"So, Finn, what's there to do around here? What do you like to do when you're not acting as a tour guide for strange girls?"

She reached out and punched his shoulder lightly as a way of letting him know that there was no mockery in the question.

"Not much," Finn said. Morgan sensed a lightening. "We have a movie theatre and two hockey rinks. Well, one hockey rink that's open, and the old one on Northbridge Road. Nobody uses that one anymore, but nobody's torn it down, either. Hockey's pretty important in Parr's Landing."

"Do you play? You know, hockey?"

"No, I'm not very good at sports." He waited for a negative reaction to this admission of failure at one of the entry-level male social rituals in Parr's Landing, but Morgan seemed nonplussed by it. Maybe not all boys played hockey where she came from. Emboldened by her neutrality on the subject, he went on. "There are a couple of churches besides St. Barthélemy and the Martyrs. In the summer time, people go swimming in Bradley Lake, but it's too cold now."

"Is that the lake we passed on the way to school today?"

"It's the only lake in town, so yeah, probably."

"Right, over by the cliffs. I can see the cliffs from my house. Well, it's not my house—the place where we're staying for a while."

"I know your house. Everyone in town knows your house. 'Parr House,' it's called. It's the only house in town with a name. It's really big. What's it like living there?"

"I don't know what it's like living there. I've just moved there. It's big, that's for sure. But I miss my house in Toronto, and I miss my friends."

"How many rooms are there?" he asked eagerly, ignoring her reference to her life before her arrival here. "In Parr House, I mean. How many rooms? Thirty? Forty?"

"I don't know," she said. She laughed. "Where did you get a number like forty?"

"That's the number of rooms in Collinwood. You know, the haunted house on *Dark Shadows*? That TV show with the vampire, Barnabas Collins?"

Morgan laughed. "We didn't have a TV at home, remember? I told you." He looked crestfallen, so she added, "I have heard of it, though. Some of the girls at school used to run home every afternoon to watch it right after school when it was still on."

"We used to get it here on Saturday mornings," Finn said. "We don't get much out here, but we used to get that."

"You like this stuff, don't you?" Morgan said, amused. "Spooky stuff? Castles and vampires and stuff like that?"

"Yeah," Finn said defensively. "I do. Is that *wrong*?"

"No, it's not wrong." Morgan said. "Of course it's not wrong. Why would it be?"

"My parents think it's weird," he said, sounding embarrassed, though whether he was embarrassed by his defensiveness or by the fact that he liked horror stuff was unclear. "I don't know why I like it, I just do. When I grow up I'm going to get out of this crappy little town and move to Hollywood and make movies. Horror movies. I'm going to be an actor, or a director or something. There's this comic book I read all the time called *Tomb of Dracula*," he said excitedly. "I get it at Harper's Drugs on Main Street. They don't get a lot of comics but they do get that one. Have you ever heard of it?"

"No, I haven't," Morgan said, keeping her amusement to herself, because she could see that his comic books meant a lot to him. She didn't want to hurt him by seeming to mock something he obviously cared about. "But maybe you could show me sometime. And maybe another time you could come and see the inside of my grandmother's house, if you like."

They had come to the place where the gravel driveway met the edge of the portico steps a short distance away. "We're here, Finn. Thanks for walking me home."

"No problem," Finn said. "Man, it's huge, isn't it? I'd get lost in there, for sure."

"Yeah, it's pretty huge. Like I said, you'll have to come in sometime and look around."

"Can I come in today?" *Nothing ventured*, Finn thought. *The worst she can do is say no.* "Or . . . I don't know. Would that be OK?"

"It's only my second day living here, Finn," Morgan said. "My grandmother is a little weird, especially when it comes to my mom and me and people in town. I don't think she'd like it. I don't know why, and I don't really know what it's about, but I promise—soon."

"She's stuck-up," Finn blurted out. "Everybody in town knows it. She thinks she's better than everyone else because she's so rich and the Parrs run everything in the Landing—" He stopped himself in mid-sentence, flushing dark red from the base of his throat to his hairline. If he'd been a cartoon character, he'd have slapped his own head and bellowed *stoopid stoopid STOOPID!* But all he could do was privately lament that the earth didn't swallow him up immediately and take him down to the very bowels of Parr's Landing. He knew he was going to be a virgin till his dying day. "I mean—God, I'm so sorry. I didn't mean that."

But Morgan surprised him by laughing delightedly. "Yeah, she is, a bit." She began to laugh again, picturing Adeline's face at the breakfast table that morning, her mouth as tight as if she'd been sipping raw lemon juice from her delicate porcelain cup instead of coffee. She steadied herself. "You sound like my uncle Jeremy. He thinks she's stuck-up, too." She began to laugh again in spite of herself.

"I'm really sorry," Finn said. He was still mortified, though awareness was dawning in him that this girl didn't seem to imagine him quite the disaster he himself saw in his mental mirror. "I didn't mean—"

"Hey, don't apologize, Finn," Morgan said kindly. "It's OK. Really. I appreciate you being so nice and friendly. Like I said, I don't know anyone here, and nobody spoke to me today in school. It's like I have leprosy or something."

She reached out and took his hand. Finn, who had never held a girl's hand, or indeed ever had any female other than his mother or his grandmother touch him anywhere, including his hand, found it unutterably sweet, soft, and warm. He felt momentarily bedazzled, as though the late-afternoon sunlight had preternaturally brightened.

"You don't have leprosy," Finn said softly. He pulled his hand away awkwardly.

Morgan smiled and readjusted the strap of her tote bag on her shoulder. "Goodbye, Finn. Thanks for walking me home." She looked at him questioningly. "Will I see you tomorrow?"

"Sure!" he said. "I mean—if you want? Do you . . . uh, do you want me to walk you home again tomorrow?"

"That'd be nice." She raised one hand and half-waved. "See you later, Finn."

Morgan walked the rest of the way to the house, opened the front door, and went inside. Finn caught a brief glimpse of the black-and-white marble foyer of the entry hall, then the door closed. He stood for a moment staring at the closed door, thinking of Morgan, memorizing her face.

Then, his chest full of stars, Finn turned and walked down the gravel drive to where the hill sloped downwards to the soft dirt road strewn with fallen yellow leaves leading to the town, and home. He half-walked, half-ran, half-skipped towards home. His hand thrilled where her fingers had been, and he whistled (something he never had done before) as he moved through the autumn-darkening streets of Parr's Landing.

Christina knocked on the door to Morgan's room, then pushed it open. Her daughter was sitting at the spindly, delicate writing desk in the corner reading from what looked to Christina like the same Ontario history book she herself had in her own days at Matthew Browning.

"Hi, Mom," Morgan said. "What time's dinner? I'm hungry."

"I think, in twenty minutes," Christina said. "I passed Beatrice on the way up here and she said that it was almost dinner time." She didn't add that Beatrice had warned her to be on time "because Mrs. Parr likes things just so, and she's peculiar about people being at the table on time, just so's you know."

"What are you reading?" Christina asked nonchalantly. "Looks familiar."

Morgan held up the book, *A History of Ontario* by Margaret Avison. It was the same one, all right. *Good Christ,* Christina thought. *My daughter is back in my hometown, attending my high school, and being taught from the same outdated textbooks as I was. It's 1972, for God's sake. Nothing changes here, nothing.*

"It's really boring," she said. "It's from 1951." Morgan closed the book and put it down in front of her. "It's like we're back in the olden days here. Even the high school looks like something from TV. It's so old fashioned."

"How was your first day at school?"

Morgan shrugged. "It was OK, I guess. Nobody was mean, but nobody talked to me, either. There was a nice lady in the front office, and the principal was OK, too." She paused, unsure of how to say what she was about to say next. "Mom?"

"Yes, honey? What is it?"

"Mom, did grandmother tell everyone that I'm illegitimate? Because it was weird, but the principal kept talking about 'life-style choices' that you and Dad made back when I was born, and it was like everyone else was walking on eggshells with me because my last name is Parr. You *were* married when I was born, right?"

Christina felt a wave of murderous fury towards Adeline pass through her, though she kept her face entirely neutral at that moment for Morgan's sake. She forced her voice to a calm register that was entirely at odds with how she felt, and swore again that if it was the last thing she did, she would get away from this town—and Adeline— at the first available opportunity. "Did someone actually say something, sweetheart?"

"No," Morgan said thoughtfully. "Not in so many words. But everyone's treating me like I'm some sort of case who needs all this special care and protection. Why are they doing that?"

Christina felt as though shards of glass were exploding inside her, but she forced herself to smile. She sat down on the edge of the bed and reached for her daughter's hand. Morgan looked desperately young to Christina just then, and her heart broke.

"Morgan, first of all—*yes,* your father and I were married when we had you. We weren't married when you were con-ceived. We told you all about that. But you weren't a 'mistake' by any stretch of the imagination, either. Your father and I loved each other very much. He wanted to marry me very much, and I wanted to marry him very much. We were married as soon as we arrived in Toronto, before I was even showing with you. You have nothing—nothing, do you hear me—to be ashamed of. I don't believe your grandmother told people that you were illegitimate," she lied, "but I do think that small-town people have a hard time, sometimes, understanding things that go differently than they think things ought to. They may be confused about things. I know this town very well, and there's a really good reason why I haven't been back in fifteen years, aside from the fact that your dad never wanted to. Would you like me to speak to your teachers about it, sweetheart? Are you worried about getting flack from the kids?"

That'll be next, Christina thought, with a familiar sickening lurch in her stomach. *That'll be next. Just like it was for Jack and me—the townie whore getting above herself with the Crown Prince of Parr's Landing. What does that make Morgan? A princess? A bastard? Or both?*

"No," Morgan replied quickly. "I'm not worried. And you don't need to talk to the teachers. It'll be OK. I just wanted to . . . well, I just wanted to tell you about school. That's all. It's all fine. I'm sorry I even brought it up. You and Dad did tell me all this stuff before, I know. I just needed to hear it again." She looked down. When she looked up again, Morgan's eyes were slick with tears. "Mom?"

"Yes, baby?"

"Mom, I miss Daddy something fierce." Morgan's shoulders began to shake. "I miss him *so much . . .*"

Christina's own eyes flooded. She stood up and took Morgan in her arms and rocked her as she had when she was a baby and they wept together, holding each other.

"I miss him, too, sweetheart. I miss him more than I ever thought could be possible to miss someone. Your daddy was everything to me, and he loved both of us more than anything else in the world. And I love you more than anything else in the world. Nothing is more important to me than you, Morgan. *Nothing.* You know that, right?"

Morgan sniffled. "Yes," she said in a thick voice. "Yes, I believe you. I love you, too, Mommy." Her face was buried in the hollow of her mother's shoulder. When Christina reached up to caress Morgan's hair, the wool of Morgan's sweater was soaked with her tears, which seemed grafted to the soft skin of her clavicle.

There was a knock on the door of the bedroom. *Oh God, please, not her. Not Adeline. Not right now. Just a few more minutes, please.* The knock came again, more gently this time, and Jeremy's voice carried through the thick mahogany door.

"Chris? Morgan? May I come in?"

Christina and Morgan parted reluctantly. Christina squeezed Morgan's hand once more, then smoothed her hair and said, "Come in, Jeremy."

"Come on in, Uncle Jeremy," Morgan called out, as though determined to show her mother that she was in control again and that her mother wasn't to worry about her any more than she already did.

"Oh . . . I'm sorry," Jeremy said when he saw their faces. "I'm so sorry, you guys. I didn't mean to interrupt. It's just that dinner is about to be served and Adeline is already down there. Just . . . well, do you want me to tell her you're not coming, or that you're sick or something?" He looked beseechingly from Christina to Morgan, then back to Christina again.

Morgan said in a clear voice, "No, Uncle Jeremy. We're all right. We're coming right down. I'm just going to put some water on my face. I'll only be a second."

She stood up and walked into the bathroom. Through the closed door, Christina and Jeremy heard the tap being turned on, then the sound of water hitting the porcelain sink.

"Is she all right?" Jeremy whispered. "Did she have a bad day at school? Goddamn it, I knew we should have taken her ourselves. This is all too much for her and too fast. I should never have let Adeline steamroll over us like that this morning."

"She's all right." Christina sighed, massaging her eyes with her fingertips. "She just had a moment."

Jeremy looked worried. "You, too, huh? Oh, Chris, I'm so sorry. Again. I keep saying that, but I really am. I feel like crap for you, really I do."

"How do I look?" she said briskly, pushing his sympathy away, knowing that she couldn't bear to feel anything at this exact moment if she was going to survive their dinner with Adeline. "I put mascara on this morning, but I think it's all rubbed off by now." She crossed to the mirror over Morgan's vanity. She squinted, touching her eyelashes gingerly. "Not very bright in here, is it? I'm sure your mother looks immaculate, like she just fell out of *Miss Chatelaine*. Well, an old issue of *Miss Chatelaine*. A very old issue."

Jeremy laughed. "You look fine. Maybe some cold water when Morgan's finished? Are you sure you want to go downstairs, you two? I'm serious, I can just tell her that you're not feeling well after the long drive. I'm sure she'd send Beatrice up with a tray."

"Listen to us." Christina laughed mirthlessly. "'I'm sure she'd send Beatrice up with a tray.' The fact that it would even be a question answers it. She might or she might not. No, better that we go downstairs and deal with her face to face. I'm sure Morgan will be all right. She doesn't have the same problems with that old bitch that we do. And somehow I have to normalize life for her, and it has to start right now. God knows what Adeline has told people about us. Morgan said that everyone was treating her with kid gloves today. She doesn't think it was for any good reason. She asked me if I thought her grandmother had told people she was illegitimate. I have no trouble seeing the hand of Adeline in that, and if she did, I'll never forgive her."

Jeremy looked at this watch. "It's six thirty-five," he said. "We'd better get down there."

The bathroom door opened and Morgan stepped out. Her face was clean and her hair was combed. Christina noticed that Morgan had darkened her lips with a trace of the black raspberry Bonne Bell Lip Smacker she'd gotten for her last birthday from Christina after much pleading to be allowed to wear makeup. Morgan hadn't worn lip gloss at all since Jack died, or indeed cared much about her appearance at all besides basic grooming and cleanliness, as though with her father gone, there was no one for whom to look particularly pretty. Jack had always told Morgan she was beautiful, so her disinterest in how she presented herself was an additional constant reminder to Christina of their bereavement. But now, Morgan looked at her mother with a lovingly critical eye and said, "Mom, you'd better clean up, too.

You know how she is. Your mascara's running. You look like a raccoon."

"You're late," Adeline said, raising her eyebrows. "All of you. It's six forty-five. I told you I expected you downstairs, on time, at six-thirty for dinner." She sat at one end of the dining table framed in candlelight from the silver candelabra that were placed on the sideboard and on the table itself. She wore a well-tailored black dress and a necklace of simple but consequential pearls. Not for the first time, Christina marvelled at how her mother-in-law managed, at whatever hour of the day or night, to look exactly like a lacquered mannequin that had just been placed in a dress shop window.

"I'm sorry, Grandmother," Morgan said, before either Christina or Jeremy could say anything. "It was my fault. I lost track of the time. It won't happen again." Christina looked gratefully at her daughter, knowing that Morgan had deliberately spoken first, intuiting correctly that if anyone would escape the wrath of Adeline Parr over the grave offence of being late for dinner, it was her granddaughter.

For her part, Adeline's smile was frosty, but there was an unmistakable sense of a storm having passed without actually touching down. "Punctuality is a very important virtue, Morgan," she said. "It bespeaks a great deal about a person's character. It's very likely that you didn't have much of a need for it in your old life, but when you are under my roof, you'll learn to comport yourself responsibly as befitting a proper young lady. Do I make myself clear?"

"Yes, Grandmother."

"Please sit down, dear." She glanced at Christina and Jeremy and nodded curtly. "You two may sit, as well."

"Thank you, Mother," Jeremy said dryly. "It's wonderful that we can all sit down as a family and enjoy each other's company like this."

Jeremy sat down and unfolded his napkin, placing it in his lap. Morgan and Christina followed his lead and did the same. When they were seated, Beatrice began to serve. Dinner that night was to be poached fish and asparagus. It wasn't until the silver lid of the monogrammed sterling silver chafing dishes were removed that Christina realized how hungry she was. The asparagus was fresh, a delicate green beneath a sliver of melting butter. She wondered where on earth Adeline Parr was able to get fresh asparagus in Parr's Landing in October.

"That smells wonderful, Beatrice," Christina ventured. "Is it haddock?"

"It's *perch*," Adeline snapped. "Haddock indeed. Does it look like haddock to you, Christina? Does it? Does it *smell* like haddock to you? Have you ever poached a fish in your life? For the Lord's own sake."

"Adeline, I just wondered—"

Jeremy laughed out loud, drawing Adeline's fire away from Christina and onto himself. "How many fish have you poached in *your* life, Mother? Ever since I can remember, Beatrice has done the cooking around here. Like Christina, I didn't know it was perch or haddock, either. I guess the best way to tell what sort of fish is being served for dinner at Parr House is to ask the cook. By the way, Beatrice," he said, deftly shifting the attention again, this time towards the housekeeper, "my sister-in-law is right. It does smell delicious. I have to tell you, all those years away in Toronto, the thing I missed most about Parr's Landing was your cooking."

"Oh, Mr. Jeremy," Beatrice said. "You were always the charmer. Have some of the veg. It's a lovely bit of asparagus."

Adeline cleared her throat and shook her head almost imperceptibly at the housekeeper. Beatrice lowered her eyes and pressed her lips together. She went on with the dinner service in silence.

"And how was your first day at Matthew Browning, Morgan? Did you have a useful and productive day?"

"It was very nice, Grandmother," Morgan said. "Thank you."

"Did you learn anything today that you'd like to share with us?"

"Not really, Grandmother," she said. "But I liked the school very much."

"Did you meet your principal? What was his name, Mr. Murphy?"

"Yes, Grandmother," Morgan said. "He was very nice to me. He made me feel very welcome."

"Did you make any new friends, honey?" Jeremy said gently, reaching for Morgan's hand. "How did you like the kids? Did they treat you well?"

Morgan turned to her uncle, grateful for the warmth of the question after Adeline's staccato interrogation. "Not at school, Uncle Jeremy. I mean," she said, glancing at her mother, "they were very nice at school. But I met this kid after school. Well . . . he met me, really. I think he was waiting for me after school and we started to talk."

"He was waiting for you? How did he know who you were?"

"I don't know, Uncle Jeremy," she said. "But it doesn't matter. He knew I was new in town and he walked me home. He's younger than me. Twelve, I think."

"A boy?" Adeline said. "You let a strange boy walk you home?"

"He wasn't strange, Grandmother. He was really nice."

"What was his name, Morgan?" Christina said. "I wonder if Jeremy and I know any of his family from when we lived here?"

"It doesn't matter what his *name* is," Adeline said sharply. "Morgan, you are never, *ever* to let young men you don't even know walk you home. It's not done. There's been enough gossip about this family over the years. I won't have more of it now, in the new generation. Do I make myself clear?"

"We didn't do anything, Grandmother," Morgan said. "We just walked. He was nice. No one else would talk to me, but he did. He walked me all the way home."

"What was his name, honey?" Christina asked again.

"Finn, Mommy. He said it was short for Finnegan."

"It doesn't matter what his name is," Adeline said. "I won't have— "

"You won't have *what*, Mother?" Jeremy said. "There's nothing wrong with Morgan making friends with a local boy. Good Lord, it's 1972, not 1872."

All of the colour had left Morgan's face, rendering it as pale as rice paper. The dark circles beneath her eyes that had been fading of late suddenly developed like bruises in a black-and-white photograph. "Mommy, may I be excused?" she said faintly. "I'm not feeling well."

"We have not finished dinner, young lady, and I—"

"Yes, sweetheart, you may," Christina said, cutting Adeline off. She shot her mother-in-law a look of such lethal ferocity that it stopped the older woman in mid-flow. "Why don't you go and lie down? I'll come up and see you in a bit. I think your grandmother and Uncle Jeremy and I need to have a grown-up talk."

Before Adeline could say anything, Morgan pushed her chair back and ran out of the dining room, looking at none of them. They heard the sound of her feet taking the stairs two at a time, then the sound of the bedroom door slamming on the next floor.

"Adeline," Christina said, struggling to maintain her composure. "Are you *trying* to push your granddaughter away? Are you trying to drive her away from you? Because I'll tell you what, before she came down here, she was crying for her dead father. Would it have been too much to ask for you to leave her alone? If you want to beat me up for my relationship with Jack, by all means, do your worst. But could you do it when Morgan isn't around? And while you're at it, could you leave her alone and let her settle in here? *She's fifteen years old!* She's *completely* innocent of whatever crime you think Jack and I committed, and except for the three of us here, she's completely alone."

Adeline narrowed her eyes. "I can see that she didn't have very much supervision in your home, Christina. But this is not your home."

She raised her glass of ice water and took a delicate sip. When she put it down again, her dark red lipstick had smudged the rim of the glass, like the mouth of a paper cut. "This is *my* home," she said. "And Jeremy's home. It would also have been my son's home if you hadn't taken him away from me and killed him. And here in my home, there are rules. I will not have her running around like a common trollop, cavorting with local boys before she has a chance to even establish a reputation for herself as a Parr."

"Mother, stop it," Jeremy pleaded. "Just stop. For the love of Christ."

"Adeline, she just wants to make friends," Christina said. "Don't you understand that? It's innocent. She's a young girl and she's all alone."

"'*Friends!*'" Adeline hissed. "'*Friends* like you were with Jack? *Friends* like Jeremy and that miner's son, that dirty McKitrick boy? Is that the sort of friends you were referring to? We've had enough of the Parrs making *friends* with the locals in this town!"

Jeremy stood up so abruptly that he knocked his chair back. He picked up his dinner plate and hurled it as hard as it could against the opposite wall. It smashed into shards, leaving a trail of butter and hollandaise that slowly dripped down the wall. He stood there pale and shaking, his hands balled into fists, looking as if he was expending every ounce of restraint he possessed to keep himself from leaping across the table and stabbing his mother to death with one of her own sterling silver dinner knives.

Adeline sat still, entirely unruffled, her back rigid, not touching the back of her own chair. "That Meissen plate was from your great grandmother Parr's wedding china," she said calmly. "It was a service for forty people. The rim of the plate is—was— eighteen-karat gold. I'll wager the plate you just destroyed with your childish outburst was worth more than the sum either of you have in your bank accounts at the moment."

"You're insane," Christina said to Adeline. "You're completely insane. No wonder Jack wanted to leave. It wasn't the town, it was you."

"We're leaving," Jeremy said to Christina. "Get Morgan. We're going. Now. We're not spending another minute in this fucking house."

Adeline said again, "Am I right? How much do you have in your respective bank accounts? Assuming," she added with a small smile, "that either of you even have bank accounts? Enlighten me, Jeremy, my independently wealthy son. Where will you go?"

"Christina, *now*! Come on!"

"You would never have come back here, Jeremy, if you had

somewhere else to go. Nor you, Christina. You are literally pen-
niless, aren't you? And you've come back here, to me, because
there was nowhere else."

"You *bitch*," Jeremy said. "You absolute bloody—"

"If I were you, son, I'd be more careful with my epithets," Adeline said mildly. "It's only my love for you as a mother that's keeping me from using a few of the choice ones that describe men
like you."

"You hate me, don't you?" Jeremy said, marvelling. "You *actually hate me*. You wish it had been me who died instead of Jack."

"No, my dear, I love you," she replied. "And I do confess that,
sometimes, I wish it had been you who died instead of Jack. But
the feeling passes."

Jeremy stumbled blindly out of the dining room. Christina
rose from her chair and threw her napkin on the table. She followed Jeremy out into the front hall, leaving Adeline alone. From
inside the dining room, Christina heard the tinkling sound of the
bell Adeline used to summon Beatrice, and the sound of the door
that connected the kitchen and the dining room swing open and
shut.

"Jeremy, where are you going?" Christina said.

"Out," Jeremy said harshly. "Away from here. Home to
Toronto. Somewhere . . . I don't know."

"You're too upset to drive. Stay here, calm down. It's too
dangerous."

"I can't," he mumbled. He reached for the pea coat he'd left on
the chair next to the sideboard in the hallway. "I need to think. I
need to get away. I need a drink. Come with me."

"I can't leave Morgan," Christina said. "I have to stay here
with her. Adeline's right, you know. We have nowhere else to
go, at least until one of us has some money. She has us right
where she wants us. We have to make it work. Or rather, *I* have
to make it work. Won't you stay with me so we can talk about
this?"

"No, not now," he said. "I'll be back in a bit. I need to clear
my head. Don't worry, she's vented now, she'll be fine for a while.
Even monsters need to rest between monstrosities." He put his

coat on and felt in his pockets for the car keys. "I'll be back," he repeated. "Don't worry."

"Just . . . well, just drive carefully." The unspoken thought that passed between them was, *Please don't leave me alone the way Jack did. I can't go through that again. Neither Morgan nor I could survive it happening twice.*

Jeremy hugged her. "Don't worry," he said. "I'll be back in a couple of hours."

He held Christina tightly for a moment, then opened the front door and walked to his car. As he turned the key in the ignition, he saw her framed in the doorway of the house, silhouetted in the lights of the hallway. Then he turned the car around and headed towards town.

The clatter of gravel against the undercarriage of the car sounded like shots.

Through the windshield of the Chevelle, Jeremy saw the stars in the night sky over Parr's Landing as though they were under-water, for he was weeping at this final and unalterable proof that his mother not only regretted his existence, as he'd known since he was fifteen, but actively wished him dead, at least if it would bring his brother back from the grave.

CHAPTER THIRTEEN

Richard Weal heard the distant passage of Jeremy's car as he crouched on a ledge above Bradley Lake and waited, invisible as any other night predator. He waited with increasing desperation for his secret voice to speak to him again, to give him one last sign that he could follow, but the voice had been silent all day.

He sifted aimlessly through his hockey bag, wrinkling his nose in disgust at the sour smell that drifted up from it. He had to admit, his hockey bag was starting to stink of blood, old hair, and bits of rotted carrion, but as he had been travelling alone for the most part, the aesthetics hadn't been much of a priority for obvious reasons. The knives hadn't been properly cleaned since before Gyles Point, and while he'd rinsed them off as best he could in the sink at the cottage, they had assumed a bronzy-red patina. The hammers were greasy and slick to the touch but, testing the sharp points of them, he didn't doubt that they could still do the job for which they had been designed—and even a few jobs for which they had not. But he doubted, at this point, that he would have much need for them.

Not after tonight. Not ever again. He would have his teeth. Weal's muscles were cramped and sore from having spent the previous night sleeping outdoors and he was chilled to the bone. And hungry. The sun had been a warming balm for the brief time he'd been able to experience it this afternoon, and he cursed the stupid cop from town who had interrupted his exploration of Spirit Rock and forced him to crouch in the cold shadows for hours afterwards.

That cop will be the next one to die, Weal swore to himself. *He's going to die for making me so uncomfortable today. And I'm going to make it hurt, too. I'm going to make it hurt a lot.*

He closed his eyes and listened for the voice, but it was silent. He felt a momentary flare of panic. His first thought was that his friend was angry at him for wasting another day, for not finding him and rescuing him. But he forced himself to calm down. He rarely heard the voice when he was upset, or when his mind was clouded with other thoughts, or worry, or panic. He mustn't panic, now more than ever, when he was so close to achieving his—*their*—goal.

"Tell me where you are," Weal whined. He lowered himself onto his knees in an aspect of prayer and folded his hands like a child. Tears of frustration welled up in his eyes and ran down his filth-caked face. "I know you're here, Father," he sobbed, closing his eyes. "I can *feel* you. I know this is the place. I know you're here. Give me a sign. Show me. Please . . . ? Let tonight be the night. I beg you, Father. Give me just one more sign. *Please.*"

And then the images came to him, redoubled in force and clarity, stronger than ever before, violent and terrifying and euphoric. The strength of them knocked him backwards and he lay on the cold ground in violent convulsion. His jaws worked, and he bit his tongue, tasted his own blood in his throat before it ran pinkly from his mouth, mixing with his slobber, staining his stubbled chin. Weal's eyes rolled back in his head, and all was darkness, except that it was a brilliant darkness, and he could see more clearly than he ever had in his life.

He saw Spirit Rock and he saw Bradley Lake, but they were *different,* surrounded by a denser, darker, greener forest, a bluer, clearer sunset sky. The air was pungent, wilder and more savagely northern than it had been that afternoon, or at any other time in his lifetime. He knew, without knowing how, that it was *not* his lifetime, that it was some other time altogether. He felt the weight of centuries hurtling around him like supernovas, and he knew that the weight would crush his soul to powder if it weren't for the protection of his friend's voice that he wore like armour in this waking dream of shredded time.

He found himself standing at the opening of a cave, not the place where his body lay shaking on the ground. He glanced around dumbly in the sunset light and saw great piles of smoking ash heaped around the opening of the cave.

He smelled the stink of burning flesh suddenly over the wild scent of the forest as the wind came up and began to scatter the ash across the cliffs. Some of it blew into his face, burning his eyes and catching acridly in his throat.

Something happened here, he thought. *Something marvellous and terrible, something not of this earth. Something beautiful.*

Weal looked around dumbly. *I'm dreaming. I'm not here. This is not happening. I fell asleep outside on the ledge on Spirit Rock. Or I'm having an episode because I threw my pills away in Toronto, and I have to wake up. There's work to do. I have to wake up!*

But his eyes burned and his mouth tasted like cinder and he felt the ground, solid and real. He felt the cold north wind that carried the stinking soot that smelled like burned meat. He felt the press of sharp stones through the worn soles of his boots.

Weal looked questioningly at the mouth of the cave, but before he could ask, he knew what the answer would be. It came and he followed it into the cave, and was swallowed whole by the shimmering visions.

He woke up underground, shivering, disoriented, and smelling of piss and shit. He was no longer cold, in fact his body pulsed with heat as though his veins were shot full of hot lead.

He raised himself on his elbow and looked around groggily. In his hand was the flashlight. He felt around for his hockey bag with his tools, but it was nowhere nearby. He switched on the flashlight and shone the beam in front of him in the darkness. The feeble light played off walls of rock and supporting arches of rotted wood. Somewhere in the distance, he heard the steady sound of water hitting stone and there was a sense of yawning emptiness ahead of him, just out of sight.

Was I asleep? Did I walk in my sleep? This isn't where I was. Where the fuck am I?

He stood up gingerly, testing the available height of the place in which he found himself. He realized that he could just barely stand without his head grazing the ceiling, or roof, of whatever this place was. He leaned forward and shone the light in front of him, and realized where he was.

He was in a mineshaft. He was underground, God knew how far, in one of the network of abandoned mineshafts that crisscrossed beneath Parr's Landing.

Weal knew about them because he had read about them, about how the Parr family had stripped this part of northern Ontario underground, blasting tunnels beneath the earth where there had previously only been caves, expanding the natural underground tunnels their mining engineers had found with artificial ones, exploiting them, abandoning them when the veins of gold had been drained dry.

He had walked in his sleep, or whatever state he'd been in, and had fallen down a mineshaft. Weal's chest tightened and he thought about screaming—screaming louder than he had ever screamed. The sense of being buried alive was instant and dreadful. He dropped the flashlight and flung his arms out, expecting to find himself entombed, but his fingers barely grazed the opposite walls. There was space, blessed space. He took a deep breath and tried to slow his breathing. When he was marginally calmer, he shook his head and tried to think.

If he had fallen down a mineshaft, his legs would be broken, he reasoned, or there would be some other evidence of injury. There was none, so he hadn't fallen. Check. He could breathe, so there was oxygen. Check. He had light, so he could see. Check. He'd felt something sharp cut into his thigh when he'd leaned to pick up the flashlight. He patted his pocket gingerly and felt the edge of one of his knives in his pocket, blade cutting inwards against flesh where it had sliced through the lining. The fabric there was sticky and wet, and he realized he was bleeding.

The knife had been in the hockey bag earlier that day, not his pocket. Either he had placed it there himself without thinking, or someone had placed it in his pocket while he'd been unconscious. Weal looked around uneasily, but he knew he was alone—quite alone. Nothing human could live down here in all this darkness, and if anyone were with him down here, he'd have sensed it already. In fact, he would have sensed it immediately.

Then he heard his friend's voice again. But beneath the sweetness of it this time, he sensed a new urgency and hunger. Weal knew where he was and why he was there. He was protected. He was loved. And he was needed.

Joyfully, Weal began to shuffle through the mineshaft, holding the bobbing flashlight in front of him, feeling his way through the maze of rotted beams and along the rock walls towards the prize waiting for him.

It was ten o'clock at night and Elliot McKitrick was off duty and minding his own business, flirting lazily with Donna Lemieux, the overblown blonde bartender with whom he'd had a brief affair when he was eighteen and she was thirty. He still carried a bit of a torch for Donna, as young men sometimes did when they thought of past conquests, if not loves. Donna realized this and was usually ambivalent, unless she was bored or horny. Tonight, Elliot thought, he might have gotten lucky if he'd wanted to, but he felt dead below the waist. He'd flirted by rote and by habit this evening. She'd picked up on his disinterest and returned it in kind. Nothing personal, as they both knew.

He was nursing his beer in the farthest corner of O'Toole's when Jeremy Parr walked in looking like crap twice warmed over. Elliot's heart sank at the sight of him.

Great, Elliot thought. *This is the rosiest possible cherry on the shit sundae that this day has been so far.*

He lifted the bottle of O'Keefe to his lips and took a long, cold pull of it, wishing he was invisible, wishing the beer was colder, and mostly hating everything about his life at that exact moment. Elliot looked away, vainly praying that Jeremy wouldn't see him, but Jeremy did see him, and he started to walk over to his table.

Elliot weighed several options, all of them calculated to salvage the airtight security of the life and image he'd built for himself here in the years Jeremy had been away.

He could get up and leave, which might look unduly abrupt and draw attention. The other danger in getting up suddenly was the possibility of leaving Jeremy in the bar alone, drunk, and rambling. God knows what he'd tell Donna—or rather confirm, since everyone had heard rumours about the two of them, but Elliot had spent the last fifteen years fucking, brawling, and goal-scoring those rumours into oblivion. No, it was better to sit still and act like he was greeting an old friend. Normalize, neutralize. Maybe buy Jeremy a beer. Slap him on the back and bullshit about the old days. Or at least make it seem that's what they were doing. It could work.

If it didn't, Elliot was royally screwed.

Jeremy approached the table and, ludicrously, stuck out his hand to shake as though they had seen each other last week. He said, "Hey, Elliot, how's it going? Long time no see."

"Hi, Jem." Elliot took Jeremy's hand without getting up from his own chair. The part of him that wanted to rise from his seat and take Jeremy in his arms and hug him had been permanently crippled years before, largely by Elliot himself. He kept that part of himself in its place and he considered it dead and buried. "I heard you were back. What're you doing here?"

"Can I join you?" Jeremy didn't wait for Elliot's answer. He pulled back the chair opposite Jeremy and sat down heavily. "So, here we are," he said. "How've you been?"

When Elliot didn't reply, he continued. "You're a cop now, I see. I saw you in the cruiser today. Do you like being a cop?"

"What are you doing back in Parr's Landing, Jeremy?" Elliot said again. "There has to be a reason you'd come back to town. What has it been, ten years?"

"Fifteen. You're not happy to see me, are you?"

Elliot shrugged. "It's a free world. You can go where you want. But no, I'm not really happy to see you. I'm surprised that you're surprised."

"It's all right," Jeremy said "No one's really happy to see me.

My mother just told me she wished I had been the one who died instead of Jack."

"I heard about Jack a while back. I'm sorry. Was that Chris I saw in the car with you today?"

"So you did see me. I wasn't sure if you had."

"Yeah, I saw you," Elliot said. "So, was that Chris? Did she come back with you, too?"

"Yeah, and Morgan, as well." Elliot looked at him blankly. "My niece, Elliot—Jack's daughter. Her name is Morgan. She's fifteen. Jack didn't leave any insurance, and Chris is broke. I brought her back here. She had nowhere else to go."

Elliot looked over Jeremy's head at Donna and held up two fingers. She signalled back the OK sign and took two fresh bottles of O'Keefe out of the beer fridge and carried them over to their table on a tray.

"Hey! Jeremy Parr!" Donna said, putting the beers down in front of them. "Long time no see, Jer! I heard you were back in town." When Jeremy looked at her blankly, she said, "It's me, Donna Lemieux. Remember? You went to school with my cousin, Rob Archambault. You remember Rob, right? I think he was a couple of years ahead of you. Maybe your brother's class?"

"Oh yeah," Jeremy lied. "I sure do remember him. Good to see you, Donna. How is Rob?"

Donna furrowed her brow. "He died. Ski-Doo accident, two years ago. It was so sad. He had a wife and kids. You didn't hear?"

"No, I'm sorry," he said. "I've been away. I've been living in Toronto."

"Long way away," she said. "And you ain't been back that whole time?"

"No," Jeremy replied. "I haven't. Been busy."

"I'm sorry about your brother," Donna said. "I heard about him. We all did. There was a thing about it in the paper. He was a good guy. I knew him in school."

"Thanks, Donna." Jeremy forced a smile. "I appreciate it."

"Thanks, honey," Elliot said to Donna. What he wanted was for her to go away back behind the bar, sooner rather than later.

He winked, dead sexy, something that usually opened doors for him with whichever woman was the recipient of the wink.

Donna rolled her eyes. "You with the winks," she said. "All talk, no action." But Donna smiled when she said it and she winked back, putting a little extra sway in her hips when she turned around and walked back to the bar. Under any other circumstances, Elliot would be looking forward to getting laid tonight, but right now he just wanted her away from him and Jeremy so he could neutralize this situation as quickly as possible. Bedding Donna Lemieux was the last thing on his mind.

For his part, Jeremy couldn't take his eyes off Elliot's face.

Late at night when he was alone in his bed, he'd let his mind wander back over the years. It was the only time he felt safe thinking about Parr's Landing and what his mother had done to him by sending him away. He was able to safely scan the memories he had, sifting through them, bypassing the cruellest ones and fingering the ones that contained traces of love, or beauty, the way someone else might lovingly caress a favourite photograph in an album. Over the years, Jeremy had found that the easiest way to access those memories was to conjure Elliot's face and body. The memories weren't *sexual*, necessarily, because that part was so associated with the pain that came later at the hands of Adeline and Dr. Janek. But they *were* resolutely romantic memories nonetheless fuelled by lovingly tended longing and desire.

Small things, flashes and mental snapshots; Elliot's tanned neck as he saw it from his desk a row behind and two seats to the left in homeroom at Matthew Browning; Elliot's dented red hockey helmet, and the way his black hair looked, wet with sweat, when he took the helmet off in the intermission between periods, his eyes never leaving the action on the ice, during the Friday night hockey games at the old Mike Takacs Memorial Arena out on Brandon Nixon Road, before the fire that shut it down.

Mostly, though, he remembered Elliot's smile which, however rare (back then at least), lit up his entire face when it suddenly appeared. His voice, his laugh. Elliot's powerful butterfly stroke as he swam out to the summer raft in Bradley Lake. The way the girls at Matthew Browning stared at Elliot when he passed in the hallway, the way Jeremy hated them for staring and knew that he hated them because he stared, too. But they could do it openly while he had to stare surreptitiously.

And Jeremy was still staring surreptitiously now, fifteen years later.

The face and body sitting in the chair in front of him, the man pretending that the two of them were just a couple of guys who had barely known each other in high school, and had now met again in a bar fifteen years later, was still Elliot's. The body had hardened and thickened with muscle, and the face had the natural bronzed look of a man who lived and worked outdoors in a northern Ontario town.

But it was still somehow the same: the same thick pelt of black-brown hair in a military crew cut, almost like mink, tapering into the barest suggestion of a widow's peak over a wide forehead; the dark eyebrows against the olive skin of his face, arching up over eyes the colour of black coffee; the strong nose and jaw, the aggressive five o'clock shadow, the sensual mouth, the white, white teeth. Jeremy's eyes reverenced Elliot's neck and throat, thick like the rest of him. More than anything at that moment, he wanted Elliot to laugh, so he could hear that joyous growl of pleasure he remembered better than any other part of Elliot. If he heard that, Jeremy believed, the rest of what had happened that night would go away, or at least not matter quite as much.

"So . . . are you still playing hockey?" He realized he was flailing for a neutral topic that might prompt even a minor thaw in Elliot's demeanour, and that he sounded desperate and the question was idiotic.

Elliot shrugged. "Some. Why?"

"Elliot, aren't we even still friends? Even just a bit? Even with everything else that happened, couldn't we just . . . I don't know, talk?" His eyes filled with tears again, and he hated himself even more for allowing Elliot to see them.

"We *are* talking," Elliot said, looking away. He took another pull of beer from the bottle. "This *is* us, talking. Jem, this isn't Toronto. People remember things here, and what we did—well, it's taken a long time for me to make it OK here, to convince people that rumours about us . . . well, you know. That they weren't true."

"Rumours," Jeremy said. "Right, the 'rumours.' Jesus Christ."

"You know what I mean, Jem," Elliot said fiercely, keeping his voice down. "Do you know what my dad did to me after your mother told him about us? Do you know what your fucking mother ordered him to *do*? He beat me with a fucking *whip*."

"Well, my mother sent me away to be tortured for six months, Elliot," Jeremy said, matching Elliot's tone. "What are we doing here, having a contest to see who got it worse? Do you want to see the scars on my body from the burns? I see them every day when I'm naked. Do you want to see them?"

"*Keep your fucking voice down.*" Elliot looked around, but no one in the bar appeared to have heard either of them. Behind the bar, Donna was washing glasses.

Jeremy said again, softly, "Do you? Do you want to see them?"

He nudged his beer bottle almost imperceptibly across the surface of the table between them until his knuckles grazed Elliot's. Their eyes met. Behind them, the jukebox played "Maggie May." Elliot allowed Jeremy's fingers to linger there for a brief second, then jerked his hand away.

"You left," Elliot said. "You ran away from home and left me here. I had to stay. You got a new life. All I had was the same one I always had, except I had to face everything by myself that you left behind. It doesn't matter anyway now," he said. "I'm *normal*. I have a *normal* life. I'm somebody in this town. The past is in the past. I don't want you fucking it up."

Jeremy looked down. "I'm sorry." He took another sip of his beer. "You know what? No—I'm not sorry. None of this was my fault, and none of it had anything to do with you. I came back to Parr's Landing with Christina, for Christina. Not for you, and certainly not for my own good. Thanks for reminding me of that, Elliot."

"Jem—"

"Forget it, Elliot," Jeremy said tiredly. He raised the bottle

to his lips and drained it in one long draught. Then he pushed
the bottle away. "I won't bother you again. But please, it's a small
town. If we do run into each other, can you just not act like . . .
well, can you just be nice? I don't think I can handle any more
shit right now from anyone, least of all you."

"Don't drive drunk now," Elliot said, trying to joke, and failing. "I don't want to have to arrest you."

If he smiles now, I'm done for, Jeremy thought. *If he laughs, I
don't know if I'm going to be able to walk out of here. Please, God,
don't let him laugh.*

But of course he didn't laugh, nor did he smile, and for that
Jeremy was profoundly grateful. It made it easier for him to stand
up without saying goodbye to Elliot, and to walk calmly out of
the bar, nodding to Donna and smiling, but otherwise drawing
no attention to himself.

And because he didn't turn around, he didn't see Elliot watching him, the longing in his face breaking through the mask of
ruthless masculine efficiency. For a moment Elliot looked seventeen, not thirty-two. The sight of it would have broken Jeremy's
heart all over again and shattered his resolve. Elliot knew this and
was likewise profoundly grateful that Jeremy hadn't seen it.

Still safe, he thought, *looking around the bar. Everything is
good. And even if it's not good, it's safe.* Elliot walked slowly and
deliberately over to where Donna was polishing glasses behind
the bar and sat down at one of the stools.

He leaned in on his elbows, laying his arms on the bar. Looking deeply into her eyes, he smiled and said, "So?"

"So yourself," Donna said. She flushed slightly and uncon-
sciously touched her hair. "So, nice evening with your friend?"

"Not a friend," Elliot drawled. He increased the heat of his
smile. "Just somebody from high school. We were in the same
class at Browning, but I really barely knew the guy. He's just passing through town."

Donna had dismissed the rumours she'd heard about Jeremy
Parr and Elliot years ago, hinting—to her girlfriends, at least, not
to men, because she didn't want them to think she was some kind
of *slut*—that she had proof he wasn't a queer. Certainly she had

entertained no doubts herself during the hours they'd spent in her bed together, with Elliot on top of her pumping away, hard as an anvil.

If she'd thought—well, not *thought*, really, just maybe *felt*, if even that—some trace of energy between them when she'd brought the beer over, she told herself she had interrupted a discussion about the death of Jeremy's brother, Jack. She'd had a little crush on Jack back in the day, but that Christina Whatshername (now *there* was a slut) had gotten herself knocked up. She'd heard that they'd run off to Toronto and that she'd forced him to Do The Right Thing and marry her. The Parrs were filthy-loaded, so Christina must be sitting pretty by now.

Donna sighed. She ran a lacquered fingernail along Elliot's index finger. "So, Elliot," she said. "Why did you never go for me?"

"I went for you plenty of times, babe," he said lazily. He wrapped his index finger around hers and held it down. "You do remember, don't you?"

"No, I mean proper-like. Why didn't you ever ask me out. You know, like on a date?"

"Well," he said, "for one thing, you were married."

She laughed. "Is that all? Lucien wouldn't have even known. He was drunk most of the time we were married. If that's all that was stopping you, you should have asked."

"We had some great times." He leaned in closer. "We had some *really* great times. Didn't we?"

"You're so conceited, Elliot," she said. "How do you know it was as great for me as it was for you?"

"I know," he replied. "And so do you." Her pupils were dilated and her lips were moist. He knew from experience that her nipples underneath the blouse she wore were now stiff. And though he felt nothing for her at that moment, either in his head or below the waist, he said, "So, Donna. Do you want to get a drink later?"

"We're in a *bar*, Elliot."

Donna liked delaying the moment as long as possible, especially with Elliot when they'd first been lovers. She was all about the slow moves and she'd enjoyed teaching the then-teenaged Elliot restraint and discipline.

But it was a cold night, and nothing was waiting for her at home but a hungry cat and a bed with cold sheets on it. And, to be honest, though she'd never admit it, she wasn't getting any younger.

He leaned into her, his cheek nearly meeting hers. He smelled shampoo and some drugstore perfume that was sexy precisely because it smelled cheap. "I mean somewhere else. Later. Some other place."

"What other place did you have in mind, Elliot?"

"Your place," he said, showing all his beautiful teeth.

Elliot covered her hand in his and squeezed gently. When he turned her hand palm-up inside his grasp, offering the softness of it to the press of his fingers, he knew he'd scored. Maybe the day was going to end on a better note than the one it had started on.

Whatever else happened, though, Elliot realized he had almost succeeded in driving any thoughts or memories of Jeremy Parr from his mind, at least for now.

It would have been impossible for him to say how long he'd been searching since he didn't habitually wear a watch, but Richard Weal knew he had two choices: he would either find his sleeping friend here, or he would die of hunger and thirst in the Cimmerian blackness of an abandoned mineshaft, not even knowing where he was, much less remembering how he'd gotten there.

He guessed that he had long since wandered off what was left of the actual path through the mine and into some sort of interconnected underground cave system formed of arches of natural rock, but the voice—and the trace imagery that remained in his brain long after he'd heard actual words—somehow continued to guide him.

Living as he did almost entirely in his own mind, memories and dreams were important to Weal—not only immediate memories, such as how beautiful his friend's voice was, but more recent memories—the slaughter of his victims, of course, and the way they suffered and bled, but also the images he'd gleaned from the pages of the manuscript he'd killed the old man for— the translation of that letter from the dying priest, Father Nyon, who'd followed his faith in God into the northern wilderness of New France in 1632.

In spite of his hatred—and he loathed the priest for what he'd done to his friend, and with as much murderous, steely hatred as if the priest had done it to Weal himself—he had to admire his faith in God.

Well, perhaps *admire* was the wrong word. He could identify with it, intellectually and emotionally. Had Weal himself not first heard his invisible friend's voice that hot day in 1952, calling to him from behind the granite walls of these very cliffs, begging for release? Had he not been listening to that voice all these years, calling him into the wilderness, and was he not as eager as any postulant, now or then, to touch the Divine?

He would still have liked to put the young priest to his knives for what he'd done to Weal's friend—to peel his eyeballs in their sockets like grapes and cut his fingers off in quarter-sections, taking his time and enjoying the screams before he took an X-Acto knife to Father Nyon's murdering tongue.

Since the manuscript he'd taken had been incomplete, he had no idea what happened to the priest from 1630, but as a scholar, he was well versed in the gruesome history of the fates that had befallen the unluckiest of the Jesuit martyrs. Weal hoped Father Nyon had met an end like that, and that it had hurt terribly.

Out of the subterranean silence, he suddenly heard the voice again. It spoke one word: *Here.*

So audible, present, and clear this time—not in his head, but directly in front of him—that Weal gasped. He swung the flashlight wildly, seeking out the recesses of the mine and the shadows between the rocks where the light couldn't reach. He gaped at what he saw standing there. It was a man, or something shaped like a man, towering, wrapped in a long black robe. Its eyes twinkled in the light, but there was no joy in those eyes, only ancient malice and an insatiable, terrifying hunger.

Weal felt his bowels let go as he fouled himself for a second time, the stench rising to his nostrils immediately, making him dry-retch.

And then, suddenly, there was no robed man standing in

front of him—no one at all. There were no eyes twinkling in the flashlight's beam. Weal blinked and stared harder into the mineshaft, trying to see. Chimerical shapes danced in front of his eyes. He rubbed them, but the shapes remained, fantastical, grotesquely cavorting. What he'd first taken for the figure of a man was nothing but an odd rock formation. The gleam of eyes was merely mica flickering as the flashlight swept over it.

There was no one there. The only monster hiding in this place was Weal himself. The thought filled him not with dread, but with impossible relief, for what he'd seen was infinitely worse than anything he could have ever imagined in his best, or worst, nightmares.

Then the voice came again, even more clearly than before. He felt an indistinguishable mix of relief and terror in equal measure, combined with nearly transcendent reverence.

Here. You have found me.

Weal knelt down in the dirt in a posture of abject supplication. He felt sharp stones cutting into his kneecaps, but he welcomed the pain as an offering of abasement.

"Where, Lord?" he wept. "Where are you? Show me. I beg you. One more sign, Lord. Please. Just one more sign."

Another image flashed through his mind and he turned his head sharply to the left. He aimed the flashlight at the place where had been told to look. A short distance from where he knelt, the natural architecture of cave rock had created an oblong depression that jutted out from the wall of bedrock like an anthropoid coffin, but too small to contain the body of man.

Lying across it almost like a lid was a long, flat slab of sedimentary shale. At first, Weal took it to be another part of the rock formation, but when he brought the light close, he saw that it had fallen, or been deliberately placed there, at an angle.

Roll the stone away.

He put the flashlight down and set his shoulder to the shale lid, pushing hard. He'd expected the slab to be heavy, but it was relatively light and brittle. It yielded readily, crashing to the ground, splitting in two at his feet. He fumbled for the flashlight at his feet. He shone it into the basin. Then the flashlight flickered and died.

"No!" he screamed. "No! No! Not now!"

He shook the flashlight, slapped it against his thigh. A bolt of agony shot through his leg as the blade of the knife in his pocket bit into his thigh again, but the impact accomplished its goal: the flashlight flickered and went back on.

Feverishly, Weal shone the light into the stone basin. It contained what he at first took to be the dried body of a small animal, but on closer inspection was a bundle of what seemed to be ashes and bone fragments inside the rotted remains of some of sort cloth, or animal skin. He reached out to touch the bundle, finding it cold and oddly dry considering the length of time it had lain underground, undisturbed.

Gingerly, he opened the bundle, gently prying apart the fabric that contained it. The fabric fell apart at his touch, leaving the pile of ashes exposed to his flashlight's beam.

"Ashes," he said aloud, remembering his vision. "These are *ashes*." He said it again, not only to confirm his findings to his senses, but also to hear a voice that wasn't in his head for once, even if it was his own.

But then, had all the voices been in his head? He felt a sickening sense of betrayal wash over him. This wasn't his *friend*, this was just an old pile of cinders. Where was his friend? Where was the voice? Where was the *treasure*? Had this whole misadventure been a series of crazy directives issued from his own diseased brain? The result of not taking the pills the doctors had prescribed him at the hospital? And now, because he'd thrown his pills away back in Toronto, he was going to die a horrible, drawn-out death by starvation and thirst.

Why is there a coffin in a mineshaft?

"What?" he said. The silence mocked him. "Who said that?" Weal looked left and right. "Father, is that you?"

It was in your head, you idiot. Crazy person. It's all in your head—all of the "voices" have been in your head the whole time. There's no "Lord." There's no "Father." There never was. You've fucked yourself good and proper now, haven't you? Are you going to keep talking to yourself until you go blind down here? Or crazier? Or die of thirst? Why don't you just cut your wrist and drink your own blood? Aren't you thirsty enough yet? You will be, give it time. You just watch.

Weal tried to swallow, but his spit had dried. He felt his throat close up, dry and hot as though it were packed with sand. He realized then that he had effectively buried himself alive, walled himself into a system of underground caves that predated the Parr family's dynamiting of this part of the country by millennia.

Yes, yes, buried alive. All very melodramatic. Typical crazy person. But by the way—not that it remotely matters at this moment—but how did ashes get into a tunnel?

Weal looked at the heap of ashes—they were ashes, weren't they? How did they get down here? Who brought them? And when? How? Traces of the vision he'd had before coming to consciousness down here floated back to him. He'd seen ash, piles of it, as though there had been a great burning. He'd smelled the burning bones and watched the wind carry the fragments into the air and scatter them across the cliffs.

Ash. Bones. *This* ash? *These* bones?

"Lord," he whispered. "Where are you? If you're real, please answer. Please only answer if it's really you. Please show me what to do." He waited, dreading the sound of the second voice, the mocking voice that sounded like his own. But there was nothing. "Please," he said again. "Please."

Wake me. Wake me.

"How?" he screamed. "Don't go away again! Tell me, how?"

You know how. I showed you many times before.

"But I can't do *that*! I'll die! I can't kill *myself*! I killed all those people for *you*!"

WAKE ME!

He bowed his head in submission and acceptance. With a sob, Weal pulled the knife out of his pocket and tested the blade with the ball of his thumb. He winced as it sliced through the skin. Blood rose to the cut and spilled down his thumb, flowing over the palm. In the light of the flashlight, it looked black on the knife blade.

He took a deep breath, then rolled up the sleeve of his shirt and jacket. He cut the flesh of his wrist with one definitive, transversal downward stroke, severing the ulnar artery. The pain was sharp and immediate, but Weal made no sound. Instead, he squeezed the upper middle part of his forearm and pumped. He raised his arm and watched the blood drain out of his body, running down his arm onto the pile of ashes in the stone concavity where the ashes had rested undisturbed for three hundred years under Spirit Rock and the cliffs that ringed Bradley Lake.

There was a sound like fat being dropped onto a hot griddle and the smell of burning meat.

Above ground, a great flock of disparate nightbirds took to the sky from every treetop on Spirit Rock—a shocked, squawking black cloud, a cacophony of harsh screams soaring into the night.

Below the mass of airborne birds, the first coyote yelped a sharp, terrified bark that became a shriek. Its mate joined in. Then another, and another, until the sound of their howling became deafening. Every dog in Parr's Landing took up the cry, including Finn's dog, Sadie, whose bloodcurdling lament was loud enough to wake Finn from a deep sleep in which he dreamed of Morgan Parr standing nude on the edge of Bradley Lake, beckoning him to join her in the black water.

"Awww fuck, Sadie," Finn groaned, his voice thick with sleep. "You *ruined* it."

Vengefully, he lobbed a pillow at the dog who was standing rigidly on point beside his bedroom window staring at the glass. "Do you want to go out, girl?" he said, feeling guilty for throwing the pillow. "Do you? Do you want to go outside? Come. Come, Sadie, let's go outside!"

She whined, bounding ahead, her claws scrabbling madly on the floor. She ran like she had to take the world's most portentous piss, and scratched madly at the metal screen door, making an even more unholy racket than she had with her howling.

"Coming, coming," Finn said. He knew that if Sadie howled like that again, his parents would wake up and then there would be hell to pay. He opened the back door and nudged her outside, shutting the door quickly. She had a doghouse out there; she could sleep in it tonight. Fucking dog.

Finn went back to his bed and tried to find his Morgan dream again, already suspecting that the moment had passed, but willing to try anyway.

Richard Weal knew he must be dying, because the cavern was full of incandescent red light and heat that streamed blindingly upward from the pile of ashes in the depression of rock. He was dying, and these were the gates of heaven. Or, more likely, hell.

He covered his face with his bloody hand and tried to shield his eyes from the luminescence that was now so bright he could no longer see the walls of the cave. His knees gave way and buckled under his weight, and he fell to the ground in the earliest stages of hypovolemic shock. Just losing consciousness, Weal realized he was no longer alone.

He lay on his side, squinting into the brilliance, trying to see. As the light began to fade, Weal became aware that the black-robed man he'd *imagined* in the moments before he'd found the ashes—the man who *wasn't*—had stepped out of his feverish brain and into the world, and was bending over him.

When the man lowered his lips to Weal's throat, he tried to turn his head to accommodate the grateful kiss—what else could it be, but a benediction of gratitude to Weal for having found him, for having saved him, for releasing him from his prison? But he was too weak to form the words. He tried to apologize to the black shape towering over him for not being able to stand, for forcing him to kneel—surely the kneeling one should be Weal, not his friend—but no words came out. Weal realized that words would be beside the point, because his friend knew everything about him already, loved him just as he was, and knew he was sorry and had already forgiven him. He felt the man's cold lips caress the tender skin below his jawline, then the scraping points of two sharp teeth.

The pain when he bit down was incredible, but it vanished almost before it had even registered. As he felt the blood drain from his body, Richard Weal felt himself pulled up into a swirling vortex of crimson and gold light. For the briefest possible moment, Weal caught a glimpse of a glittering necropolis of souls, a dimension of pure love and endless wisdom. Its inhabitants reached out, their arms outstretched to embrace him, to join him to them, to forgive him and to guide him into their inanimate dimension that was opening before him and beckoning his soul to join the mass of others.

Not this! Make me like you! Make me like you! You promised! I want to live forever! This isn't what I killed for! This isn't what I died for! YOU PROMISED!

The crimson sky turned black and cold and violent.

The dead recoiled in horror at his fury. They recognized him for what he was, for what he was becoming, and they fled in terror lest they, too, found themselves sucked into the black circumgyration of supernatural energy that dragged Richard's enraged, insane soul back into the prison of his own dead body—the body lying on the stone floor of the cave where the creature he'd resurrected was still feeding on the last drops of his life.

After the bar had closed, they had gone to Elliot's place instead of Donna's, because Elliot said he had to get up early in the morning. She didn't find it particularly chivalrous on his part, but Donna wanted his company more than she wanted to be in her own bed, so she'd acquiesced. He'd asked her to stay the night and offered to drive her home afterwards, but she'd brought her own car and didn't relish the prospect of leaving it in front of Elliot's house overnight, advertising her whereabouts to the entire town. For the same reason, she didn't want to leave her car in the O'Toole's parking lot overnight so they could all wonder where she'd been instead of knowing.

In the past, sex with Elliot had always been a deeply pleasurable experience. He was a devoted, attentive lover who took her satisfaction as a point of personal pride. He'd bend his body to her pleasure while taking his own, always leaving her satiated.

Tonight had been different.

It had all started the way it always did, the way she liked it, with his hands and mouth deftly playing her body, with Elliot offering his own body for her exploration, gratification, and pleasure. But when she'd slipped her hands between his legs to stroke his shaft, she found it soft.

It's me, Donna thought, abruptly and self-consciously aware of the slackening of her body and the way it must have changed, how different it must feel to him since they had first slept together years before. What she saw in the mirror at home looked just fine to her, but here, with Elliot McKitrick on top of her . . .

She guided him onto his back and knelt between his legs, using her mouth on his cock, gently squeezing his nipples between her fingers until she felt him harden, then laid back herself and urged him along using the filthy words she knew he liked. She arched her back, offering her mouth and her breasts to his kisses the way she had always done, which he'd always liked before.

"Turn over," he'd said in a muffled voice she'd never heard before—a compressed, harsh, entirely unfamiliar but oddly thrilling voice. "Roll over on your stomach."

When she did what she was told, he entered her from behind. At first his movements were languorous and rhythmic and she moaned with familiar pleasure. But as the strokes quickened, he thrust harder and with more force.

Then Elliot pulled out and slipped his cock into her ass.

Donna gasped at the sudden invasion. Wanting to please him, she willed herself to relax and take him in. His fingers dug into her hips as he pushed. When he entwined his fingers in her hair and yanked on it as though it were a bridle, she cried out in shock and pain. She felt his body buckle and he collapsed against her, driving her into the bed with him on top as wave after wave of his climax shuddered through his body.

"We've never done it like that before," she said. When there was no reply, she asked, "Was it OK? I mean, doing it that way?"

"It was great," he said.

Afterwards, he'd sat naked on the edge of the bed with his face in his hands. She ran her fingers along the scallops of muscle between his shoulder blades. When she'd touched his shoulder, he'd flinched.

She'd asked him if he was crying and he said, "No, of course not, why?" as though it was the stupidest question he'd ever heard, which hurt Donna's feelings more than anything else. When she asked him what was wrong, he told her he'd had a bad day, then apologized for snapping at her and offered to drive her home.

"I brought my car, Elliot, remember? You have to get up early, you said."

"Right, sorry," he said. "I'm sorry, Donna. Really, I am. I have a lot on my mind. Work, you know. I'll make it up to you next time."

Donna said nothing. She kissed him on the cheek, then picked her jeans and pink blouse off the floor where she'd left them.

I'm too young to feel like this, she thought bitterly. *Like something secondhand, like something in the fridge that's turned.* Her clothes smelled like beer and cigarette smoke after the fresh-laundry scent of Elliot's sheets, but she couldn't dress quickly enough to suit her purposes. The only thing Donna wanted was to be out of Elliot's house and back in her own bedroom, with her cat and her cold sheets, where at least there was no one to make her feel the way she felt right now.

"Next time," Elliot promised as she said goodbye. But they both knew there wouldn't be a next time. And Donna, for one, was fine with that.

In the car, she lit a cigarette, then turned the key in the ignition and pulled out of Elliot's driveway, heading towards her house on the other side of town, thinking that Elliot McKitrick was a prick of the first order, but that it still hurt like hell.

At 4:30 a.m., Donna had parked her car in her driveway and put the keys in her purse. A light, cold rain had begun to fall and she hurried up the driveway to avoid getting drenched. *The perfect ending to a perfectly awful night,* she thought.

She was nearly at the front door of her house when she heard something pass through the air above her head. The sound disoriented her. When she was eight, her mother took Donna with her to visit an elderly aunt who'd spent her life in a convent outside of Montréal. The sisters kept a working farm, and while her mother visited with the aunt, one of the younger nuns showed her the dovecote attached to the barn. Donna had lain on her back in hay and watched the doves fluttering above her. She'd closed her eyes, listened, and imagined they were angels.

That's what this was like—the ripple of wings, but louder and heavier than doves' wings. Instinctively, she looked up towards the sound, but saw nothing in the night sky except stars and the distant mass of the cliffs.

Then the sound came again, directly over her head this time. The last thing Donna Lemieux ever saw was something huge, something with wings—no, not something, *someone*, and not wings, outstretched arms—fall from the sky, smashing her into the gravel of her driveway. Her mind had time to register only two things: first, that the body on top of her was male and that it—*he*—was fiercely strong. And secondly, that she was about to die here on her own driveway in sight of her own front door. She tried to scream, but the impact of the body crashing down on top of her back had driven the air from her lungs and she lay on the driveway gasping for air.

Then her world went white.

All around her was the scent of hay and clover, and the musk of barn animals. She lay back on the straw and watched the doves wheel and flit above her like angels. She listened to the beating of their wings. Wonderfully, even though her eyes were closed, she could still see: the doves were indeed transforming into angels— the most beautiful angels imaginable, angels with strong, gleaming naked men's bodies and opalescent-feathered wings.

She felt a warm gust of heavenly air as one of the angels separated from the others and swooped down to where she lay prostrate on the hay. She gazed at the angel's face, awed by the perfection of its body—a face and body she recognized.

"Elliot," Donna said weakly. "What are you doing—"

The angel opened its jaws and cocked its head to the side, and Donna saw its two rows of sharp white teeth. She realized then that the angel wasn't Elliot at all—how had she ever confused them? This angel's hair was white, and he was wearing a long black robe that covered him from neck to ankles. Rain streamed from his hair, running down from his high forehead and into his eyes, which burned like coals. But Donna didn't care because she knew at that exact moment she was desired—desired and desirable, more desired than she'd even been by Elliot, or indeed any other man. She felt the angel's cool lips on her throat for a moment and a sharp, momentary pain. Then a spreading coldness that felt like heat, in spite of the cold rain that soaked her clothes and her skin, as she lay there in the driveway.

When the angel—or whatever it was—enfolded her in its black wings, she gave herself up to its hunger, and knew that whatever it cost to be loved like this, she would gladly pay that price a hundredfold or more.

CHAPTER FOURTEEN

As usual, Finn woke before dawn.

There was an unfamiliar sticky wetness inside his pyjama pants. For a moment, he was terrified that he'd peed the bed, something he hadn't done since he was a little boy, but the wetness was localized in his bottoms, not anywhere else in the bed, which was dry and warm with sleep. Then the dream of Morgan Parr naked in Bradley Lake came back to him.

Oh, yeah. That.

He smiled shyly and rolled over on his stomach, grinding the mattress with his pelvis. It had been a very good dream. Suddenly self conscious about staining the rest of the sheets by accident, he took off his pyjama bottoms and carried them downstairs to the laundry room and buried them underneath the rest of the family's dirty laundry, before taking the stairs two at a time to get back to his room quickly, in case his mother saw his bum. Safe in his room, he pulled on a pair of clean underpants and some jeans. He took his sweater from where he'd left it on the chair by his desk. He put it on over his T-shirt and went to look for Sadie.

Finn remembered the howling he'd heard last night and remembered putting Sadie outside in the yard when she'd started howling herself. He hated leaving her in her doghouse overnight, but he hadn't been about to wait around for her to come back in when he was cooking a dream like the one he'd been having.

He opened the back door and peered into the pre-dawn gloom of the fenced-in yard. The doghouse Finn and his dad had built for Sadie when she was a puppy was in the far corner of the yard.

"Sadie," he called softly. "Good morning, Sadie! Come, girl! Want to go for a walk?" Finn waited expectantly for Sadie to slither out of the doghouse like a long black breadbox, stretch, and wag her tail, shaking her entire hindquarters along with it. But she didn't come through the doorway of the doghouse, nor was she anywhere else in the yard. "Sadie!" Finn called again. "Sadie, come!"

Finn stepped out of the house and crossed the yard. The grass was wet between his bare toes. He jogged over to the doghouse and leaned down to peer inside. It was empty. Again he looked around the yard, but there was no sign of the Labrador anywhere. The fence was too high for her to jump—his parents had learned that lesson when she went into her first heat and almost wound up becoming another Parr's Landing unwed mother statistic.

Fighting rising panic, he ran back to the house to look for her. Perhaps his parents had gotten up in the night and let her in. Yeah, that must be it. She was probably upstairs on the landing, or down in the rec room, behind the couch where the heating vents were. Sadie liked to sleep there in the winter sometimes.

Finn searched the house from the basement to the top floor, but there was no sign of his dog anywhere. The only place he hadn't checked was his parents' bedroom. They wouldn't be happy to be woken up at six in the morning, but this was an emergency. He approached their bedroom door. Before he knocked, he said a prayer to himself.

Please, God, if you're real, let my dog be sleeping in my parents' room. Please don't take my dog away from me. Let her be all right.

Finn knocked on their door. There was no answer, so he knocked again. From the other side, he heard his father's querulous sleep voice asking him what he wanted. His heart sank, because there was no scratching on the other side in response to his knocking.

He turned the knob and pushed the door open. His parents were cocooned in their blankets, each of them with their own set. He looked on either side of the bed, but there was nothing on the floor but their bedside rugs and a pair of his dad's grey sweatpants balled up in the corner near his dresser.

"What is it, Finnegan?" he demanded, not bothering to lift his head from the pillow, much less open his eyes. "This better be good." When there was no answer, because his son's throat was working too much for him to form the words needed to answer, he opened his eyes and sat up. "Finnegan? What is it, son?"

"Sadie's gone, Daddy," Finn said. "She's gone from the yard and I can't find her anywhere." And then he burst into tears.

Billy Lightning woke from a fitful sleep full of bad dreams in his room at the Gold Nugget. His head ached, and his back felt as though he'd been sleeping on a blacktop highway.

He'd woken twice in the middle of the night: once because he'd heard what sounded like a thousand dogs howling all at once outside his window, and once again because of the nightmare he was having, a familiar one that usually visited him during periods of profound stress. He'd had it constantly through his childhood at the residential school. It stayed with him until the second year of his adoption by Phenius Osborne and his wife, after which time it visited him more and more rarely. It didn't come back till he was at the University of Toronto doing his undergrad. It occurred less frequently throughout his Masters and PhD studies as his sense of his own vulnerability to exploitation diminished and, for all intents and purposes, even disappeared.

In the dream, he was six years old and crying for his father. Not Phenius Osborne—whom Billy considered his real father—but rather his biological father, Tom Lightning, the man from whom he had been forcefully taken by the truancy officers who would deliver him into the hell of St. Rita's Catholic Residential School in Sault Ste. Marie—the man who had been compelled by law to leave him there so Billy could be saved from being an Indian.

It was always the same dream, by turns poignant and awful, like the most scarring nightmares are, pregnant with symbolism overlaid with memories as fresh as cuts.

The narrative of the dream was always the same: he was standing at the gate of St. Rita's, which was locked. On his side of the gate stood Billy and his father, flanked by the two truancy officers. On the other side, two priests in long robes, both pale with hard faces, were walking towards it with keys. In the dream, the priests were enormous, gigantic, moving in inexorable slow motion towards Billy, swinging the ring of keys like a pendulum.

In the dream, Tom pleaded with the truancy officers to let him take Billy home, explaining that his mother had died the previous year and that it was *too soon, too soon!* for this. Tom begged the two men to let him bring Billy the following year, when he would be seven, or maybe even the year after that, when he'd be eight. With Billy clinging to his father's leg, the truancy officers told Tom to be a good Indian and let them do their job, or they'd have to arrest him, which they didn't want to do.

In the dream, the sound of the iron key in the lock was like a freight train, and the gate swung open with torturous slowness. When the priests reached for him, he clung even tighter to his father's leg and screamed, and he kept screaming as they pried him away and dragged him across the threshold. The dream always ended with the same mental images weighted with symbolism—the expression of decimated impotence in Tom Lightning's eyes as the truancy officers restrained him and he was forced to watch while Billy was dragged across the threshold of the school, the burn of the priest's grip on Billy's shoulders and wrist. And most importantly, the searing sense of his own irrelevance in the face of forces beyond his control—powerful forces that had identified him as inferior and damaged and powerless.

He knew why he'd had the dream—he had it a week running after his adoptive father's murder in Toronto. In that instance, it had obviously been about losing another father. He'd had it last night because he'd been forced to deal with the two white policemen, the younger of whom had come just short of calling him a criminal.

Billy stood up and walked into the bathroom. He switched on the overhead light and studied his face in the mirror above the sink. There were dark circles beneath his eyes, and his face was puffy. "You look like crap, Dr. Lightning," he said to his reflection. "You need to get it together, and quickly. You've got a lot to do."

He stripped off his T-shirt and turned the shower on. He needed breakfast and really needed coffee.

When there was no answer at Donna Lemieux's door at ten in the morning, her mother, Madeleine Tarrant, rapped on the glass of her front window. Still no answer. She cupped her eyes with her hand and peered in. The lights were off in the living room and the cat, Samantha, was crying in the kitchen, which meant she hadn't been fed—which meant that Donna had likely not been home last night. And yet her car was in the driveway.

Madeleine thought, *Well, my stars. What are we to make of that?* Donna not being home at ten in the morning after a shift at O'Toole's the night before was not, in and of itself, a problem. The problem—if you wanted to call it a problem, and Madeleine was not ready to do that just yet—was what an unlikely occurrence it was. While Donna was no prude—not by any stretch, and never had been—as far as her mother knew, Donna had always focused on work in the years since her worthless drunk of a husband, Lucien, had run off and left her and moved to God knew where.

She hadn't "gone steady" with anyone for years, though she certainly was popular with the men who came into O'Toole's. On the other hand, most of them were married and Donna had gone to school with their wives and, as far as Madeleine knew, was friendly with most of them. All the single men of datable age were likewise accounted for in Parr's Landing.

In the past, when Madeleine had expressed regret that Lucien hadn't at least left her with a grandchild, Donna had laughed and asked her mother who she thought would support them? Lucien couldn't even support himself, let alone a child. But Madeleine knew her daughter, and she knew that behind the dismissal of the notion, there was genuine sadness.

Lately, too, Donna had been talking about getting older and wondering aloud what she had to show for it, which was ridiculous since Donna was still as pretty as a picture and as popular as she ever was. But she was still a small-town woman in her late forties in a town full of married people.

Madeleine unlocked the front door with her extra key and called out, "Yoo-hoo! Yoo-hoo! Anybody home? You home, honey?" There was no reply from anywhere in the house, except for Samantha's plaintive wailing. "I'll get to you in just a minute, puss. I promise."

The sound of her own voice in the stillness of the house startled her.

She went down the hall to Donna's bedroom and found the door halfway open. She peered inside. The bed was made, the blinds were open. Nothing appeared to be amiss. Donna's makeup (she used a little too much, Madeleine thought) was lined up on the dresser alongside her bottles of Jontue and Muguet des Bois.

The bathroom was likewise empty—the sink and the bathtub were both dry, as was the mat.

In the kitchen, Madeleine opened a tin of cat food and scraped the can into Samantha's bowl, which was blazoned with the slogan *Frankly, I deserve 9Lives!* and a photograph of a supercilious-looking yellow cat that looked nothing like Samantha, who was adorable. As she dropped the can into the garbage, Madeleine caught a whiff of something in the hallway that reminded her of the smell of a dead mouse behind a refrigerator. She fished the empty can out of the garbage and sniffed it to see if it had gone bad. It smelled awful, but that was cat food for you.

She stepped out into the dim hallway and sniffed again. She thought she smelled the mouse-smell, then she wasn't sure. She felt a prickle of fear as she had a notion. Madeleine walked back through the kitchen to the back stairs, where the entrance to the cellar was. She opened the door to the cellar and peered down into the darkness. She flicked the switch. No light. She flicked it back and forth a couple of times. Still no light.

"Donna?" she called. "Honey, you down there? Hello?"

Of course there was no reply. Donna wouldn't be in the basement. She hated going down to the basement for any reason at all. And if the light was burned out, forget it. Donna had always been afraid of the dark. She didn't even have a washing machine down there. Madeleine closed the door to the cellar and went back through the house. She was going to feel pretty darn silly when Donna called her this afternoon and told her she was—well, wherever she was. She felt the prickle of fear again, but forced it down. She was a practical woman, if nothing else.

Madeleine filled Samantha's water dish and left the house, closing the door behind her. She thought briefly of locking it, then decided not to. No one locked their doors in Parr's Landing. Then she drove back across town to her home on Blossom Street to make some phone calls.

Billy sat in a back booth at the Pear Tree Café and Breakfast Nook on Main Street eating his breakfast when the young cop parked his cruiser outside and walked up to the counter. Billy heard the cop order two coffees to go: one black, and one double-double.

What Parr's Landing needs is a doughnut shop, Billy thought dryly. He would have liked to make the joke to the cop's face, but suspected that Constable McKitrick was lacking a sense of humour where Billy was concerned. He went on eating his breakfast and hoped McKitrick wouldn't notice him. But the café was small and McKitrick was a cop, and you didn't get to be a cop—even in Parr's Landing, Ontario—without at least rudimentary observational skills, so he braced himself.

McKitrick gave the room a once-over. His glance lighted on Billy at the far table and he walked over, leaving the takeaway coffee cups on the counter.

"Dr. Lightning," Elliot said.

"Constable McKitrick." Billy replied with cool politeness. "How are you this morning?"

"Very well, sir. Thank you. Still here, I see."

"Well, I try not to rush my breakfast, constable," Billy replied. "At my age, it's not good for the digestion."

Two red spots appeared high on McKitrick's cheekbones. "I mean in Parr's Landing, Dr. Lightning," he said stiffly. "How long are you planning to stay, exactly?"

"I don't know, constable." Billy had already taken as much of this as he was going to take from this stupid redneck cop. "As I understand it, it's a free country, and I am a citizen of that free country. Are you enacting the War Measures Act in Parr's Landing, constable? Has there been another October Crisis, except involving visitors to Parr's Landing this time instead of rogue French Canadians? Or is it just that I'm an Indian?"

"Think you're tough, do you, sir?" Elliot said, too softly for anyone at the surrounding tables to hear. He leaned in close to Billy's face. "I'm warning you—"

Billy raised his own face to Elliot's level and met his gaze. "No, constable, *I'm* warning *you*. If you continue to harass me, you're going to find out the hard way that your harassment is a mistake on your part. I'm sure that in this town, your word is law. But I'm not from here, Constable McKitrick. I'm a tenured professor at a major university. I am also well connected. There's a telephone in my motel room that makes long distance calls. Unless you want to find yourself transferred to some shit ass northern outpost that makes Parr's Landing look like Paris, France, my advice to you is that you back off."

Billy was bluffing a little bit, but he was gambling on the cop not knowing by how much. Apparently, it worked: Elliot dropped his eyes and took a half step backwards. Billy leaned back in his seat.

So intent on their standoff were the two men that neither noticed the blonde woman in the dark green sweater until she tapped Elliot on the shoulder and said, "Excuse me, are you Elliot? Elliot McKitrick?"

Billy looked up, surprised, and Elliot turned around.

"You don't recognize me, do you?" The woman smiled at Elliot and said, "I used to be Christina Monroe. Now I'm Christina Parr. You know—Jeremy's sister-in-law? I think you're a friend of Jeremy's, aren't you?"

Billy, whose first thought had been that this woman was too beautiful to be a local, was watching Elliot's face for a reaction, wondering how anyone who looked like Christina Parr—presumably some member of that family of Parr's, the local gentry—could have any possible connection to a buffoon like Elliot McKitrick. He was surprised by Elliot's reaction. In lightning-fast succession, the colour drained from the cop's face, then returned with a vengeance, rising from the line where his uniform collar met his neck to the top of his hairline. Elliot hadn't made a sound. But if his reaction had been audible, it might have sounded like the sharp, automatic intake of breath the human body makes when it's plunged into a lake that's colder than expected on a hot summer day. Billy immediately liked Christina Parr, if only because she'd inexplicably managed to ruffle this smug bully's veneer of authority. Billy wondered if they'd ever been a couple, but dismissed the notion, as much out of enlightened self-interest as his growing conviction that Christina Parr was so far out of this cop's league as to render the notion beyond absurd.

"Oh, hey—of course," Elliot said, recovering some composure. "Chris! Good to see you. I was sorry to hear about Jack."

"Thanks, Elliot." Her neutral gaze never left Elliot's face. "You look well."

"Thanks, Chris," he said. "You, too. It's been—what, fifteen years?"

Christina nodded. "About that. So," she said. "You joined the police force. I'm not surprised. Good for you. I knew you'd make something of yourself."

"So—how's Jeremy? It's been at least as long since I've seen him. How's he doing?"

Christina smiled again, but Billy noted that there appeared to be subtitles to the entire conversation between her and Elliot. This particular smile didn't seem entirely friendly.

"He's fine, I guess. I could have sworn he told me this morning that you and he had a beer together last night at O'Toole's, out on Davenport Road? Did I get the name wrong? Was it one of his other friends he ran into?"

Again, Elliot blushed. "Oh, yeah, right! Sorry, Chris—yeah, I did run into him there last night." He indicated the takeaway coffee on the counter with a sideways jerk of his head. "Long day yesterday. Not enough coffee yet today." He laughed, as though he had made some sort of joke. When Christina said nothing in reply but only continued to smile that peculiar, knowing smile, Elliot cleared his throat and said, "Well, back to the station. Good to see you, Christina. Welcome back. I wish it were under different circumstances, though. Again, I'm sorry about Jack. He was a good man."

"Yes, he was," she said. "Thanks, Elliot. I'll tell Jeremy I ran into you."

This seemed to fluster the cop even more. He nodded briskly and went back to the counter to collect the two cups of coffee. He didn't look back at either Christina or Billy when he pushed open the door of the café. In silence, they both watched the cruiser drive off down Main Street.

Billy exhaled. "Whew," he said. He looked at Christina and said, "So, friend of yours?"

"He is—was—a friend of my brother-in-law's," she said, her eyes still on the departing cruiser. "I haven't seen him for a long time. I've been away."

"Not the friendliest sort," Billy said neutrally. If there was a backstory here, he didn't want to get off on the wrong foot with her by accidentally putting that foot in his mouth. He was still wagering that there wasn't one, but there was no point in risking it. It had been a long time since he'd been as attracted to a woman as he was to this Christina Parr.

You're an idiot, Billy chided himself. *You're not a romantic, you're a cynic. And this woman isn't just out of the cop's league, she's out of yours. She's too beautiful for either of you.*

Christina shrugged. "This is a hard place," she said sadly. "Life is tough up here in these little northern towns. It's mean. It does things to people. It's one of the reasons my husband and I left. My late husband, I mean. I'm sorry. I'm still not used to saying 'late husband.'"

"I'm sorry," Billy said sincerely. "For your loss, I mean." He half-rose from his seat and extended his hand. "I'm Billy Lightning."

"Christina Parr," she said. Billy was acutely aware of the softness of her hand in his, and of its apparent fragility. Everything else in Parr's Landing had been hard, or rough, from the people to the topography. Her hand felt like a sparrow had landed in his palm, one he might accidentally crush if he squeezed it too hard.

"Forgive me if I'm being too forward," Billy said, "but would you care to join me? I'm not from here. I'm just visiting."

Christina glanced around the café. While she and Elliot had been talking, the two remaining tables had been taken and she had no desire to sit at the counter with her back to the rest of the patrons. Some residual sense of small-town sensitivity to gossip rolled over in its sleep in the back of her mind, but since nothing good had ever come to her from this particular small town—and because if her "reputation" was that vulnerable to gossip, it was likely already toast when she got pregnant and ran off with Jack Parr—and mostly because she'd never been lonelier or more eager for a neutral conversation with another adult that wasn't fraught with subtext—she found herself saying to Billy Lightning, "Thank you, yes. I can't stay—I'm just going to have a cup of coffee. I have errands to run."

"Please," Billy said, indicating the empty seat in front of him. "I'd enjoy the company."

Christina sat down at the booth. For a moment the two of them sized each other up in the way that men and women meeting for the first time under potentially complicated circumstances do—Christina trying not to be conscious of the looks they were getting from a few of the patrons of the café, and Billy not giving a damn about them, except for her sake. He hoped he hadn't made a mistake in inviting her to sit down like this. Of course, all of this happened without either of them giving each other any clue of what they were thinking.

"So," Christina began. "You're not from here, obviously. How do you like it?"

"Not much," Billy said honestly. "They're not very friendly to outsiders." He didn't add, *especially outsiders who look like me,* but Christina seemed to understand what he meant. She favoured him with a smile that was sympathetic but noncommittal, as though she were acknowledging the root of his problem—the fact that he was an outsider, and a Native outsider at that—but allowing him the space to elaborate, or not, as he saw fit or was comfortable. He was touched by her sensitivity.

"My husband and I left when we were very young," Christina said. "We moved to Toronto just before our daughter was born. We raised her there, so nothing about this place is familiar to her. It has no memories."

"Did you come back to be with family?"

Something passed over Christina's face. "In a way. My mother-in-law is here," she said. "My daughter hadn't ever met her, and I thought it would be a good time for her to get to know her a bit. It's a big house, so we'll be staying for a while."

"Of course—the big house on the hill. The one that looks a bit like a Norman chateau."

Christina raised her eyebrows. "A Norman chateau? I have to say, I've never heard it described that way before. Lots of ways, but never like that." Her curiosity was piqued and she took a second, closer look at the man in front of her who spoke so politely and made references to Norman chateaus. "Where are you from, Mr. Lightning?"

"Please, call me Billy," he said. "I'm originally from Benson, a tiny little town way outside of Sault Ste. Marie. When I say 'way outside,' I mean 'way outside.' I was adopted when I was twelve by a family from Toronto. I grew up there, except for graduate school—so basically, I guess, the short answer to that question is, Toronto. Like you," he added.

"Graduate school?"

"You sound surprised."

"No, it's not that," she said. Now it was Christina's turn to be flustered. "It's just . . . my husband—my *late* husband, Jesus I need to get used to saying that—and I never went to university. We barely escaped high school here by the skin of our teeth. What did you study in graduate school?"

"Lots of different things," he said neutrally. "A lot of history. I'm a cultural anthropologist at Grantham University, in Michigan."

"Now I'm impressed!" she said, laughing.

She has a beautiful laugh, Billy thought, feeling absurdly flattered to be the source of it.

"So, you're not 'Mr.' Lightning, you're 'Professor' Lightning."

"Only to my students. And then, only in the classroom. I've always preferred 'Billy' to anything else. My father was the first person to call me 'Billy.' At the residential school, they always called me 'William.' It took a long time for me to hear 'William' without a lot of bad memories."

"Billy it is, then. So, Billy, what on earth are you doing here? I know why I'm back, but what would bring a university professor to this shi . . . I mean, godforsaken town? Sorry, I've only been back a couple of days and my language is already starting to suffer."

"It *is* a shitty town," he confirmed. "There you go. I said it so you don't have to." He signalled to the waitress, then said to Christina, "You still don't have any coffee."

When the waitress had refreshed Billy's coffee cup and brought Christina a cup of her own, Billy continued. "To answer your question," he said, "I'm here because my father passed away recently. He'd done an excavation up here at Spirit Rock in the early 1950s, on the site of the St. Barthélemy Ojibwa mission, the Jesuit mission from the 1700s. My father was a cultural anthropologist as well, at the University of Toronto. I was on his crew in 1952. Some strange things happened on that dig. My father's death . . . well, my father's death wasn't accidental. I have some notion that it might be somehow connected to the work he did in Parr's Landing in the fifties."

She paused. "Not the kid who went crazy and heard voices coming from inside the cliffs and killed all of those people?"

"The very one," Billy said. "He was on our crew that summer."

"You mean that really happened? I mean, we all heard that story, but I always thought it was just made up to scare kids."

"No, it happened," he said. "But he didn't kill any people—that part must be from the campfire story version. But he did attack one of the other guys on the team and hurt him pretty badly."

"But why did you come back? What does this have to do with your father's death? I'm sorry," she said, chastened. "I don't mean to pry. I know what it feels like to be asked these questions. I should know better. I'm sorry."

Billy's first impulse was to tell Christina the story he'd shared with the two cops, Thomson and McKitrick, but thought better of it. He had no doubt that Christina would treat it with respect, unlike the two officers had. At the same time, he realized that every time he told the story in Parr's Landing, it stood a better chance of getting circulated as gossip in a way that didn't flatter him. While he didn't give a damn whether or not he was thought of in flattering terms by the residents of the Landing, if he was going to find any answers here, his personal credibility and status would have to stand on its merits and history in the face of people's prejudices. His encounters with McKitrick and Thomson had shown that the ice was thinner than it looked where that was concerned.

"I don't know," he said. "Just a hunch. Probably nothing to it."

"You don't want to talk about it, do you?"

"Not really," he said, sighing. "Is that OK?"

"Sure," Christina said. "But can I at least ask about what happened in '52? I've never had a chance to hear the story from anyone who wasn't actually just trying to scare me with some dumb ghost story."

Good compromise, he thought. *And I don't really want her to leave, anyway.* "Of course. What would you like to know?"

"Well—what happened?"

"In a nutshell," he said, "the young graduate student, Richard Weal thought he heard voices coming from inside Spirit Rock. He attacked one of the team members and put him in the hospital."

She sounded disappointed. "That's it? That's all there is?"

"Pretty much," he replied. "The interesting thing is the history *behind* Spirit Rock. That's something that would make a good campfire story for the locals."

Christina perked up. She leaned forward, and Billy caught a whiff of violets when her hair moved. "What history?"

"Well," he said, "there have been some similar incidents reported over the years—and by 'the years' I mean over the course of the last three hundred years or so, so we're talking in historical terms now, so maybe 'legends' is better than 'history,' since the source of some of the stories are a little obscure, not to mention unverifiable."

"Now you really sound like a professor," she teased, but it was teasing of an unmistakably gentle variety. "Go on, please."

"The St. Barthélemy mission was attacked and decimated by an Iroquois raid in 1629 or 1630," Billy explained. He was trying not to sound professorial, but doubted he was succeeding very well. "Everyone was killed, including the priest, a Father de Céligny, There seems to be precious little information on what actually happened, which is odd considering what great historians the Jesuits were when it came to their missions in New France. They never rebuilt on that site—as far as my father could tell, the site encompassed the area around Bradley Lake. More or less where Parr's Landing is today."

"Go on," Christina said again. "Please." This time, there was no teasing, only what appeared to be genuine interest on her part. "This is really interesting."

"Well, it's interesting stuff," he said, warming to the topic. "Around 1702, two members of a brigade of trappers were camping on the shore of Lake Superior and wandered inland—the area in the account suggests that if it wasn't actually nearby, it was close to here—and disappeared for a week. Only one of the pair found his way back to his brigade, and he was half-starved and raving about demons—do you know what a 'Wendigo' is?"

"I think so," Christina said dubiously. "It's some sort of evil spirit, isn't it?"

"Something like that," Billy said. "It's a spirit that possesses a man and makes him crave human flesh. Anyway, the trapper told them he'd murdered his friend and drank his blood. At least that's what the story says happened. The other members of the brigade were terrified and they turned on the fellow and killed him. When they returned to Québec, they were exonerated at trial because all of them testified that the man who murdered his friend had been insane. The court believed them. It wasn't unusual in those days for people out here to lose their minds because of the isolation."

Christina shuddered involuntarily. "What a horrible story."

"There are more," he said. "In 1850, a minor British men's adventure writer and explorer named Timothy Gentry came to this area to produce a revised map of the lake systems and islands in this part of Lake Superior. His brother, Adam, came with him as a sort of secretary and record-keeper. When neither they nor their guides had returned by the expected time, another set of guides was dispatched. The guides found Adam roaming the forests at night with his brother's head in his rucksack. Adam's fingertips had literally been worn down to bloody stumps. Before he died of his infected wounds, he told the Indians that he'd been trying to claw a hole through the rock." Billy pointed to the window of the café. "Up there. Those rocks."

"How do they know it was those rocks?"

"There were Gentry's maps and diaries—none of which mention what happened to him and his brother, mind you, because the entries stop after they landed. But the Indians described the area perfectly, including the cliff paintings." He paused. "There is at least one verifiable account from the nineteenth century of occurrences involving miners working up there, including one that dates from the early years of the Parr family—your family— buying the land and starting to develop it.

"In the 1895 instance, the miner in question disappeared. It was considered to be an accident, and the mining company was held liable. In another separate instance in 1902, a brawl apparently erupted underground between two of the men. One man killed the other with a rock and hid his body for three days before another member of the crew found it. They charged the miner in question—Rod MacNeil, I think his name was—with the murder. They hanged him in 1903, even though his lawyer argued at trial that he was insane. The body was described as 'torn and plundered, as though by furious beasts.'

"And yes," he added, winking. "That's a direct quote from the *Port Arthur Chronicle* in 1903. I don't talk like that in real life."

"Jesus," Christina said in a hushed voice. "I had no idea. I grew up here all those years and didn't have a clue about any of this." She took another sip of her coffee. It was cold, so she put the cup down. "Is this what your father was studying in 1952?"

Billy laughed, a big full-hearted laugh that made Christina smile, and made a few of the other patrons of the café turn around to see what the ruckus was about. Billy waited until they'd turned back to their own companions before answering her. "No, he was studying the settlement itself, looking for artefacts," he said. "My father had a great passion for that part of Canadian history. He always felt that the Jesuits, though well-intentioned, did a lot of damage when they arrived on these shores."

"May I ask . . ." Christina began, then blushed. "I'm sorry, it's too personal and invasive. I apologize. Never mind."

"No," he said kindly. "What is it?"

"Is that why . . . well, is that why your father adopted you? Because of what . . . well, because of history?"

Billy was quiet for a moment. Christina was sure she'd offended him and was ready to apologize again, and leave before she said anything else equally stupid. Then Billy said, "No, he adopted me because he loved me. Really. Don't feel bad, it's a natural question after what I just told you. Don't worry about it. It's OK."

Christina was moved by the simple, unadorned love implicit in Billy's statement. She thought of Jack and Morgan, naturally, and how much he'd loved his daughter. She looked down at the plain gold wedding band on her left hand and, when her eyes began to fill in a way that was becoming altogether too familiar and commonplace, she mentally shook her head, *No*.

"Oh, I really have to get going," she said briskly, looking at her watch. "It's later than I thought. Billy—thank you for the coffee. It's so nice to speak to somebody from Toronto."

He hesitated, then thought, *What the hell? Nothing ventured, nothing gained.*

"Christina, do you think . . . I mean, would you like to have dinner sometime while I'm here? You know," he said, "just to hear some more horrible Wendigo stories, if nothing else?"

"Billy—things aren't very good at the house right now," Christina said. She saw the disappointment in his face and kicked herself for being the cause of it. "My mother-in-law is a difficult woman."

"I know," he said. "I remember."

"You remember?" She frowned. "What do you mean, you remember? You know my mother-in-law?"

"No, not personally," he said. "But she gave my father a pretty hard time about permits in 1952, when he was setting it up. I know they spent some time together that summer at the beginning of the dig. He didn't ever talk about it so I assume it was more of the same."

"She's not an easy woman to get along with. And we're on tenterhooks up there at the house. My brother-in-law, Jeremy, has a difficult relationship with her, as well."

"I understand," Billy said, feeling embarrassed for having put her in the position of turning him down, let alone for having put himself out on a limb like this. "Don't give it another thought."

After they had shaken hands and parted, each went about their own particular business, Billy walking back to the motel to change into his hiking gear, and Christina aimlessly circling the town limits of Parr's Landing in the Chevelle to delay her inevitable return to the house. Both were surprised that each could still feel the other's hand in theirs. For his part, Billy had memorized her face and heard her voice in his head as he walked.

Christina felt only that she was the tiniest bit less vulnerable since Jack's death and her arrival in Parr's Landing, and that Jack would have really liked and trusted Billy Lightning.

CHAPTER FIFTEEN

At the moment Billy Lightning and Christina Parr went their separate ways, Elliot McKitrick was parking his cruiser behind the Parr's Landing police station in his accustomed spot. The distance between the Pear Tree and the police station was less than five minutes, but when he'd left the café, he was too angry to get back to work, so he did what he always did when he was angry—he drove.

He circled the town limits once, twice, three times. As he was about to go around a fourth time, it occurred to him that the visibility of the cruiser was making him conspicuous to anyone who happened to look up as he drove, loop after unvarying loop, along the same route. He turned the cruiser towards the town limits and drove out in the direction of Bradley Lake and the cliffs.

His town was suddenly getting far too small for his comfort. With Jeremy Parr in Toronto all these years, and the past . . . well, in the past, he'd made a good life for himself in Parr's Landing. He commanded respect. It wasn't an exciting life, but all Elliot had ever wanted to be was normal. Now, he *was* normal. And he occupied exactly the echelon he wanted to occupy, and no one challenged it.

Now, in a matter of days, the entire structure of his world seemed under attack from all sides. This mouthy, jumped-up

Indian—whom, he'd just realized, he actually hated—was chal-
lenging his authority and had actually threatened him—an
Indian had threatened *him*. Jeremy Parr was back in town trying
to stir up the past, Elliot's past. It didn't occur to Elliot to think
of it as Jeremy's past, too, because Jeremy had gotten away, leaving Elliot to do all the work of self-recreation and the rewrit-
ing of his—their—history. Even Jack Parr's girlfriend, Chris—his
wife, or widow, whatever she was—was back in town. It had been
obvious from the cold tone she'd taken with him that Jeremy had
gone home last night and cried on her shoulder about what had
happened between them at O'Toole's. Typical. So *she* knew, too.

A sudden thought occurred to Elliot. *What if she told the
Indian?*

He'd seen them talking through the window of the Pear Tree
as he drove off. What if she'd inclined her head towards the Indian
and said, "Don't worry about that cop—he's a fag. He and my
brother-in-law had a 'thing' ten years ago, and as you may have
heard, the cop never married anybody." What if she'd laughed
at the point, laughed with high, shrill insight—and what if the
Indian had joined her in her laughter at his expense, promising
to himself that the next time Elliot crossed his path, he was going
to let Elliot know *exactly* what he knew and threaten him again,
this time with the one thing that truly terrified Elliot—exposure?
His knuckles on the wheel of the cruiser were white. Elliot made
a sound somewhere between a sharp intake of breath and a soft
yelp, startling himself. For a moment, all he heard was the sound
of his own heartbeat and the blood thundering in his temples.

Elliot pulled over to the side of the road and waited until his
heartbeat slowed down and his breathing returned to normal.
He opened the driver's side door and stepped out into the cold
late-morning sunlight and took a deep breath, then another. As
he did, his vision cleared and he felt the panic recede.

The sword cut both ways, he realized. Jeremy wasn't back in
town to threaten him. Jeremy was back in town because Chris
needed him there. The Parrs didn't want another scandal. Old
lady Parr had sent Jeremy to a lunatic asylum. She'd threatened
Elliot's old man with ruin if he didn't beat a lesson into Elliot that

he'd never forget. The cuts had healed, but the feel of the whip cutting through his clothes into his flesh was one Eliot would never forget.

No, whatever else was going to happen, there would be no concerns about exposure from the Parrs, any of them. They had as much to lose as he did, scandal-wise. No way was Mrs. Parr going to let either Jeremy or Chris make any trouble for him.

The thought comforted him, and slowly Elliot grew calm again. The wind suddenly came up and the trees around him shivered,

releasing clouds of orange and red leaves against the hard blue sky. Elliot shielded his eyes against the sunlight with his fingers and watched the leaves blow away across the treetops towards Bradley Lake.

In fairness to Jeremy, there had been nothing threatening or angry in his demeanour last night at O'Toole's. On the contrary, Jeremy had shown traces of the very gentleness and vulnerability that had drawn Elliot to him in first place when they were boys, so many years ago. Last night, Elliot had tried to hurt Jeremy, to drive him away. He'd succeeded in hurting him, but Jeremy hadn't been angry at all. There had been nothing in his eyes but a terrible sadness that Elliot had tried very hard not to see.

But he had seen it, even if last night he told himself he hadn't. And at that moment, in his privacy by the side of the road, with nothing around but the reddened forest and the cliffs of Spirit Rock in the distance, he could admit it.

Perhaps if Jeremy *had* been angry, if he'd shown Elliot hatred instead of that terrible gentleness, Elliot would have been able to get it up for Donna Lemieux right away instead of failing, for the first time in his life, to get wood until he did her from behind.

He realized that the thought should disturb him, but he found himself smiling instead. To think of Jeremy and to smile felt good. The muscles of his face relaxed. He hadn't realized he'd been clenching his jaw until he unclenched it and released all the tension he'd been holding there. He felt the release of that tension spread to every part of his body. He breathed in the cold air easily and deeply. He'd give Jeremy a call this evening, or drive up to Parr

House, and talk it out. There was no reason why they shouldn't be friends, or at least on some sort of conversational terms. They were just a couple of guys who had been good friends once a long time ago—OK, maybe a bit more than friends, maybe, but it was a long time ago. Then was then and now was now.

Elliot climbed back into the car and turned the key in the ignition. He needed to get back to the station and back to work. He was a cop. There would be time for all this personal crap later.

On his way back into town, Elliot passed Donna Lemieux's plain white house on house on Hobbs Street and felt a stab of guilt. On a whim, he pulled into her driveway. He'd been an asshole to her last night as well as to Jeremy Parr. Fixing the Jeremy situation was going to take some time, but an apology, some charm, and some reassurance of her desirability would go a long way towards making things right with Donna. Elliot prided himself on being a hard-ass, but he'd never thought of himself as an asshole, and didn't plan to start now. He wished he'd brought flowers, but realized immediately what an idiotic thought that was.

Elliot pulled into her driveway and got out. Instinctively he looked both ways to see if anyone had seen him. A police car parked in someone's driveway was a universally acknowledged symbol of trouble in the neighbourhood and the last thing he wanted to do was compound last night's romantic disaster by embarrassing Donna, making her a spectacle to her neighbours. But there was no one in the street, and no one was peering at him from behind the curtains, at least so far as he could tell.

He knocked on her door and waited. Then, receiving no answer, he knocked again, more loudly. He glanced over his shoulder to where her car sat in the driveway. She'd left his place at—what, three-thirty in the morning? Four? She'd obviously driven home in one piece because the car was right there. Had she gone out already? Not likely. Not without the car. He knocked again, and peered in through her front window. The living room beyond the window was dim. There was no movement at all.

She's sleeping, Elliot thought practically. *She came over to my house after a night shift and probably didn't get back here till four a.m. And she was pissed. She's probably sleeping, and the last thing I want to do is wake her up and have her answer the door with her hair all messy and her face puffed up and give me shit for waking her up, on top of everything else.*

Elliot walked back to the cruiser. He glanced back over his shoulder at the silent white house with the dark windows. A thought came and went so quickly that he barely registered it as a thought before dismissing it: the thought that the house felt empty to him. No, not just empty— absent of life.

It was an irrational thought—emotional, illogical, very unlike Elliot the police officer, therefore, in his mind, very unlike Elliot, period. His rational, logical thought, on the other hand, was that Donna Lemieux was inside, sleeping like the dead, after a rough night for which he was at least partly to blame. That was reality. He would drive out to O'Toole's tonight and make amends. Maybe even bring flowers. Perhaps flowers would seem like a better idea once the sun had gone down.

Elliot sighed again, thinking in abstract terms that having a conscience was a burden he hadn't had to consider until very recently, and one he could happily do without.

He got back into the cruiser and drove to the station as quickly as he could, realizing that nearly two hours had passed since his encounter with Christina Parr and Billy Lightning, and he was going to have to think on his feet if he was going to come up with a plausible excuse for Sergeant Thomson as to where the hell he'd been all morning.

CHAPTER SIXTEEN

Sergeant Thomson was sitting at his desk, talking on the telephone, when Elliot walked through the door of the Parr's Landing police station. He looked up irritably and motioned with his hand for Elliot to sit down. The gesture pushed Thomson's coffee cup perilously close to the edge of the desk. Elliot lunged forward and grabbed the coffee cup just before it pitched over the edge of the desk. Pleased with himself for this act of minor heroism, he grinned and mimed relief. Elliot whispered, "Whew!" but Thomson was jotting down notes on a pad of paper and didn't even look up.

"You say the yard was secure? Right, of course. Well, you know how some dogs are. What kind did you say he was? *She,* sorry. A Lab? Well, was she in heat? Spayed. OK, I see. Well, maybe . . . no, I don't know. But we'll definitely keep an eye out. Of course. No, I wouldn't worry. Yes, we're going out a bit later. We'll do a loop of the town and take a look. Yes, I promise. Of course. Yes, it's hard. Had one myself when I was a boy. Yes, they do, don't they? All right Mrs. Miller. Thanks. We'll let you know. All right. Bye, now." Then, to Elliot: "Where the hell have you been? The phone has been ringing off the hook. What the hell happened last night? Was it a full moon?"

"Sorry, Sergeant," Elliot lied, thinking fast on his feet. "Someone thought they heard guns up at the lake. I thought, hunters. Didn't see anything."

Thomson was brusque. "Never mind, I don't care. OK, aside from the call I just took from some woman about her son's lost dog, I also had a call from the mother of that waitress from O'Toole's—Donna something. Donna Lemieux."

Elliot froze. "What about Donna Lemieux? What happened to her?"

"What happened? Nothing, probably. Her mother went to her house this morning and she wasn't there. I told her—nicely—that it's not suspicious for someone not to be at home during the day. Her car was in the driveway, too, according to her mother, so she probably went out with friends or something. Her mother said she had 'a feeling about it' and wanted us to know. Mothers, Jesus."

"We all have them," Elliot said automatically, treading water. "Did she say anything else?"

"Just that she went into her daughter's house and said it didn't look like she'd slept there last night."

"But the car . . ."

"That's what I told her. The car is in the driveway. All we can do is wait and see what develops. I'm sure it'll be nothing. It's too early to raise the panic alarm at this point. Besides, we have other things to think about. Early this morning I was talking with my contact at the RCMP in Toronto. Surprise, surprise—Dr. Lightning's story about his father's murder and the fact that he thinks it was committed by that student of his father's—the crazy one, Weal—just got a bit more complicated."

"Oh, yeah? How so, Sergeant?" Elliot hoped that the forced neutrality of his tone had effectively camouflaged his relief at the fact that they had moved on, away from the minefield topic of the possible disappearance of Donna Lemieux.

"According to the RCMP, Richard Weal is dead," Thomson said. "Has been for a bit less than a year now."

"Dead?"

"Dead as a damn doornail," Thomson said. To Elliot, he sounded more satisfied than bemused. Maybe the Indian had pissed him off, too, more than Elliot had realized. "Car-over-the-cliff crash, apparently. Suicide. In January of this year. A car went off the Scarborough Bluffs in Toronto. They found a pile of clothing and Weal's identification. Neat little folded pile, just like a crazy person would do on a bloody cold winter night. He must have gotten into the car naked and just driven it over the edge, right onto the beach. Metro Police in Toronto said the body inside the wreck was pretty burned up, but the I.D. was right there on top of the pile of clothes. Old I.D.," he added. "From the time when he was locked up in the loony bin, years ago. But it was definitely him. Metro said it was an open-and-shut case, once they contacted the nuthatch where he'd been locked up. His doctors said they weren't surprised."

Elliot said, "So where does this leave the Indian's story?"

"Well," Thomson said. "I'm thinking we can pretty much put the notion of Richard Weal running around committing murders in Gyles Point and roaming around Parr's Landing to rest. Whoever did that to that old man on the Point, it wasn't Richard Weal."

Elliot paused for a moment. "Sarge?" he said.

"What?"

"Sarge, the other day I was out at Bradley Lake looking around."

"So?"

"So," he said. "I think I saw something."

"You *think* you saw something? You *think* you saw something, or you *saw* something?"

"No, I did see something," Elliot said firmly. "Up by the cliffs. It was a man, I think. Prowling up on the ledges. I thought it was a kid, or some hikers or something. I didn't really think anything of it at the time." *Not strictly true,* Elliot admitted to himself. *It spooked me something fierce.* "I'm just wondering if . . ."

"If what?" Thomson said impatiently. "Come on, McKitrick, get to the point."

"Well, in light of this new development, my question is, why is the Indian in Parr's Landing, and isn't it kind of a coincidence that he arrives here with some story about a guy who just so happens to be dead, right around the time that somebody commits a murder a few miles from here?"

"Still nothing solid connecting Billy Lightning to what happened at Gyles Point," Thomson said. "And the assumption is that there was a murder, but we can't rule it a murder since there's no body," Thomson said. "The dead man wasn't connected with either Lightning, his father, or Weal—Weal, who we now know to be deceased. As far as the law is concerned, Billy Lightning may be an odd duck, but he's not a criminal. Not yet, anyway."

"Something doesn't add up here," Elliot said stubbornly. "I just feel it. I feel it in my bones that there's something wrong here."

"There could be something wrong, but until there's some evidence, there isn't anything I can do. Look, Elliot," Thomson warned. "I know you don't like Dr. Lightning, but I don't want you jumping any guns, or making any accusations you can't back up that are going to come back and bite you—or me—in the ass. The man's a professor; he's not just some random vagrant. Be careful."

"But—"

"If you find something solid, we can move on it," Thomson said with finality. "Until then, hands off. I don't want any problems."

Elliot remembered Lightning's threat to him that very morning and kept his mouth shut.

Thomson's own instincts, honed over many more years of police work than Elliot's, signalled to him that there was something going on, not with Billy Lightning, but with Elliot himself. He looked like he hadn't slept in a couple of days, and there was a sullenness and a tension to the younger man that was entirely alien to his character as Thomson knew it. Disappearing for two hours under some bullshit pretext of looking for illegal hunters wasn't like Elliot McKitrick at all. He wasn't dating anyone in particular, as far as Thomson knew, which more or less ruled out woman trouble. But then again, who knew? Something was very clearly bothering the younger man.

Thomson said, "McKitrick, is everything all right?"

"What do you mean, Sarge?"

"Just what I said. Is everything all right?"

Elliot looked at him neutrally. "Yeah, everything is fine, Sarge, why?"

"You seem like you have something on your mind," Thomson replied. "Anything you want to talk about? Anything bothering you?"

"No, Sarge," Elliot said. "Just thinking about that murder in Gyles Point. And about what you just told me, about that crazy guy killing himself in the car in Toronto."

Thomson sighed. "OK, McKitrick." Clearly whatever was bothering him, Elliot would be keeping it to himself for the moment, which was fine. But the next time he disappeared for two hours, Thomson was going to hand him his head. Steering the conversation back to the business at hand, he said, "Have you been back up to the cliffs where you saw . . . well, whatever you saw? Did you check it out?"

"No, Sarge," Elliot replied. "I haven't. No reason to, I guess."

"Well, now you have a reason. Why don't you drive up there and take a look around? Check it out. Just to rule everything out. It's probably nothing, but it never hurts to be sure."

"No, sir. When do you want me to go?"

Thomson sighed again. As irritated as he had been by Elliot being AWOL this morning for two hours, the tension was coming off the younger man in waves, and it was irritating as hell. Maybe a hike up to Spirit Rock would help him realign his priorities, or at the very least adjust his attitude a bit. The murder at Gyles Point wasn't officially Thomson's headache—yet—so he could afford to focus on the stack of paperwork that had been building up on his desk.

"No time like the present, McKitrick. Shouldn't take you more than an hour or so, I should think. Just check it out." He briefly considered joining Elliot, thinking that it had been a while since he'd done that particular hike on a fall morning, before realizing that the prospect of traipsing through the bush this morning on what was likely a make-work mission was entirely without appeal. And it was getting colder outside, too. He was starting to feel the coming winter in his joints, though Thomson wouldn't have confessed to that under torture. "This time," he added pointedly. "Keep in touch."

"Yes, sir, will do." Elliot said.

To Thomson, he sounded relieved. Whatever the kid was going through—girls, or whatever—Thomson hoped he'd get it out of his system soon, because it would become a pain in the ass very quickly if he didn't.

Still, as he watched Elliot leave, he was barely aware that, as the father of two daughters and no sons, he was far more fond of the kid than he'd ever admit, even to himself.

Well before the lunch bell rang, Finn had made his decision. He knew that there was an excellent chance that he'd catch holy hell, and very likely get suspended, but he didn't care. Sadie was lost and no classroom could hold him this afternoon.

He'd barely heard anything that his teacher, Mrs. Marshall, had said all morning, though he'd kept a bright, pleasantly neutral expression on his face. Only his eyes, red from crying, would have given any indication that there was something wrong. Since he'd deftly avoided one-on-one contact with anyone else in his class (and because Mrs. Marshall tended not to look too hard at students unless she had to) no one had any idea that he was teetering on the verge of his own personal hell.

He needed to find his dog, and he needed to find her before something terrible happened to her. There was no one in his life he loved more than Sadie—not even his parents. No one. Sadie was his baby. She was his world.

When he'd woken his parents that morning, his father was initially irritated—hardly unusual for his father in the morning, especially before he'd had his coffee and locked himself in the upstairs bathroom with the newspaper—but that irritation had quickly turned to a level of concern that stunned and comforted Finn. His father had even driven around the neighbourhood looking for Sadie. Finn had waited by the picture window in the living room for any sign of his father's car, praying that he'd see Sadie, grinning foolishly in the back seat when he came back. When his father had returned alone, looking frustrated, Finn had burst into fresh tears.

His mother was almost as frantic as Finn, calling the neighbours on either side to see if, by some miracle, Sadie had wandered into their yards. But even as she did, in between calls, his mother kept muttering,

"There's no *way* she could have gotten out of that yard. No way *at all.*"

"Do you think she . . . do you think some sort of animal might have . . ." Finn couldn't bring himself to finish the thought.

"Don't be silly, Finnegan," his mother said, dialling the next number in her book. "Sadie is too big for an owl or a hawk to have carried her off. And any other animal would have had to get in—and out—with her. She probably found some way to jump the fence."

"There was a lot of barking last night," Finn said hopefully. "Maybe she wanted to join in with the other dogs?"

"Was there? I slept right through . . . Laura?" his mother said brightly. "Hi, it's Anne Miller. Good morning! Yes, fine, thank you! Listen, Laura, I'm sorry to bother you, but Sadie's missing. Yes, I know. I don't know. Would you mind taking a look in your back yard and see if she's there?"

His mother looked up at the ceiling, tapping her fingers along the counter by the wall as she waited for Mrs. Smythe to come back on the line. The finger tapping was something Finn knew she did when she was more upset about something then she wanted to let on. When she spoke again, Finn heard the disappointment in her voice and his heart sank. "No? Isn't that strange. No, we have no idea. Thanks for looking, though, Laura. Oh, would you? That would be so nice. Yes, I hope she turns up, too. Finn is a little upset. All right, give my best to Al. Yes, goodbye, Laura."

"Mom," Finn said. His bottom lip had begun to quiver. "I want to stay home from school today. I want to look for Sadie."

"Finn, there's nothing you can do. Go get dressed for school. You can look for her when you get home. I'll call around. I'll even call the police station and let them know to keep an eye out for her."

"Mom, I don't *want* to go to school! I want to stay home and look for my *dog!*"

"Finn, please." His mother sighed. "I know you're upset, but you being upset isn't going to bring Sadie home any sooner. It'll all be fine, you'll see. I'm sure she hasn't gone far. We'll find her. I'll take you out in the car after school and we'll look together."

Finn wanted to shout that his mother didn't care about Sadie, and if she cared, she'd let him stay home, but he knew that wasn't true. She did care. He also knew that he was already as upset as he could stand to be, and that a fight with his mother over whether or not he could stay home was a fight he was bound to lose.

He'd gotten dressed and left for school, Sadie's red rubber ball tucked into the pocket of his jacket, thinking he could keep it together. By noon, he realized he wasn't going to be able to do it, because Sadie was all he could think of.

All morning he'd mentally explored the horror show of possibilities of what might have happened to Sadie—some more realistic than others, but all equally awful.

He was haunted by one particular image—Sadie wandering, injured, lost in the cliff area around Bradley Lake, perhaps with a broken leg, or worse. Somehow the mechanics of how this might have occurred was less important than the absolute *vividness* of the image.

He could see her, as though he were gazing into the Wicked Witch of the West's crystal ball in *The Wizard of Oz,* a movie his mother had taken him to in Sault Ste. Marie when he'd been eight, and which had both terrified and thrilled him. One particular scene in the film returned to him now: the scene in the witch's castle, where Dorothy sees Auntie Em in the crystal ball, plaintively crying out her name, unable to find her. At the time the scene had spoken to him about the terror of loss, of separation from his mother, his home, and everything safe. But now it just filled him with dread.

He pictured Sadie in the crystal ball instead of Auntie Em— lost, hurt, terrified, and looking for Finn to protect her and bring her home. The scene repeated itself in his mind all morning at school until the possibility of sitting in his seat and listening to Mrs. Marshall drone on about the geography of countries he knew he'd never visit made him want to scream.

When the lunch bell rang, he waited till no one was looking, then climbed the chain-link fence behind the schoolyard and ran like hell along the streets behind the school, heading for Bradley Lake. He'd considered meeting Morgan in their usual spot and telling her that he wouldn't be able to stay and eat lunch with her today because Sadie was lost and he was going to go look for her, but he realized he didn't even want to waste the extra ten minutes it would take him to detour to Matthew Browning.

In truth, Finn was wracked with guilt over his selfishness last night in leaving Sadie out in the yard to fend for herself against whatever had taken her away, just so he could get back to his horny dream about Morgan naked in the lake.

For a treacherous fraction of a second, he considered blaming Morgan for Sadie's disappearance, then realized it was his dream, not hers. She'd had no part in it. If there was any blame for abandoning Sadie—and that was what he was now convinced he had done—the blame was Finn's alone, and he hated himself for it.

Elliot heard the boy calling for his dog before he saw the flash of his red jacket moving through the yellow leaves.

He had spent the last hour scouring the ledge area where he thought he'd seen the crouching figure the previous day, but there was nothing at all—none of the usual indicators of passage: no cigarette butts, no obvious footprints, no noticeable disturbances of the foliage and undergrowth. He hadn't really expected to find them, but he still hoped there would be something there he could tie to the Indian, even tangentially. Nothing would have pleased Elliot more than to nail that smug bastard in such a way that none of his fancy academic credentials and smooth talking would help him out.

Elliot wasn't a stupid man, nor was he unaware of the fact that his feelings about Billy Lightning had as much to do with what he represented—like Jeremy, a threat to the established social order of the world with which he'd compacted—as they did with the Indian's snooty way of talking to him, as though the fact that he was a university professor made him anything more than an Indian or, more to the point, anything more than Elliot himself.

Still, even separating all of those variables from the mix, it still seemed a noteworthy coincidence that Billy Lightning should just show up in Parr's Landing the day after what had happened in Gyles Point, and be talking about murders and crazy people (as it turned out, dead crazy people) and local legends.

And now, it appeared that what he'd seen had been a trick of the light, after all, or maybe a hiker. Or a kid, like this one who was calling *Sadie! Sadie!* in a high-pitched, ruptured voice as though he were being broken on the rack.

Elliot gauged that the kid was about 200 yards directly above him, close to the highest accessible point of the cliffs around the lake. It was a dangerous place for a kid to wander for any reason, and not just because of the ever-present danger of accidentally falling through some grown over mineshaft entrance, but because of the time of day—especially now, at this time of the year when the dusk came so much earlier.

Elliot turned towards the sound of the kid's voice and walked towards it. He called out, "Hey, kid! Stay where you are—I'm coming for you. I'm a police officer. Don't move. It's dangerous up there. Let's get you down."

He still couldn't see the kid, but he'd stopped calling for his dog. Elliot figured that he might have startled him, so he called out again, "It's OK, kid. Just hold on. I'll be there in a minute."

Silence answered him. A sharp arrow of late-season Canada geese streaked southward across the sky. The light was burnishing as the late afternoon slouched towards evening. Elliot rounded a sharp turn on the hill and, with three wide steps, he reached the plateau. He vaguely recognized the kid standing there from one of his annual Elmer the Safety Elephant police visits to the primary school, but couldn't think of his name—Frankie? Fenny? The kid's face was pale and he'd obviously been crying. His red windbreaker was muddy and there were pine needles in his hair.

"Hey, kid, you all right?" Elliot said in his best Officer Friendly voice. "What are you doing up here all by yourself?"

But the kid wasn't looking at Elliot. He was staring into the opening of a filthy hockey bag—a heavy one, too, judging by the way he was holding it. Even from six feet away, Elliot caught a whiff of something rotten coming from inside it. At the same moment, the kid seemed to smell it, too, and he dropped the bag. It landed on the ground, making a jangling metallic sound as it struck the earth.

The boy took two steps back, away from the bag. He pointed at it and said, "That's not mine." He wiped his hands frantically on the legs of his jeans as though he were trying to scrub them clean.

"Whose is it?" Elliot's question was automatic, reflexive. When the kid didn't answer, but instead kept wiping his hands, Elliot walked over to the bag, knelt down, and pulled open the flaps.

At first he didn't know what he was looking at—metal, paper, grease. No, more than just metal. Knives, some hammers. The blades were stained, and there were streaks of red on the T-shirt inside. The stench was awful—old blood, obviously, and something like putrescent raw chicken skin, but also shit and sweat. He moved the bag away from his face and held his breath. When he was sure he wasn't going to throw up, he took a deep breath of fresh air.

First and foremost in Elliot's mind was that this was very likely connected to the murder in Gyles Point. He knelt down and pulled his hand up inside his sleeve, forming a cloth barrier against his hand. It wasn't gloves, but it was better than touching the bloody knives and catching God-knew-what disease from the stinking T-shirt. He nudged aside the metal and saw that there was a bound typescript underneath. The title page was smeared with blood and dirt, but he was able to read part of it:

Being the Last True Testament and Relation of Father

The rest of the text was unintelligible. The paper was warped from exposure to water, the ink smeared and bedaubed with rain and mud. It was a hefty manuscript. He judged there were at least 70 double-spaced typed pages in all. Awkwardly, he nudged the papers with his cloth-covered knuckles, but it was futile. To see more, he was going to have to turn the pages with his fingers, and he wasn't going to do that without gloves. At the very least, Thomson would kill him for messing up evidence with his own fingerprints.

Turning his attention to the boy, he said, "What's your name, kid?"

"Finn Miller," the boy replied. "Am I in trouble?"

"No, you're not in any trouble," Elliot said in a reassuring voice. "What are you doing up here? Shouldn't you still be in school?"

Finn's eyes brimmed. "I was looking for my duh-duh-dog," he said. His eyes spilled over. "My dog is lost. She's been lost since last night."

"Don't cry, Finn," Elliot said. "I'm sure your dog is all right. What's her name?"

"Sadie," he replied. Elliot saw that Finn was struggling to regain his composure. He admired the kid for that. "Her name is Sadie."

"Is this where she usually likes to play?" he asked. He was consciously easing the conversation so he could ask about the bag without spooking the kid.

"We were up here a few days ago," Finn said, glancing around. "Sadie was scared by something up here."

"Scared? Scared by what?"

"I don't know," Finn said. "By something. She was really upset. I thought maybe she came back here to . . . I don't know, to check it out or something."

"Is this where you found the bag?" Elliot said calmly. "Right here? Or did you move it?"

Finn pointed to a clump of rocks and overgrowth a few feet away. "There," he said. "I found it there."

Elliot walked over to the spot and nudged aside some of the branches and broken tree limbs with the toe of his boot. It looked like a crack in the rocks, about four and a half feet long, maybe six inches across. It could be the opening to some sort of animal's burrow, perhaps, or a snake hole. Nothing out of the ordinary, certainly not somewhere a man could hide. And yet, as he glanced around again, he knew that somewhere the owner of this bag was very likely hiding. For the first time in two days, he reached down to his holster and touched the gun, just to feel its reassuring solidity against his hip.

"Finn," Elliot said. "I think you'd better come with me. We can stop off at your house and see your Mom and Dad, and they can come to the police station with us. Is that OK with you?"

"What's in the bag? I saw knives and stuff. It sure stinks, too."

"Yeah," Elliot said casually. "Knives and stuff. Probably left behind by a hunter. But we have to make sure it's all OK and that nobody got hurt up here. Gave you a scare, did it?" Elliot tried to chuckle, but he realized it sounded fake and this kid wasn't stupid. Elliot knew he would see right through it.

"I'm not scared by a stupid hockey bag full of knives," Finn said. "I'm scared about not knowing where my dog is."

"You said I wasn't in trouble," Finn continued. "Right? You *said*."

"Right," Elliot said soothingly. "You're not in trouble. It just looks like you might have found something important, and my sergeant would probably like to hear how you found it."

"But what about Sadie?" Finn said urgently. "I can't leave. I have to look for my dog. It's getting dark. I can't leave her out here." He looked around wildly. For a moment Elliot thought he was going to bolt back off into the woods.

"I'll tell you what, Finn," Elliot said, reaching out and putting his hand on Finn's shoulder. "After we go to the police station and you talk to the sergeant, I'll drive you home, then I'll take a drive around and look for Sadie myself. I'll even come back here— well, maybe not all the way up here, since you've already looked, but around the lake. I'll see what I can find. I bet she's home by tomorrow, one way or another. But we really have to get to the police station, just in case what you found is really important."

"Promise?" Finn looked doubtful. "You promise you'll come back and look for her?"

"I promise," Elliot said. "Now let's get back down to the car. Have you ever been in police car before? It's kinda fun."

Finn didn't answer. Instead, he pushed past Elliot and started down the path from the cliff towards the lake without looking back.

When the police cruiser pulled into the driveway, the first thing Anne Miller thought was, *They found Sadie!* Finn would be so relieved. That is, he'd be relieved after he was told he'd been grounded for a month. Mrs. Brocklehurst, the school secretary, had called her that afternoon to ask if Finn had her permission to leave school.

Anne had told Mrs. Brocklehurst that Finn had just lost his dog and was very upset. No, he didn't have her permission, Anne explained, but she'd appreciate it if the school would look the other way just this one time. She'd speak to Finnegan when he got home and she personally guaranteed he'd be in school tomorrow.

Mrs. Brocklehurst, who had been the primary school secretary for twenty years, loved animals, said it would be fine, and she hoped Finnegan found Sadie soon, too. She'd lost a collie named Mingus when she was a little girl and it just about broke her heart. "I think a cougar got him," she said sadly. "I have nightmares about it even today."

Anne hadn't even considered cougars, or jackals, or anything of the kind, and her heart sank. But she'd thanked Mrs. Brocklehurst and hung up the phone. Then she went to the kitchen and fixed herself a stiff rum and coke, even though she never drank during the day.

When she saw Finn in the back seat of the police cruiser, her hand flew to her chest and she gasped in shock. She opened the front door and said, "Finn, what happened? Are you all right?" The driver's side door opened, and the policeman stepped out. Anne recognized him, of course.

"Constable McKitrick, what's going on ? What's my son doing in a police car?"

"It's nothing serious, Mrs. Miller," Elliot said politely. "Finn here was up by Bradley Lake looking for Sadie. I found him and brought him home. That's all."

"Well, that's a relief," Anne replied. To her son, she said, "Finn, the school called, young man. You left early today. You and I are going to have a talk once your father gets home from the mill. Go on up to your room."

"Actually, Mrs. Miller, Finn found something up on the slope near Spirit Rock, and we'd really appreciate it if you and he could come down to the police station and have a talk with Sergeant Thomson and I about how that happened."

"I'm sorry, I'm confused—he 'found something'?" Anne said. "What did he find? And what does that have to do with him coming down to the police station? I thought this was about him playing hookey. Or that you'd found Sadie. That's his dog. I called the station about her earlier today."

"No, ma'am," Elliot said. "No sign of Sadie yet, but I'm sure she'll turn up. In the meantime, I'm sure it's nothing to be concerned about, Mrs. Miller, but there was an . . . incident up at Gyles Point recently, and we just want to make sure that what Finn found isn't connected in any way to that incident."

"What on earth did he find? Finn? What did you find?"

"It was a bag of *knives*, Mom," Finn said. He wrinkled his nose. "They're all bloody and stuff, and they *stink*."

"Oh my God," Anne said, gasping. "And you think they're . . ."

"We don't know anything yet, Mrs. Miller," Elliot said. "But if you and Finn would come down to the police station, we might be able to put this together and make some sense of it. Then," he added winningly, winking at Finn, "we can get back to looking for Sadie."

Anne hesitated. She looked at Finn standing awkwardly beside the police car. His hair was askew and his clothes were filthy. The emotional fracture of his separation from Sadie seemed to have actually bent Finn's posture, and there was something *broken* in his demeanour that she'd never seen before. The last thing she wanted to do was go down to the police station right now to discuss Finn's gruesome discovery just before dinnertime—it was probably nothing but hunters' debris anyway. At the same time, she realized that if they cooperated now, she'd have the attention of the Parr's Landing constabulary, which might chivvy them on when it came to looking for Sadie.

"I'll just call my husband and let him know where we'll be," Anne said. "That way he can meet us there. I'd really prefer if my husband was present if you're going to question Finnegan."

"Would it be all right if we called your husband from the station, Mrs. Miller?" Elliot countered. "This is sort of important, and I'd rather not waste your time any more than we have to. And we're not going to 'question' Finnegan, we're just going to ask him some things and take a statement. There's nothing to worry about."

Anne looked from Elliot to Finn, then back to Elliot. "All right, if it's that important. Is it?"

"It is, ma'am," Elliot said firmly. "It is. I'd appreciate it."

Without another word, Anne went into the house and took her purse off the hall table and took her coat out of the closet. When she came back out, Finn was already in the back seat of the car, waiting for her, and Elliot was holding the passenger-side door open.

As they drove through town towards the police station, Anne realized she'd never been inside a police car in her life and, fancifully, that Parr's Landing looked different through its windows. The plain houses and shops they passed—houses and shops she'd passed her whole life— suddenly seemed alive with the possibilities of secret lives occurring behind their closed doors. *This must be the way policemen see the town,* she thought. She supposed that was what the police were for—to make sure that the secret lives of other people remained, if not pure, then at least *contained.*

The more practical part of her hoped against hope that none of her neighbours would see her and Finn in the police car and start gossiping.

Anne glanced at Finn, who was staring out his window. He was lost in his own thoughts—doubtless thoughts about Sadie. Anne was also grieving for Sadie's disappearance, and worried, but she knew better than to break down in front of Finn.

She reached over and gently squeezed his hand.

When Finn didn't respond, Anne held his hand until he extricated it from hers. Finn did this gently, as though to reassure his mother that it wasn't *her* hand, per se, that he found unbearable, but rather that any human contact at all right now was a sorry substitute for the feeling of Sadie's head under his chin, the soft black fur tickling his neck as he held her body close to his and inhaled her warm dog scent, and felt her heartbeat.

Later, at the station, while Anne tried unsuccessfully to reach her husband on the telephone, Finn told the police everything he could think of about how he'd found the bag up by Spirit Rock. The two cops listened closely, but gave no indication one way other another what they were thinking.

The older one—Sergeant Thomson—put on plastic gloves and looked through the bag. He'd kept his back turned to Finn and his mother while he did so, and all they heard was the clink of metal on metal, and then the sound of the hockey bag being zipped closed.

When he turned around again, Thomson asked Finn a series of questions that Finn answered as best he could while the younger one—McKitrick—took notes.

No, Finn said, he couldn't think of anything else. No, he hadn't seen anyone. No, he hadn't been alerted by any noise—he'd only gone up that far because of Sadie's terror of it when they'd walked there that morning a few days ago. He thought maybe she'd gone back up there. He didn't know why he thought that—it was just a possibility.

"That's what dogs are like sometimes," he'd said with a shrug. "I thought maybe I'd find her there. I hoped I would." He paused, his voice thickening. "I didn't."

"I think that's all, Finn," Thomson said. "I think we've pretty well covered everything we need to know. Mrs. Miller, thank you so much for coming in with Finn. Constable McKitrick will drive you home now."

"You'll look for Sadie?" Finn said hopefully. He turned to Elliot and said, "You said you would, remember? You promised."

"I will, Finn," Elliot said. He glanced uneasily at Thomson. "I promise."

"Mrs. Miller, Finn?" Thomson said. "If you don't mind, I'd appreciate it if you didn't talk about this for a bit. Don't tell your neighbours or—especially you, Finn—your friends. Let's consider this our secret for a while, until we figure out what's going on. It wouldn't do for rumours to be circulating about something that may well be . . . well, nothing."

"*May* well be?" Anne demanded. "It's a hunter's bag, isn't it? You're not suggesting it might be something else? You don't think that someone was . . . well, that people were hurt, do you?"

"Very likely it's a hunter's bag, Mrs. Miller," he replied calmly.

"But you know how these stories grow in small towns. Like I said, I'd appreciate it if you folks would just keep it under your hat for a little bit. I will personally call you when we know for sure what's going on."

After Elliot had left to drive Finn and Anne home, Thomson stared thoughtfully at the hockey bag for a long moment. Then he put the plastic gloves back on and reexamined the contents. The knives and the hammer had obviously been used to achieve a violent end. If it hadn't been for the presence of the hammers, he might have considered the possibility that they'd belonged to a hunter, and that the blood was animal's blood, not human blood. There was hair on the head of the hammer and thin matted clumps of it where the base of the knife blade met the handle.

Thomson lifted the bound typescript from the bottom of the bag and read the first few pages. It was obviously the document that Billy Lightning had told them about, Professor Phenius Osborne's translation from the original French that he claimed had been stolen from his father's desk by Richard Weal after Weal had murdered him. Except it couldn't be Richard Weal, since Weal had apparently committed suicide months before the murder, according to the Toronto police.

Which left Billy Lightning as the only link between the bag and its contents and—very likely—the recent events in Gyles Point.

Whatever else was true, the fact that the bag had been found at Spirit Rock meant that its owner had to be in the vicinity. Thomson sighed— his gut told him that Billy Lightning was no murderer, and he tended to trust his gut in cases like this. But facts were facts, and facts trumped gut feelings when it came to him doing his job.

He considered calling Bill Lefferts, the senior officer over at the Gyles Point detachment, to let him know what they'd found, but he told himself that the situation was still unfolding and he had more questions that needed answering before bringing anyone else into the mix.

Thomson reminded himself to commend McKitrick on

having found the bag—or, if not actually having found it, at least having identified and brought it in. He had been checking out the area based on something he'd seen, so if there was to be any credit given, it was rightfully Elliot's.

As soon as Elliot was back from the Miller house, they'd take another run out to the Gold Nugget to talk to Billy Lightning. Thomson hoped that the professor would be cooperative, because under the circumstances, if he wasn't, it wasn't going to go well for any of them, least of all for Billy Lightning.

CHAPTER SEVENTEEN

Night falls swiftly in Parr's Landing in late October. The sunlight is there, then it's gone.

It's not that night comes unannounced, but rather that the announcements themselves manifest in a rapid sequence of shifting light and temperature fluctuations that might be missed by someone not born and bred in the north country. By late afternoon, the sky is already darkening to orange and pale violet, with bands of dark blue and black hunkering down behind the line of trees and cliffs ringing Bradley Lake and Spirit Rock, and the biting, hyperborean wind blowing in off Lake Superior chills everything in its path.

At night, Parr's Landing breathes in its population and doesn't exhale them until the morning.

Morgan Parr, who was used to Toronto's perpetual neon twilight, found the sudden darkness both intimidating and oddly enchanting.

She'd waited for Finn at lunch, and was surprised by how much she missed him when he didn't show up. After school was over, she walked from Matthew Browning over to the primary school in the hopes of finding Finn and walking home with him, but he wasn't among the crowd of kids milling about after the bell.

Disappointed, she walked home alone, aware of the change in the light even at four-thirty in the afternoon.

At Parr House, she found the impossibly thin Parr's Landing phone book in a drawer of the marquetry cabinet in the foyer and looked up Finn's phone number. There was only one "Miller" in the book, an "H" on Childs Drive. She copied down the address on the small yellow pad of paper by the telephone and pocketed it, then went upstairs to do some homework. By dinnertime, it was nearly full dark.

As she descended the staircase from the upper hallway, Morgan noted that even with the night pressing against the other side, the baronial stained glass windows in the foyer seemed to catch and hold whatever light existed, seeming to burn with a singular lambency all their own, even at night. At Parr House, it seemed to Morgan, even the encroaching darkness was subject to the whims of Adeline Parr.

For once, dinner around the long dining table was more or less civil. Adeline seemed sanguine, as though her excoriation of her son and daughter-in-law the previous night had fed some ravenous private hunger, filling her up and leaving her full and bloated. She asked perfunctory questions of Morgan, easy-to-answer questions about school and how she liked the town. Morgan noticed that Adeline didn't raise the topic of Finnegan Miller, nor did she ask if Morgan had met any new friends. Morgan doubted this was accidental, but far from being disappointed by her grandmother's lack of curiosity about her social life, Morgan was relieved by it. It meant at least one fight was not going to break out again over dinner.

For his part, Jeremy seemed entirely lost in his thoughts. Judging by his face, Morgan guessed they weren't very happy thoughts. Morgan worried about him. She wasn't sure what exactly had happened to Jeremy growing up here—the specifics had never been discussed with her, nor did she have any indication that questions about his past at Parr House would be welcomed by her uncle— but she sensed that they had not been easy years.

Her mother, on the other hand, seemed to be in a genuinely good mood for the first time in weeks, certainly since they'd arrived in town. Christina smiled encouragingly at her daughter as she answered Adeline's questions about her day, adding a few comments of her own—comments that Adeline, for once, neither disputed nor mocked. Morgan dared to hope that the evening might well pass without any sort of incident, but it was early yet.

"I met someone very interesting today," Christina said brightly to Jeremy. "At the Pear Tree. A professor, from Michigan."

"A professor? Really?" Jeremy brightened. "In Parr's Landing? What on earth was he doing here?"

"He didn't say, really," Christina said thoughtfully. "He mentioned something about his father passing away. His father worked here some years ago. He's Native," she added. "He knew all about the Landing and the Wendigo legend. It was fascinating."

"An *Indian*?" Adeline said. "An Indian *professor*?" Her mocking laughter rang out from the head of the table. "Christina, you're so gullible. A man could tell you anything and you'd believe it, wouldn't you. And you met this . . . 'professor' at the café in town, did you? Why were you speaking to strange men in cafés, Christina? I should think you'd know better than that, considering."

"What was his name?" Jeremy asked, desperate to keep the conversation between his mother and his sister-in-law from going in the direction it was most certainly headed. "Did he say where he taught?"

Christina smiled gratefully at Jeremy. Before Adeline could say anything else, she said, "He said his name is William Lightning. He teaches at Grantham University. It's somewhere in Michigan. I think he told me where, but I don't remember."

Both Christina and Jeremy expected another sharp rebuke from Adeline—were braced for it, in fact. When she said nothing, they looked to the head of the table. The colour had drained from Adeline's face.

"Mother," Jeremy said. "Are you all right? What's wrong?"

"Nothing, Jeremy," Adeline said, her voice was faint. She fumbled for her water glass, and then took a few sips before shakily putting it back down. "Christina, what did you say his name was?"

Christina looked quizzically at Jeremy who returned her look blankly, as if to say, *I have no idea.* "His name is William Lightning. Why?"

"You said his father passed away, did you?" Her studied casualness seemed entirely at odds with her pallor. "Did he mention what his father's . . . what he taught?"

"I think he said his father was an anthropologist, too. His name was something Osborne. He was part of some archaeological excavation here in the fifties. As I said, Billy—Dr. Lightning— said his father just died. Why, did you know him?"

"I believe we may have met when he was here in 1952 for his dig," Adeline said. Still deathly pale, Adeline seemed to have regained some of her composure, though her voice sounded unusually brittle, even robotic.

Adeline placed her napkin on the table and pushed her chair away. "If you'll excuse me, I have some correspondence to attend to this evening. Please don't dawdle over dinner in my absence. It's not helpful to Beatrice when you make extra work for her by tarrying."

Jeremy sighed. "For that matter, we wouldn't want to risk enjoying Beatrice's cooking by 'tarrying,' much less endanger ourselves by digesting it properly, Mother."

Instead of lashing back as was her usual wont, Adeline got up from the table without a word and walked out of the dining room. She looked straight ahead. They heard the sound of her high heels on the marble foyer and the sound of the door to Adeline's study being shut. Then, silence.

"What the hell was that?" Jeremy asked in complete mystification. "What just happened? What did you say to her?"

"I have no idea," Christina said, equally baffled. "Did I say something that offended her? She just walked out." Christina turned to Morgan. "Honey, did you notice anything strange about your grandmother just now? Did I say something weird?"

"I don't know," Morgan said. "It looked like something hurt her feelings."

"She doesn't have 'feelings,' Morgan," Jeremy said dryly. "And if you offended her, Christina, good for you. I don't know how you did it. For a minute there, it was almost as if she had a heart. Which, as we all know, is bullshit."

"Mom," Morgan said tentatively. "Would it be all right if I went out? I mean, since Grandmother is . . . well, you know . . . not here for me to ask permission?"

Christina raised her eyebrows. "Where do you want to go, honey? It's late, and it's dark."

"It's not that late," Morgan said. She showed her mother her watch. "It's just a little after seven. I want to go and see if Finn is all right. He wasn't at school today."

"You don't know the town very well yet, Morgan. It's only been a few days. Why don't you go and see him tomorrow afternoon?"

"Mom, please! I'll be back in an hour or so. I just want to make sure he's OK."

"Do you even know where he lives?" Christina wasn't sure if it was the notion of Morgan wandering around Parr's Landing at night that bothered her, or the fact that she was going to see some local boy Christina hadn't even met yet. *You sound like Adeline right now,* Christina chided herself. *It didn't take you very long to start worrying about 'townies,' as though you weren't one yourself.*

"I looked up his address in the phone book when I got home today," Morgan said. "It's not far from here."

"Then why don't you phone him?"

"Come *on,* Mom," Morgan said, her voice brimming with teenage scorn. "If I were going to the library to study, you wouldn't be saying a word. I walked around Toronto at night and you weren't worried about that. What do you think is going to happen to me here? I'll only be gone for an hour. I want to take a walk, anyway. I'll just knock on his door, say hi, and come right back."

Jeremy said, "Do you want me to drive you, Morgan?"

"No thanks, Uncle Jeremy. I really want to take a walk. I'm fifteen, you know," she said. "I'm practically an adult."

Christina sighed. "All right. But be back by nine, OK? And we won't tell your grandmother where you are, or what you're doing." Now it was Morgan's turn to sigh. "All I'm doing is going for a walk, Mom," she said. "It's no big deal, really." Morgan kissed her mother on the cheek and practically danced out of the room.

"Take a sweater!" Christina called after her, but the front door had already swung shut. Christina hoped Adeline hadn't heard it. She didn't relish another lecture on propriety from her mother-in-law. But there was no sound from Adeline's study. If she'd heard Morgan leave, she gave no indication of it.

"What do you want to do?" Jeremy said. "Shall we watch TV? Do you want to go to O'Toole's and have a drink? Or go for a drive?" He seemed unsurprised by either Adeline's departure, or Morgan's, as though vicious hostility and unexplained behaviour shifts were simply a matter of family life. *Jesus,* Christina thought. *No wonder Jack wanted out.*

"Let's go for a drive," Christina said brightly. "Let's go for a drive, all the way back to Toronto."

Finn was lying sprawled across his bed rereading his *Tomb of Dracula* comics, trying to recapture some familiar joy in them, when his mother knocked on his door and told him there was a girl downstairs in the living room asking for him.

His cotton pillowcase was soaked and his eyes were red and sore. He hadn't been able to eat much at dinner, which was already a sombre affair, since neither he nor his parents could forget that there was no furry black presence lying in the doorway where the dining room met the kitchen, front paws folded in front of her, head resting on paws, amber eyes watching the table in case her master dropped any food.

Even the story about the visit to the police station to report the discovery of the bag of knives failed to rouse much of a conversation. When Finn's father said that hunters probably left the bag, there seemed to be a tacit, general agreement to let it go at that. No one wanted to talk about blood and slaughter up at Bradley Lake with Sadie missing.

As to Finn specifically, the emptiness of that doorway cut him so deeply that he'd had to excuse himself from the table, feeling he might be sick.

His parents excused him and he went up to his room to read, but the familiar images struck him as harsh and garish tonight. If Finn had been older, he'd have realized that he was receiving his first abject lesson in the cruel architecture of love and loss, and how no depicted horror— even in *The Tomb of Dracula*—could ever hope to match the awfulness of a real one, but he was just a twelve-year-old boy who loved a dog that was missing.

What was the point of being able to turn himself into a bat, or mist, or live in a ruined castle in Transylvania without Sadie sleeping next to him? What use was a crossbow, or a silver compact, or a crucifix in fighting Dracula and his minions without his best friend bounding ahead through the bush on one of their pre-dawn walks out by Bradley Lake, fetching her red ball and bringing it back to him as though it was the most precious token of love imaginable?

"What, Mom?" He leaned up on his elbow. "What did you say?"

"I said, there's a young lady downstairs to see you," Anne said. "She said her name is Morgan Parr, and that she's a friend of yours."

"Morgan is here?" he said, surprised. "She's downstairs?"

"She seems a little old to be a friend of yours, Finnegan," Anne added. "Which one of the family is she? How old is she?"

Finn sat up and wiped his face with his sleeve. "I don't know how old she is. We sometimes walk home from school together," he said, finessing the truth a little bit, knowing that his mother would be happier if Morgan were his age. "She just moved here, from Toronto. She lives at Parr House with her grandmother. Her mother lives there, too."

Ah, Christina, of course—Christina Monroe. That was her name, at least back then. The one that got knocked up by Jack Parr and ran off to Toronto under the cover of darkness. That one. The tramp. So, not a real Parr after all, a shotgun Parr.

Anne Miller, who was not in the habit of gossiping, or thinking ill of other women, immediately regretted her mean-spirited bitchiness, even in thought, and rightly decided it was beneath her. All the girls had crushes on Jack Parr, truth be told, so no girl that landed him would ever be immune from the jealousy. *Besides,* she chided herself, *it was all a long time ago. And it wasn't this girl's fault, anyway.*

Anne noted that Finn had brightened since the news that Morgan Parr was downstairs waiting for him. Until Sadie came home, or was found, she'd be happy for anything that would take her son's mind off his lost dog.

"She's very pretty," Anne said. "She looks like her dad. I knew him in school."

"I guess," Finn said, blushing. "Her dad's dead, anyway."

Anne blanched. "Jack's *dead*? When? How?"

"I don't know," Finn said. "Don't ask her about it, OK? I don't think she wants to talk about that stuff. At least not yet."

"Well, don't just sit there," Anne said, recovering. "Put some cold water on your face and come downstairs and greet your guest like a gentleman. We don't want her running back and telling Mrs. Parr she visited a barnyard."

Finn rolled his eyes at his mother. "She's not like that," he said, suddenly protective of Morgan. "Mom, please just— I'll be right down, OK?"

He went down the hallway into the bathroom and closed the door. Anne heard the water running and the sound of splashing as Finn washed his face.

She went downstairs to tell Morgan that Finn would be down directly, and to offer her a soft drink while she waited. When Morgan smiled and thanked her politely, she felt even worse for her churlish thoughts about Christina Monroe and Jack Parr.

What an awful, awful day, she thought. *First Sadie, then that horrible hockey bag, now this news.*

Anne decided that another rum and coke—a strong one this time— might hasten sleep and bring it to a close a little sooner, which would be just what the doctor ordered.

"Your parents are nice," Morgan said as she and Finn sat in the basement drinking Cokes. "Especially your mother. She asked me how I liked the town. I told her I liked it a lot, but it was hard to get used to."

She glanced around as she spoke. On the fireplace mantle there was a framed photograph of a much younger Finn on the edge of a lake with his arms around a wet black Labrador retriever shaking water from its fur. Curling trophies, likely his father's, flanked the photograph. Morgan took in the fake wood panelling and the wet bar, and the hockey and travel posters on the wall, thinking how nice it was not to be at Parr House where everything seemed to be a brittle antique, including her grandmother—to be in someplace normal for the first time since leaving Toronto.

"They're OK," Finn said, shrugging. Then, thinking better of it, he said, "No, they're great. My mom, especially, yeah. I like them. Do you like your mom?" He mentally kicked himself for asking such a stupid question. "I mean, you probably do, right? Everyone likes their mom."

Morgan laughed, but not unkindly. "Yeah, I love my mom. My uncle Jeremy, on the other hand, probably doesn't love his—my grandmother is a bit hard to take sometimes. She's a bit mean. She wasn't really happy about you and I becoming friends, I guess."

Finn sounded indignant. "How come? What's wrong with me?"

"It isn't you," Morgan said. "It's anyone from here. I think she'd like to think of me as this princess or something, and that I shouldn't be associating with the peasants, which is how she sees the people who live here."

"Well, she owns the whole town," Finn said scornfully. "Of course she'd think like that. How come she let you come here, then?"

"She doesn't know I'm here—and I can't stay long." Morgan looked at him more closely. Finn's eyes were red and swollen. He looked as though he had been crying for hours. "Where were you today?" she asked gently. "I didn't see you at lunchtime, or after school. Is everything OK?"

"My dog ran away. Her name is Sadie. I woke up this morning and she wasn't in the yard," he said simply. "She's lost. I cut school early to go look for her. I went to Bradley Lake and looked all over, but I didn't find her."

"Oh, God," Morgan said. "I'm so sorry, Finn. I didn't know. Why didn't you come get me when you got home? I would have helped you look."

"It's OK," he said. "I didn't want to get you into trouble. I almost got into trouble myself for cutting school but . . . well, something else happened this afternoon."

"What do you mean?"

Finn looked towards the stairs leading to the living room where his parents were watching television. "If I tell you a secret, will you swear to keep it?"

Morgan shrugged. "Sure, I guess so. What is it?"

"No, don't say 'I guess so,'" he said urgently. "You have to *swear*."

"OK, I swear." She forced herself to keep from smiling. "What is it?"

Then he told her about the bag of knives and hammers he'd found at Spirit Rock.

Billy was pulling into the parking lot of the Nugget when he saw the flashing lights of the police cruiser coming towards him from the opposite direction. *No siren*, he thought mirthlessly. *I guess they don't think I'm a high-speed chase risk.* Then, *Enough is enough with this harassment by these goddamn yokel cops.* The cruiser pulled sharply into the spot next to Billy's allocated parking spot, the light still flashing.

He parked his Ford XL smartly and opened the door. The two cops— both of them this time, which surprised him—were already waiting for him beside their cruiser. The younger one actually had his flashlight out, shining it at the truck.

Billy put his hand up over his face, blocking the light. "Sergeant Thomson, would you please ask your colleague to put the light away? I'm not going anywhere and, as you can plainly see, I'm me. There's no need for it."

Thomson turned to Elliot and said, "Constable McKitrick, I don't think we need that light on Professor Lightning." Then back to Billy, "I apologize, sir."

If Thomson's intent in calling Billy "sir" and apologizing had been to reassure him, it had the opposite effect. In Billy's experience, the only thing more ominous than a redneck cop being verbally abusive was a redneck cop being ostentatiously polite.

"What is it this time, Sergeant Thomson?" Billy said calmly. "What are you charging me with? Driving a Ford? Being an *Indian* driving a Ford? Staying in a motel in your town? Or maybe having dinner at O'Toole's, which is where I have been all evening? It surely wasn't speeding—and that was a paragon of parking I just did."

The younger cop—McKitrick—didn't smile, but Thomson did, however wanly. "Dr. Lightning, I wonder if you'd be so good as to accompany us to the police station for a word?"

"We're having 'a word' right now, Sergeant Thomson," Billy snapped. "Why do we need to go to the police station to do it? I've done nothing wrong. There's no reason for me to go to the police station with you. As I explained to Constable McKitrick earlier today, I'm getting very tired of this harassment, and am prepared to take action to make it stop."

"There's been a . . . development," Thomson said. "It relates to your story about your father's death, as well as some other things. I'd really appreciate it if you'd come along with us and help us clear some things up. It won't take any time at all, I'm sure. But we'd like to talk with you."

"I think not," Billy said coolly. "I think I'll decline."

"Sir," Thomson said, this time with an edge, "if you don't come along with us of your own volition, I'm prepared to arrest you. I don't want to, but I will."

"*Arrest* me? On what charge?"

"Please, Dr. Lightning," Thomson said. "Trust me, I'd rather just speak with you down at the station. But I will take whatever measures I need to ensure that happens."

"What are you going to do," Billy demanded, "make something up? Some trumped-up charge?"

Thomson merely shrugged. "Would you please come along with us, Dr. Lightning?"

"You're both going to hear from my lawyer about this," Billy said in a cold fury. "The minute I get to a telephone, I'm calling Toronto."

"It's the middle of the night, Dr. Lightning, and we're a long way from Toronto. Now," Thomson said, opening the passenger door for Billy, "if you please—just a chat."

*   *   *

At the police station, Thomson showed Billy the hockey bag. It was zipped closed, with no hint of its contents visible. He watched Billy's face closely for a reaction, but none was discernible, other than a calmer version of the same irritation he'd shown in the parking lot of the motel.

"I've never seen that before in my life," Billy said. "What on earth does it have to do with me?"

"It was found up by Spirit Rock this afternoon by a boy looking for his lost dog," Thomson said. "Constable McKitrick brought the boy back to town. Do you know what we found inside?"

"I have absolutely no idea what you found inside it, sergeant," Billy said. "Nor—and I know I'm repeating myself here, so forgive me—do I have any idea what any of it has to do with me."

Thomson opened his desk drawer and withdrew a clean pair of latex gloves. He put them on and unzipped the bag. He withdrew the manuscript and held it up for Billy to see.

"Do you know what this is, Dr. Lightning?" Thomson said quietly.

Billy leaned forward in his seat and peered at the papers Thomson held in his hands. He looked confused for a moment, then he blanched. If the confusion was some sort of act, Thomson thought, it was a damn good act—better than any he'd seen, anywhere. When Billy spoke, his voice was hushed.

"Where did you get that?" he demanded. "Where the *hell* did you get that?"

"You recognize it, do you, Dr. Lightning?"

"It's my . . . it's my father's manuscript." As Billy stared at it, the look of bafflement on his face was replaced by one of dawning horror. "Is that *blood* on those pages?"

"I think so," Thomson said in a neutral voice. "Blood, some mud. Grease. We haven't had it tested yet—it was just found this afternoon. Do you know what else we found in the bag?"

Billy shook his head. Thomson beckoned him over and opened the flaps of the hockey bag. The stench that rose from the interior of the bag was thicker and greasier than it had been even a few hours earlier. Thomson felt his stomach lurch. The hammers and knives gleamed dull brown and silver in the overhead light of the police station.

Billy looked inside the bag, then vomited into the trash can next to Thomson's desk. When he had finished retching, he stood up and steadied his hand on the side of the desk. "May I have a glass of water, please?"

"Elliot?" Thomson said. "Would you mind?"

"Those hammers are archaeological tools," Billy said, wiping his mouth with the back of his hand. "Those are the kind of hammers we used here in 1952. I told you, it's Weal. He's here in Parr's Landing, like as I said. Now will you believe me?"

"Dr. Lightning, the problem is this—Richard Weal is dead. Those couldn't be his tools, and he couldn't be in Parr's Landing. He died in a car crash earlier this year, in Toronto."

"Not possible," Billy said, shaking his head. He took the glass of water Elliot brought him. "It's not possible," he repeated. "That's the manuscript that was taken from my father's desk. The one I told you about. Those are Richard Weal's tools. What else could it be? I *knew* he was going to come here. You've got to search for him. I *told* you. He's here."

"Dr. Lightning, I spoke with the investigating officer in Toronto myself. They found his identification near the wreck. It looks like it was a suicide."

"Did they identify the body?" Billy demanded. "How did they identify the body? Dental records?"

"There weren't any dental records," Thomson admitted. "The body was burned beyond recognition, but the police were satisfied it was Weal. So, as far as we're concerned, certainly officially, he's dead. Which means that we have a problem. Can you see what that problem might be, sir?"

Billy laughed harshly. "You think *I* . . . You're joking, right? You think that bag is mine, and that those are my tools, and I . . . what, drove across northern Ontario with a copy of my father's manuscript in a hockey bag doing God knows what, carving people up, then walked into the Parr's Landing police station and introduced myself to Constable McKitrick? Are you *serious*?"

"Would you give us a sample of your fingerprints, just to clear this up?"

"Absolutely not," Billy snapped. "After the way I have been bullied and harassed by Constable McKitrick practically since I arrived, and shanghaied into coming in here tonight with implied threats of arrest, I'd have to be very stupid to fall for that one. I'll be telephoning my lawyer in the morning. When you send the contents of that bag to a fingerprint lab, you'll find that I haven't touched them. I'm going to raise such a holy stink that you'll be lucky to find work as security guards in the Northwest Territories."

"Dr. Lightning—"

Billy ignored Thomson, cutting him off in mid-sentence. "Now," he said, "if there's nothing else, I'm going back to the motel. In the morning, I'm going to go look for Richard Weal, with or without your help. Unless he was working with some sort of accomplice—which I doubt—he's here in Parr's Landing."

Without waiting for a response from either Thomson or Elliot, Billy walked out of the police station, letting the door slam behind him.

Thomson and Elliot were both silent. Then Thomson spoke.

"I think we have a problem," he said slowly. "I don't think it's Lightning's bag. I don't know whose bag it is. But I think he's telling the truth."

"Too much of a coincidence, Sarge," Elliot said stubbornly. "And you said this Weal was dead, so who else could it be?"

"I don't know," Thomson admitted. "I don't know what the hell is going on here, but it's about time we called Gyles Point and told them about this. In the meantime, Elliot, do not bother Dr. Lightning in any way. We need to let him cool off a bit."

"But Sarge—how can it *not* be Lightning? I mean, we have evidence—"

"For God's sake, McKitrick, for once, just listen and do as I'm telling you!" Thomson was practically shouting. "We have evidence of *something* having happened, probably something bad.

But it doesn't directly implicate Lightning except for the fact that it's his father's manuscript. If anything, it supports *his* god-damn theory about what happened. It supports his theory that Weal came back here to the Landing, just like Lightning said he would. Now, would you please, for the love of *Christ,* just leave him alone until we get some fingerprints, at least? Lightning isn't the only one who needs to cool off here. I don't know what sort of bug you have up your ass about this guy, but don't let it get in the way of you doing your job—the right way. You have a lot to learn about police work, son. Don't go off half-cocked and make us look like back-country idiots."

Elliot stared. He'd never heard Thomson raise his voice before. He felt himself blushing and he lowered his eyes. "Yes, sir," he said. "I understand."

Thomson softened. "Look, Elliot, you're a good cop. You have a lot going for you. I understand how you're feeling right now about this. You did good, bringing in the bag. No one is going to forget that when this gets solved. But the rest of this has to go by the book. There's too much riding on it. I'm going to call Gyles Point and get this bag off to the lab A S A P."

"Yes, sir, I understand," Elliot said again. "By the book. I'll give Lightning some space."

"Good man," Thomson said. "Now, go get some sleep, Elliot. I have some calls to make."

Just before midnight, Finn was lying in his bed when heard a soft scratching at the back door. He sat bolt upright in bed and listened. The scratching came again, this time accompanied by a soft, familiar whining sound. Finn's heart leaped in his chest. *Sadie! It's Sadie! She's come home!*

He threw back the covers and ran to the back door. He fumbled with the latch, opened the door wide, and looked down. By the back yard lights, he saw a familiar shape huddled by the door.

"Sadie! Sadie! You're home!" He shouted for his parents. "Dad! *Mom!* Sadie's home! Come quick!" He heard muffled voices from upstairs, then the sound of his parents' feet on the hardwood floors, then pounding down the stairs.

"Finn, is she back?" his mother said breathlessly. "Is she home?"

Finn's rapturous joy rendered him incapable of any speech other than his dog's name, repeated like a mantra. "Sadie! Sadie! Sadie!"

"Finn, bring her in," his father said. "Why is she still out there?" Hank Miller reached out for Sadie and tried to pick her up. The Labrador yelped in pain and cowered back. His hand came away slick with blood and fur.

"Dad, don't hurt her!" Finn cried. "Be careful!"

"She's hurt," Hank said. "She's been in some kind of fight, I think." Then, to the dog, "Here, Sadie, come. Come inside, girl."

The Labrador looked fearfully behind her, and then scooted into the house, dragging her left leg behind her slightly as though it were broken, or sprained. Once inside, she collapsed on the floor beside the back door, lying on her side and breathing in shallow hitches.

Finn bent over her and gingerly explored her fur with his fingertips. His parents stood back as though they instinctively understood that their son was the authority in this case.

When he inhaled sharply, the sound he made releasing it reminded Anne of a punctured birthday party balloon. Both she and Hank leaned in to see what Finn was looking at.

Sadie was covered with bites. Finn counted two, three, four clumps of matted fur and blood along her thick neck and flanks. In those places, the fur had been torn away, exposing the ravaged pink flesh beneath. The bite marks were about two inches apart and, to Finn's inexpert eye, looked deep and nasty.

"Mom, she's been bitten all over," Finn said, horrified. "She's been in a fight with some animal or something. Look! It's horrible. Sadie," he crooned, petting her head. "It's all right, girl, you're home now. It's OK. Shhhh, it's OK."

"Be careful, Finn," Anne said. "She might be . . . well, whatever animal she fought with might have been rabid."

"Rabies doesn't work that way, Anne," Hank said. "It's not that fast acting. We'll take her to the vet tomorrow and check her out. She's had all of her shots this year, so she'll be all right, I'm sure.

Finn, see if you can get her to come upstairs where there's some proper light. Anne, get the first aid box. It's in the medicine cabinet. There's some hydrogen peroxide there. At least we can clean these cuts and bites a little bit."

"*Don't hurt her!*" Finn screamed.

"Hydrogen peroxide doesn't hurt, Finn," Anne said soothingly, putting her hand on his shoulder. "It'll be fine, you'll see. And in the morning, we'll get her to the vet and get her checked out."

Finn put his fingers in front of Sadie's muzzle and rubbed his thumb against them, a familiar invitation to her to follow him, one that usually implied treats.

Sadie, if you get up and follow me now, I'll give you anything you want. Please, God, Finn prayed silently. *Make my dog better. Please let her get up and follow me.*

He heard the sound of Sadie's tail thumping weakly against the floor before he saw it. Sadie rose shakily to her feet, tail swinging from side to side, and slowly followed Finn upstairs.

In the kitchen, Hank swabbed her bites with hydrogen peroxide. His wife and son noticed the gentleness with which he ministered to the injured dog, and it surprised even him, truth be told. It wouldn't be till much later, when he was in bed with his wife sleeping next to him, that Hank Miller would weep his own tears of relief at Sadie's return—modest tears, to be sure, because men didn't cry, at least not in front of women and children, but he'd been a boy once, too, and he remembered what it was like to love a dog the way only a twelve-year-old boy really can.

Anne brought a crocheted afghan downstairs from the cedar chest in their bedroom and laid it on top of Sadie to keep her warm during the night. She kissed Sadie's muzzle and said, "Good night, sweet dog." Anne wiped her cheek with the back of her hand and stood up. She cleared her throat. "All right, Finn. Back to bed. Sadie will be all right here by the stove. In the morning, I'll drive her over to the vet clinic right away, I promise."

"Can I come, too?" Finn pleaded. "Please? Even if I miss the morning part of school? Please?"

"Of course you can, honey," Anne said. "She's your dog. She'd want you there."

Hank turned off the overhead light. Sadie lay her head on her paws. Her breathing was still shallow, but it slowed as they stood in the doorway, then became deep and regular in peaceful sleep.

When Finn heard the sound of her leg twitching on the floor in the way it did when Sadie was dreaming of running, he sighed in relief and silently reassured God of his intention to honour his part of the deal he'd made, as long as God honoured His.

It was well after midnight by the time Elliot stopped at O'Toole's on the way home from the police station. He needed a drink, but more importantly he was hoping for a chance to speak with Donna Lemieux and make things right. But the only person behind the bar tonight was a supremely pissed off Bill O'Toole, the owner.

"I don't know where she is," he fumed. "She didn't open tonight, and she didn't call. She won't answer her goddamn telephone. I couldn't get Molly to take her shift tonight because she's off for the week visiting family in Wawa. So guess who that leaves? Me, the owner, washing glasses and tending bar. Well, we'll see if she still has a job when she waltzes back in here. We'll just *see* about that."

Elliot doubted very much that Bill O'Toole meant a fraction of what he was saying about firing Donna, who was the primary reason—besides the liquor—that men came to O'Toole's in the first place.

"Maybe I'll take a run by her place and make sure she's all right," Elliot said to Bill O'Toole, thinking to himself how unlike Donna it was to miss work. Sleep late, yes. Be pissed at Elliot, yes—take a number. But she wasn't an irresponsible eighteen-year-old girl; she was a divorced adult woman with a carved-in-stone survivor's work ethic.

Bill paused. The notion that anything could be wrong with Donna clearly hadn't occurred to him. "You don't think anything's really the matter, do you?"

"Dunno, Bill, but it's worth checking out," Elliot said gruffly. "You didn't go over there yourself, I take it?" Elliot knew full well that he hadn't, and felt a flash of remorse that he was taking out his own guilt over last night on Bill O'Toole.

"No, I just figured she . . . well, I don't know what I figured. It's not like Donna, is it, Elliot? You think she's OK?"

"Tell you what, Bill," he said. "I'll check on her. If you don't hear back from me, you can just assume that she's under the weather. If something's wrong, I'll give you a call, I promise."

Bill looked at Elliot with relief. "Good deal," he said. He took a bottle out of the beer fridge behind him and proffered it. "One for the road, Elliot? On the house?"

Elliot shook his head. "Another time, Bill." He winked. "I'll let you know about Donna. I'm sure it's nothing."

When he pulled into Donna's driveway, the first thing he saw was that the house was completely dark. Not even the porch light had been switched on, something Donna, like most people in Parr's Landing, did reflexively once night fell. The house, set back from the street—ordinary in every possible way—tonight had the aspect of a cenotaph.

Elliot rang the doorbell. He heard the cling-clang of it on the other side of the door. Somewhere in the back region of the house, likely the kitchen, he heard what sounded like the plaintive mewling of a hungry cat. Elliot hated cats as a rule, but this one—Samantha—he had grown fond of over the course of his visits to Donna's bedroom. Nice cat. Hungry, it sounded like. Donna would never, ever neglect feeding Samantha, whatever else she might or might not do.

The image of the bag of bloody knives and hammers from Spirit Rock suddenly flashed through Elliot's mind in a crimson streak.

He reached for the doorknob and turned it. The door was unlocked and swung open. Switching on his flashlight, he played the beam over the empty living room. On the wall adjacent to the doorway, Elliot located the light switch and flicked it up and down. Nothing. He stepped over the threshold.

"Donna?" Elliot called out softly. "Donna, it's me. It's Elliot. Are you here?"

The darkness and silence seemed to mock him. The sound

of Samantha's mewling came from the next room, louder than before.

Elliot crossed the living room and stepped into the kitchen, his flashlight beam playing in front of him, picking up objects here and there without illuminating the room as a whole. The kitchen was immaculate, the sink dry. He tried the light switch on the wall. It was dead here, too.

He played his light along the floor. Samantha sat in front of the stove, silent now. Her eyes reflected back in the light of his flashlight. "Samantha," Elliot whispered. "Where's Donna?"

Behind him, the sound of something falling over, but muffled, as though from a near distance. He spun, shining the light in front of him. It found the closed door leading to the basement. Elliot strained to hear, but there was no further sound. Beads of sweat dotted his upper lip and gathered along his hairline and under his armpits.

Elliot thought of the Wendigo legends of his childhood—the stories of cannibalism and Indian witchcraft and malefic spiritualism associated with Spirit Rock. He remembered the expression on Finn Miller's face when he first looked into the hockey bag and saw its gruesome contents. *The blood on those knives still smelled sour,* he thought. *They weren't used that long ago, and they weren't washed.*

Tucking the flashlight under his arm, he drew his gun with one hand and turned the handle on the cellar door with the other.

"Hello?" The loudness of his own voice startled him. "Is anyone down there? This is the police. I'm armed."

Elliot listened for an answer. Receiving none, he stepped down into the cellar, taking the stairs one at a time. The darkness here was even deeper than it had been upstairs where there had been at least the tangential glimmer of lights from the street, or from neighbourhood porches.

Like a grave, Elliot thought. Then, he rebuked himself: *Don't be such a moron. You're a cop. Get your shit together.* He licked the sweat off his upper lip and continued his descent till he reached the bottom of the steps and stood on the floor of the cellar.

Playing his light along the walls, Elliot identified the hulking shape of the washing machine and the dryer below a wooden shelf of laundry detergent and miscellaneous odds and ends. The beam of light passed through dusty jars of jams and preserves on the opposite wall, the light transfixing the glass, the contents of the jars casting red and gold and green shadows against the stone walls.

He half-turned, shining his light on the alcove leading to the area off the main part of the basement, the place where Donna kept the enormous deep freeze that had been her husband's pride and joy. Slowly, he walked towards the freezer, then stopped in his tracks. The contents of the freezer were spread all over the floor around it, as though someone had been so desperate to find whatever was inside that they'd tunnelled through the frozen meat and packaged vegetables to reach the bottom.

Elliot cocked his gun, the click ricocheting loud and sharp against the stone walls of the cellar. He approached the freezer, opened it, and shone his light inside.

"Donna . . ." Elliot breathed. "Jesus."

Donna Lemieux was curled up on the bottom of the freezer in a foetal position. She was wearing the same jeans and pink top she'd worn the previous night when he'd left her house. The clothes were stiff now, and frozen. Her skin was blue with cold, and ice crystals blossomed like white flowers in her long hair. It seemed impossible that her body had been able to fit into the confined space without broken bones and dislocated joints, but there was no evidence of any breakage or dislocation. Her body had merely folded like a puppet in a shoebox, fitting itself to the rectangular confines of the empty freezer as though it were a single bed.

Then, Donna Lemieux opened her dead, frozen eyes and sat up.

Elliot jumped back, startled by the sudden flurry of movement. Instinctively, he swung his gun in her direction, resisting the urge to fire just in time, and cursing himself for his stupidity in aiming a loaded gun at an obviously injured woman.

Donna crawled out of the freezer in a sequence of crab like movements that disoriented Elliot, because they seemed to occur almost too quickly for his eye to follow. Then, suddenly, she was standing directly in front of him, and her hands were on his shoulders.

"Donna, are you all right?" he said. "Jesus, you gave me one fuck of a shock. What the hell are you doing down here?"

"*Elliot, you came back. . . . I knew you would.*"

"Donna, let's get you upstairs where it's warm," he said, putting his arm around her. "Then we need to get you to a hospital. What happened to you? What are you doing here?" The coldness of her body burned through his windbreaker, and only then did he realize that there was something very, very wrong, besides the obvious wrongness of finding the woman you couldn't get it up for last night—until you fucked her in the ass—sleeping in a deep freeze in the basement of her house. It felt as though he had his arm around a frozen carcass in the meat locker of an abattoir.

There's no oxygen in that freezer, Elliot, and no way to open it from the inside. Remember the kid when you were in the third grade, the one who suffocated to death because he was playing in his parents' deep freeze and couldn't get out? Something's wrong here, Mr. Cop. So much for your instincts.

"Donna?" He pulled back. "Donna, how did you—"

She reached out, snakelike, and grasped his arm in a grip that made him wince and suck in his breath. Her eyes weren't blue, as they always had been. Now they were a deep dark red, the same garnet colour as the full jelly jars when he'd shone his light through them moments ago.

Donna took his other arm and pinned him to the wall. "*Elliot, I want you to love me.*"

Though Elliot could see her lips move, the sound of her voice seemed to be coming from inside his head, not from her mouth. It rippled through his body, liquefying his arms and legs, crumpling him to his knees, then to the floor.

The part of his mind that governed fight-or-flight tried to inform Elliot that he should scream—wanted to, in fact—but he didn't have access to that part of his brain. It was as though something outside him had identified it, isolated it, and cut it off from being able to communicate. Elliot floated on a cloud of luminous red mist and infinite space full of flickering points of light.

His knees buckled and he fell backward. The base of his head struck the concrete floor and he saw fireworks at the contact.

"*I only ever wanted you to love me.*" Donna's voice shivered in his brain. "*You never did. I always knew you didn't. Will you love me now? I want you inside of me, Elliot.*"

Elliot felt the blood thundering through his body. His cock was harder than it had ever been, straining painfully inside his uniform pants. Donna straddled his crotch and ground her pelvis against his erection. His limbs were paralyzed, but he'd never been more sexually aroused in his life. He tried to think, to focus, but his brain was disconnected from every other part of himself, and his body was on fire with sensation. The universe was composed of Elliot, his engorged cock, and Donna Lemieux writhing on top of him, suddenly the most desirable woman—the most desirable creature, male or female—he could imagine.

"Donna," he whispered. Tears ran down his cheeks. "Donna . . . please . . ."

When she placed her lips against his neck, the pressure of her sharp teeth behind her frozen lips was the most erotic sensation he could imagine. Even the sharp pain of those teeth slicing through the soft skin below his jawline only stung for a moment, then the pain was replaced by spreading heat he felt at every extremity. Seconds before he lost consciousness, his body was wracked by the most shattering orgasm of his life.

His last thought before blacking out was that he was sorry Jeremy wasn't there to see this *proof* that he really was a normal guy, and that the past really was past.

Finn wasn't sure what woke him. The iridescent green hands of the clock on his night table read two a.m. The clock itself ticked softly and the house was deathly quiet.

Instinctively, he put out his hand beside his bed and felt for Sadie's head. Then he remembered that she wasn't there, that she had been lost, then come home, and was now sleeping in the kitchen. He was suddenly possessed of a powerful need to see with his own eyes that she was there, that their reunion hadn't been some sort of fantastic dream that would leave him heartbroken when he realized it was, in fact, just a dream. He swung his legs over the side of the bed and reached for the light switch and turned it on.

Sadie was sitting a foot from his bed staring at him, silent, unmoving. At her feet was the red rubber ball.

Finn realized that she'd dropped it there. The sound of the ball hitting his bedroom floor was what had woken him.

He rubbed his eyes and stared at his dog.

Sadie's posture was not the posture of the broken thing that had limped in through the back door a few hours earlier. The hydrogen peroxide had clearly done its work, because the bite marks in Sadie's fur were already healing, even fading. Finn doubted there would even be scars, at this rate. Maybe God really *had* been listening tonight when he prayed for his dog's life to be spared. He tried to remember the terms of his part of the bargain, but realized that, whatever they were, he'd honour them.

"Sadie, are you feeling better?" he whispered joyously. "You're a good girl. Sadie's a *good girl*!" Almost as an afterthought he added courteously, "Thank you, God. I appreciate it." Finn patted the bed beside him, their time-honoured signal for Sadie to jump up on the bed for a cuddle, or a sleep. Sadie didn't move. "Sadie, come up! Come up!" Finn said, more loudly. He patted the mattress again. "Come up on the bed!"

Sadie lay down at his feet, keeping her distance from him. When he reached out to pat her paw, she made a sound low in her throat, somewhere between a whine and a growl. Finn pulled his hand back in shock.

When he did, the Labrador's tail swished back and forth, as though she were telling him she would lay there beside him, but warning him not to touch her. Sadie had never, ever growled at Finn. Not once.

"What is it, Sadie?" he said, alarmed. "Are you still hurt?"

Swish, swish, swish.

"Fine, Sadie." He was somewhat mollified by the tail-wagging, which said to him that whatever else was wrong, she still loved him, and was likely still feeling the pain of her ordeal. He'd see how she was tomorrow— she was going to the vet tomorrow, anyway, to check out the bites. Would his parents ever be surprised at how much better she was looking. Maybe they wouldn't even need to go to the vet, after all. Miracles were obviously at play, and Finn had a personal investment in them.

He switched off the light and fell back asleep to the comforting sound of Sadie's soft breathing from the place on the floor from which she never once moved all night.

CHAPTER EIGHTEEN

On the last morning of his childhood, Finn woke up in his bed exactly as he always had. He yawned and stretched as he always did. He looked at his clock, figured that his parents were still fast asleep, and would be for hours yet. He looked around for Sadie. She had moved from the spot beside his bed and was now sitting on her haunches in the doorway connecting his bedroom and the downstairs hallway.

"Good morning, Sadie," he whispered. "How's the good girl? Did you have a good sleep?"

Sadie didn't come to him as she usually did, but she wagged her tail slowly back and forth.

Finn got out of bed and padded over to where she sat. It was dark outside, but by the light of his bedside lamp, he beheld the miracle fruit of his bargain with God: Sadie's bites had entirely healed. Her fur was glossy and black, and the patches of hair that had been torn out of her flesh during the fight with whatever animal had done this to her had almost completely grown back. She looked as she had looked three, maybe four years before, when she had been much younger, almost a puppy again.

Indeed, a miracle. He thanked God again, just to make sure He'd heard it the first time and knew how grateful Finn was for this second chance with his beloved Labrador. He couldn't wait to tell Morgan after school later.

Sadie's mouth hung slightly open, her brilliant white teeth lying over her bottom lip, pink tongue quivering. She panted gently as though she wanted to go outside.

At her feet was her red ball. She looked down at the ball, then back at Finn. It was their personal signal for playtime, an instance of Sadie training him rather than the other way around.

Finn smiled hugely, feeling as though his heart would burst with the sheer euphoria of having her back, well and healed. "You want to go outside, Sadie?" he said. "You want to go for a walk?"

Swish, swish, swish.

As he had every day when he took this walk in the late fall, Finn dressed quickly and warmly. At the front door, he put on his coat and boots, tucked the ball into his jacket pocket, and called Sadie. She trotted up the stairs and followed him out the door into the pre-dawn darkness of Parr's Landing.

He looked up and breathed the cold, clean air deep into his lungs.

For the rest of his life, Finn would remember the particular clarity of that morning sky: Venus still visibly glowing in the western reach above the ridge of cliffs on the far edge of the horizon, past Spirit Rock; the stars, hard like jewels; the variegated shades of dark blue that hinted at the coming sunrise. He would remember how he skipped and ran with a buoyancy so pure that the pavement itself seemed to release him from the constraints of anything as pedestrian—or adult—as gravity, with Sadie trotting ahead, her black body a barrel-shaped shadow bobbing over the pavement on legs that were remarkably delicate and slender for such sturdy work.

Like always, he cut across the streets, through back lots, till the land flattened out and grew more timbered as they approached the road that led to Bradley Lake and the cliffs of Spirit Rock. When the lake was in sight, he turned west and began the upward ascent along a path he could navigate with his eyes closed if he had to.

But he didn't close his eyes. He kept them open, trained on Sadie who trotted in front of him, not bounding ahead as she usually did, but seeming to savour this new beginning as much as Finn was. He relished the sight of her as though it were their very first walk. Occasionally, she stopped and looked back, as though to reassure herself that Finn was right behind her, as he always had been, and always would be.

Higher and higher they climbed. The land underfoot grew harder as soft earth gave way to pine needle-covered patches of shale and granite shield. In the sky, the dark blue was lightening by degrees. Finn gauged that the sun would begin to rise in approximately five minutes. He could practically set his watch by the colour of the sky.

Sadie stopped abruptly and sat down on the path. She sniffed the air and whined.

"What is it, Sadie?" he said, catching up to her. He reached down to pet her, and she snapped at his hand. He jerked it back. "Sadie, what's wrong?" *She's afraid of something,* Finn thought. *Not me, surely? She can't be afraid of me.*

He reached down to pet her again, and this time she snarled with unambiguous menace, showing all her teeth. Finn backed away slowly, thinking about rabies and wondering how quickly a dog could be infected with that virus, and how quickly it would change her.

Once again, as soon as he backed away, she closed her mouth and wagged her tail, whining apologetically, as if to tell him she was sorry. The thought came to him, suddenly and with near-telepathic clarity that, for some reason, Sadie wasn't afraid of *Finn*; rather, Sadie was trying to keep *him* away from *her*. She was afraid for him.

Then, she turned and bounded off into the forest as if pursued.

"Sadie, no!" Finn shouted, thinking, *No, not again. Please, God, don't let her run away again.*

He chased her straight up the hill. He'd never known Sadie to run so swiftly and nimbly, even as a puppy. Finn was panting as he tried to keep up with her. He watched her tail disappear around an outcropping of boulders directly above him, slightly to the left of where he was trying to navigate the slippery rock.

Reaching level ground, he looked left and right and called her name. He saw the land around him clearly now. The light was pale blue and pellucid, shot through with gossamer threads of yellow. He looked around again and called out, "Sadie! Come on, girl! It's OK, don't be afraid. We'll go home now!"

Stupid, stupid, stupid, he berated himself. *It was too soon for her to come back up here after what happened to her. We should have slept in.*

Then he remembered her waiting in the doorway of his bedroom with the red ball, begging to play. He felt for the ball in his pocket. It was there. He took it out and held it in his hand.

"Sadie, I have your ball," Finn called out winningly. "Come and get it. Come on, girl—come and get your red ball!" He bounced it on the ground—Sadie could always identify that sound, no matter where she was in the house.

He heard a soft whimper come from behind the boulders. *Thank God,* he thought, adding a casual prayer, though no less earnest for its casualness. *Thanks, God. Please, just one more thing? Could you make her come to me, so I can take her home? Sorry to keep bothering you.*

The whine came again, and Finn walked around the boulders.

Sadie was cowering in a deep rock shelter behind a copse of low growing white pine, almost hidden from sight. He saw her eyes gleaming in the dimness—more red than amber in the brightening light, he noted, dismissing the observation even as it occurred to him—and he spoke to her in a soft, soft voice.

"Sadie, come out. Please, Sadie. Let's go home now. Come on, baby."

He bounced the ball twice, then three times against the ground. From inside the grotto he could have sworn he heard the sound of her tail swishing against stone.

He held out his hand with the ball in it, and she crept towards the opening of the rock shelter. Finn heard her panting before he saw that she was slick with sweat—sweat that hadn't been there a few moments before—trembling violently. Sadie looked at him imploringly, as though desperately trying to push her thoughts into his mind.

He felt a wave of pure love coming from Sadie. Love, and something more.

Finn's pupils dilated and he swayed on his feet, struggling for balance.

Amorphous, sibylline images tumbled through his brain—vivid impressions of Sadie as a puppy, but not images of his own recollect, not images of *himself* with Sadie, not the privileged god's-eye view from which even the most benign and loving human beings experience their interaction with animals.

No, these were images of *Sadie* with *him*: the gift of a glimpse of the world as experienced from Sadie's perspective—a mosaic of smells no human nose would ever experience; the literature of light on grass and snow; the secret language of birds and squirrels and cats; the true meaning of unconditional love, something no human being would ever truly understand; the perfect ecstasy of Finn's fingers combing through her soft black fur, the utter completion of falling asleep at the foot of his bed. Pure and uncomplicated gratitude for every affection ever shown to her. Vigilance for Finn's safety. Self-sacrifice.

The sound of the red rubber ball being dropped on the bedroom floor. Thump-thump-thump. Bounce, bounce. Good! Chase! Me chase! Throw!

As if in a trance, Finn threw the ball. Sadie scrambled out of the grotto and leaped into the sunlight.

Finn saw the flash of white light and felt the searing blast of unearthly heat before his brain could record what was happening. In one second, Sadie's body had launched itself into the air in pursuit of the red rubber ball. In the next second, there was a ghastly smell like ozone and burned hair, and his dog burst into flames before his eyes, shrieking in agony and crashing to the forest earth in front of him, writhing in the flames of an incandescent calefaction; a fire that seemed to come from *inside* Sadie's body, consuming it with merciless efficiency, melting fur and flesh and bone.

As Finn watched, her body rippled and crumbled to ash, leaving a charred skeleton that continued to burn even after the flesh was gone. Then, the fire abruptly went out, seemingly drawn inward by the skeleton itself, leaving only thick black smoke and the horrifying images seared into his brain.

It had taken seconds—seconds that, to Finn, felt like centuries repeating themselves in a cycle of agonizing revelation. The skeleton collapsed, became ash that blew away into the forest on the dawn breeze. In the east, the sun continued to climb in the sky, golden light touching the crest of the pine trees and the cliffs surrounding Parr's Landing, promising the most beautiful of late autumn days.

Finn stared, his mouth hanging open, his mind refusing to reconcile with what his eyes had just recorded. He opened his arms in the supplicant posture of a cheated embrace. Then he screamed louder than he had ever screamed in his life, a harrowing shriek of impossible betrayal, one that ripped away his innocence, his childhood, and his faith forever.

"SADIE!"

Finn stumbled, half-blind, towards the pile of smoking ash that had been his dog and reached out blindly to touch it, to hold it. Still hot, it seared his hand. He screamed again as painful blisters rose on the skin, a last, final insulting damnation from whoever the author of this counter miracle had been.

He said Sadie's name over and over again, part mantra, part keening, part pleading for this unimaginable horror to be revealed as some terrible cosmic mistake, or a scientific impossibility that would be unmasked as a sick joke at any moment.

But it wasn't. Nothing came, neither relief nor absolution.

As Finn knelt alone in the forest, rocking and weeping, the smoke dwindled down to wisps, and then died out entirely. Sunlight dappled the forest around him, and in the trees above his head, Finn heard the gentle lamentation of birdsong.

Anne Miller stood at the kitchen window wearing the pink velour winter bathrobe she'd gotten last Christmas from Finn "and Sadie." She was pouring her first cup of Maxwell House when she heard the front door click open. The house had been cold when she'd woken up half an hour before. Sadie wasn't in the kitchen, and Finn wasn't in his bed.

Damn it, she thought furiously. *Couldn't he have at least waited till we got home from the vet before he took her outside for a walk? Didn't he see how sick she was last night? That boy doesn't have the brains God gave a grasshopper sometimes, I swear.*

Coffee cup in hand, Anne marched into the living room. "Finn? Is that you? I can't believe you took Sadie out knowing that she—"

The coffee cup fell from her hand and smashed against the hardwood as her son slowly shuffled into the living room.

Finn's face and neck was a Kabuki mask of grief; smudged white ash scored with the tracks of Finn's tears. His right hand was badly burned, and he reeked of smoke and something infinitely worse.

She gasped. "Finnegan, what on *earth*. . . ? Where's Sadie?"

"Mom," Finn said in a dazed, swollen voice. "Mom. Mommy..."

He reached out his arms to his mother, but stumbled and fell. Anne caught him before he hit the floor. She held his unconscious body against her own, finding it clammy and cold. His breathing was shallow, his lips and fingertips bluish. She shouted for Hank to hurry up and come out of the bathroom right away, and to call a doctor because something was terribly, terribly wrong with Finn.

CHAPTER NINETEEN

Adeline Parr had not gone down to breakfast. She suspected that the rest of the family would enjoy her absence, but this one time she didn't care. She looked at her Piaget. It was ten o'clock in the morning. Breakfast would be long finished. Morgan would be at school. Christina and Jeremy would be . . . who knew where they'd be? Likely out somewhere, making spectacles of themselves in town. Both had shown a marked preference for being absent from Parr House during the day. Since Adeline could barely stand the sight of either of them for reasons unique to her view of each of them, their absence suited her perfectly.

She'd had Beatrice bring her coffee in her bedroom. Adeline sat in a yellow brocade chair by the window smoking a steady line of du Maurier cigarettes from a sterling silver monogrammed cigarette case that had been a gift from her late husband. Blue smoke shimmered like a low hanging cloud over the room, caressing the glass of the closed window like the fingers of ghosts.

Her eyes were red and sore, partly because of the smoke, but also because, even though she prided herself on not being the sort of woman who cried as a reaction to shock or even immediate grief, her own body didn't always remember to obey her. When she stubbornly refused to cry, her body reacted on her behalf, without her permission. Adeline's tears were like the tears of some men, the ones who'd grown up and forgotten the mechanics, the technique, of weeping. Adeline's tears seemed to bleed from pinpricks in her eyes instead of flowing naturally, let alone with healing.

She had locked herself in her study after dinner the previous evening. She'd heard Morgan leave the house and she'd heard Christina and Jeremy laughing in the dining room, probably laughing at her. After a time, she'd heard them leave the dining room and go upstairs. The sound of the television came from one of the upper bedrooms. Adeline assumed they were watching it together.

Shortly after nine, she'd heard the front door open again, stealthier than it had the last time. Morgan had obviously returned from wherever she'd been gadding. Adeline made a mental note to deal with Morgan later. One slut in the family was more than enough. She wasn't having a repeat performance of Christina's harlotry in the current generation, not in a year of Sundays. When the house was entirely quiet, when they were all in their beds, only then did she unlock the door to her study and glide noiselessly up the stairs to her bedroom, locking that door in its turn, and remaining in the room all night and into the morning.

Had anyone pointed it out to her, it wouldn't have occurred to Adeline Parr to find anything unusual in the fact that she had been able to monitor the entire evening's comings and goings from the leather chair behind the desk without ever leaving her study. Like a bejewelled, lacquered, well-tailored spider, Adeline Parr felt every tug on every strand of her web, which included not only Parr House, but the town of Parr's Landing itself. Nothing and no one arrived or departed without her knowing about it.

Except this time. Except for the arrival of Phenius's adopted Indian boy, Billy Lightning. News of his arrival in Parr's Landing had eluded her, as had news of Phenius's death. She felt the impact of this the way she might have felt the impact of an explosion on the other side of town— the ground had shaken, the air had shimmered and eddied for a moment, and while there was an intellectual awareness of devastation, the damage itself had not yet been internalized or quantified.

Phenius. *Phenius.*

When she closed her eyes against the haze of smoke in her bedroom, it wasn't the entirety of him she remembered—she didn't see him completely, not from head to toe—but rather a pastiche of memories that somehow added up to Phenius: the back of his tanned neck, his legs protruding from the rumpled khaki shorts he'd worn every day on the dig in 1952. The pattern of his chest hair, the way the blond blended with the silver almost imperceptibly. The surprising hardness of his arms— surprising in a man of his age, entirely unlike the soft, plump arms of her husband, who had been the same age when he'd married her as Phenius Osborne had been when he'd taken her in his arms for the first time. The wiriness of his body, the feeling of his cock brushing up against the inside of her thighs. The feeling of his calloused hands warming her body, the secret thrill of being touched in places she'd never been touched in her life, certainly not by her husband, and by no one since he'd died.

Phenius had taught her what it felt like to be a woman instead of the inviolate queen of Parr's Landing.

As to her guilt—not only her guilt over her own adultery, but also over making an adulterer out of Phenius Osborne—she could barely access a memory of her feelings of guilt over what they'd shared that summer. But she knew it was there, hovering like the twinge of a broken bone that still occasionally aches when the weather is damp. She'd never spoken of it to anyone, of course. Nor, to the best of her knowledge, had Phenius, who had still been married when they last saw each other.

Adeline stood up and walked over to her dressing table. There was a small mother-of-pearl box sitting between the cloudy amber bottles of Joy and Arpège perfumes and her monogrammed silver vanity brushes and mirror. Adeline opened the box and withdrew the bronze key that lay against the faded green velvet lining.

As she did so, she turned her husband's photograph face down on the lace runner. Then, almost as an afterthought, she opened the middle drawer of the dressing and tossed the picture inside, slamming the drawer shut with the back of her hand. She didn't want to think about Augustus Parr at all right now, or even look at his face.

She held the key to her lips for a moment, deep in thought.

Then she crossed the floor and opened the door to her bedroom. Hearing no one on the landing, or downstairs, she stepped out into the hallway and took the staircase downstairs to the foyer. In a hallway off the main rooms, she opened the door to a flight of stone stairs that led into one of the basement wings of Parr House where there was no electricity. Adjacent to the basement door, a flashlight hung on a chain.

Adeline removed the flashlight and switched it on. She played the beam of light across the walls, but it was an instinctive response. She could walk through Parr House blindfolded at midnight and never miss a step. Adeline knew the house the way another woman might know a lover's body. Leisurely, as though savouring the pressing darkness, she walked to the end of the hallway. She reached for the doorknob, opened the door, and stepped into the room.

Against the far wall were grouped a collection of boxes and storage trunks in various sizes. She shone the light through the curtains of dust that seemed to sway as she stepped towards them.

When she found the box she was looking for, she knelt down and unlocked it. Inside were a packet of letters, some photographs, and a bound sheaf of papers in an envelope with a Toronto postmark. These she tucked under her arm.

Adeline retraced her way down the stone corridor to the stairway leading up to the main floor and the privacy of her study, again locking the door behind her, even though she had encountered no one on her way there, nor heard any sounds coming from anywhere in Parr House.

Sitting at her vast mahogany desk, she perused the contents of the package thoughtfully for a time. Then she reached for the telephone and dialled the number of the Golden Nugget Motel.

When Darcy Marin, whose family had owned the motel for fifty years or more, picked up the telephone, Adeline identified herself, then asked to be connected to Billy Lightning's room. As always, she was obeyed immediately, and the phone on Billy's desk in the motel room rang, startling him from the notes he was writing about the discovery of the bloody hockey bag, and the ones he'd been reading about the history of murder and madness associated with the land Adeline Parr considered sanctified by the martyrdom of the priests of St. Barthélemy three hundred years before.

To say that he was surprised to receive a telephone call from Adeline Parr inviting him to lunch would have been an understatement of some magnitude. Billy had a dim memory of having met Adeline in 1952. He had a clearer memory of Phenius Osborne's frustration at the hoops she'd made him jump through in order to secure the permits that Phenius needed for his archaeological dig.

Adeline had cited the "holiness" of the land around Spirit Rock, as though the fact that the Jesuits had been martyred there three hundred years before, while trying to convert the Ojibwa of the area to Christianity before being wiped off the face of the earth by an angry rival tribe, had somehow rendered holy the land that used to be her family's gold mine.

Even as a teenager, Billy had found the hypocrisy galling, as had his father—the fact that Adeline Parr claimed to be concerned about the sacrilege of an archaeological dig to locate the ruins of the St. Barthélemy settlement, but had not had any such qualms about her husband's family raping and exploiting that very same land for profit in the nineteenth century, and amassing the very fortune that allowed her to put roadblocks in his father's way. It was as though the notion that the land might be sovereign unto itself had never occurred to any of the people who had occupied it—not the French who came to Christianize Billy's ancestors, not the English who'd taken it from the French, and not the oligarchs and land barons who had purchased it and made it their own.

And now Adeline Parr wanted to have lunch with *him*?

"May I ask what this is about, Mrs. Parr?" he'd asked politely.

"It's not 'about' anything, Dr. Lightning," had come the reply, metallic-sounding in the telephone receiver. "I knew your father slightly when he was here twenty years ago. While I was surprised to hear that you had returned to Parr's Landing, it occurred to me that you might not know anyone in town. I understand you're now a professor in your own right, like your father. I'd be delighted to entertain so distinguished a visitor in my home. We rarely have the benefit of such company in Parr's Landing. And I think your father would have approved."

"*Would have*?" Billy said warily. "You heard about my father's death?"

"Only that he had passed away, Dr. Lightning. My daughter-in-law mentioned it at dinner last night. I understand you met her in town. She told me nothing of the circumstances. I'm so very sorry."

"Thank you, Mrs. Parr."

"Shall I expect you at noon, Dr. Lightning? I can assure you that Beatrice, my cook, has a skill in the kitchen that you'll find unparalleled anywhere else in town, let alone the available dining establishments." There was silence on the other end of the line as Adeline Parr waited. When Billy hesitated, she snapped, "Well? Are you coming or not?"

His own curiosity overrode his qualms—qualms whose source he couldn't identify, but which he chalked up to residual distaste for the high-handed way the Parrs had treated his father in 1952. Besides, he'd never been inside a robber baron's house before. And Christina might be there. He would dearly love to see her face again.

"Yes, Mrs. Parr," Billy said. "I'd be delighted. I'll see you at twelve noon."

"Splendid." Adeline's voice was crisp, once again the voice of a woman used to being obeyed. "Do you know the address?"

Billy smiled into the telephone receiver. "I do indeed, Mrs. Parr. I know the house. It's the only one in this broken-down Ontario mining town that looks like a Norman chateau."

Two hours before Adeline Parr called Billy Lightning, Jeremy Parr drove his niece to school.

Without his mother at the breakfast table to countermand

him, Jeremy had asked Beatrice to tell her husband that he didn't need to take Miss Morgan to school that morning because he and Christina had some errands to do in town, and they'd drop Miss Morgan off at Matthew Browning before they did them.

"That's fine, Jeremy," Beatrice had said. "I'll tell him. The weather feels a bit raw today. Nice sunrise, you know, but it's gone all damp and bitter. I'm sure Jim will be happy to hear it." Beatrice lowered her voice and glanced at the ceiling, almost by reflex. "Did you ask your mother?"

"No, Beatrice. I haven't seen her this morning. Have you?"

"I took some coffee up to her earlier. She said she didn't want any breakfast." Beatrice clicked her tongue on the roof of her mouth. "I hope she's not coming down with something."

Christina shot Jeremy a warning glance from across the table, and he bit down on the sarcastic retort about to spring forth. Christina was right—it wasn't fair to involve Beatrice in his ongoing war with his mother, especially since she would still be there with Adeline in that house long after he and Christina had gone back to Toronto, or wherever they wound up going.

"I'm sure she's fine, Beatrice," Jeremy said sweetly. "I'll mention it to her when I'm back later."

Both Beatrice and Christina had smiled gratefully at that, and the tone at the breakfast table grew light and carefree. By unspoken agreement, none of the three were going to comment on how much they were enjoying Adeline's absence, as much for Beatrice's sake as anything else. Morgan chattered about school and about her friend Finnegan, who'd lost his dog. Christina seemed lost in her own thoughts, though they seemed to Jeremy to be happy enough thoughts.

As for Jeremy, while he listened to his niece with apparent interest, and contributed his own comments here and there as was appropriate, his mind was running on an entirely different, and entirely private, track.

It had been two days since his disastrous encounter with Elliot McKitrick at O'Toole's. Jeremy had convinced himself over the years that he was no longer in love with his friend and he still believed it, even after the other night. But he was disturbed by

Elliot's coldness, even near dislike. Jeremy told himself that they needed to clear the air because they were living in the same town and things could get unpleasant very quickly if they didn't.

But in his more honest moments, moments that had been increasingly consuming him in the last forty-eight hours, Jeremy realized that they needed to make up because Jeremy felt Elliot's disdain like an acid burn on his heart.

If they weren't to be friends ever again (something he'd never worried about when he was living in Toronto and visiting Parr's Landing only in his dreams—or nightmares) he could live with that, but only with Elliot's absolution of Jeremy for being the one who escaped, or whatever else had kept Elliot's anger towards him simmering all these years. They needed to have it out, whatever that was going to take. And it had to happen today.

"All right, Morgan," Jeremy said cheerfully. "Let's get you off to Parr's Landing's illustrious institute of higher learning. We're burning daylight."

"It's a stupid school," Morgan said, just as cheerfully. "It's like someone put me in a time machine and sent me back to the olden days. But it's OK, I guess." She took one more bite of her toast, and then pushed her chair back. "I'll go get my books. I'll be down in five minutes."

When Morgan had left the room, Jeremy turned to Christina. "So, do you want to come for a drive? I need to do some things in town."

"What things? Oh, never mind. I bet I know." Christina sighed. She had always been able to read her brother-in-law like a book. "Just be careful, Jeremy," she said. "I'm worried about you. I know you want to . . . I don't know, make friends with him again or something. But you didn't see his face when I told him you'd mentioned meeting him at O'Toole's. It was like he didn't know who you were. Something isn't right there."

Jeremy said stubbornly, "I know. But I still need to . . ."

"'To make it right.' Yeah? To talk? You're just like a girl, Jeremy, I swear."

"Thanks a lot," he grumbled. "What a great vote of confidence, Chris."

"Don't pout." Christina laughed gently. "You know what I mean. You know what I'm talking about. It's part of what makes you . . . well, you. It's why I love you. It's why we all love you."

Morgan appeared in the doorway of the dining room. "I'm ready to go," she announced. She was wearing her dark green jacket and holding her books in her arms.

Jeremy turned his head so Morgan couldn't see and mouthed *thank you* to Christina. She smiled back at him and winked.

In the car, as Jeremy drove the Chevelle through the falling leaves on the winding roads into town, Morgan said, "Mom, could we stop by my friend Finn's house on the way to school? I want to see if they found his dog yet or not. He was feeling really bad about it last night."

Christina frowned into the rear-view mirror. "I think he'll be at school, too, won't he, honey?"

"Please, Mom," Morgan pleaded. "Just for a minute? It's on the way."

"I don't think we have time, Morgan," Christina said firmly. "But I'll tell you what. If you want, you can stop off and see him after school. If he's not there, you can call him and I'll drive you over tonight after dinner. What do you think?"

"You never let me do anything," Morgan said sullenly, staring out the window. "I hate this town."

Christina and Jeremy exchanged a knowing look. This time it was Christina who mouthed the word. *Hormones.*

"That's enough, Morgan," she said automatically. Softening, she added, "I'm sure your friend's dog is home by now. You can go see him after school. I'm glad you're making new friends. He sounds like a very nice boy. Why don't you invite him over?"

"Are you *kidding* me, Mom? After that scene with Grandmother about 'townies' and 'sluts'? No way. He asked me if he could come and see the house, but I told him that it wasn't a great idea, at least not now."

"Tell you what," Jeremy interjected. "I'll talk to your grandmother about it. I'm sure we can make it OK somehow. Like your mom says, he sounds like a nice boy."

"He is," Morgan said sadly. "And I'm worried about his dog. He really loves her."

Christina looked at her watch, but there really wasn't any way to allow for a stop before school without making Morgan late. And her mother-in-law would hear about that, she had no doubt whatsoever.

"We're almost there, sweetheart," Christina said. "Do you want us to pick you up after school?"

"No, thanks, Mom. I'll walk. And I think I will stop by Finn's house on the way home, unless I see him at lunchtime. He usually meets me. I hope he has good news."

"I hope so, too, sweetie."

Just before they pulled up to the front of the school, Morgan asked Jeremy to stop and let her out so she could walk the rest of the way. "Just like all the other kids do," she said, almost apologetically. "Is that OK?"

"Sure it is, honey," Jeremy said. He stopped the car and Morgan stepped out. She gave them a little wave, then hurried up the street to Matthew Browning without turning back. When she was out of sight, Jeremy asked Christina where she wanted to go.

"Why don't you drop me at the library? It's decent enough, as I recall. You can go and see Super Cop and I'll amuse myself in the stacks."

"I don't know how long it's going to take, though. Will you be all right?"

"Oh, please," Christina said. "I'll read for a bit. If you're back in an hour or so, we can go have lunch or something, or head back to the house. If you're not, I'll walk home. It's a nice morning. I could use the exercise. Who knows, maybe by the time I get home, Adeline will have taken a fall off the roof of Parr House and she will have left us all her money, and we can get the hell out of here once and for all."

"Dreamer," Jeremy said. "But I admire the scope of your ambition. Tragic death and inheritance. We'll make a real Parr out of you yet."

After Jeremy had dropped Christina off in front of the Parr's Landing library, he drove along Dagenais Street in search of a pay phone to call the police station.

Jeremy doubted Elliot would be amenable to anything as normalizing as a cup of coffee, much less lunch at the Pear Tree but—nothing ventured. Who knew? Besides, it wasn't like Jeremy had anything else on the agenda.

The man who answered the phone at the police station identified himself as Sergeant Thomson.

"Good morning," Jeremy said politely. "May I speak with Constable McKitrick?"

"May I ask who this is, sir?"

Jeremy took a deep breath. He leaned back against the wall of the phone booth. "This is Jeremy Parr. I was . . . I am a friend of Constable McKitrick's. From school. I've just come back to town. From Toronto," he added, feeling like the biggest babbling jackass that ever troubled daylight. At the same time, he noted how artlessly he'd slipped back into the entitlement of his family name. Not *My name is Jeremy Parr,* but *This is Jeremy Parr,* conveying the automatic expectation that the person on the other end of the line should recognize his name and be able to identify him. He suddenly missed the anonymity of the city even more.

There was a pause on the other end. "Of course, Mr. Parr. Welcome home. We'd heard that you were back in town."

The policeman's voice was as polite as ever, and if Jeremy had expected to hear some note of derision or condescension in it, he was relieved not to have heard any such thing. Even though he knew rationally that Elliot would never have willingly talked about what had happened between them—and its terrible consequences—Jeremy's dominant memory was of the scandal, and he assumed everyone else in town shared the same memory. Paranoia, obviously, but not necessarily unfounded paranoia. To his mother, it was as though it all happened yesterday, as she had reminded Jeremy every minute since his return to the Landing.

"Thank you, sergeant," Jeremy said. He waited a beat, then asked again, "Is Constable McKitrick in the office?"

"No, I'm sorry," Thomson said. "He's not. He's not on duty for a few hours yet. I don't expect him till early afternoon."

Jeremy frowned and looked at his watch. It was almost eleven. He didn't cotton to waiting around town for two or three hours till Elliot came on shift. "Thank you, sergeant," he said again.

"Any message?"

"No, sergeant." He was suddenly struck by how ridiculous he sounded. *Who calls a police station and asks for a particular cop, but doesn't leave a message? Are you trying to sound weird?* "Actually, yes," Jeremy said firmly. "Would you tell him I called? And that I'll try him again?"

"I will indeed, Mr. Parr. And again, welcome back to town."

"Thank you, sergeant," Jeremy said for a third time, then hung up.

What to do, he pondered. Then he picked up the telephone directory hanging from the ledge next to the phone in the booth and looked up the phone number and address of *McKitrick, E.* The phone number was there, right beside the address on Martina Street.

His mouth was suddenly very dry, and his heart sounded like the echo of a trip-hammer in his ears. *No guts, no glory,* he thought, even though he'd always hated that phrase, associating as he always had, with clubs he would never, ever be part of. But it still rang true.

The worst case scenario would be that Elliot refused to see him, or threw him out, or decked Jeremy for daring to show up at his house, especially if he was with a woman. On the bright side, maybe in the privacy of his own house, Elliot might be able to talk about his feelings. *Christina is right. I am just like a girl.*

Jeremy pushed open the door of the phone booth and walked over to where his car was parked. No guts, no glory, indeed. He slipped behind the wheel and turned the key.

Anne Miller had decided against taking Finn to the hospital even though when he'd regained consciousness he'd been hysterical. He'd only been out for a few minutes, but to his frantic mother it seemed as though he'd been in a coma for six months. She'd shaken him and patted his face, trying to wake him.

When he'd woken, in between great arcs of crying, Finn had

tried to tell Anne and Hank something about Sadie catching fire. It made no sense to Anne, but the fact that he'd come home distraught and nearly delirious without his beloved Labrador was a fact that asserted itself in the midst of his agitation. Also, he was covered in ash, an incontrovertible fact that chilled Anne Miller to her heart's core.

"Finn, slow down," she begged. "Tell us again. What happened? Where's Sadie?"

"I threw the buh-buh-ball," he wept. "And she . . . she *burned up*. My dog burned up into *smoke*."

"Finn, that's not possible," Hank had said, slipping automatically into the reasoned tone of fathers, a tone that usually had the power to right the world's wrongs and bend reality with the sheer power of its unquestioned authority. "Did someone shoot Sadie? Was it maybe a gun you heard? Did you see smoke?"

"*I threw the ball and she burned up! She burned up! SADIE BURNED UP!*" Hank went to slap Finn's face—not out of anger, but merely a lifetime of watching movies where hysterical people are slapped across the fact to calm them. Before he could, however, Anne stepped between Hank and their son, holding Finn tightly to her breast. Over the top of Finn's head, Anne shot her husband a look that clearly telegraphed, *Oh, for heaven's sake, Hank.* Finn buried his face in her bathrobe and sobbed till his entire body shook, but even Hank could see that his mother's embrace had a calming effect on him.

"Shhhhhh," said Anne. "Shhhhh, Finn. It's all right. Take your time. It's all right. We'll figure out what happened to Sadie. Shhhh . . ."

And yet Finn was inconsolable. "I told you what happened. I told you."

In his bedroom, Finn curled against his pillow as though it were Sadie's body. She hadn't seen that posture in her son since he was a baby, and if Finn had suddenly popped his thumb in his mouth and began to suck it, she wouldn't have found it out of place. As his mother, Ann knew every position of his sleeping body, every curve, every mood-based physical cue. What she saw here terrified her. It was as though Finn was retreating into himself, reverting to a preconscious infantile state. And Sadie was definitely missing—again. There wasn't any way around it.

Finn lay on top of the coverlet. Anne took a blanket from the foot of his bed and covered him. As she watched, his shallow breathing deepened and he closed his eyes. If he was not actually sleeping, she thought, he was at least slowly calming himself. Ann ran her fingers through Finn's hair. Her fingers came away matted with a combination of ash, sweat, tears, and snot. She wiped her hand on her bathrobe. *Ash. Sadie? On fire? It's not possible.*

Back in the living room, Hank was waiting for her, pacing the floor. "Anne, what the *blazes* . . . ? Where's Sadie? Did Finn say anything else?"

"He's resting," she said. It was as though she hadn't heard the question. "Not sleeping, but resting. He'll sleep."

"Anne, where's Sadie? Where's the damn dog? Last night she could barely walk. This morning he takes her out for a walk and comes back without her, and with some crazy story like something out of a horror movie. Did he do something to her? Did he hurt her?"

"Jesus Christ, Hank. What do you mean, 'did he hurt her'? Are you insane? He loves—loved—that dog like a baby. He'd never hurt her. What the hell are you asking me? Did he hurt her? What's wrong with you?"

"Anne," Hank said, with a patronizing patience that would normally have driven his wife to thoughts of murder, "the dog is missing. You don't believe she burst into flames all of a sudden, do you?"

"Hank, Finn is covered with *ashes*! And Sadie isn't here! You *bet* something happened! But what?"

Hank thought for a moment. "A gunshot? Did a hunter shoot her, maybe? Did he imagine the rest? You know the way he is, especially with those bloody Dracula comic books of his. His imagination can be the very devil."

"Hank, if Sadie had been shot, he'd have blood on him. He doesn't have blood on him. He has ashes on him."

"Summer lightning, maybe . . . ? It does happen. It's rare, but it does happen. I can't think of any other explanation. Can you?"

Anne was silent. Then she said, "Hank, can you go out there and see if you can find her . . . her body? Even if she was struck by . . . by summer lightning, she should still be there, shouldn't she? Can you bring her home? So we can bury her in the yard? I think it would be a good thing for Finn, don't you?"

Hank sighed. "I can't go now, Anne. I have to be at work. But I'll try to cut out earlier today and head up there before sunset. I just can't manage it any sooner than that."

"How will you know where to look?" Tears filled her eyes at the thought of Sadie lying untended on some rock ledge somewhere up near Spirit Rock. "How will you find her?"

"Shouldn't be hard to find her," Hank said, his throat suddenly full. "I'll find her. I'll bring her back home. You're right. It'll be good for Finn to see that she . . . that he didn't . . . well, that something else didn't happen to her."

When Hank left for work, and Finn was finally asleep in his room, Anne did two things in quick succession. First, she telephoned the Mrs. Brocklehurst at the school and told her that Finnegan was running a high fever and wouldn't be at school for at least the next day or two. She was keeping him home, for everyone's sake. Yes, it *was* a pity. Yes, these sudden changes in temperature were indeed the dickens. Yes, she'd make sure his bedroom window stayed closed. Of course. Yes, thank you Mrs. B. When Anne hung up the phone, she locked herself in the bathroom and turned the cold water tap full-blast in the sink so Finn wouldn't hear anything. Then she sat down on the edge of the bathtub and wept her own tears, the ones she'd kept from Finn and Hank because if she fell apart, they would, too. And now Finn had fallen apart, and there was no more reason to keep the tears inside. At least not in private. She cried for Sadie, whom she loved as though Sadie were her dog, not Finn's. She cried harder than she had since she was a little girl, so hard that her shoulders and her abdominal muscles throbbed with it.

But mostly, she cried for Finn, because whatever had happened this morning out there on the cliffs—whatever it was— it had destroyed something in her son she feared he'd never get back. Whatever other tragedy had happened here, something had been shattered beyond any possibility of repair.

Later, around lunchtime, through an upstairs window, she'd seen the Parr girl come up the driveway. Anne had heard the knock on the door, but hadn't answered it. She'd prayed Finn hadn't heard it. He was finally asleep. For her part, Anne didn't have the faintest clue how to tell the Parr girl about Sadie, even if she'd had the heart to try.

She looked out the window again and saw the girl walking back in the direction of Matthew Browning. *A nice girl,* Anne thought, relieved that she'd left so quickly. *She reminds me of Jack. I'll tell Finn she was by when he wakes up. He'll appreciate that she stopped by. So sweet of her to do that.*

CHAPTER TWENTY

Jeremy double-checked the address on Martina Street as he manoeuvred the Chevelle to a parking spot next to the curb. He found he'd forgotten that even towns like Parr's Landing had streets like this one—rows of narrow, rectangular prewar shotgun houses with peeling paint and small chain-link fenced front yards where nothing beautiful ever grew, with fenced back yards that housed dogs who were never allowed to experience the warmth of the indoors. Houses that were smaller and meaner than even the other small, mean houses in a town full of them.

Christina grew up on one of these streets, Jeremy thought. *Her father died alone in one of these houses while she was in Toronto with Jack, and no one told her until six months after he was in the ground, probably because they were too afraid of my mother to find out where she lived. God, what must we look like to Christina, really, up there in that house, throwing eighteen-karat gold dishes at each other and stomping across marble floors and slamming mahogany doors. Good fucking Christ.*

To Jeremy, even the light seemed dirtier on Martina Street. It was as though the generations of men and women who'd offered their youth, their hopes, their dreams—indeed the entirety of their lives—to the Parr family gold mines as a sort of terrible, ultimate rent had only their own despair left to plant in the patchy, ugly side gardens between the houses. If that was the case, it was a crop that had thrived both in the heyday of his family's violent use of the land and its people and later, when the mines closed, throwing a town full of miners on the mercy of government welfare, and their own hardscrabble ability to survive. His own family's fortune had been long ago secured, of course, which had allowed his mother to continue to live like royalty, albeit lonely royalty, in her house on the hill on the other side of Bradley Lake.

Visible even here, from Elliot McKitrick's front steps, the jagged line of cliffs loomed in the distance, gathering the town in its brutal fold of wings. Though not usually given to flights of philosophy, Jeremy suddenly wondered whether the hills and the honeycomb of mines beneath them had been consuming the bodies and lives of the townspeople for more than a hundred years, or whether the townspeople themselves had been the predators and the once-pristine boreal forest and the earth beneath it had been the prey.

There were two mansions in Parr's Landing: Parr's House, and the Roman Catholic Church of St. Barthélemy and the Martyrs on MacPherson Street, arrayed in the self-referential sanctity of its own history as a shrine to the French priests who had died here attempting to colonize the people to whom the land actually belonged.

Everywhere else, it seemed, there were variations on the houses on Martina Street. In one way or another, both Parr House and the church had consumed the lives and the lifeblood of the townspeople and had been nourished by it.

This is my inheritance, Jeremy thought. *This is my legacy. This land and the people my family has been feeding on for over a hundred years. Whatever seed was planted in those hills and under that earth, it's been held for me in trust all these years. It's been waiting for me to claim it. Or for its chance to claim me.*

And right now it has me exactly where it wants me.

Jeremy shuddered. He shook his head, then reached out and knocked on Elliot's door. When there was no answer, he knocked again. He tried the doorknob, finding that it turned easily and swung open.

"Elliot?" he called. "Are you there? Elliot? Hello?"

At first there was silence, then out of the silence came a thump, like someone swinging their legs over the side of a bed and planting both feet firmly on the floor. In the air was a not-unpleasant scent of sweat and cigarette smoke, and something else—Jeremy recognized it immediately. It was Elliot's own musk, the unique, personal signature of his skin and hair. And his sex. Jeremy closed his eyes and breathed it in, suddenly flooded by a rich flush of memories that excited and shamed him in spite of himself.

"Elliot? Are you in there? It's me, Jeremy."

The bedroom door opened, and Elliot stood framed in the doorway. Behind him the bedroom was dark, the windows closed. In the half-light of what Jeremy assumed was a bedside lamp, Elliot's body was etched carved in shadow. At first, Jeremy thought Elliot was nude, but he was wearing a pair of white cotton boxer shorts that clung to his legs as though dried sweat had plastered them to the sinewy curves of his thigh muscles. Elliot was half-erect. The wiry scrub of black pubic hair crested the waistband of the white boxers, hanging off his lean hips, and the tip of his cock was visible through the fly.

Elliot squinted in the dimness. "Jem? Is that you?"

Jeremy's breath caught in his chest. "Yeah, it's me. Are you OK?"

His voice was rough with sleep. "What time is it? What are you doing here?"

"I called the station, they said you weren't in till later. I . . . I knocked. I thought we could maybe talk or something."

"Talk. OK, we'll talk, sure." Elliot went to rub his eyes and flinched. Gingerly he felt the area under his jawline. He explored it with his fingertips, feeling for something Jeremy couldn't see. "Where am I? Wait, what are *you* doing here?"

"You asked me that already, Elliot. You're in your house. This is where you live." Jeremy took a step towards him. "Is everything OK?"

"Bad dreams. *Fuck*, my head hurts. I feel like shit."

"Do you want me to get you a glass of water?"

"Yeah, please." Elliot indicated the kitchen with a general sweep of his arm. "In the kitchen." Almost as an afterthought he added, "Thanks."

Jeremy found a clean glass in the midst of the unwashed crockery in the sink and poured Elliot a glass of water. When he returned to the living room, Elliot was no longer standing there, though Jeremy saw his legs over the side of the bed through the doorway of his bedroom. Elliot was sitting on the bed with his face in his hands. As Jeremy drew closer, he saw that Elliot was pale—no, more than pale, actually waxen. The thatch of dark chest hair stood out against the whiteness of his skin. His thick black crew cut was askew with jagged spikes.

Jeremy handed him the water. Elliot took a sip, then handed the glass back to Jeremy, his mouth puckering in distaste. "Guess I didn't need water," he said. "How did I . . . do you know how I *got* here? How did *you* get here?"

Jeremy sat down next to him on the bed and put his hand lightly on Elliot's shoulder. "Hey, are you all right, Elliot? This is where you live. This is your house. I assume you came home last night and went to bed, and that's how you got here. How else would you have gotten here?"

"Dunno," Elliot muttered. "I don't remember. I was . . . I was . . . I think I was at work, then I drove . . ."

"You drove home," Jeremy said soothingly. "Here. Were you drinking last night?" Jeremy looked around for empty bottles or glasses, but there were none around Elliot's bed, or anywhere in the room, for that matter. Nor had he smelled alcohol when he entered the house.

"Bad dreams," Elliot said again. "Donna . . ."

"Donna?"

"From the bar, Donna. That Donna. The . . . the . . . girl. Woman. Donna. From the bar. That one."

"Were you at O'Toole's, Elliot? Were you drinking at O'Toole's, maybe? Did you pass out last night?"

"I told you," Elliot said irritably. "No, I didn't drink." He lay back on the bed and put his hands over his face. When turned his face away from the light of the bedside lamp, Jeremy saw that there were bruises on the side of his neck, along the jugular.

Jeremy looked closer. Elliot had obviously cut himself shaving, more than a week ago, judging by appearance. The abrasions looked almost healed, the pink skin gleaming through the aureole of surrounding bruises. While the contusions themselves were dark purple, with no sign yet of the yellowing that came with healing, the cuts—which now looked more like punctures to Jeremy's untrained eye than scratches—seemed to have already closed up. *Not possible. Not bruises that dark. The skin underneath should look like roadkill.*

"Elliot," Jeremy said. "What did you do to yourself? What are these marks?"

Elliot grinned. His eyes were still covered with his hands. It wasn't a pleasant smile. "What marks?"

"There, under your jaw. Did you hurt yourself? Did you cut yourself?"

"Feels like . . ." Elliot touched his neck. "Feels like love. Some chick, maybe? Some hungry chick?" His voice, though tired, was mocking. "Chicks dig me, and I dig chicks."

Jeremy drew back from Elliot's words as though scalded. "Fine," he stiffly. "I got it. I was just curious. I wanted to see if you were all right. You're obviously all right. I'll go now and let you get ready for work."

Elliot took his hands away from his face and smiled again, different this time. All the malice had vanished and, for a moment, Jeremy doubted he'd even seen it. "Don't be like that, Jem," he said. "Stay awhile. You wanted to talk. Let's talk." He ran his index finger along Jeremy's upper arm, caressing it. "Stay for a while."

"Elliot, what are you doing?"

"Stay for a while." He voice was warm and insinuating. He reached over with his other hand and switched off the bedside lamp, bringing the room to near-darkness. "Isn't this better? It's better in the dark, right? Remember? In my room?"

"Elliot, I don't think this is a good idea. I think we should stop. You were right, it was a long time ago." Even as he said it, Jeremy knew he was lying.

Elliot propped himself up on one arm and kissed Jeremy full on the mouth. With the weight of his body, he pressed Jeremy down on the bed and swung his leg effortlessly over Jeremy's midsection, pinning him to the mattress between his thighs.

Jeremy felt Elliot's erection through the boxer shorts pressing against his own groin. His body responded immediately. Jeremy's erection grew until he felt it straining against the fabric of his jeans.

Elliot leaned down and kissed him on the mouth, full and insistent. Elliot's mouth was surprisingly soft—no, not surprisingly. Everything was familiar, and becoming more so by the minute. All he had to do was close his eyes and let the encumbrance of years break away from him like clouds after a violent storm. Elliot was right. Jeremy *did* remember.

He reached around behind Elliot and pulled the waistband of his boxer shorts off his ass, feeling the smooth, cleft halves of hard muscle covered flesh under his hand. This time it was Jeremy's turn to groan. He leaned up to kiss Elliot again. The feeling of Elliot's teeth beneath his lips was shockingly erotic. Elliot pressed himself against Jeremy's body in an aspect of unquestioned dominance, and Jeremy felt himself yield to it naturally.

"Take off your shirt," Elliot whispered. "Come on. No one needs to know about this. This is just you and me here now—come on. You still dig my body, right? You want me, don't you?"

"Yes," Jeremy breathed. "Yes, I . . . I still want you."

"You can have me. I've always been yours. Take off your clothes."

Without moving from underneath Elliot's weight, Jeremy unfastened the buttons of his 501s and shrugged them down to his knees. He pulled his briefs down as well, then kicked them both off his legs. Elliot kissed him again, on the lips, on the side of his face.

In the darkness of the bedroom, Elliot was a looming, bulky shape grinding on top of him. Jeremy saw Elliot's face only blindly, ridges and bone and hair under his fingers. Elliot's breathing came more quickly now, in torturous, jagged hitches that, to Jeremy, could only signal passion. His kisses grew even more insistent, moving from the side of Jeremy's face, along the side of his neck, across his throat, and back again.

"Elliot, hold up," Jeremy gasped. "Let me take off this turtleneck. Hold on. Slow down."

He leaned back to let Jeremy slip the turtleneck off, which he then tossed to the floor. Their bodies were pressed against each other. Jeremy scissored his legs around Elliot's waist, pulling him close, giving himself joyfully up to what now seemed an inevitable, blissful conclusion.

Elliot reached out with both his arms and grasped both of Jeremy's wrists in a crushing grip, kissing him brutally on the mouth. Jeremy screamed as the pain from Elliot's grip shot up his arms. On top of him in the darkness Elliot's body temperature suddenly rose, spiking to feverish levels of heat. Jeremy felt the heat from Elliot's body bake into his own skin, warming it uncomfortably. Then it plunged hypothermically, as though some internal thermometer in Elliot's body had gone haywire. It rose again sharply, and this time the heat of Elliot's body felt as though it could actually burn Jeremy.

"Elliot, get off me! Elliot! What's wrong with you?"

In the darkness, Elliot's voice sounded as though it was coming through a mouth full of sharp nails. His breath was suddenly foul in Jeremy's face, and Jeremy gagged.

"Kiss me," Elliot said hungrily. "Kiss me, Jeremy."

"Jesus, Elliot, *get off me!* What's wrong with you?"

Jeremy flailed wildly for the switch to the bedside lamp, terrified of what he would see straddling him when he turned on the light, but even more terrified by what was hidden by the dark. He felt Elliot's lips on his throat, and something else—he felt Elliot's teeth. Elliot's mouth opened and Jeremy felt his tongue tasting the flesh of the jugular area, and now there was no question of seduction or desire. Jeremy felt like an animal being scented as prey. Elliot's grip was implacable.

"Elliot, for God's sake, *get off me!*" Jeremy gave one mighty shove with his knees into Elliot's abdomen. He felt Elliot's body react with stunned surprise, recoiling just enough for Jeremy to roll over on his side. As he thrashed his head back and forward trying to dislodge himself from Elliot's grip, he felt something thin and cold slither across his throat from where it had been tucked away behind his head, felt it lodge itself between his chest and Elliot's shoulder. An unengaged part of his brain dully wondered what it could be, then realized. Jeremy never thought of it, mostly because he hadn't taken it off since his confirmation years ago, however many times he thought he ought to, all things considered. The St. Christopher's medal his mother had given him, telling him not that it would protect him, but rather that terrible things would happen to him if he ever dared remove it.

There was a sudden dazzling flash of blue light in the bedroom, and a popping sound, like a sparking electrical plug.

Elliot screamed and leaped off the bed with supernormal agility, clutching his shoulder and crouching against the wall like an injured animal.

Jeremy scrambled off the bed and turned on the bedside lamp. In the nanoseconds between the act of switching on the lamp and his eyes growing accustomed to the sudden brightness after the darkness before, what he saw seemed to shimmer and transform as he watched. A naked monster squatted in front of the wall, a monster with a bloodless white face, a mouth full of sharp white teeth, and an expression of terrible, thwarted hunger and injury as it clutched the place where it had been burned, its eyes full of hate.

Jeremy's vision swam, blurred, and then cleared as his eyes adjusted to the light. *No, it's not a monster. How did I see a monster? It's just Elliot, holding his shoulder. Elliot burned himself on something. A wire? Did something happen with the lamp cord?*

Elliot's breath hissed painfully through his clenched teeth—normal teeth, not wolf's teeth.

"Elliot, what the hell? Are you all right? What were you doing?"

"Jem, get out of here. I mean it. Leave. Now."

"Your shoulder. What happened to your shoulder? What the *fuck* happened just now? Did you burn yourself on something?"

Elliot tore the cover off the bed and wrapped it around himself. "Jeremy, get out of here! I mean it! Get your fucking clothes on and go! I don't want to see you here; I never wanted to see you here! Why can't you take a fucking hint! Leave me alone!"

He lashed out, his fist catching Jeremy across the chin. Jeremy felt the impact thrum though his face, making his eyes water and his ears ring with it. Jeremy touched his face in pain and shock, and stepped back. He stared at Elliot for what seemed like a very long time.

"You don't know what you want, Elliot," Jeremy said quietly. "That's always been your problem. It was your problem when we were kids, and it's still your problem now. I'll leave. Believe me. I won't ever bother you again."

Jeremy turned his back on Elliot and dressed quickly, pulling on his jeans and turtleneck in a sequence of short, angry movements. Behind him, he heard Elliot begin to sob.

"I'm sick, Jem. I'm really, really sick. Help me, Jem. Help me. I'm changing into something terrible. I can feel it."

"You're not sick, Elliot," Jeremy said tiredly. "You're just a coward. Maybe I was a coward, too, for running away. Maybe I was an idiot now for coming to your house and falling into . . . well, what we did just now. Trying to go back in time. But you know what? I really loved you. I thought we could at least be friends. But I'm done. I wish you well—I mean that. But I'm finished."

"Jem, please . . . I'm sorry I hit you! I'm sorry about . . . well, what happened. But please don't leave me alone here. There's something wrong with me. I'm sick. I'm afraid that something awful is going to happen to me if you leave. I'm not strong like you are, Jem. Don't leave me here."

"Elliot, I'm sorry, too. I really and truly am. But I never should have come back."

Jeremy walked out of the bedroom into the living room, and then out the front door to where the Chevelle was parked. It took everything in him not to look back.

In the time he'd spent with Elliot, the sky had darkened and now a cold rain was falling. Martina Street looked dirtier than it had when he'd pulled up.

Above him, Jeremy heard a thunderclap. He tucked his head down and ran for the Chevelle just as great knives of icy rain began slicing from the sky. He hoped Christina had stayed put in the library where it was warm and dry. He'd stop by and pick her up on his way to Parr House, and tell her that they were leaving the Landing as soon as humanly possible.

Jeremy swore to God that even if he had to steal the money from Adeline, or even kill her for it, he was going to get himself and Christina and Morgan out of Parr's Landing, away from the sundry monsters that had been waiting for them for all these years.

"The rain is here," Adeline Parr announced to Billy Lightning, as though she were speaking of an outdoor servant who tended her gardens fortnightly but who came to the back door and never crossed the threshold. "It was inevitable. Fall is so fickle this far north." Adeline pressed her lips together in a delicate moue of regret. The expertly applied dark red lipstick and her sky-blue tailored wool dress, to which was affixed a parure of sapphires and diamonds in the form of a brooch shaped like a maple leaf, provided the colour in the gloom of the dining room. "We've been having too many good days in a row," she added. "It's been *such* a lovely autumn so far."

Adeline had greeted him at the door of Parr House herself, ushering him into the dining room as though he were a visiting dignitary. On the way, she'd given him a brief lecture on the history of the house. She'd touched on this history of the mines, and pointed out the oil portraits of the various men in her husband's family who had brought it to prominence, and when they'd lived and died. Over lunch, she'd expounded on the history of the town, demonstrating a remarkable knowledge of the history of the doomed Jesuit mission of St. Barthélemy.

Billy had eaten some of the jellied freshwater eel that the cook, Beatrice, had placed in front of him ("So yummy!" Adeline had trilled, rubbing her small white hands together in a way that somehow managed to communicate mirth, but which struck him as faintly ogrish, and which made Billy wonder if, somehow, Adeline was mocking him.) He ate it out of politeness, but Mrs. Parr didn't seem particularly surprised or bothered when he helped himself to two more rolls of bread from the basket, leaving the plate of eel—to Billy's tastes, disgusting—more or less untouched.

He had remained quiet when she opined that he was likely grateful for the sacrifices of the Jesuit martyrs who had died in an attempt to help his "people" come out of ignorance and savagery and into the light of Jesus Christ. He didn't remain quiet out of intimidation, as he surmised she would think, but because he was curious about why she'd invited him to this gothic fun house on the hill. His academic training had been significantly involved in research, and an essential component of research, especially when it came to oral history, was to let the subject talk, no matter what.

And if the pretentious, arrogant white woman at the other end of the table wanted to go on about the weather, she was welcome to, at least for now.

He smiled politely. "I didn't hear the rain, Mrs. Parr," he said. "How do you know it's raining?"

"Young man," she said. "I know every creak and patter in this house. I can practically hear the seasons changing. I heard the rain on the roof when it began—on several of the roofs, actually." She laughed self deprecatingly as though she'd made a witticism. "It's a rather large house, as you can see. Some members of my family have come to stay, including my granddaughter." Adeline took a small bite of the jellied eel. Her lips barely moved when she chewed. "It's all been tremendous fun, and so lovely that they've all come to see their old granny," she added, touching the heavy linen napkin to her lips. "Any house is so much less grim and vast when it's full of family, don't you think?"

"Of course," Billy replied. "And I met your daughter-in-law in town. I believe you already know that. I was so sorry to hear of your son's passing. He sounds like he was a fine man."

"Indeed he was," Adeline said curtly. Her face suddenly blank and uninviting of any further discussion on the topic. "Thank you." With visible effort, she softened her face and smiled. "Dr. Lightning, I understand that you, too, have recently suffered a bereavement. Your adoptive father?"

"My *father*," he corrected her gently. "Yes, Mrs. Parr. He died earlier this year."

"I'm so sorry," she said. Billy thought he detected something shift in her face. For an instant, he could have sworn that he'd seen something real break through Adeline Parr's honed-to-perfection

Lady of the Manor routine. And then it was gone, if it had been there at all. "Had he been ill?"

"No, he was in fine health." Billy paused. He was unsure of how much more personal he wanted to get with this woman until he had a clear idea of what she wanted.

Adeline's tone managed to be both solicitous and peremptory at the same time. "Then . . . ? How did he . . . what happened to your adoptive father?"

"He was murdered, Mrs. Parr," Billy said, ignoring her second reference to his adoptive status. "He was killed by someone who broke into his house near the university. Whoever it was killed him and stole some personal artefacts related to his work." Billy paused, studying her face. "He was working on a book pertaining to the history of this region—the mystery surrounding the destruction of the Jesuit mission of St. Barthélemy, in particular. And the history of the unexplained occurrences."

Adeline blanched. "*Murdered?*"

"Mrs. Parr, are you all right?" Billy leaned forward across the table as though to catch her. She appeared to have aged twenty-five years in the span of seconds. Billy saw her skull beneath the flawless makeup and carefully styled hair. Her skeleton, wearing flesh and an expensive sky blue dress, slumped in the dining room chair. The falling silverware clattered loudly on the polished floor of the dining room.

"Mrs. Parr? What's wrong? Are you all right? Shall I call someone?"

Slowly the colour returned to Adeline's face. When she spoke, her voice was weak. "Do they know who . . . do they know who it was?"

"No, the police don't," Billy said. "Mrs. Parr, again—are you all right?"

"I knew your father, Dr. Lightning. We . . . he was a fine man. I remember that awful business with that student of his, what was his name? The one in 1952?"

Billy suddenly felt the room was oppressively warm. "Richard Weal. His name was Richard Weal. Why do you ask?"

"Your adoptive father was . . . we stayed in touch, Dr. Lightning. Not often, mind you. More out of *courtesy*. He was a very courteous man. He was quite . . . he was quite disturbed by what happened that summer. He expressed it to me several times."

"Mrs. Parr, why are you telling me all this? Do you know something about what happened to my father? Did my father . . . were you and he frequently in touch?"

"No," she said sharply. "As I *said* . . . we were very sporadically in touch."

"Mrs. Parr, you just said that my father expressed to you several times that he was 'disturbed' by Richard Weal. The dig ended when Richard was arrested. *When* did you and my father discuss Richard Weal? And for how long? Recently? Please tell me!"

Adeline closed her eyes. "I'm sorry, Dr. Lightning. I feel rather faint. I'm going to go and lie down now." She reached for the silver bell next to her plate and rang it. From behind the swinging door that connected the dining room to the kitchen, Beatrice approached to clear the table. "I'm so sorry about your adoptive father," Adeline said.

The hostess voice was back, weaker of course, but evident. Billy pictured a curtain being drawn. In a few seconds, any chance of getting any information out of Mrs. Parr would vanish.

"Mrs. Parr, if you know something about Richard Weal and my father, please tell me," Billy said urgently. "I believe Richard Weal killed my father. The police don't believe me—they insist he's dead. I don't believe he is. I believe he's come back here, looking for whatever he thought wanted him in 1952. At least one person is dead in a town not far from here, and a boy from Parr's Landing found a bag full of bloody archaeological hammers up on Spirit Rock yesterday. Please. I'm begging you—tell me what you know, if you know anything."

But the curtain had closed. Adeline's eyes were again bright, her expression impermeable. "Ah, Beatrice," she said brightly. "Yes, you can clear now. The eel was absolutely delicious. You've outdone yourself yet again."

"Thank you, ma'am," Beatrice said dutifully.

Adeline smiled at Billy, inclining her head slightly like a queen preparing to accept a visiting ambassador's gratitude and admiration for her kingdom's hospitality. "Did you enjoy your lunch, Dr. Lightning? The eel? Oh, I do hope you did. Dr. Lightning is a famous professor from Michigan, Beatrice," Adeline continued, turning to the cook. "He spent some time here in the Landing as a young man. It just didn't seem right to let such an illustrious guest pass through our little town without visiting Parr House, don't you agree?"

"Yes, ma'am." Beatrice began to clear away the plates. She bent down to pick up the cutlery at Adeline's feet, placing it without a word on the empty plate she carried.

"Beatrice, would you be so kind as to see Dr. Lightning out? I would do so myself, but I'm feeling rather sleepy and may toddle upstairs for a nap. Dr. Lightning," she said, turning to Billy. "Again, thank you for having lunch with me. I very much enjoyed our discussion about your work, and the mission that was in Parr's Landing. We're very proud of the town's history, as you know—both the development of a barren region as a source of industry, and of course the introduction of Christianity and salvation to a heathen race. You're a perfect example of the success of that introduction, Dr. Lightning. Your adoptive father's charity allowed you to rise in the world. You should be very proud."

Billy stared at her blankly, his mouth open in disbelief. *This woman isn't real,* he thought. *There's no way this is a real person. Surely not. What the hell is going on here? I'm in a madhouse.*

Adeline extended her hand, as though expecting it to be kissed. Dumbly, Billy shook it.

"Goodbye, Mrs. Parr," Billy said. "If you can think of anything else, I'll—"

Adeline cut him off swiftly. "Please enjoy the rest of your stay in Parr's Landing, Dr. Lightning."

When Billy turned around, Beatrice was waiting with his coat. "This way, Dr. Lightning," she said, stepping ahead of him out of the dining room, into the foyer.

When Billy looked back, Adeline was staring at a fixed point in front of her, at something Billy couldn't see.

Again, he was struck by how much she seemed to have aged in the short minutes between hearing about his father's murder, and now. She stared ahead of her, not seeing him watching. Billy had the sudden uneasy notion that she was watching for ghosts. He wished he knew whose ghosts they were, and what secrets she was keeping for them.

The cold rain turned to wet snow, then back to rain, eventually slowing to the present drizzle, but the skies were still dark with low-hanging storm clouds, and the road was slick and wet. The air was full of the scent of pine and rain, and the near-distant overture of winter. It was a scent that Jeremy had always loved, one he secretly craved in late October, in the city.

If anything could have pleased him right now, could have soothed the rage and pain and desolation he'd felt after leaving Elliot's house, it might have been that subtle but unmistakable turn of the seasonal wheel, but Jeremy was incapable of seeing beauty anywhere this afternoon, and if either truth or passion had greeted him by name on any one of the ugly streets of Parr's Landing this afternoon, he wouldn't have recognized them. That, or he would have suspected they were imposters.

There could be nothing good in this town—nothing decent thrived here, and never would. And if he and Christina and Morgan were to thrive, they'd have to leave. Every moment they remained was draining some essential part of their souls in a repetitive pattern that he suddenly understood was carnivorously cyclical, a pattern that had been woven into his history, the town's history, and the history of their ancestors. Parr's Landing fed on itself like the Ouroboros devouring its own tail. It had almost devoured Christina and Jack. It *had* devoured Elliot, draining him of all hope and tenderness, leaving him a shell, a hard, brittle revenant, a small-town cop in a dead-end job, in a town on the edge of the world where nothing ever changed. A place where the one thing he could never be was the person he actually was.

Parr's Landing might even have swallowed Jeremy himself if he hadn't fled that night fifteen years ago, hitchhiking to Toronto under the cover of darkness to ensure that his ogress of a mother wouldn't ever find him again. And now here he was, right back where he started.

His eyes on the road, his mind sifted through this history and his own place in it.

Simple, really, Jeremy mused. *I come from a family of ghouls. We've been feeding on the town for more than a century, in the same way the people who came from the old world to claim this corner of the new world fed on the people who lived here before us. My mother has fed on her own children. The "eternal return" in Parr's Landing isn't renewal, it's damnation.*

Jeremy picked up Christina at the library. She was waiting inside, by the door. She saw him, waved, and made a dash for the car to avoid the drizzle.

"How'd it go with Elliot?" Christina asked.

"Not well. I don't want to talk about it right now. Later, though, I promise, okay?" Jeremy said, paused for a moment, then continued, "We've got to leave here, you know. This was a very bad idea. This town isn't a good place for any of us."

And the way she had of always seeming to understand him as few others had ever been able to, Christina grasped his hand and squeezed it. She said nothing, but that nothing was everything to Jeremy with her hand on his as they drove back to his mother's house in silence, except for the steady patter of cold northern rain on the roof of the car.

"Who's that?" Jeremy said as the Chevelle pulled up into the circular driveway of Parr House. A tall man in his late thirties or early forties, wearing a leather jacket, was stepping out of the front door, which he then closed decisively behind him. The man's thick black hair was gathered in a ponytail.

Christina said, "It's Billy Lightning. The professor I was telling you about the other night."

"Handsome," Jeremy said with more than a little envy. "*This* is the guy you picked up in the café?"

"Shut up, Jeremy. I didn't pick him up in the café. We talked. Stop the car."

"Well, *obviously* I'm going to stop the car. We're *here*, aren't we? Hmmm," Jeremy said, peering through the windshield. "He doesn't look very happy. He must have encountered dear mama. He must have asked her for money, or blood, or water or something."

"Shut up, Jeremy," Christina said again. "Seriously, though, what could he be doing here?"

She opened the car door and stepped out onto the gravel driveway. When Billy saw her, he brightened perceptibly.

"Hi there," he said. "Fancy meeting you here."

"Hi yourself," she said. "I didn't expect to see you again, especially not here of all places."

"I didn't expect to be here, of all places," Billy replied. "Your mother-in-law phoned me and asked me to lunch. It was . . . strange."

"She *what*? You're kidding, right?"

"No, she invited me to lunch," Billy said. "She called me this morning at the motel and said she knew my father—or rather, she'd known him— and that I should come to the house."

Jeremy came from behind and extended his hand. "I'm Jeremy Parr," he said. "You must be the famous Dr. Billy Lightning."

Billy's face was wry. "Famous here for all the wrong reasons, it seems. I seem to have antagonized the police, I seem to have upset your mother, and I sincerely hope that this young lady," he added, indicating Christina, "will forgive me for showing up on her doorstep and surprising her."

"I'm surprised, but it's not my doorstep," Christina said. "It's fine."

"Christina," Jeremy said. "I'll just go inside and check on things with Mother." He smiled almost imperceptibly, then turned to Billy. "Nice to meet you, Dr. Lightning."

"Nice fella, your brother-in-law," Billy said as the front door closed behind Jeremy. "Are you sure that's really his mother in there? I don't see the resemblance."

"Neither do we. My husband wasn't much like her, either."

"Listen, Christina." He paused. "I know we agreed not to . . . to see each other again because of . . . well, you know. Our respective situations. But I really need to talk to you. Your mother-in-law said some very strange things this afternoon."

"Everything my mother-in-law says is strange. Why should today be any different?" When she saw that Billy was serious, she stopped. "Strange in what way?"

"She talked about my father. She claims they knew each other, but wouldn't elaborate. When I told her about his murder, she almost had a heart attack. Now look, I could be wrong, but something about Mrs. Parr leads me to believe that hearing about a murder isn't going to rattle her cage too much. But she nearly pitched a fit."

Christina tried, and failed, to picture Adeline as vulnerable in any way. Raging, yes, even murderous. But not vulnerable to the news of someone else's death, unless she was celebrating it in some way.

"Would you have dinner with me tonight?" Billy said tentatively.

"Billy . . ."

"Not a date. Just to talk. Really, I mean it," he said with conviction. "You're the only sane person I've met in this town, and I need to thrash out some ideas. I'll answer any question you want in exchange for you listening to what I have to say, and maybe helping me make some sense out of it."

What am I afraid of? Christina asked herself. *What Adeline thinks? What the town thinks? I already know what they think. Morgan will understand—she knows what it's like to have her grandmother disapprove of her making friends. What do I think? I think I could use a friend—that's what I think.*

"Christina . . . ? Would you? It could be an early dinner. There's a diner next to the motel. We could go there. Or we could go to the Pear Tree in town. Or even O'Toole's, if you'd prefer?"

She hesitated, then said, "Yes. That'd be fine. I'd like that. I could meet you at seven. I have to be home before nine."

"Not a problem," Billy said, stifling his pleasure and gratitude with difficulty. "Would you like me to pick you up?"

Christina laughed. "God, no. If you thought she pitched a fit over lunch, you wouldn't want to picture what kind of a fit she'd pitch if she knew I was going to meet . . . if she knew I wasn't going to be at the dinner table on time. I'll get Jeremy to tell her something. I'll meet you at the Nugget at seven."

As she watched Billy drive away in the Ford, she checked herself for feelings of guilt over having dinner with a man less than a year after the death of Jack Parr.

Finding none, she probed deeper. The only remorse she felt, if it could properly be called remorse, was that Jack hadn't met Billy, as well. They would—as she had thought earlier—have liked each other immensely.

Jack—better than anyone except, perhaps, his brother— would have understood what it was like to feel alone and friendless and vulnerable at Parr House, and he wouldn't have wanted that for anyone, least of all the woman who had given him a reason to save himself by leaving.

When Finn's subconscious mind registered that his sanity would not survive his obsessive replaying of Sadie's last moments—the flash of red arcing air in the orange and pink dawn sunlight, Sadie rocketing into the air in pursuit of her favourite ball, her body igniting *from within* as though a fire had started under her skin, and her terrible, near-human screams as she was burned alive in the sunlight—it eventually overrode his conscious mind, shutting it down and causing him to fall asleep.

It was not a restful sleep, but one full of random, dreadful images selected by his half-sleeping brain.

He dreamed of Sadie, of course, and the images of her as a puppy, or licking his face, or watching him solemnly, waiting for a piece of cheese to fall off the kitchen counter, having her wounds daubed with hydrogen peroxide by his father the other night, a million years ago. His own voice, *Don't hurt her!* These were agony and somehow infinitely worse than the flashes of Sadie's actual death that flickered at the periphery.

He moaned in his sleep, rubbing his eyes. Sweat sealed his hair to his forehead, which was hot and shiny with nightmare-sweat.

Images of Morgan, of course. Images of his parents' faces, the scent of fresh laundry and coffee as she held him against her warm body this morning. Bits of movies, the sky over Spirit Rock, the smell of bacon frying.

And images selected from his *Tomb of Dracula* comics—the streaks of lightning inked in bold yellow, indigo blue for black, black only for shadows and highlights. The faces of Frank Drake and his beautiful fiancée, drawn by the artist whose name he'd memorized: Gene Colan. Vampires in slumbering coffins, vampires rising nightly to suck the blood of the living. . . .

The weakly handsome face of Clifton Graves, the weasel who betrayed Frank Drake, his best friend, trying to steal his girl from him and unwittingly pulled the wooden stake from Count Dracula's rotting skeleton deep in the dungeons of the castle, thus releasing the risen vampire into the night.

These were his friends, and his mind whispered their names like a calming mantra: *Frank, Clifton, Jeanie. Frank, Clifton, Jeanie. Dracula.*

Poor Jeanie, a shard of splintered wood driven through her body by her brokenhearted fiancé in the hotel room in London. That terrible comic book scream as she died a vampire's death—AIIEEEEEEEEEEEEEEE. No exclamation point was ever required, not with that glorious, lurid green lettering.

Jeanie crumbling to dust, burning in the sunlight. Pleading for forgiveness, absolving Frank Drake of not having been able to protect her as a man ought to have been able to from the ghastly things that crept through the shadows when the sun went down.

"Frank . . . ? I'm dying, Frank. The sunlight."

. . . vampires burning in the sunlight . . .

. . . Sadie burning in the sunlight . . .

Finn sat bolt upright in his bed, gasping for breath. The damp blanket his mother had draped over him fell from his shoulders as he pinwheeled his arms, pushing the dream away, flailing for wakefulness. He looked down into his left hand. In his sleep, he'd sought out the red rubber ball as though it were a talisman to ward off nightmares. It was still smeared with ash. Finn uttered a sharp cry and let it fall on his coverlet. It rolled across the bed and bounced on the floor.

Next to his bed, Finn kept his stack of magazines and comics. He leaned down on his stomach and tore through the stack until he located Issue Two of *The Tomb of Dracula*. Frantically, he flipped through the pages until he reached the end, page twenty-one—seven panels, the dawn tones of orange and yellow like the sky above Bradley Lake this morning playing against the dark blue and black of the ever-present darkness.

Finn looked out his window. It was dark. Rain beat against the windows, a harbinger of colder, more murderous weather on the way as winter raked skeletal fingers through the darkening sky for the first time that fall. His bedside clock read five p.m. He had slept for six hours.

He looked again at the comic book in his hand, then down at the ash-covered rubber ball on the floor.

When his mother turned around where she stood in front of the stove, she was readying an aluminum-covered cookie sheet upon which three Swanson's chicken pot pies would be placed into the preheated oven. Finn loved Swanson's chicken pot pies—they were his favourite.

"Hi, sweetie. How are you feeling? We're having Swanson's for dinner! And mashed potatoes, and creamed corn." She made a smacking sound with her lips. Finn hated it when she made the sound, but he loved his mother too much to tell her. "Delish, right?"

Finn looked better, she thought. He had washed his face and changed his clothes. Some colour had returned to his cheeks, but he still had those god-awful dark circles, and his eyes looked freshly sandpapered. It was going to take a while for him to feel better. But the chicken pot pies would be a good start.

Anne smiled expectantly and smoothed her apron with her hands.

"Mom, I know what happened to Sadie," Finn said. "A vampire got her. That's why she burned up. A vampire got my dog. And I'm going to find him, and I'm going to kill him. I'm going to drive a wooden stake into his heart, and I'm going to make him pay for what he did to Sadie."

* * *

A branch slapped Hank Miller across the face in the gathering gloom, stinging his cheek and making him yelp. Hank was a proud man, and didn't think men ought to show pain. But since he was alone, and it was dark, he shouted, "Holy old *fuck!*" as loud as could. He rubbed his face, which hurt like a whore, but no blood came off on his fingers. "Sadie, where the *hell* did you get to, goddammit?" he muttered. "Where the hell did you two walk this morning, the fucking moon?"

The sun was well over the yardarm, as his father used to say, and it was most definitely going down behind those clouds, whether he could see it or not. He looked at his watch. Six frigging o'clock. The sun wasn't just over the yardarm, it was halfway in the drunk tank. It was early night, not early evening. He felt in his pocket for the flashlight and turned it on. The beam was molded by drops of thick, swirling night fog and the aftertaste of this afternoon's deluge.

Hank had hoped to tell his wife and child that he'd found Sadie's body and brought it home to bury her before the ground froze, which it would before long. His hope had been to keep the dog's corpse in the garage until Finn had gone to bed, then put her in the ground and present his son with a *fait accompli* in the morning. Finn never doubted his father, so Hank could have buried anything in his garden and told his son it was his beloved Labrador, but he would never do that to Finnegan.

At four p.m., he'd clocked out an hour early. He'd left the mill and taken his car up to the highest point of ground he could reach in his sturdy truck. He tried to check the position of the sun in the sky, but the storm clouds from the earlier downpour had remained. He had about an hour of daylight left. He squinted up the cliff, guessing more or less where Finn and Sadie had taken their walk.

Finn had rarely allowed anyone to join him on those walks, but he'd let Hank come along one morning this summer, and Hank had excellent recall. If worse came to worst, he wouldn't find Sadie and would have to come back the next morning and deal with whatever carrion mess the forest scavengers had left of his son's gentle dog. The thought sickened him, but not for squeamish reasons. He'd loved Sadie far more than his wife or his son knew.

A twig snapped somewhere above him. Hank stood stock still. He shone the light above him, but saw nothing except branches and rock. Hank rubbed his eyes. Something had moved up there beyond the copse of trees. He felt a momentary stab of fear, thinking of bears.

Bears, bullshit. Get a grip, you idiot. There hasn't been a bear attack here in thirty years or more. The bears and the mineshaft openings are the two stories we tell kids to keep them out of the woods. It didn't keep Finn out, and you're no kid. So get some sack.

The sound came again, two more twig snaps, coming from different places close by. This time, the sound unnerved him deeply. "Hello?" he called out. "Hello? Is anyone there?" He whipped his head from side to side trying to locate the source of the sound, to no avail.

The very last emotion Hank Miller would ever feel was a fear so desolate and hopeless that it was almost chemical. He felt a sudden kinship with every cornered animal he had ever hunted, in the moment right before he pulled the trigger. *So this is what it feels like,* he marvelled, as though from a great distance, even as he felt the piss running down the leg of his work pants.

Hank knew beyond a shadow of a doubt that he was living his last minutes before he physically saw the woman in the muddy jeans and the stained pink blouse drift towards him out of the darkness, her feet not touching the ground, her eyes incandescent and her mouth open and full of teeth like he'd never seen on anything from this earth. For a moment, he thought he recognized her, from school maybe? No, from the bar. It was that sexpot bartender from out at O'Toole's. But no, Hank thought, his mind in a state of confusion. *It can't be her—what would she be doing out here in the forest at this hour?*

And when the scrawny man with the wild, greasy hair and red matted beard crawled out from between an impossibly narrow wedge of rock beside him like a spider coming out of its hole—a great stench of shit and blood and rotted meat unfurling in his wake like a shroud— Hank knew that there was no shame in dying.

Terror, yes. Terror, absolutely. Who wanted to be eaten by monsters in the forest without even kissing his wife and son goodbye? But no, there was no shame, nothing ignominious in falling before this implacable, limitless blackness.

"*But you* will *see them again,*" the man said. "*You will kiss them goodbye. We promise.*"

They fell on him in a fury, burying their faces in the soft parts of his body and biting down, hard and sharp until he shrieked so loudly that even the nightbirds scattered.

Above him, Hank heard the beating of heavy wings and saw a shadow pour itself down from the treetops, lengthening, becoming columnar and corporeal.

The last thing Hank saw before Richard Weal and Donna Lemieux tore him apart, splitting his spine between them like a wishbone, was the tall black-robed man with the long white hair raising his hands in a gesture of benediction.

And because some deaths are crueler than others, Hank Miller never knew that he *had* found Sadie's body, after all. Indeed, he had died three feet away from where the remainder of the Labrador's bone and ash had been sluiced down the rock face by the rain.

Hank never realized that Sadie had already entered the ground— here at Spirit Rock instead of his back yard—and she had become part of the earth in a way that Hank never would.

Forty-five minutes after the desolate death of Hank Miller above Bradley Lake, five miles inside the Parr's Landing town limits, Elliot McKitrick woke from the dreamless sleep into which he had fallen when Jeremy Parr had left, finding himself hungrier than he had ever been in his life. His mind was filled with cloudy, half-formed images flowering silver and red, and the air was full of whispering, dead voices calling his name. When he turned to look, the shadows seemed to leap back from his sight, and when he tried to focus on them, there was nothing there but the bare walls of his bedroom which, though pitch dark, he could see as clearly and sharply as if it were high noon.

One voice in particular caught Elliot's attention. It was a familiar voice, and Elliot cocked his ear to listen. He smiled in acknowledgement, then walked naked to the small bedroom window and opened it, extending his arms in clear welcome.

The mist rolled in from the lightless black on the other side of the glass, and night entered, filling his bedroom with silver-blue fog in which vaguely human shapes shimmered and eddied.

Donna Lemieux, her mouth brown with Hank Miller's blood, gathered Elliot in her arms and kissed him where she had kissed him in her cellar, claiming him, caressing his nude body with what might have been merely the memory of possessive human desire. Elliot leaned into her, one arm across her shoulder, submissive, supine in her arms as she drank away the remainder of his life, taking his confusion and pain along with it. Elliot tried to speak, but could only murmur, and even that effort caused his eyes to roll back in his head.

"Thank you," Elliot said, then died.

CHAPTER TWENTY-ONE

The Gold Nugget diner was nearly deserted, and Christina couldn't decide if this pleased her because of the privacy it afforded, or made her feel more conspicuous in Billy Lightning's company. Ultimately, she decided she didn't care, which proved to be a relief to both her and Billy as they picked at their Salisbury steak special. The waitress assured them that the tapioca pudding was included in the price, then asked them if they wanted it after the meal, or with it.

"After, please," said Billy, speaking for them both. Though ravenous, not having eaten since Adeline's aborted jellied eel luncheon, Billy was still too upset to do more than move it around on his plate. Also, he hated tapioca pudding, which reminded him of St. Rita's, where it was considered a special treat for the residents, even though the milk used to make it was usually sour and the tapioca often rancid.

In the background, a radio played softly. Christina caught the strains of B.J. Thomas singing "Rock and Roll Lullaby," a song about a teenage mother and her child, which made her think of Morgan. The smell of grease in the air was oddly warm and comforting, not off-putting.

Christina had dressed carefully, and had applied lipstick. She told herself that it was because she was tired of Adeline making her feel like the bottom of a grimy lunch pail by swanning through her empty mausoleum in Mainbocher dresses and diamonds. But the truth was, Christina wanted to look pretty tonight, for Billy.

Odd, that, Christina thought. She'd mostly forgotten what it felt like to care.

They had spent an hour or more discussing Adeline's bizarre behaviour at lunch, but Christina was sick to death of talking about Adeline Parr.

"So, Billy," she said. "Tell me about you."

He shrugged. "I've told you about me. There's not much else to tell."

Christina smiled. "I don't believe that for a second," she chided him gently. "You've lived such an impressive life. I can't even imagine what it took to become what you've become. What drove you? Was it your father? I know he was a professor, too—did you always want to be like him?"

"Becoming like my father wasn't something I really thought of when I was a kid," he said. "I suppose having a father who was an academic, who valued learning, was an inspiration. But no, I didn't always want to be like him—that came later."

"So, what did you want to be?"

Billy paused. "I wanted to be dead," he said. "I wanted to not exist. I wanted the pain to stop. I wanted to be safe. Since it appeared I would never be safe, as a child, and since pain was a daily part of my life, I didn't see a lot of merit in being alive."

Christina was confused. "Billy—I'm sorry. I don't know what you mean."

He shook his head. "Never mind. I'm sorry I brought it up. I don't usually talk about it. Please forgive me—forget I said anything."

"No," she said, reaching for his hand, laying her own on top of his. "Tell me. What are you talking about? I want to know . . . that is, I want to know if you want to tell me. Do you? I mean . . . I'd like us to be friends, you know?"

"Friends," he said. He tested the word, probed for sharp edges. Finding none, he said, "I'd like that, too, I guess. I mean, yes. I *would* like us to be friends, Christina."

"So . . . tell me," she said. "What happened when you were a child, Billy? What made you wish you were dead? Death is obviously very much a part of my life these days since Jack has been gone. Yours, too, to be fair. I can tell you miss your dad as much as I miss Jack. I wish they were both still alive, still here for us. I can't imagine anything better than life right now."

"Do you know what my least favourite colour in the world is, Christina? Red. I hate it. I absolutely loathe it."

"I'm glad I didn't wear red tonight, then," she said lightly. She paused. "Why red?"

"Red is the colour of the uniforms we had to wear at St. Rita's when the priests took us out on Sundays, or to show us off in public. Do you know what a residential school is?"

"Not really. A school for Indian children, right?"

"Yes," he corrected her gently. "That's right."

"I'm sorry," Christina said. "I don't know much about them. We were taught that the schools were an example of the generosity of the Church and the Canadian government. Charity. They told us that we were lucky to have been born white."

"Yeah, the priests taught us that you were lucky to be born white, too." Billy realized that it sounded cruel when he said it. He forced himself to smile because it wasn't Christina's fault and she was obviously trying to understand.

"I remember when we were in school here, we had to memorize that poem from Kipling. The one about other children. What was it called?"

Billy smiled bitterly. "You mean, 'Foreign Children.' That was the title. 'Foreign Children.' They taught it to us, too. But we had to learn to recite it after we were punished. After the strap. Or worse." Billy looked away and recited. "*Little Indian, Sioux or Crow/Little frosty Eskimo/Little Turk or Japanee/O! don't you wish that you were me?*"

"Billy . . ."

"You asked," he said with another shrug. "You wanted to know me. Well, this is part of me. The government took me away from my birth father when I was a little boy. My mother had just died. My dad was all I had. I still have nightmares about that day—I was *six years old.* The priests shaved my head and put me in a dormitory with twenty other little boys. The first night, all I heard was crying from the other beds. When my hair grew back, they put a bowl on my head and cut around it. The priests started every day with a sermon about the love of Christ and the grace of the Catholic Church. They taught us that the price tag for acting like an Indian was an eternity of torment in Hell. But that was just after we were dead and away from the priests—they made sure that we had a taste of what was coming to 'bad Indians' in the afterlife right then and there. One kid I was friends with was given thirty lashes with a leather strap for speaking his own language. The food was rotten— literally rotten, sometimes. But not eating it could get you chained to the dining room table for days at a time."

"Billy, my God. My God."

"I ran away once," Billy said. "Do you know what they did to me when they caught me and brought me back to St. Rita's? The principal pushed me down a flight of kitchen stairs. And when I couldn't get up, he and another priest dragged me to his office, stripped me naked, and beat me unconscious. Afterwards, they took me to the infirmary and found out I had a broken arm. They weren't sure if it was the stairs, or the stick they used to beat me with." He laughed mirthlessly. "I got off easy. Other kids ran away and didn't make it. They'd bring their bodies back frozen with parts missing. I don't need to tell you how godforsaken cold it gets up here in the winter, or how hungry the animals get when the snow comes."

Christina's horror couldn't have been more obvious if someone had written it across her forehead with a grease pencil.

In many ways, Billy was appalled at himself for telling Christina about St. Rita's. She could not possibly have expected to hear what he was telling her when she asked him about his childhood. On those levels, he was ashamed of himself for using the truth as a cudgel, always knowing that, if push came to shove, he could always exonerate himself using her sheer decency and his terrible childhood history to grease those wheels.

On several other levels, including his own heart's measure, he wanted this woman to know him. He wasn't sure why, but he did. And he wanted her to know the worst as well as the best. He could see that she was impressed with his credentials—maybe too impressed, in that it seemed to cost her some dignity, maybe causing her undeserved shame about her own relative lack of formal education. He didn't want Christina Parr to think his life began as a tenured college professor without also knowing about what he had endured at St. Rita's, and how the blows of that hammer and chisel had helped shape his life.

"Didn't you say anything? Didn't anybody check up on the children? How could this happen right under the noses of the authorities? I mean, didn't anyone *tell*?"

He shrugged again. "We didn't tell," he said flatly. "We didn't say much of anything at all. If anyone did, after the inspectors left, the punishments were brutal. It was worse to tell than not to tell. They wouldn't have believed us, anyway. Everyone knew Indians were lazy, and that they lie. Especially bad Indian kids."

"What about your mother and father? Did you ever tell them about it after you were adopted?"

Billy shook his head. "No, I didn't. I kept it to myself. They loved me so much, I didn't want them to have those images in their heads. It would have been too horrible for them. Sometimes I wanted to tell them, but I always stopped myself in time. At St. Rita's, we learned the value of keeping quiet. Some lessons are hard to unlearn, even today. I can't believe I'm telling you this. I've never told anyone about his before. Christina, I'm sorry— please, don't cry. I'm sorry I even brought it up. It wasn't fair."

"You didn't bring it up, I did," she said. She blew her nose on the paper napkin beside her plate. With the clean end of it, she dabbed her eyes. "I wanted to know. Now I know."

"Yes," he said simply.

"I don't know where you buried all of this, Billy. I don't know how you got past it."

"I was lucky," he said. "Two wonderful people took me out of it and did their best to raise me as their own. They didn't try to make me 'not be an Indian.' They just loved me as I was. When they found out I was interested in history, they bought me books and took me to museums. They gave me the best education they could afford. And then they encouraged me to reclaim my Ojibwa heritage, and to be proud of it. But you know," he said thoughtfully, "all it takes sometimes is someone like your brother's friend—that G.I. Joe white cop, McKitrick—to look me up and down the way he does, like I was just a dirty, falling-down drunk, mouthwash-swilling nitchie, and suddenly it gets really hard to remember who I actually am. Or to have to sit in that funeral parlour your mother-in-law calls a dining room, eating her creamed snake, or whatever the hell she served me for lunch today, and listen to her tell me how 'grateful' I should be to the priests who 'founded' this town—her words, not mine—in 1631 for saving my soul and making me civilized. All I could think of was my birth father not being able to keep me safe from the government when they took me away from him. Thank you *very much*, Mrs. Parr."

"My mother-in-law is such an *asshole!*" Christina gasped. Shocked at her own audacity, she burst into horrified laughter. Billy, equally shocked at her use of the very unladylike word "ass-hole," joined her.

They doubled over, their laughter leavening the horror of Billy's story as nothing else could have. Instinctively, he reached for her hand and held it. When their eyes met, they realized they'd breached some perimeter of distance that neither of them had believed was permeable. Christina didn't pull her hand away from Billy's until she saw the waitress shambling over to their table, and then she withdrew it reluctantly, her cheeks warm with flush.

But when the waitress asked in a bored voice if they wanted their tapioca now, all bets were off and they laughed till they wept.

When the waitress asked them what was so funny, their laughter redoubled, and all Billy could do was wheeze, "Nothing, nothing is funny. Nothing is funny." Which, naturally, made them laugh even harder—so hard that Christina excused herself from the table to powder her nose before she had an accident.

Adeline Parr was outraged. *Why, there's a man standing in my driveway!* She gathered the collar of her cashmere bathrobe close, instinctively pulling away from the window. *And he's staring up at my bedroom, bold as can be. It's nearly ten o'clock at night. For the Lord's own sake.*

Adeline found it very difficult to believe that any of the locals would dare trespass on her property at any time of the day or night, but the fact remained that there was someone standing in her driveway. The moon and the stars that broke out from behind the rain clouds were bright white. They lit the driveway and the grounds with resolute clarity, and there was indeed a man standing there, looking up at her bedroom window.

The figure wasn't Jeremy—he was upstairs in his room. Adeline could hear her son's radio playing behind his closed bedroom door. Her whore of a daughter-in-law wasn't at home. She was out cavorting in some gutter somewhere. Jeremy had given Adeline some codswallop about Christina visiting high school friends for the evening, but Adeline knew better. The whore was getting her bug scratched in some basement or back alley somewhere. And Beatrice and her husband lived in town, so it wasn't either of them.

So, who on *earth* was standing in her driveway?

Adeline shrugged off her bathrobe and took her twenty-year-old sable coat off the padded hanger in the armoire. She slipped it on over her nightgown and stepped into a pair of shoes. Then she stalked out of the bedroom and swept down the stairs.

As she crossed the marble foyer, she wondered if she shouldn't perhaps alert Jeremy or Morgan that there was a man outside and that she was going to investigate it herself. *Yes, indeed,* she thought. *Which member of my illustrious, stalwart family shall I call to protect me from intruders? My pansy son? Or my fifteen-year-old granddaughter, who's already showing the moral laxity of her mother, the whore?*

Adeline smiled to herself. She realized that, at the end of the day, it would always be up to her to settle things. It had always been that way and always would be.

Her husband had been weak. One son was a pervert and the other had been a traitor. Adeline had only ever known one real man in her life, and even he hadn't been man enough to leave the simpering titmouse to whom he was married, much less his jumped-up adopted redskin brat, now a so-called "professor."

In the meantime, there's a man standing in my driveway.

When Christina came back to the table, Billy saw that she had indeed powdered her nose. Himself the son of a fastidious woman, the gesture touched him and reminded him of his mother, in the best possible ways.

He checked his watch and said with mock reproach, "It's well after ten. Didn't you have a nine o'clock curfew, Mrs. Parr?"

"Good God, is it, really?" Christina looked shocked. "I didn't even wear a watch! I have to get back home. I want to see my daughter before bed." She shook her head in disbelief. "I can't believe I let the time get away from me like that. What was I thinking? God, I'm such an *idiot*!"

"I'd guess you were thinking that you needed a break, Christina," he said gently. "Don't make this into something it wasn't. You're entitled to some time off from being what everyone else in that house needs you to be, for good or bad. Remember that."

Billy walked her to her car. As they said goodbye, he had the preposterous notion to kiss her on the cheek—a notion he overrode, shaking her hand instead. He told himself it was because of gossip, but he suspected it was really that he wouldn't want to stop kissing her. He wanted to take her away with him, back home to Toronto, even back home to Michigan with him. Somewhere he could watch over her. Anywhere, as long as it wasn't here.

Adeline pushed open the front door of Parr House and stepped out onto the portico.

"You there!" she called out. "What are you doing on my property? Identify yourself at once!" She waited, hands on hips. But the man in the driveway didn't move, nor did he speak. "Are you *deaf*? Answer me! This is *Adeline Parr* and you are trespassing on my land. Identify yourself at once."

When the man still didn't move, Adeline stepped off the portico and took a step towards him. She leaned forward and squinted, but the moonlight was behind him and she couldn't see his face.

"This is your last chance to identify yourself and state your business," Adeline said coldly. "In one minute, I shall go back inside my house and summon the authorities. And you'll find out exactly what it means to trespass on my land."

The man took a step towards her. Then another. Adeline squinted, but the shadows seemed to follow the figure as he walked towards her. The moonlight seemed to fall *around* him without once touching his face, or lighting on his clothes. He was dressed in from head to toe in black, however—that much she was able to ascertain, if only by the way the night seemed to fall away from him as he moved, the shades of black separating and reforming themselves in his wake. She felt dizzy watching him . . . *drift*? No, he was *walking,* she was sure of it. He was wearing some sort of long black robe—that's why he seemed to be floating, his feet not appearing to touch the ground. She hadn't been able to see his legs.

Is that . . . a priest? Why is there a priest on my front lawn in the middle of the night?

Adeline felt light headed. She closed her eyes tightly for a moment and shook her head.

When she opened them, the man was still there. But he had stopped moving and was standing close enough that she could touch him, his face still wreathed in shadows.

Adeline hissed, "Get out of here, whoever you are! I am going to turn around immediately and summon the authorities."

"*Laissez-moi entrer.*"

"What did you say?" she seethed. "Speak up. Speak English. I have no idea what you're saying."

Adeline stopped. The moon was behind where he stood beside the denuding phalanx of topiary bushes. Their shadows lay against the gravel drive, but where the priest stood, there was no shadow at all.

Too, she'd heard his voice—a beautiful, cultured voice, speaking . . . French? A language she didn't speak or understand herself, but she hadn't seen his lips move, and somehow she'd understood him anyway. He wanted her to invite him into her house. Into *Parr House,* of all the insolence!

His voice was rich and full and masculine, very much the voice of a real man—not a pansy's voice at all, she noted. Not like Jeremy's voice, not like the voices of all the weak men she'd known her whole life. Could this really be a priest?

Adeline felt a sense of vertiginous disorientation, a sensation of being probed, being *read,* as though her mind had been taken down off a bookshelf, her memories turned and rifled like pages in an album. She touched her fingertips to her eyes and pressed, moaning softly at the invasion. She felt an unfamiliar and nearly forgotten warmth spread between her legs, a phantom dampness that she knew couldn't possibly be real—not standing out here on the lawn on a cold October night with some strange intruder threatening her.

But he wasn't really threatening was he? Not really. He was just cold. He just wanted to come inside. He'd been sleeping in the caves above Bradley Lake for a long time. It made sense he should want to come inside. It was a reasonable request, and one she could easily grant by saying: *Come in. You're welcome in my house. Enter freely.* Those were the magic words. He was too much of a gentleman to enter without an invitation from the lady of the house.

Images spun through her brain, her own most private memories, coming faster and faster like a rickety black-and-white silent film. Her memories of Phenius. Her secrets, all of them, the light and the dark ones interchangeably. Some of them made her giggle—ridiculous, she knew, in a woman of her age. Others made her feel violated. He had no right to those. No . . . right . . . at all.

No, get out of my mind! You have no business here. Go away! I'm Adeline Parr! *How dare you—*

Pourrais je vous faire l'honneur de ma presence?

Adeline felt somewhat mollified by his courtesy. *May I honour you with my presence?*

Let me in. I'm so cold.

"Let me in, Adeline," Phenius said. "Let me in. I'm so cold."

She could see his face now, as though the man had somehow deigned to allow the moonlight to fall upon it.

It was *Phenius's* voice she'd heard, she was sure. Phenius speaking French. No . . . English now. But it was a *priest*, not Phenius. Phenius was dead, and the priest was—

He was grinning.

"*Adeline, my love.*"

She took three more stumbling steps forward, towards the man with Phenius's voice, the man who opened his arms to her.

No, not *his* arms, *Phenius's* arms. It was Phenius, looking exactly as he had in the summer of 1952 on the night he took her to Spirit Rock and showed her the site of his dig.

Adeline stumbled and fell. She felt the sharp gravel cut into her kneecaps, scraping them bloody. The house behind her was a million miles away and the world was reduced to Phenius's beautiful voice, and the moonlight was now bright enough to drown in.

Behind him on the driveway, the shadows divided and sub-divided, shifted, formed, shaping and reshaping. *Phenius hasn't come alone. He's brought friends.*

It was a disappointing thought to Adeline. It had been years since she'd seen him, and she'd hoped for some time with just him alone—a reunion.

"Let me in," Phenius said again, his voice jagged and sharp as one of the stalactites hanging from the roofs of the caves at Spirit Rock, and this time there was no hint of courtesy, let alone entreaty. It was an unambiguous command. The implicit invitation to self-abasement in his tone thrilled her with the filth of it. No one but Phenius had ever succeeded in making her feel that way—cheap, like a whore. Like a woman. Desired, and desirous. His voice was a hand between her legs, squeezing and probing with authority and ownership.

Adeline looked up at him from where she knelt at his feet in the sharp gravel like a supplicant. "Come in. You're welcome in my house," she said, the pain in her bloodied knees coming to her as though from a great distance. "Enter freely."

When Phenius took her in his arms, she saw that she was

alone with him on the lawn, that there was no one else there, that no one had come back with him from the grave—for surely he must have travelled that great distance just to be with her, smelling of dirt and caves and centuries under the earth.

No greater proof of love could there be than that, Adeline thought with satisfaction. *Phenius didn't come back to his adopted redskin "son," he came back to me.*

By the time she saw the old man with the bone-white face and the long white hair that blew around his head in the night wind, she was beyond caring that it wasn't Phenius at all—she just wanted the man with Phenius's voice to kiss her, to hurt her, to claim her.

And in the cold October moonlight, he did all those things, and more.

TOMB OF DRACULA

CHAPTER TWENTY-TWO

The marble foyer of Parr House was dark when she got home just after ten. Christina heard the door click softly behind her as she stood in the entryway listening to the rhythmic tick of the grandfather clock near the entrance to the dining room.

In the darkness, the place felt cavernous. For the first time since she'd returned to Parr's Landing, she was aware of the true vastness of her mother-in-law's house. It wasn't just a big house, or even a mansion—it was a small castle on a hill. *A very dark castle right now,* Christina thought.

As her eyes adjusted to the gloom, she perceived that a bit of redtinted moonlight shone through the stained glass windows on the landing of the grand staircase upstairs. In its dim light, she felt around on the marble-topped hallway table for the Waterford crystal lamp she knew was there.

Finding the lamp, she switched it on and the foyer was flooded with yellow light. Familiar objects came into view. It looked like a house again, albeit a monstrous house.

Christina crossed the floor and looked up the stairs. "Hello? Jeremy? Morgan? Anyone still up?" She didn't expect a reply—Adeline's house hadn't proven to be the sort of house where people ran down the stairs to greet each other, or shouted from floor to floor. But still, Christina couldn't ever recall the house being *this* quiet. The complete absence of noise—the apparent absence of *life*, really—struck her for the first time.

She crossed the floor quickly and climbed the stairs, taking two at a time. Outside Morgan's door, she knocked and called out softly, "Morgan? Are you still up? It's Mom." She opened the door as quietly as she could and peered inside.

Morgan lay in her bed—fast asleep, by the look of it. The room was freezing. Christina went to the window to close it, but found it tightly shut, the latch securely in place. *So where the hell is that cold coming from?* She looked at the glass. It was dirty, smudged with fingerprints. Christina rubbed at them with the edge of her sweater. *What on earth was Morgan doing this evening? Planting a garden? Adeline would be furious if she saw this.* Christina rubbed again, harder, but the smudges still didn't come off. She pressed her fingers to the window, aligning them with the smudges there. She frowned.

The marks were on the other side of the glass. Christina looked down at the moonlit lawn. Morgan's room was a twenty-foot drop to the ground.

What the hell? How can there be fingerprints on the other side of the glass? Impossible. She shook her head and gave herself a mental swift kick in the rear end. *Well, then, obviously they aren't fingerprints, you idiot—unless you think maybe Morgan was hanging from the outside wall by a trapeze harness, trying to get into her own bedroom.*

Christina crossed to the bed and pulled the blankets up to her daughter's neck. She leaned down and kissed her softly on the forehead. She deeply inhaled Morgan's scent. When she slept, Morgan still smelled like a baby to her mother.

She paused outside Jeremy's door one floor up, then knocked. Light streamed from under the door. From inside, Jeremy said, "Come in?"

She pushed open the door open. Jeremy was sitting up in bed, wearing a T-shirt and boxer shorts, reading. Self-consciously, he reached for the sheet to cover himself, which made Christina smile in spite of herself. He blushed.

"Don't worry, I can't see anything," she said. "Your mystery is still intact."

He laughed. "Old habits, I guess. This isn't the house in which to be caught naked, as you know. Bad consequences." He tried to smile, but failed.

"Are you OK, Jeremy? I mean, really OK?"

He shrugged. "Sure, I guess. How was your night?"

"It was really nice," she admitted. "Billy was a perfect gentleman. He told me about his life. He went to a residential school in Sault Ste. Marie. It sounded awful. Brutal. I had no idea. It makes his success even more amazing. But mostly he was just a really, really nice man. He reminded me of—" she trailed off, embarrassed by the treason implicit in what she had been about to say. "Well, he was a nice man."

"Christina," Jeremy said gently. "Do you . . . did you enjoy spending time with him? I mean—that way? It's OK if you did, you know. It doesn't mean you're being disloyal to Jack. It just means that you're human."

She paused, struggling for composure. "It's too soon, Jeremy," she said. "Even if I wanted to enjoy it that way, it's still too soon. But thank you for saying that. I know what you meant, and I appreciate it."

He smiled. "I'll always be here for you, Chris. No matter what. I know how much you loved my brother, and I know how much he loved you—and all of us, especially Morgan."

"God, how did everything get so messed up? How did it all come to this?"

Jeremy paused, then said, "Chris?"

"Yeah?"

"Chris, we're leaving tomorrow."

Christina raised her eyebrows. "Really? That's news to me. Last I heard, we were dead broke. Did you win a lottery?"

"No," he said quietly. "But today, when you were talking to Billy Lightning on the driveway, I went into Adeline's room and looked around. I found some money. A *lot* of money. She keeps it in the bottom of her vanity. There's almost a thousand dollars in twenties. More than enough to get us the hell out of Parr's

Landing and back to Toronto. I would have taken it this afternoon, but I didn't want to risk her finding out."

"Jeremy!" Christina was shocked in spite of herself. "You can't do that! What are you thinking?"

"I'm thinking that Adeline will be the death of us, and I'm thinking that it's time we face it," he said calmly. "This town is a bad place. After this afternoon—after Elliot—I realized that. We need to leave. If we don't, either the town or my mother will eat us alive. She's enjoying torturing us, you know. Can't you tell? Can't you feel it?"

"But you can't steal almost a thousand dollars from her!"

"Why not?"

"Well, for one thing, she'll have you arrested and thrown in jail."

"We'll be gone before she even knows the money is missing," he said. "And once we're outside of northern Ontario, she has no power or authority, whatever else she'd like you to believe. And when we're gone, we'll never, ever come back."

"Jeremy . . . ?"

"Never mind, Christina. I'm deadly serious. Pack your things tomorrow, just don't let her see you do it. Morgan's, too. We'll make a dash for it mid-afternoon. We'll tell her we're . . . I don't know, having a talk with Morgan's principal. We'll think of something."

"Are you sure? Are you *sure* this is the only way?"

"Aren't *you* sure yet, Christina? Do you really want to risk Morgan turning into someone like Elliot? Someone broken and ashamed of who they are? Because my mother will do it to her, you know she will. She'll destroy your daughter just like she's tried to destroy everyone else who isn't the person she demands they be."

Christina looked hard at her brother-in-law. "OK. I'll pack tomorrow morning."

"You don't even need to bring everything, just what's necessary. We can pick up anything else once we're the hell out of here."

Near midnight, Finn still heard his mother crying in the living room, but he didn't think he could bear to come upstairs from his room to comfort her, nor did he believe she wanted him there—not after she'd shouted at him and sent him to his room in such a fury an hour before. He knew that her worry over his father not being home was the source, but he also knew he could be of no comfort to her at that exact moment.

The house felt huge and empty to him with just Finn and his mother in it—the ceilings higher, his bedroom walls farther from the bed, the autumn darkness outside deeper, the shadows longer, the silence as soft as a thunderstorm.

Anne hadn't ordered him to stay in bed all night, something quite unprecedented in his twelve years of bedtimes. And both of them were on tenterhooks, listening for the sound of his father's car in the driveway.

Finn had left her—at her request—alone after dinner, sitting in the orange corduroy slip covered easy chair that Anne had angled facing the front door, almost as though she were afraid that she if she didn't see Hank's car pull into the driveway in addition to hearing it when he pulled in (a sound she was acutely attuned to, after seventeen years of marriage), it wouldn't be real.

They'd eaten dinner in silence after Finn's preposterous announcement that a vampire had killed Sadie. Anne had stared at him open-mouthed and then said, "Oh Finnegan, stop it. Please, for heaven's sake."

But the look in her eye wasn't botheration, which Finn was accustomed to from his mother when he went on about vampires, or his *Tomb of Dracula* obsession.

No, it was *horror*—not horror at the thought of vampires snatching up Sadie, but rather at the idea that Finn would even joke about something like that at a time like this.

Then she'd turned back to the stove, her posture rigid enough to snap in a high wind. Finn sensed that his mother was waiting for his father to come home before she even broached the topic of his preposterous comment with him.

As excited as he was by his new awareness of what had happened to his dog, Finn felt shamed by his mother's silence. He knew it wasn't what she wanted to hear, because he suddenly saw the strain on her face that Sadie's death had caused. Selfishly, perhaps, he hadn't considered that anyone could be as affected by Sadie's death as he was. Sadie had been Finn's dog, Finn's great love, and Finn's grief.

But at dinner, as she pushed her chicken pie around on her plate, his mother appeared to be maintaining her composure by frayed, bloody tendons.

Anne kept looking up at the kitchen wall clock with the carved grapes on a vine, with "Bless This House" in elaborate cursive letters around the clock's face.

"Where can your father be?" she'd said, repeating it twice more during the meal. But it didn't sound like it did when she'd said it a thousand times before. There was no good-natured exasperation in the tone this time, no housewifely impatience about burned dinners, or food getting cold. It was an actual question: clinical, tinged with the metallic frostbite of growing panic. "He's never this late."

"Mom, he's probably just working late at the mill. Or he stopped off on the way home."

"Finn, he . . ." She stopped herself in mid-sentence. "He went . . ."

Something in her voice pierced his self-distancing absorption in his own thoughts of Sadie and vampires and grief. "He what, Mom? Where did he go after work?"

"Eat your dinner, Finnegan." Anne's face had gone the colour of milk. Her voice was robotic. "Your father will be home soon."

But of course, he hadn't been home soon. He hadn't come home at all. And now here it was, practically midnight.

From upstairs, Finn heard his mother calling a few of his friends from down the Legion. None of them had seen Hank. Finn heard the reluctant-to-disturb-your-family's-dinner-sir deference in her voice when she called his foreman at the mill, but he didn't know where Hank was, either.

No, no, no, sorry, no, Anne, we haven't. . . . No, sorry. I'm sure he'll be home soon. . . . No, maybe he had car trouble? Stopped for a beer? Had to finish something?

With every phone call, with every new confirmation that Hank had cut out from the mill an hour earlier but that no one had seen him since, Anne's voice grew incrementally tighter and shriller. After the last call, she slammed the receiver down hard enough for Finn to hear it downstairs in his room.

Halfway up the stairs, he said, "Mom, are you OK?"

"Finn, I'm fine." She sounded like she was crying. "Your father should have been home hours ago. I'm at my wit's end. Where the hell is he? Why isn't he home with us?"

He climbed the stairs and stood a few feet away from where she was standing, the phone poised in mid-air as though she were about to make another call. When she saw him, she put the phone down.

"Mom, where did Dad go after work? You started to tell me at dinner, but you stopped. Why? Where did he go?"

"Finn, he said he was going to go find Sadie and bring her home so he could bury her." Anne began to weep. "He was going to stop by after work and bring her back to us. I'm so very afraid he hurt himself up there or something in the woods."

Now it was Finn's turn to blanch. "Mom, why did you let him go up to Spirit Rock after I told you what happened to Sadie? You let him go up there *at night*? After what I told you tonight? Are you *crazy*?"

For an instant, terror passed across Anne's face like the shadow of a cloud moving overland. In that moment, Finn saw everything he had seen that morning on Spirit Rock reflected in his mother's face. Their synergy electrified him.

In that moment, she believed him, he could tell. That knowledge both terrified and thrilled him, ripping asunder the security veil that was keeping his twelve-year-old fantasies safely locked outside the back door of reality. If his mother believed him about Sadie, or about the vampires, then they could be real.

Then, the moment was over. Her adult face came back, and she said, "Finn, stop it. There are no such things as vampires. Nobody killed Sadie. I don't have time to waste on this nonsense right now. Your father is missing. What happened to Sadie this morning was . . . well, it was something else."

"What was it? Tell me!" he demanded. "*Tell me what I saw wasn't what I saw, Mom!*"

"Summer lightning!" Anne practically screamed. "I don't know! Go to your room *right now*! I can't deal with this crap of yours right now, Finnegan! Your father is *missing*! Do you understand me? I don't have time for all your Draculas and the rest of it!"

Finn's face flamed. He turned on his heel and fled to his room, slamming the door behind him. He flung himself across his bed feeling impotent rage—but not at his mother, of course, even though she had hurt his feelings by shouting at him, and even though he understood that she was upset about his father.

He half hoped, half expected to hear the sound of her feet on the stairs to his room to comfort him, or apologize, or to admit that she, too, was deeply and gravely afraid that his father had been taken by the same malefic force out there in the dark that had taken Sadie—but there was nothing.

When he quietly opened the door to his room and listened, he heard her talking to someone at the Parr's Landing police station—maybe that liar of a cop who had promised he'd look for Sadie, or maybe the old one who had told them not to say anything to anyone about the bag of bloody knives.

From the rising, near-hysterical crescendo of his mother's voice, whoever had answered the phone at the station wasn't being very helpful at all.

"He's *never* late!" she shouted. "I'm not shouting! *Don't tell me not to shout!* My husband is missing!" And then, "My son found that bag of bloody knives up there by the caves and you're telling me that . . . I don't *care* if Constable McKitrick didn't come in to work today! That's not my problem! Do you mean to tell me that you can't . . . Yes, I know it hasn't been twenty-four hours yet!" There was a long pause, then Anne said. "So, I'm supposed to just *wait* . . . ? All right, if you promise you'll take a ride out there and take a look. Tonight! Yes, thank you." She hung up.

"Mom . . . ?" She turned and saw her son back on the stairs. "Mom? I'm sorry."

"Come here, sweetheart," Anne said. She opened her arms to her son, and he ran into them. She felt his face against her shoulder and she squeezed him tightly.

"Mom! Ow! You're squishing me!" Finn yelped, not meaning it. He snuggled in closer. "I love you, Mommy."

Anne closed her eyes and pressed her face against his hair. It still smelled like Prell from his shampoo before dinner. "I love you, too, Finnegan." She looked at the clock. It was nearly midnight. "OK, bedtime, vampire hunter," she said, obviously trying to take the sting out of her earlier chastisement. "I'm going to stay up for just a little while and wait for your daddy to come home. I want you to go to sleep."

"You called the police, didn't you, Mom? Was that the police?"

"Yes, sweetheart," I did. "Just to be sure. You're daddy is fine, don't worry."

"Mom?"

"*What*, Finnegan?"

"Mommy," he said solemnly. "You're fibbing, aren't you? Why are you fibbing?"

"~~Finnegan—please, sweetheart. Please just go to bed now. Be~~ a good boy for your mom." She ruffled his hair. "I'll wake you up when Daddy gets here, I promise."

"OK, Mom," he said. He turned to go back downstairs. Then he turned around. His mother looked very small sitting in the orange corduroy-covered chair. Impulsively, Finn walked back over to the spot by the window and hugged her as tightly as he could. "Night, Mommy."

"Night, baby," Anne said. She patted his bottom through his pyjamas and bathrobe. "I love you. Sleep tight."

Finn reluctantly let his mother go, then went downstairs to his bedroom to try to sleep while he waited for his father to get home.

Before switching out his bedside lamp, Finn glanced over at Sadie's empty dog bed across the room. When it hurt too much to breathe, he switched off the bedroom light and let the darkness swallow him up and carry him away from this terrible day.

What the blazes is that young dunderhead doing? For Christ's sake. He drops out of sight, then has the nerve to drive around the goddamn town in his cruiser with the lights off? And to drive past the window of the police station, practically flipping me the bird? Is he on drugs?

Dave Thomson slammed his coffee cup down hard on his desk, spilling some of it on his blotter. He pushed his chair back from his desk and ran to the door of the station. He threw it open and stepped out onto the sidewalk.

"Elliot," Thomson bawled. "Goddammit, Elliot, get back here! Right now, boy! I mean it!"

The police cruiser paused, as though waiting for Thomson to shout something else. Then the brake lights winked redly in the blackness— once, then twice, as the driver tapped the brake. *Well I'll be a goddamned jumped-up monkey-fucker!* Thomson seethed. *He's actually* playing *with me!*

The car sped ahead, pausing a ways up the block. Again, the tapping of the brake light—flick-flick.

I'm going to break his fucking ass!

Thomson grabbed his keys off the desk and let the door of the police station slam shut behind him. He jumped behind the wheel of his own brand new Impala and took off in pursuit of the police cruiser that was now taunting him by maintaining a pace just slow enough to follow, but still too fast for Thomson to catch up to without speeding—something Thomson was loath to do in his own town, even at this hour.

Elliot—and he had no doubt it was Elliot, probably stark raving high on pot, or God only knew what else he'd been getting into lately that had made him act the way he'd been acting—led him on a merry chase through the streets of Parr's Landing, and out towards the edge of town, driving without lights and making Thomson squint.

"Where are you going, you crazy bastard?" Thomson muttered. He leaned his arm out the window and tried to signal to Elliot that he should pull over. Instinctively, he reached down to activate a siren, but of course there was no siren to activate. "Get back here, goddammit!" he shouted again out the window. "Shit on a goddamn *stick!*"

Just when it looked like Elliot was headed for the road that led to the cliffs (and on those roads, Thomson promised himself, he *would* open her up and pull even with the little bastard and then break his fucking ass), he turned off Percy Street and onto Brandon Nixon Road.

Where the hell *is he going?*

The cruiser sped up. Thomson floored it again, cursing his lack of siren. He could think of no better use for the siren than right now—then, when he caught Elliott, he was going to shove it so far up his goddamn ass, Elliot would shit pieces of red cherry-top glass all the way to the welfare office. He honked his horn several times, but to no avail. The cruiser kept speeding ahead.

In the distance, Thomson saw the taillights of the cruiser abruptly veer right, then wink out and vanish altogether. *What the blazes? Where the hell did he go?* Thomson floored the accelerator till he reached the spot where he'd lost track of Elliot. He craned his neck, trying to see where the little bastard had gone.

Then, suddenly he saw the car. He also saw why the taillights had disappeared. Elliot had parked it in front of the burned-out shell of the Mike Tackacs Hockey Arena. *Got you, you little fucker,* he thought, gloating. *Your ass belongs to me.*

Thomson pulled in behind and parked the Impala. He took his flashlight out of the glove box and shone it alongside the cruiser.

The early morning electrical fire that had taken the hockey rink down in '59—killing a maintenance worker named Eric McDonald and his young son, Timmy, who was skating while his father worked, thus adding two more souls to Parr's Landing's already ample supply of ghosts—had burned fiercely and efficiently, leaving only a husk that somehow still smelled like smoke after all these years.

Why no one had torn it down in all this time was a mystery to Thomson. It was as dangerous as all get-out. They'd rebuilt a new arena on the other side of town—the Brenen Gyles Arena, so named after Parr's Landing's one and only semi-famous contribution to the 1962 Ontario Junior A League, paid for in no small part by the Gyles Family, who owned most of the town of Gyles Point—so there was no reason for the ruins of the Takacs Arena to be standing at all.

The Parr family could have afforded to tear the Takacs down and rebuild it themselves—hell, the old bitch could have paid for it out of her change purse, but it would be a week of frosty Fridays in hell before Adeline Parr would lift a finger to help the town do anything but work for her.

As for Elliot, he must be high, Thomson decided. There was no other reason for this entirely out-of-character behaviour.

"Elliot, you there?" he shouted. "Come on out, now. Stop this foolishness. We can talk about it, whatever it is. But we can't fix it until we do. You need to come out right now, son. Don't make me go in there and find you."

But there was no answer. Thomson took a few tentative steps into the ruined arena, playing his flashlight along the charred baseboards, cumbrous slats, collapsed walls, and rotting ceiling beams.

Goddamn deathtrap. The thought hovered in his mind with the weight of a portent. Thomson was oddly glad he hadn't said the words out loud.

Elliot's voice echoed from deeper inside the ruins. "Sarge, I'm in here. Follow my voice. Use your flashlight—you can find me. Just listen to my voice."

"Elliot, what the *hell* are you up to? What are you doing in here? Cut this shit pronto, mister, and come out right now!"

"Sarge, come over here. I found something you need to see. I think I know what happened in Gyles Point. I think I know who that hockey bag belonged to. It's worse than we thought."

Thomson's heart quickened. "Elliot, what are you on about? And why are you here?" A thought suddenly came to him. "Is it the Indian? Is it Lightning?"

"No." Elliot's voice sounded as though he were standing right in front of Thomson now, though he still couldn't see anything except what was directly in font of him, illuminated by the flashlight beam. "It's worse. It's much, much worse than that."

Then Elliot stepped into the beam of his flashlight. He was nude, his body smeared with a brownish-red substance that looked like dried blood.

Thomson dropped the flashlight. He barely had time to shout "Jesus fucking Christ!" before Elliot, almost casually, reached out with one bare arm and tossed his sergeant halfway across the arena.

Then Elliot was astride his chest. The fingers of one hand gathered Thomson's hair and brutally yanking his head to one side, while the fingernails of the other hand ripped through his uniform shirt and jacket like they were wet toilet paper.

Thomson kneed Elliot as hard as he could, using the force of his legs to throw him off balance. Gaining a momentary advantage, Thomson scrambled to the side, reaching for his revolver by instinct and pointing it at the indistinct shape crouching in front of him.

He fired twice, again on instinct. In the flare from the gunfire, he saw the bullets slam into Elliot's torso, and then heard them thud into a wall somewhere outside his limited vision. In that short glimpse, Thomson feared he had lost control of his own senses, because as far as he could tell, the bullets had left no trace of a wound.

Thomson's subconscious mind registered that Elliot was not alone, that there were other shapes crouching there behind him in the blackness, horribly patient shapes that undulated and twisted languorously as though undecided about what form they would ultimately choose to take.

Then Elliot stood up and said, "Coming for you now, Sarge."

"Elliot, get back!" he gasped. He aimed the gun in the general vicinity of Elliot's voice. "I mean it! *Get . . . right . . . back . . . !*"

Those were the last words Dave Thomson ever spoke before Elliot McKitrick—whom Thomson hadn't even seen move—tore out Thomson's throat with his teeth. The last thing Thomson felt was the wet warmth of his own blood on his face, and Elliot's mouth fastened on the wound, sucking the arterial spray as his life ran out of his body and into the body of the thing astride him whom he'd once wished was his son.

Finn woke to the sound of breaking glass and his mother's screaming. He had been dreaming that his father had come home with Sadie riding in the passenger seat of the car, her nose out the window and her wet red tongue lolling foolishly from the side of her muzzle, tasting the wind. In the dream, it was daylight—which proved the dream's ultimate undoing, because Finn suddenly remembered in his sleep that it was night, and that Sadie had burned up in front of him that morning above Bradley Lake.

He sat up quickly and listened to his mother shrieking in pain and terror. There were crashes that sounded like furniture splintering, and the sound of more shattering glass. *Oh, please, God,* Finn prayed. *Not again! Enough already, please.* Aloud, he screamed "Mommy!" and jumped out of bed, wrenching his bedroom door open and taking the stairs two at a time until he was standing in the living room.

What Finn saw, by the light of the table lamp on the floor casting crazy shadows on the wall, was that his father had indeed come home to them. Around him, shards of broken glass from the front picture window twinkled in the light like icicles growing out of the green wall-to-wall carpet.

Hank Miller's body skewed at a horrible angle as though his bones had all been broken and somehow reassembled in haste, with no concern for either aesthetics or practical mechanics. Finn had barely passed science last year in school, but even with his deficient knowledge of human anatomy, he knew that there was no possible way the shambling, disjointed, horror movie staple standing behind his mother, holding her by the shoulders could possibly be able to stand up, let alone move towards him—even at such a tortured, dislocated pace, pushing his mother in front of him like a wheeled dolly.

And yet, he—it—did exactly that.

"Finn," said his father through a mouthful of teeth that Finn had only ever seen in the pages of *The Tomb of Dracula,* "you should be asleep. Go back to bed. I'll come and tuck you in after I've finished speaking with your mother."

Then Hank Miller opened his mouth wider than Finn could ever have dreamed possible and buried those terrible new teeth in his mother's neck.

Finn and his mother shrieked at exactly the same time—and Finn again felt that odd communion with her that he'd felt hours before when his mother briefly appeared to consider the possibility that vampires had carried off Sadie and his father.

This time, however, when their eyes met, the automatic, dismissive adult façade didn't descend and obliterate the moment.

Rather, as Anne Miller's eyes rolled up in her head, almost regretfully, Finn imagined her saying, *Well, Finn, you were right. There are such things as vampires. I guess one of them did get Sadie. Now, you'd better run before your father gets you.*

Hank dropped his wife's lifeless body on the floor, the bottom half of his face wet and red. He licked his teeth almost curiously, seeming to Finn as though his father were feeling them for the first time, like a child on Christmas morning with a new toy—a dangerous one that he wanted to enjoy before some nosey adult figured out just what to do with it.

"Finnegan," Hank said, opening his arms. Finn noticed that his nails had grown. "Come here. Let's go find Sadie. She's up at Spirit Rock waiting for us." He stepped over his wife's body and took a step towards his son. "*Come here.*"

"You're not my father," Finn said backing away. "Get away from me."

He looked around wildly for a weapon, but could find nothing on the floor, or on the table, or the walls. His father took another step towards him, and Finn caught the smell of Hank's breath, the copper whiff of his own mother's blood on his father's lips.

"Our Father which art in Heaven," Finn shouted, pointing his finger at his father. "Hallowed be Thy name! Thy kingdom come! Thy will be done on earth as it is in Heaven!"

Hank clapped his hands over his ears and roared, stumbling backwards, his awkward, broken body tripping and falling over the upturned, blood-spattered orange corduroy easy chair.

"Give us this day our daily bread, and forgive us our trespasses as we forgive those who trespass against us!"

Finn reached down and snatched up two pieces of a broken table. He swung them together in the shape of a cross and pushed it into his father's face.

It's like a picture tube just blew up in a television, Finn thought from somewhere far outside his own deadly panic, wincing in the sudden bedazzlement of blue light.

Acrid smoke burned Finn's eyes and seared his nostrils as he stepped back, coughing.

Finn wasn't sure if he heard the piercing ululation come from his father's own throat, or whether it was merely, suddenly, everywhere at once, from some outside place beyond the parameters of the world as it was. Finn felt the air move with it, and he felt the sound in his teeth. There was pure agony in that sound, and Finn was viciously, triumphantly glad of it.

And then Hank was . . . something else.

Through the blue mist emanating from his father's body, Finn saw wings grow where his father's arms had been, wings that extended the length of the living room before they began to shimmer and dwindle even as Hank stumbled forward to where Anne's body lay crumpled on the green carpet.

As he watched, his father knelt down and scissored his legs around his mother's waist, cinching it tightly between his thighs. There was wind in Finn's face and his hair blew backwards as his father's wings flapped, then flapped again. Hank backed away towards the window, awkward and spraddle-legged with the weight of his mother's body still clenched between his legs.

He leaned against the jagged mouth of broken glass where the window had been shattered and tilted his broken body at an impossible angle, half-in, half-out of the living room, craning his dislocated neck forward so he could look Finn in the eye.

"Goddamn you, you little piece of fucking shit," Hank said. "I'm coming back for you."

Then Finn saw his father tumble backward, outside, airborne, rising into the night with the lifeless body of his mother hanging from his talons like dreadful ballast.

He rushed to the window, but it was too late—he thought he caught one last glimpse of his mother's blonde hair in the moonlight, but the flash of it was gone before he could be sure of anything except that his hands were bleeding from the broken glass, and he was alone in the house, and it would be hours yet before the dawn.

CHAPTER TWENTY-THREE

Morgan, who usually slept like the dead, was the first person to be woken by the sound of Finn banging on the front door of Parr House half an hour before dawn.

She rubbed the sleep from her eyes and squinted at the clock beside her bed. It was six forty-five. Outside her window, there was a barely perceptible sense of lightening in the sky, but the darkness was still nearly absolute.

The banging came again. Morgan swung her feet over the side of her bed and picked up her bathrobe where it lay on the chair beside her nightstand. Then she went into the hallway and started down the stairs.

Jeremy's sleepy voice carried from the landing above. "Morgan? Is that you? What's going on? Who's at the door?"

"I don't know, Uncle Jeremy. I just heard it now. It woke me up."

"Wait for me," he said. "Don't open the door. I'll do it, hopefully before your grandmother hears it and makes Beatrice dish up whoever's pulverizing that door for breakfast."

Christina's door opened. "Morgan? Jeremy? What's going on? Who's at the door?" She belted her own bathrobe and ran her fingers through her hair, less through vanity than by reflex.

Jeremy hurried down the stairs past both Christina and Morgan. "I don't know, Chris," he said over his shoulder. "But whoever it is, he's playing with his life if my mother gets to him first."

Jeremy stared at the boy standing in the doorway. He'd never seen him before. The boy's fist was poised as if to bang on the door again. His face was puffy and pale, his hair askew. Like them, he wore pyjamas, but his were muddy and ripped at the ankle as though he had torn them running. Clutched tightly in the boy's other hand was a jar full of some sort of clear liquid that looked like water.

"Hi," Jeremy said, confused. "Can I help you?"

"I need to see Morgan," the boy said. "Please?"

"Morgan?" Jeremy glanced at the staircase where Christina and Morgan stood waiting for him to identify who had woken them. "Morgan, honey, there's a . . . you have a visitor. Uh, come in, kid."

Jeremy looked from Christina to Morgan, and then back at the boy, who took a few tentative steps across the threshold, onto the marble floor. Jeremy noticed that his feet were bare and bleeding.

Morgan hurried down the stairs and stopped in front of the doorway. "Finn? What are you doing here? Are you OK?" She stared at him blankly, as though trying to reconcile Finn's bedraggled appearance in the foyer of Parr House before dawn. Morgan looked at her mother. "Mom, this is Finn Miller, my friend. The one I told you about? The one who walked me home?"

Christina stared at the dirty, half-dressed boy in the foyer. "Of course," she said automatically, extending he hand. He stared at it blankly. "Hi, Finn," she said. "I'm Morgan's mom. This is her uncle, Jeremy. Come inside where it's warm."

Then Christina took his full, unkempt, tattered measure with instinctive maternal tenderheartedness. She was horrified by what she saw—dirt, blood, dried tear-tracks on his cheeks sluicing through the grime. "Are you OK, Finn? What happened? Where are your clothes? Why are you in your pyjamas? Where's your mom?"

The last question turned the key in the lock of Finn's composure. He stumbled into Christina's arms and collapsed there, weeping. Again, instinctively, Christina gathered Finn in her arms and held him tightly while he sobbed. She could barely understand what the boy was saying, but she made out the words *Mommy, my father, Sadie, window broke,* and *dead.* Then there were more sobs, even more wracking this time than before.

"What's going on?" Jeremy whispered to Morgan. "Who is this kid? Where are his parents?"

Morgan shrugged and shook her head. "He's Finn. He's my friend. He lives over on Childs Drive. He lost his dog a couple of days ago."

"Sadie died." Finn turned his wet face away from Christina's shoulder. "She burned up. We were going for a walk and she went to catch a ball I threw, then she burned up."

Jeremy said, "What do you mean 'she burned up'? Finn? That doesn't make sense. What are you saying?"

"Hush, Jeremy, let him talk," Christina said over the top of Finn's head. Then, to Finn, "Sadie is your dog, is she? Did she get lost?"

"No, she's dead. She burned up." His voice was calm now, and matter-of-fact.

Shock, Christina thought. *Just like my voice when I first heard about Jack's car crash. Whatever has happened to this little boy is obviously very, very bad.*

"And then my dad went to look for Sadie last night," Finn continued. "He didn't come home for dinner, or even later. My mom was so sad, and she waited up for him. She was worried. She called the police. Then she told me to go to bed. And then . . . and then my dad came home. *He killed my mom.* He came in through the window. He broke it. There was glass all over the place, and then he . . . then he bit my mom and he . . . he . . . took her with him. Out. Out the window!"

"Finn," Christina said carefully, looking only at him. "Were you in the house all night? When this . . . well, when this happened—whatever happened to your mom and dad? Were you there all night, in the house?"

"No," he said in a hushed voice. "I got away—I hid."

"Where did you hide, Finn?"

He hesitated. "I went to the church. I went to St. Bart's. I got in through the basement window. I waited there till I knew grown-ups would be awake. When the sun was going to come up."

He held out his hand, still clutching the jar full of liquid. When Christina tried to take it out of his hand to examine it, he held on more tightly. But when she said, "Shhhh, let me look," and gave him another little squeeze, he let her take the jar.

Christina held it up. "What is this, Finn? What's in here?"

"Holy water," Finn said. "It's holy water. In case my dad comes back."

"The phone's out at Finn's house," Jeremy said, replacing the receiver in its cradle.

"Are you sure you got the right number, Uncle Jeremy?" Morgan looked down at the open Parr's Landing directory on the table. "Do you want me to read the number to you again?"

"No, sweetie—I've tried it twice now. No answer. His folks aren't picking up."

Morgan's voice quavered. "What if it means they—what if it means they're hurt or something?"

"I'm sure they're fine," Jeremy said. Even has he spoke, he realized how ridiculously adult and fake-rational he sounded. *Yes, of course, by all means—a little boy stumbles through the door of Parr House at seven in the morning and says his dog burst into flames and that his father broke through a window and murdered his mother, and you assure your fifteen-year-old niece that you're "sure" they're "fine." You sound like your mother right now, Jeremy Parr.* "I'll take a run over there in a few minutes, Morgan. I'll knock on the door and see what's what."

"OK," she said. "Can I come?"

"Absolutely not," he said. "You stay here with your mother and your friend. I'll be right back. And Morgan?"

"What?"

"Go on upstairs and knock—very gently—on your grand-mother's bedroom door and tell her we have a bit of an emergency situation going on here."

"What'll I say?"

"Tell her . . . tell her you have a friend who got hurt." When he saw the trepidation on Morgan's face, he smiled comfortingly and said, "It'll be all right. She's not going to bite your head off. You're the one she loves, even if she doesn't like the rest of us much."

"Yeah, right," Morgan said. "She hates me, too. Why can't Beatrice do it?"

It suddenly occurred to Jeremy that there were none of the usual pre-breakfast sounds coming from inside the kitchen—no cutlery being laid out, and no clatter of china plates being placed on the mahogany sideboard in the dining room. Where *was* Beatrice? He'd never known her to be late—not in a lifetime of meticulously orchestrated breakfasts at Parr House.

"I don't think Beatrice is here yet," he said slowly. "And no, your grandmother doesn't hate you. Now, wait till five minutes after I leave, then knock on her door."

Morgan sighed. "OK, Uncle Jeremy. I will."

"Good girl. Now, go wait in the sitting room with your mother and your friend. I'm going to run upstairs and get dressed, then go and check out his story. Go see if your mom needs anything for Finn."

The Miller house on Childs Drive was exactly as Finn had described it—entirely nondescript except for the fact that the picture window facing the street was shattered.

When Jeremy entered the house—trying the door handle and finding it unlocked and, indeed, empty—he saw that the broken glass from the window was sprayed all over the carpet. There was none on the scrubby lawn outside. In other words, whoever had broken it had done so by smashing it from the outside.

Jeremy looked dubiously at the lawn. *How did he get in here, assuming someone had? On a trampoline? Did he pole-vault in?* He examined the glass on the floor, nudging it with his foot. Under an orange corduroy cushion he saw that the carpet was stained a brownish-red. He reached down and touched it. The carpet was still sticky, and his finger came away smeared red. Uh-oh, Jeremy thought. *This isn't good. Not good at all.*

Fighting rising panic, Jeremy called out, "Hello? Is anyone here? Mrs. Miller? Mr. Miller?"

There was no answer. Jeremy would have been surprised had he received one. In a corner of the dining room floor, he saw the wall telephone. The jack had been ripped out of the wall, the exposed wires protruding like bones. He thought of checking the rest of the rooms in the house, but he already knew they would empty and he didn't want to spend one more minute here than he had to.

"OK," Jeremy said aloud. The rawness of his own voice in the grey dawn light filling the living room from the broken window startled him. "OK," he said again, trying to sound calm and reasonable, if only to himself.

"Morgan, I know what happened to Sadie," Finn said weakly. "I know what happened to my parents."

"What happened, Finn?"

They were seated together on a divan in Adeline's sitting room off the foyer. Finn had calmed down somewhat, but was still shaking from head to toe. Little bodily earthquakes, unsettling him.

From the kitchen, Morgan heard Christina making breakfast in Adeline's vast kitchen. Her grandmother was still not up, and Morgan had not gone up to check on her as Uncle Jeremy had asked. Instead, she'd sat in an uncomfortably spindly chair next to the divan where Finn sat.

Finn turned his face away as though he changed his mind. "You wouldn't believe me," he said. "No one will. You'll just say I'm crazy, or fibbing. My mom didn't believe me, and now she's dead."

"Finn, try me," she prodded. "Tell me. I'm your friend. I'll believe you."

"No, you won't."

"Yes, I will," she said urgently. "Just tell me."

While Christina made breakfast in the kitchen, Finn, trusting her, told Morgan everything.

He told her about Sadie's gruesome end in the sunlight two mornings ago above Bradley Lake. He told her of his father's disappearance, and his return.

He told her about his mother's murder, how he drove his father out of the living room with the Lord's Prayer and the two pieces of smashed table leg in the shape of the cross. He told her how he crouched in his bedroom for an hour afterwards, watching his bedroom door, his pyjamas stained with gouts of his mother's blood, clutching the two shards of broken wood, thinking he heard footsteps pacing the floorboards through the living room and the kitchen above him but not being sure, not daring to move from his spot to find out.

Finn told her about fleeing the house on his Schwinn, watching the skies as best he could, all the while knowing that if something came to carry him off, he would be powerless to stop it. He told her of spending the night crouched near a statue of the Virgin Mary near the baptismal font at St. Barthélemy and the Martyrs, only leaving when he was sure dawn was right around the corner, and that there would be adults awake in the houses around him, adults that might be able to protect him from whatever was surely hunting him even as he cycled like the wind all the way up the hill to Parr House, and the safety of Morgan.

Morgan was silent for a long moment. The she said, "Finn, this is like something out of one of your comic books. You realize that, don't you?"

He raised himself on his elbow and said furiously, "I *told* you, you wouldn't believe me! I *said*!"

"Finn—"

"Never mind! I mean it! Never . . . *mind*!" He stood up abruptly, almost knocking over his jar of water—holy water, Morgan supposed, since she believed him about having spent the night in the church.

"Finn, are you feeling better?" Christina stood in the doorway with a glass of orange juice. "I've made some breakfast. Are you hungry? Morgan's uncle isn't back yet, but he will be soon." She extended the glass of juice, but he didn't move to take it.

Finn looked from Morgan to Christina, then back again. His expression was hard for Christina to read—thwarted anger, longing, terror. Grief, definitely. But mostly, it seemed, terrible frustration.

Christina said, "Finn?"

He picked up his jar of holy water and ran out of the sitting room. They heard the sound of his bare feet on the marble foyer floor, then the sound of the front door being flung open, then slamming shut.

"Morgan, what happened? What did you say to him?"

"Nothing! He started telling me this story . . ."

"What story? What did he tell you?"

"Something about . . ." Morgan looked at her mother's bewildered face, and faltered.

It was one thing for Morgan herself not to believe Finn. She was a kid, too—well, a teenager, but still. It would be something else to for her to tell her mother the crazy story and have Christina think Finn was crazy. It seemed disloyal, somehow.

Finn had been the only friend she'd had since they arrived, and all he'd ever been was kind to her. And how had she repaid him? By doing the one thing she knew would hurt him—treating his vampire comic book obsession like a joke. She hadn't intended to, of course, but he clearly believed what he had told her. The least she could have done was listen to Finn and trust that he believed what he was saying, and keep her big fat trap shut. She was such an idiot.

"Morgan Louise Parr, what *did* that boy say before he ran out of here? You tell me *right now*!"

"He said . . . he said something about his mom and dad."

"What did he say?"

"I don't know. He wasn't making sense. And then you . . . and then he just ran out of here. You saw him. I don't know why, he just did."

They heard the door click open again, then shut. Christina called out, "Finn?"

"No, it's me." Jeremy's voice came from the foyer. He walked into the sitting room. From his face, Christina and Morgan knew the news wasn't going to be good.

"Where's Finn?" Jeremy said, looking blankly around the sitting room.

"He left," Morgan said. "He just ran out of here."

"What do you mean 'he ran out of here'? Where did he go? His bicycle is gone, too. Weren't you watching him?"

"Yes, we were watching him, Jeremy," Christina snapped. "But he just jumped up and bolted out of here a few minutes ago. We couldn't stop him. We tried."

"Well, I went to his house. It's not good, Chris. There's glass everywhere, all over the floor. And I think . . . Morgan, would you excuse your mother and I for a minute?"

"I'm *fifteen*," she said. "I'm not a baby."

"You think what?" Christina snapped, ignoring them both.

"I think there's blood on the carpet. It looks like something pretty awful *did* happen—maybe a fight between the mother and the father that went wrong. Got violent."

Christina said, "Did you call the police?"

"The phone was ripped out of the wall. No way to call. I thought of finding a phone booth, but I decided to stop by the police station in person on the way back here and report it instead."

"And? What did the police say? Are they going to check it out?"

"Well," Jeremy said, "it was the damnedest thing. The station was empty."

"What do you mean the police station was empty? How could it be empty? It's a police station!"

"I don't know how it could be empty, Christina. But it was. The lights were on and the front door was unlocked. It's like they went out for coffee last night without even bothering to close up, then just didn't come in for work today."

Christina sat down heavily on the divan. "None of this makes any sense. And now that poor boy is running around outside in his pyjamas. He obviously saw something happen to his parents that upset him. Morgan, does he have any relatives in town, do you know? Or friends? Why did he come here?"

"I think he came here because I'm his . . . well, I think I'm his only friend," she said. "He's never mentioned anyone else. All Finn does is read Dracula comics and play with his dog. Her name's Sadie. She ran away a couple of nights ago. Remember, I went over to see him? He was really upset about it. I wanted to go see him yesterday, too, on the way to school, but you were too busy to take me." She added reproachfully, "Remember?"

Christina sighed. "Morgan, would you just stick to Finn? Did you see him again? Was he OK?"

"I went over his house at lunchtime. I knocked, but no one answered. That was the last time, until this morning."

Christina took a deep breath and tried to marshal her thoughts. "All right. OK. One step at a time. Morgan, shouldn't you be getting ready for school?"

"It's *Saturday*, Mom." Morgan rolled her eyes. "There's no school today, even in Parr's Landing."

Jeremy frowned. "Morgan, did you check on your grand-mother like I asked you to?

"No, Uncle Jeremy. I was talking to Finn. I'm sorry."

"It's almost nine and I haven't seen her at all this morning. Have you, Chris?"

"No," Christina said. "She hasn't been down. And Beatrice didn't come in this morning, either. I made breakfast, and no one came into the kitchen to tell me what a disaster I was, or how I was doing it wrong, or what a mess I was making."

Jeremy smiled wanly, then sighed. "All right, I'll go up and check on her."

Jeremy rapped lightly on the door of Adeline's bedroom and called out, "Mother? It's me, Jeremy. Are you all right? It's almost nine o'clock."

He expected to hear a stinging rebuke of some sort issuing through the mahogany door, but there was only silence in the gloom of the upstairs hallway. He gently turned the cut glass doorknob and pushed. The door swung easily into the room. Jeremy blinked.

The bed looked like it hadn't been slept in. The bedspread was smooth, the pillows—fluffed up every evening by Beatrice before she was allowed to leave for the day—were propped against the ornate headboard of Adeline Parr's bed. Her perfumes and brushes were lined up on her dressing table the way they always were.

More, though—there was a sense of dry airlessness in the room, as though the door had been left shut for much longer than just the night.

"Mother?" he called out again, in case she was in her bathroom. But no, the door was open. He saw that the bathtub was dry, as were the sinks and the floor.

Glancing guiltily around him, Jeremy crossed to Adeline's dressing table and opened the bottom left-hand drawer. He lifted up the file folders he found there and saw that the money he'd found yesterday— almost a thousand dollars, as he'd told Christina—was still in place.

Joy rose in him. The money was still there, which meant that they could leave whenever they wanted to. Adeline's absence would have been completely fortuitous in this regard, except that now this Miller kid had disappeared and he doubted very much that he would be able to pry either Christina or Morgan away from the Landing until he surfaced again.

Jeremy only prayed that his mother didn't return anytime soon from whatever errand or assignation had taken her away from the house so early this morning. It would just make stealing her money and escaping from her house that much easier. He considered pocketing the money now, but realized that if Adeline came home abruptly and saw that the money was missing, the consequences of her fury would be unthinkable. No, better to take it at the last possible minute, before Adeline had time to even realize it was gone.

In the least emotionally involved and most tangential way, Jeremy wondered where his mother was. But Jeremy was a child of Parr House, and he realized that the times when he could enjoy Adeline's absence had been few enough in his years here that he should appreciate them when they occurred. Better not to risk breaking the spell by asking questions.

The three of them ate breakfast in the kitchen, not the dining room. They mostly ate in silence, each deep in his or her own thoughts.

Jeremy tried to signal with his eyes to Christina, to remind her about their escape plan, but she stared at her plate of scrambled eggs and barely touched them.

Morgan was thinking about betrayal and how her thoughtless dismissal of Finn at his most vulnerable had sent him fleeing from the house at the moment he needed Morgan the most. And now he was somewhere outside, afraid to go home, terrified that the vampires in his comic books were real, and that they had laid siege to his family and his dog.

Then Christina said, "I'm going to call Billy Lightning. I'm going to call him at the motel and meet him in town and talk about this."

Jeremy looked surprised. He laid down his coffee cup. "You are? Why?"

"Because I trust him, Jeremy. Aside from you and Morgan—who frankly don't know any more than I do about what's happening here—he's the only person in this town I trust. He knows a lot about this town and the things that have happened here over the years. And he has a truck. We may need it to look for Finn later, especially if he's gone into the woods to look for his dog or something."

"Mom, I told you, his dog is dead," Morgan said. "Finn said the dog burned up."

"Morgan," Christina said patiently. "Finn's dog didn't 'burn up.' Dogs don't 'burn up.' He's probably so rattled by what he saw last night—and I can't believe we're not talking to the police about this because the Parr's Landing police detachment forgot to come in to work today—that he's imagining it. He's probably had a spell of some sort. Anyway, Billy might know what to do, so I'm going to call him."

"Christina," Jeremy said, rolling his eyes surreptitiously. "Remember what we talked about . . . ?" He mouthed *today*, his head angled in a way that Morgan couldn't see his face. Christina shook her head almost imperceptibly and walked out of the room, towards the phone.

Morgan and Jeremy heard her dialling, then asking to be connected to Billy Lightning's room. There was a brief, muffled conversation, then Christina returned to the dining room carrying her purse.

"I'll be back soon," she said. "Morgan, would you please stay here until we figure out what's going on? Jeremy, would you keep an eye on her?"

"Mom! I'm not—"

"Yes, Morgan, I know you're not a baby. So please, do as I ask and don't leave the house until I get back. All right?"

Morgan sighed theatrically, then softened when she saw the fear on her mother's face. "All right, Mom, don't worry. I'll stay here."

"You can take advantage of your grandmother's absence to do some exploring," Jeremy said. "It's a big house, and you haven't seen much of it so far. With Adeline away, the mice can play."

"Thanks, Jeremy," Christina said gratefully. "I won't be long."

CHAPTER TWENTY-FOUR

Behind the wheel of the Chevelle, Christina noticed how empty the streets were for a Saturday morning—how she passed no other cars on the road and there was no one hurrying along the sidewalks. Even with weather this raw, there ought to be people living their lives. Parr's Landing was a tough town—weather was what they lived with, not what dictated how they lived.

That damnable cold rain began to fall again, and she turned on the windshield wipers.

When she pulled up in front of the Pear Tree, she saw Billy Lightning huddled under the awning by the front entrance, waiting for her. When he saw her, he brightened visibly and hurried over to the car. She rolled down the window. "Why are you waiting out here in the rain? Climb in before you get soaked."

Billy shrugged, opening the door and sliding into the passenger seat. "It's closed, I guess. Locked up tight as a—" He blushed furiously. "Well, it's closed."

"Really?" Christina was surprised. "The Pear Tree is always open for breakfast."

"Closed today," Billy said. "Let's go to the Nugget. I passed Mr. Marin sitting at the counter having coffee on the way here." He grinned. "How about a lift? I walked over there before the rain started."

"Sure thing."

"Pretty dead today, isn't it?" Billy said mildly, looking out the passenger-side window. "I haven't seen many people out today, even with the rain. Is there some sort of town ordinance about people staying indoors on Saturday mornings in the Landing?"

Christina squinted through rain streaming across the windshield as the sign for the Golden Nugget came into view. "I noticed that myself on the way over here. I don't know what the hell is going on."

Again, they were alone in the diner. Billy wondered idly how poor Darcy Marin, the owner of the Nugget, made enough money to live, between his nearly empty motel and this albatross of a diner than never seemed to have any customers in it. But the coffee was hot and it was warm inside, in sharp contrast to the rain that was now falling in earnest, and cold enough to become snow before sunset.

"Something very odd is happening in Parr's Landing and I don't know what, exactly. But I need to talk to you," Christina said.

Billy raised his eyebrows. "I love a mystery. And it sure wouldn't be the first mystery that ever occurred here."

"It's sort of serious," she said. "Have you seen the police today?"

He smiled. "No, why? Am I in trouble—again? Is McKitrick going to arrest me for having dinner with you the other night?"

"Billy, please," Christina pleaded. "I'm serious."

Billy sighed. "OK, I'll bite. No, Christina, I haven't seen the police today. Why?"

"Early this morning, a friend of Morgan's woke us up at the house," she began. "Finn, his name is. He said his parents had been killed—to be precise, he said that his father had murdered his mother. Jeremy went over to check the house. He said the front window was broken and that there was blood on the floor. He went to report it at the police station, but no one was there— not Elliot, not his sergeant. Jeremy said the lights were on and the door was unlocked."

"So someone *was* in the station at some point that morning?"

"Jeremy told us it seemed like the lights had been left on all night."

Billy regarded her skeptically. "How does he figure that?"

"He said all the lights were on," she said, "When you come in, in the morning to open up an office, you don't turn all the lights on—just the ones you'll be using."

"So what are we to assume, then? That the Parr's Landing police department has taken a holiday?"

"I don't know, Billy," she said fiercely. "But I do know that there's a little boy out there who claims he saw his mother get killed by his father, but there're no police around to report it to."

Billy was silent for a long moment. To Christina he seemed about to share something, but the moment passed. Instead, he reached for his coffee cup.

"Billy, what is it?" She reached for his hand and touched it lightly. "Why did you come back here?" Christina said. "What did you hope to find here? I mean, in Parr's Landing. You hinted at it the other day, but you said you didn't want to talk about it. Do you still not want to talk about it?"

He sighed. "You'll think I'm crazy and paranoid."

"No," she said. "I won't. I don't think you could be either of those things."

"I think my father was murdered by that graduate student I told you about, Richard Weal. I think Weal was the one who killed him, and I believe he either has, or will, come back to Parr's Landing. I feel it in my bones. Listening to this story scares the crap out of me."

Christina looked at him dubiously. "Billy, even if that's true—even if it's true that this guy killed your dad, why on earth would he come back here?"

"You didn't see him that summer, Christina," Billy said impatiently. "You didn't hear him raving about the voices he heard coming from under Spirit Rock. You didn't see his face when they found him hiding out after he hurt Emory Greer. This is where he first 'lost it,' as they say. This is where he went crazy. Like a lot of other people over the years have gone crazy here and killed people."

"Again—I'm sorry, Billy, but how would you find him, even if he did return? What would you do with him? You're not a cop; you're not a private detective. You're a university professor." Christina hesitated, unsure how best to phrase what she was about to say next. "I don't have a home to go back to. You do. Wouldn't the best way to honour your father's memory be to go back to your teaching life? I wish I could leave here, but Jeremy and I are stuck, at least for the moment. You're free as a bird. Is this town really where you want to be?"

"Christina," he said slowly. "I saw a hockey bag. Some kid found it up by Spirit Rock when he was looking for his dog, apparently. It was full of hammers and knives. There was blood on them. And there were some—some personal artefacts of my father's. Some documents. The police have the bag. They've sent it off for fingerprints. I think they hope they'll find mine on it, but they won't. They'll find his."

"Wait a minute. Oh my God. Did you say the kid was looking for his dog? Is that what you said?"

Billy was confused. "Yeah, that's what the cops told me. Why?"

"Because that's Morgan's friend—the one who came to our door this morning." Christina's voice had jumped an octave. "He lost his dog up there on the cliffs. Sadie, her name was Sadie."

Billy let out a low whistle. "You've got to be kidding me. The same kid who found Weal's hockey bag was banging on your door this morning claiming he saw his mother murdered, but there are no cops around? They're around to harass me for just daring to be in Parr's Landing, but when there's an actual crime, they take a break from police work?"

"Can you really picture Elliot McKitrick taking 'a break' from being a cop, Billy? Do you really think he just flaked off the job? My God."

Privately, Billy couldn't picture it, no. Not a chance. That young tight ass wouldn't know how to take a break from being a cop, not even for money. *Especially not with me in town,* Billy thought. But neither did Billy want to escalate this situation— whatever it was—by giving Christina any further reason to panic. At least not yet.

Billy didn't believe the kid had mistaken Richard Weal for his father, but it was 1972, not 1872, or even 1952. Surely whatever madness had historically afflicted the inhabitants of this place wasn't still afflicting them after all this time? The anthropologist in him had always been intrigued by the persistent legends of this part of northern Ontario, but Billy didn't believe in ghosts or demons or the Wendigo.

"I think we need to find a cop, Christina. I can't believe I actually just said that, but we need some help. I suggest we pay up here, then take a drive past the Parr's Landing police station and find either the young jackass or the old one. Any cop in a storm," he said lamely, trying to make a joke.

But Christina didn't laugh and, of course, neither did Billy.

Outside, the rain had turned to wet snow, and the skies were bitter and dark with low-hanging clouds, the same argentite colour as the cliffs.

The police station was as Jeremy had found it that morning—still empty, still illuminated. Billy thought briefly about searching for the hockey bag with his father's manuscript in it, but there was a fine line between checking out a bizarre story about an abandoned police station and committing an actual crime by tampering with tagged evidence.

He looked through the station window where Christina watched him anxiously from the Chevelle. He shook his head at her: *Nope, no one here.*

After Billy got back in the car, Christina said, "What now?" Billy thought for a moment, then said, "Let's go back to your mother-in-law's Norman chateau. It might be worth talking to Morgan about her friend, Finn. He may have told her something that might help us find him before he—"

"Before he what?"

"Before it gets any colder," Billy said quickly.

They found Finn huddled by the side of the hill leading up to the driveway to Parr House as though he was trying to decide whether to proceed up to the house itself.

Finn was leaning against his Schwinn, his pyjamas stiff with icy rain. In the basket of his bike, Christina saw that he still had the mason jar of water he'd brought into the house that morning—'holy water,' he'd called it, whatever that meant. Finn's body was shaking dangerously. He was clearly skirting hypothermia.

"For the love of *God*," Christina said, slamming on the brakes. "What on earth is he doing out in this rain?"

Billy said, "That's the kid? That's Morgan's friend?"

"Yes! Billy, get him, would you? Put him in the back seat? Mother of Christ."

Billy opened his door and ran out to where Finn stood. Christina couldn't hear what Billy said, but she saw Finn flinch away, then draw in close to him. Then she saw Billy take off his leather jacket and wrap it around the boy.

Billy picked him up in his arms—effortlessly, she noted—and carried him to the car. He opened the back passenger-side door and put him on the seat.

Christina turned around in the driver's seat and said, "Finn, for heaven's sake, what are you doing out here? Let's get you up to the house, and warm. You'll catch your death!"

"I'm cuh-cuh-cuh cold," Finn said through chattering teeth.

"Of course you're cold," Christina said. "Good Lord, let's get you into a hot bath right away and warm you up. Why did you leave?"

Finn looked down, refusing to meet her eyes. His narrow shoulders rocked with repeated waves of shivering.

"Never mind," she said, flooring the accelerator. In that moment, she didn't care whether Adeline was watching her through the upstairs window, ready to berate her for whipping up the gravel drive. She needed to get Finn inside. Whatever else was going on, Christina was still a mother.

Morgan could just make out Finn's face under the high stack of blankets atop Christina's bed. Finn had let Christina bathe him in a hot tub, and had let her dry him with rough Turkish towels and put him to bed.

Christina knew that boys could be strange about being nude in front of anyone, let alone females, related or otherwise, but Finn hadn't been strange. He'd been compliant and docile with

Christina, looking anxious and fretful when she stepped out of his line of sight. He even called her "Mom" once.

She didn't believe the story he'd told her in the bathtub, the story about vampires and monsters and sunlight burning up his dog, but whatever had happened to this boy—whatever he'd seen—had clearly shattered him.

"Finn," Christina said softly when she'd cleared away his bowl. "Is it OK if Dr. Lightning—Billy—comes in and talks with you? He wants to hear what you told Morgan and me?"

Finn nodded. "OK," he said. "But he won't believe me."

"It's all right, Finn. Just tell him what you told us."

Christina nodded to Billy, who had been standing in the doorway.

He entered the room and sat down in an armchair across from the bed. Christina had made Billy promise not to ask about the bloody hockey bag. Billy asked, "How are you feeling, son?"

"Fine, I guess," Finn replied. "Cold."

"You'll warm right up," Billy said. "Now, would you mind telling me what happened? Just like you told Morgan and her mom? Morgan told me it's a bit of a scary story. I don't want you to be scared, because you're safe here. But I know a bit about spooky stories myself. I'm a teacher, you know. At a university. Do you know what a university is?"

"Of course I know what a university is," Finn said weakly. "Just because I'm a kid doesn't mean I'm stupid."

Billy laughed, a full-throated, warm laugh. "Of course not, Finn. Sorry, it was a stupid question. Grownups can be the dumb ones sometimes. Now, can you tell me what happened?"

"OK. Well," Finn said, "a vampire must have taken my dog, Sadie. I put her out in the yard and the next morning she was gone. When she came back, she was all bitten up. When I took her for a walk, the sun came up and she went on fire. Then my dad went up to look for her body and he didn't come home. When he came home, he was different. He was horrible. He had long sharp teeth and he bit my mom in the neck and killed her."

Billy spoke calmly and neutrally. "How do you know he was a vampire, Finn?"

"Because he had long sharp teeth and he bit my mom in the neck and killed her," Finn said patiently. "Because when I put a cross in his face, it burned him," Finn said. "My dad screamed when it touched him. That's the only way you can hurt them—crosses, holy water. Stuff like that. And you can only kill them with wooden stakes or by dragging them out into the sunlight. Everybody knows that."

"Finn, have you ever thought there were vampires here before? I mean, in Parr's Landing?"

Finn's expression was scornful. "You don't believe me," he said. "You're just fibbing."

"I'm really interested, Finn," Billy said softly. "There have been some strange things happening up here over the years. And, most of all, I believe you that something pretty awful happened to your mother and father. Now, why do you think that there are vampires in Parr's Landing?"

Finn thought for a moment. "Once when I went for a walk with Sadie, we were up by Spirit Rock and she was really scared. She was barking and whining. She never made that much noise. She was *scared*."

"Do you remember where you were, Finn? I mean, pretty close?"

"Up under by the paintings, on the cliffs. In my comics, sometimes dogs can tell when there's a vampire's grave around. I think this vampire's grave was there. I think the vampire woke up somehow."

Billy sat very still. "Finn, do you know any other stories from around here? You know, scary ones?"

"No," he said. "What kind of stories?"

"You know, legends?"

Finn paused. "Not really. I once heard some of the older guys talking about a Wendigo. But that's just a spook story to scare kids," he added scornfully. "Nobody believes that one. It's so fake."

"What do you think?"

Christina and Billy were sitting in front of the fire Jeremy had built in Adeline's ground-floor study. Even though Jeremy had assured her that Adeline wasn't in the house—no one knew where she was, nor much cared at the moment—Christina was still uncomfortable there. She was convinced that Adeline was going to come walking through the door any second, eyes blazing, demanding to know how they *dared* make themselves so at home in her study. Jeremy, for his own reasons, couldn't bear to remain in the study, and Christina had sent Morgan to her room to read.

Billy said, "Are you asking me if I think Finn's father is a vampire?"

"Of course not! For heaven's sake, Billy." She shook her head. "I'm asking what you think actually happened?"

"I have no idea," he admitted. He stood up and walked over to the fire. "But Finn believes his story exactly as he told to us. I'm no psychologist, Christina, but he really believes it. As an anthropologist, I have to take into account that Finn—who has no connection to Richard Weal, other than finding the hockey bag—seems to be suffering from another variation of the documented Wendigo psychosis, minus the anthropophagy."

"The *what*?"

"The desire to eat human flesh," Billy said. "It's an established element of Wendigo psychosis. In Finn's case, he just believes the myth without wanting to be part of it."

"Jesus Christ, Billy," she said, shuddering. "He's a child. And he's not talking about the Wendigo, he's talking about vampires. Actual ones, like in the Dracula movies."

Billy shrugged. "One legend or another," he said, sounding embarrassingly professorial, even to himself. "Finn has just grafted his version on the myth in response to the trauma he experienced." He looked at his watch. "Christina, it's four in the afternoon. We need to find a cop. This is ridiculous. We have a boy upstairs in bed with no parents. I'm not sure that's even legal. I'm going to drive into town. If Thomson and McKitrick still aren't in the goddamn station, I'll drive around until I find someone. You stay here. I'll be back with the cavalry."

"Billy?" Christina said. "Please be careful?"

He thought of making another lame joke, or a glib retort, but

Billy realized two things: that Christina meant it, that she cared. And that he felt warmed by that care.

Not for the first time, he cursed the circumstances of meeting this woman so early in her widowhood, when mourning was still so fresh. But he still felt warmed.

"Hold on," Christina said. "I'll drive you back to the motel so you can pick up your truck. I'd let you take the Chevelle, but we may need it for Finn later."

Billy had done two loops through the empty streets of Parr's Landing before, entirely by haphazard chance, he turned onto Brandon Nixon Road and found himself pulling up in front of the scorched-out jumble of charred buildings with the police cruiser parked in front of it.

How did I never see this before? Billy thought, surveying the darkened ruin. *What a goddamn fuck-ugly mess, even in a town full of goddamn fuck-ugly messes.*

Wet snow had begun to fall heavily, and it was starting to cling to the ground, flowering the autumn oaks and maples along the side of the road. The snow had begun to layer the burnt boards, highlighting them with streaks and clumps of white.

Billy approached the police cruiser and peered in through the windows. He rapped on the glass with his knuckles—softly, but with tredpidation.

Of course it was empty. He hadn't expected to find McKitrick or his boss in it, crouched wolfishly on the edge of the road in their police car on this lonely road, had he? Or *had* he? And what was the cruiser doing parked here in the first place—empty like the police station, like the streets of the town itself?

Billy called out, "Hello? Constable McKitrick? Sergeant Thomson?" The wind suddenly picked up, scattering the wet snow and carrying away the sound of his voice. He looked up at the darkening sky, then down at his watch. It was now nearly five. It would be dark soon, and there were no lights on Brandon Nixon Road.

Who do you report an abandoned cop car to? Well, to the cops. But if there aren't any cops around, what then?

He hesitated, then went back to his truck and took the flashlight out of the glove box. Billy Lightning had never been a coward in his life, and he didn't plan to start now.

He reached behind the back seat and picked up the crowbar he kept there, telling himself it was for just in case.

Billy smelled something inside the rink that made his stomach twist inside him. It was a smell that brought back a memory from St. Rita's with horrible vividness. It was the smell of rotten pork.

There had been a sausage plant inside the school. All the boys had been forced to work in it at one point or another, manufacturing pork sausage that the priests would sell locally to earn extra money for the school. The priests told the boys their labour was pleasing in the sight of God, and might help redeem them from their fallen Indian state. There was no question of paying the boys, the priests explained, since the Indian children were already subsisting on the charity of the Canadian public and the Church.

Occasionally the pork went bad and had to be thrown out when it was too far gone even to feed to the children.

Fuck, that awful stench, Billy thought, covering his face in the crook of his arm and gagging. But the smell, putrescent though it was, was the smell of active decay. It had no place out here in a charred hockey arena on a snowswept northern Ontario road on the edge of dusk where nothing lived.

Billy felt his foot strike something soft. He shone the light on the ground.

Dave Thomson, still wearing his uniform, lay at Billy's feet, curled up in a foetal position, eyes closed, apparently fast asleep.

Billy played his light along Thomson's face and neck, stifling a scream with difficulty. The wounds to Thomson's throat had been mortal ones: the flesh had been grated away from his jugular area, the flaps of skin hanging like a string of maggots from two ghastly, jagged holes. There was no way Thomson—anyone—could have survived those wounds.

But ghastlier still was the suppleness and rosy texture of the rest of his skin—face, neck, even his hands. It glowed with vitality.

When Billy shone the light at just the right angle, he could see the red veins beneath the surface.

To Thomson's left, Elliot McKitrick slept, nude, his limbs lewdly entwined with those of a blonde woman in a stained pink top and blue jeans.

Billy backed away carefully. As he did, he saw the shadows of still other bodies in similar states of repose, as though the dark arena was some sort of dormitory, or a nest. Billy counted—what, fifteen? Twenty? No, closer to thirty bodies or more scattered around the arena, all of them assuming Thomson's same restful posture. There were men with the rough, rawboned faces and hands of miners. He saw children lying against the burned boards, arms and legs askew in the way children sleep, some still wearing pyjamas as though they had been plucked out of their beds as they slept. There were women, some nude, some wearing nightgowns, some dressed in bloodstained parkas—not heavy parkas, but just the right temperature for a walk on northern Ontario night on the death-edge of autumn.

Billy's flashlight picked out the bodies of a man and woman in their early thirties. His body was broken and his face was charred with an ugly cinderous scar that was vaguely cruciform in shape. The woman's body was curled against the man's body. Her head lay on his chest in a loving, wifely aspect. Cruel new teeth protruded and lay against her lower lip, lending a vaguely lupine mien to an otherwise loving and maternal face that Billy could easily picture comforting a boy grieving for his lost dog, for Billy had no doubt at all that he'd found Finn's parents.

Not possible, thought the anthropologist. *There are no scientific or material grounds for any of this. Not possible. I refuse to accept this scientific impossibility. I am a tenured university professor. I teach legends and myths. I don't believe them.*

But another voice, colder and infinitely more realistic said: *Look around you. Finn was right.*

Something swayed above him in the shadows and Billy shone his light towards the roof of the arena. The yellow beam caught a familiar face, a face he had not seen for twenty years almost, but one whose contours and hollows he would be able to pick out of any police lineup, in spite of the wild long hair and the matted red beard—no, not a red beard. Just *red.*

The body hung from its toes by a broken beam as though he weighed nothing more than a handful of bad dreams, scrawny arms folded across its chest as though it were cold.

"Richard," Billy whispered. "What the hell?"

Then Weal opened his shining dark red eyes and dropped from the ceiling with balletic grace that struck Billy as beautiful. "Hello, Billy," he said, opening his arms. "Welcome back."

Billy said, "You killed my father, you crazy fuck."

"Yes," Weal said, winking. "I did. He didn't put up much of a fight. He was old and frightened. Phenius Osborne was *weak.* I wanted to use the knives on him, but I didn't have enough time. Luckily for him, he gave me what I needed. His papers. The book he was writing about the history of St. Barthélemy. I just needed the pages that showed me where to find the Master and how to wake him. And I *did* wake him. And now," Weal said, "I'm a god." He covered his mouth with his fingers and giggled—a horrible, mirthless squealing that made Billy think of nails being dragged across a china dinner plate. "He was a bit of a coward, wasn't he, your father? He wouldn't have made a very good Jesuit martyr. No tolerance for pain." Weal paused, grinning. "How's your tolerance for pain, Billy? Shall we find out?"

Billy swung the crowbar as hard as he could at Weal's head. His skull cracked open in a red grapefruit *whoomph!*, spraying blood and brain matter against the standing beams. Weal's body pitched backwards on the ground, jerking spasmodically.

Then he sat up and Billy watched the skull reform atop his neck, bones miraculously reassembling themselves, flesh layering upon flesh.

Even his hair is growing back, Billy noted with awe, feeling around in the dark around him for something—anything—to use as a weapon for when this fucking bastard dead thing had decided to finish growing fully back together, which Billy already knew was imminent. His groping hands found something that felt like a charred shovel. *Thank God!* Billy thought. *It's about time things started going my way here.* As Billy raised it to swing at Weal's body, the weight of the blade of the shovel snapped the wooden handle in two. The blade fell uselessly to the ground, leaving Billy holding a broken pole.

"Jesus fucking Christ!" Billy shouted. "Son of a *bitch*!"

Fully restored, Weal rose to a predatory crouch. "Now you're going to die," he said. "No one is going to miss another dead Indian. At least when I'm finished with you, you'll have served some useful purpose, as food."

At the exact moment Weal leaped for his throat, Billy thrust the shovel handle in front of him, plunging it into Weal's chest as hard as he could.

The skin of Weal's torso split as easily as had his skull, but this time there was no reforming flesh or miraculously healing bone. Weal shrieked—a high, undulating trill that Billy felt move through the air like electricity. Weal fell back against the rink boards, writhing like a harpooned fish.

Billy picked up the flashlight and shone it at Weal's body. Black blood gushed from the chest wound, slowing to a trickle as the thrashing stopped and he lay still.

In the shadows beyond the flashlight's reach, Billy heard the shivering and twitching of the sleeping bodies around him begin to stir and wake.

Oh fuck, he thought. He looked around wildly for another shard of unburned wood to use as a weapon. He still had the crowbar, but he'd already seen how useful that had been against these things.

Without thinking, he reached over and pulled the broken shovel handle out of Weal's chest. It came out surprisingly easily. He turned away from the body. Using the flashlight's beam to pick his way through the debris, Billy retraced his way towards the entrance.

By his reckoning, he had almost reached the front of the building when he heard the unmistakable sound of a board being accidentally kicked.

Billy swung the flashlight in the direction of the sound, but there was nothing. He broke into a run. Then he tripped, landing heavily and painfully on the ground, the air driven out of him. The flashlight pinwheeled into the air. It landed with a clatter a few feet away, the light extinguished.

Dark-blind and gasping for breath, Billy crawled in the dirt, feeling around for the shovel handle.

There it is! he thought, the relief bringing him to the verge of pissing himself. *Thank God.* His fingers closed around the shaft.

From above him, he felt rather than saw the arm that reached down and plucked the shaft of wood out of his grip and tossed it away. Billy heard it land, but he couldn't gauge where.

"You should have left that inside me," Richard Weal said. "Poor Billy."

Jeremy Parr stood under the hot spray of the shower in his bathroom at Parr House and thought about his life.

It had begun here in this town and had been shaped by forces beyond his control. As soon as he had been old enough to control his own life, he'd fled.

Elliot had called him a coward for leaving, but leaving was his first completely courageous act. While he would have liked to think that there had been many other courageous acts in his life, he realized that returning to this place with Christina and Morgan was very likely only his second completely courageous act.

He'd returned here for them, for Christina and Morgan—to be the man he knew Jack would have wanted him to be. When he had fled from Parr's Landing and Adeline, his brother had taken him in and protected him, keeping him safe until Jeremy was strong enough to take care of himself.

As Jeremy saw it, the best way to honour Jack had been to return the kindness—to take care of his wife and daughter. It still was, which was why he was taking them away tonight, whether they liked it or not. He was already packed, and it would take Christina and Morgan no time to follow suit.

All he needed was the money from Adeline's dressing table drawer; the thousand dollars that would get them home to Toronto and away from this awful place. It was past time. They would take Finn with them if they had to, drop him off in the care of some hospital or other, or even a police station—any-where other than Parr's Landing. Finn wasn't safe here, either. No one was.

Jeremy stepped out of the shower and dried himself off. He wrapped a thin white towel around his waist, then opened the bathroom door and stepped out into the dim hall.

From downstairs in Christina's room, he heard the televi-sion—a comforting sound, since he couldn't ever remember Adeline allowing it to be turned on when she was in the house, all through his childhood years. Tonight, the sound recalled the living room in Jack and Christina's house in Toronto, which made him smile.

Jeremy walked quickly down the hallway to his mother's room and pushed open the door. The room was dim, but there was enough light from the hallway behind him.

He was surprised to see the snow on his mother's bedroom windows—he hadn't even noticed the change in weather. He crossed to Adeline's dressing table and pulled open the bottom drawer, where he knew the money was carefully hidden under-neath the neat bundle of letters and file folders.

The drawer was empty.

Outside, the wind and the snow hissed against the glass of Adeline's bedroom window.

Jeremy felt a cold hand on the small of his back, tugging once. The towel around his waist fell to the floor. In the reflection of his mother's dressing table mirror, Jeremy was alone, naked. Behind him was reflected the entire bedroom and doorway lead-ing to the hallway, where light and safety was, where Christina and Morgan were. He felt the cold hand slip under his buttocks, between his legs.

Directly behind him, he heard his mother's dead voice. "Jer-emy," she said. "My son."

CHAPTER TWENTY-FIVE

Of the three of them, only Finn had grown used to the sound of screaming.

Consequently, when Jeremy's high-pitched shrieks ripped through the preternatural silence of Parr House, Finn didn't startle, or even flinch. He just looked up at the ceiling, pointed, and said, "They're here in this house, too. They're real. I told you."

Christina's head snapped forward and jerked upwards to the place Finn was pointing.

She jumped up from the chair next to her bed where Finn was still buried under the blankets. Morgan had been lying across the foot of the bed. She raised herself to a sitting position and instinctively moved closer to Finn and her mother, and away from the screaming, which had risen in pitch since Finn first spoke.

Uncle Jeremy sounded the way Morgan had always imagined an animal being slaughtered would sound.

"Stay here!" Christina commanded, pointing her finger at Morgan and Finn. "Do not move from this spot, do you understand me?"

"Mommy," she whispered. "It's Uncle Jeremy."

"Morgan, stay here with Finn! Promise me!"

White-faced, Morgan nodded her head in assent. Finn, also pale, nodded briefly but with much less conviction. He squeezed Morgan's hand.

Christina took the stairs two at a time, shouting, "Jeremy, I'm coming! I'm coming!"

She reached Jeremy's bedroom and pushed the door open. The room was empty, his suitcase on the bed, half-packed. The rest of his clothing was folded in neat piles. The screaming wasn't coming from his bedroom; it was coming from Adeline's room.

Christina ran down the hallway. She threw open Adeline's bedroom door. The room was dark. Instinctively, she groped for a light switch and stepped inside.

At first she wasn't sure what she was looking at. There were three figures in the room, arrayed in a tableau that made Christina think of the ecclesiastical paintings of Christ's crucifixion she'd seen in books—not the Passion itself, but the taking-down from the cross.

Jeremy was lying nude, spread-eagled on Adeline's yellow silk bedspread, arms outstretched in a posture of martyrdom. The blood from his throat wound streamed down his broken neck, soaking the yellow silk pillowcases upon which his head lay at a terrible angle.

An old man with white hair, wearing some sort of cassock, was crouched at the head of the bed, his face buried under Jeremy's jaw. And Adeline knelt at the foot of the bed, head bowed like Mary, mother of Christ.

From somewhere outside her own body, Christina idly noted that her mother-in-law was—ostentatiously, even for Adeline— wearing a fur coat indoors. Underneath the coat, Christina saw the grimy hem of a nightgown. Adeline's bare feet on the immaculate carpet were black with filth, and there were dirty footprints leading to—no, back from—the window.

Adeline's back was to Christina, her arms extended, her hands clamped on Jeremy's drenched thighs, holding them apart as implacably as if they were secured in an iron grapple. The yellow silk bedspread was sodden with Jeremy's blood, which had started to pool on the carpet in an outward-spreading stain.

Christina made a sound high in her throat, somewhere between the whine of a trapped animal and a moan. "Adeline . . ."

Adeline turned her crimson-smeared face towards Christina. She smiled as casually as a hostess who'd been disturbed in her embroidery, and spat her son's penis out of her mouth like an hors d'oeuvre.

"MOMMY!" Morgan stood in the doorway to Adeline's room, her mouth an open circle of horror. Behind her, one hand on her shoulder, Finn stared, likewise open-mouthed.

"Oh my God, Morgan!" Christina wailed, turning around. "I told you to stay downstairs! Get downstairs *right now!*"

Adeline rose jerkily to her feet, looking from Christina to Morgan. Her mouthful of teeth was stained and needle-like in the overhead light.

"Whore," Adeline croaked. "Dirty, dirty *whore.*" She took two shambling steps towards the doorway where Christina stood protectively in front of Morgan.

"Get away, Adeline, goddamn you!" Christina shouted. "Get away from my daughter!"

"Or else what, Christina?" Adeline crooned. "This is my house. I come and go as I please, and do as I like. Haven't you learned your place here yet?"

Adeline reached out with one hand and slapped Christina across the face, sending her crashing into the polished maple Philadelphia highboy next to the doorway. Agony sang through Christina's shoulder. She felt blood trickling down the back of her scalp where she'd cut it on the edge of the dresser, and she groaned.

Adeline turned her blazing eyes on Morgan and said, "Morgan, come here to your grandmother. Come and give me a kiss. You're a real Parr. You're the only real Parr in this house except for me. All of this is for you—this house, this town, and everything in it. It's your birthright. *Come here.*"

Morgan flinched. Then her arms dropped limply to her sides. Her eyes glazed over and went blank. She took a blind, stumbling step towards Adeline, who crooked her arms and opened them in a grotesque parody of grand-maternal devotion.

"Morgan, no! Don't go to her!" Finn shouted. "Don't look at her! That's how they get you!"

Morgan, empty-eyed, took another step towards her grandmother.

At the exact moment that Adeline's arms snaked out, her fingers grazing the sleeves of her granddaughter's sweater, Finn placed his palm flat in the middle of Morgan's back and shoved her as hard as he could.

Morgan spun off-balance and fell, sprawling on the floor near where Christina had fallen. Christina scrambled for Morgan and dragged her daughter across the carpet towards her.

Blind fury passed across Adeline's face. From her open mouth came a shrill, sibilant buzzing, vaguely insectile or serpentine.

Her teeth actually click when she hisses like that, Finn thought in wonderment, fascinated in spite of himself. *Just like in the comics.*

Then Adeline threw back her head and laughed. "Little idiot," she said. Her voice brimmed with contempt and malicious, dark mirth. "Dirty little townie boy. A dirty townie, just like my cunt of a daughter-in-law."

Very clearly, Finn said, "Fuck you, you snob. This is for my dog."

He unscrewed the lid of the mason jar of water he was holding behind his back and threw its contents in Adeline Parr's face.

Finn's father had once let him hold a candle up to a blowtorch. The candle had literally been uncreated in front of Finn's eyes, liquefying and becoming viscous in the heat of the blowtorch.

That was what happened to Mrs. Parr's face when the holy water splashed into it—*into it,* not *across* it. The water burned into Adeline's face, flushing away skin, troughing bone, until the liquefied mixture that had been her face ran down in an oily red and yellow stream of blood and fat. Adeline dropped to her knees and then fell on her side, clawing at her face and rending the air with her agony.

She's melting just like the Wicked Witch of the West, Finn mused. *Good. I hope it hurts like hell.*

It seemed impossible that she could still make that agonized highpitched sound with her throat melting away like it was, but

Finn's ears rang with the sound of her excruciation. Acrid, stinging white smoke poured from Adeline's dissolving face, filling the room. It burned Finn's throat and eyes, making him cough and retch.

Temporarily blind, Finn stumbled into the cavernous bedroom, feeling his way as he went. He flailed his arms in front of him, trying to stay balanced.

He didn't see Adeline's spindly dressing table chair, but he surely felt it when he collided with it. He said, "Ooooh!" Then his legs buckled and he collapsed on the floor at the foot of the bed, disoriented and unable to see.

He heard Christina screaming his name, but—still smoke-blind—he didn't understand why, and he couldn't see what they saw until it was long past too late.

The old man in black streaked toward Finn with the speed of a deadly underwater snake. Christina screamed Finn's name as she saw the man's blackrobed arms with their long-fingered white hands uncoil from his sides and seize the boy in a possessive grip, yanking Finn back towards him, enfolding him in his arms. He slipped his elbow around Finn's throat in a crushing chokehold. Finn's face turned a dull, airless red as he began to suffocate. As he dragged Finn towards the French doors leading to Adeline's balcony, the old man's eyes met Morgan's.

"Let him go!" she screamed. "Let Finn go!"

Christina shouted, "Morgan, stay away from him!"

But if Morgan could hear at all, she gave no sign of it. She launched herself at the old man, her fists raised. But she never reached him *or* Finn.

Finn's face was the colour of the dark pink flush of an overripe peach, and his eyes bulged and watered from lack of oxygen. He reached out one arm and choked out one ragged, pleading word that sounded like *Morgan* at the same time as Morgan reached out to him, fully intending to wrench Finn from the old man's death grip.

Their fingers brushed, once.

Then the old man threw himself back against the closed French doors. The glass shattered around him in his wake, and the momentum sent them tumbling over the edge of the balcony, thirty feet above the ground. Clouds of wet snow and cold rain blew into the bedroom from the broken doors and the night outside, curtains flapping into the room like flags.

But instead of the sound of their bodies striking the lawn below, Morgan heard the sound of giant wings churning the air outside the window—and Finn screaming her name, over and over again.

When she ran to the balcony and tried to follow the sound, Morgan saw a great dark mass, nearly indistinguishable from the general blackness, rising into the night sky.

She might have missed it entirely except for the helplessly flailing figure of a small, screaming boy in white pyjamas it carried in its claws, growing smaller and smaller as they drifted almost lazily into the deeper darkness towards the outlying forests and the cliffs beyond. Then it was swallowed up entirely by the rain and the sheets of snow.

Adeline Parr's bedroom reeked of blood and acid smoke. Christina stood up carefully, but spears of white-sharp pain still shot up her left leg from the impact of her collision. Her head throbbed. Morgan, her hair wet with melting snow, stood on the balcony, wailing Finn's name over and again.

Adeline Parr's headless body was motionless on the carpet. Where her head had been, there was only a nimbus of boiled slush and bits of stubborn bone fragment that had survived the annihilation of the holy water.

Christina had a great longing to kick the body as hard as she could, but there was still some lingering fear in her that, even now, Adeline would reach out and grasp her ankle, diamond rings and red-lacquered scimitar fingernails digging into Christina's soft skin. Instead, she stepped over Adeline's body and went to the gory tangle of silk sheets where Jeremy had bled out and died.

Christina couldn't breathe. She looked down at the familiar face, so much like Jack's, and felt a band of grief tighten around her chest so strongly that she feared she might literally suffocate from the pain of this second tragic severing from their lives of the second of the two men who had meant the most to her and Morgan.

Oh, Jeremy, she thought. *Oh, my poor, sweet Jeremy. What did they do to you?*

Christina pulled one of the sheets out from under him—a cleaner one than the others, at least—and carefully and lovingly covered his broken and torn body with it.

As she did, a glitter of silver on the carpet caught her eye. It was Jeremy's St. Christopher's medal. The chain was broken as though it had been ripped off his neck and thrown down. Christina bent and picked it up. She put it in the pocket of her jeans.

By the window, Morgan had stopped calling Finn's name, but her body still shook with sobs. Her shoulders were hunched forward and her hands were loosely clasped in front of her, as though praying.

Christina called out softly, "Morgan? Honey?"

Morgan turned around. Her face was white and stiff with shock. "Hi, Mom," she said. "What did you say? Mom . . . he took *Finn. He carried Finn away.*" Fresh tears streamed from her eyes. "There really are vampires. Just like Finn said there were. It was all true."

She shook her daughter gently. "Morgan, we have to leave," Christina said, struggling to keep her voice calm without sacrificing the force of her words, words she needed Morgan to hear and heed. "We have to leave *right now.* Are you OK to walk? Can you make it downstairs to the car?"

"But what about Finn?" She stared frantically through the broken French doors.

"Morgan, listen to me," she said urgently. "We have to leave the house. It's too dangerous here. We can't worry about Finn now. Finn would want you safe."

"OK," Morgan said. She glanced down at Jeremy's body on the bed and started to shake again. "Oh, *Mom . . .*"

"Don't look at it, Morgan. Don't look at him. Come on now—here, look at me instead. Look at my face." When she did, Christina smiled encouragingly. "That's it. Just keep your eyes on me."

She put her arm around Morgan's shoulders and gently herded her past the carnage in the bedroom and out into the hallway. Once there, she hurried her daughter down the stairs. The keys to the Chevelle were where she left them—on the console table near the front door, next to her purse. The only light downstairs came from the embers of the fire in Adeline's study bleeding through the half-closed doors, and a greenshaded library lamp on the other side of the hallway.

Christina took one last look back at the foyer of Parr House, which seemed to have gorged itself on the darkness, both natural and unnatural, until it was bloated. Whatever the source of the monsters that seemed to have stepped out of the storybooks and into her world, they had all been drawn here, to Parr's Landing and to this awful place. Nothing could live here—could *ever* have lived here, she corrected herself—except anguish and misery.

Christina wished she had a can of propane and a match. She thought briefly of looking for just that in one of the pantries off the kitchen, but she realized that there just wasn't time. Every moment she remained in this house, they were in danger. She had to get Morgan to safety, whatever "safety" meant in the middle of this horror.

"Come on, sweetheart," Christina said. "Let's go. We never have to come back to this place again."

CHAPTER TWENTY-SIX

The Gold Nugget motel was dark when Christina pulled into the parking lot in the snow.

The Chevelle's headlights played across the windows of the diner, illuminating empty tables and shining through empty water glasses that went dark again when the high beams veered away as she parked the car.

Morgan opened the passenger-side door and looked around fearfully. "Mom, what are we doing here? Where is this place?" She leaned close to her mother, away from the snow and rain that was now falling in an even mixture of both.

"It's the motel, Morgan," Christina said, with a calmness she didn't feel. "It's the Nugget. It's where Billy is staying." She stepped out and locked the car, realizing at once what a futile gesture it was. If those things wanted to get in somewhere, they seemed to just do it. They didn't ask questions or worry much about locks.

At some point, when I can think about it without going insane, I must take some time to sit down and consider the fact that my gay brother-in-law was just killed by his mother. Oh, but it gets better: he was killed by his mother who drank his blood and then bit his cock off with teeth the size of fingers. Then spat it out.

At which point, a twelve-year-old friend of my daughter's threw a jar of holy water in the bitch's face and melted it right off because he'd read it in a vampire comic. Then—wait for it!—my daughter's friend was carried off by an old man dressed like a seventeenth-century Jesuit priest in one of our history books from school.

I'm living in a monster movie—which is crazy, of course. But crazy or not, here we are.

And it's dark and I'm cold and there's no one anywhere around here who can help me except a man I barely know. And if I think about any of this right now, I'll go right off my goddamn head.

She reached for Morgan's hand and pulled her along as quickly as she could. "We need to find him, quickly. Let's hope he left his room unlocked. It'll give us a place to stay where it's safe, at least for now."

"What if he's not here? What if we have to go back to Grandmother's house?"

"Morgan, we're not going back there to that house, ever—no matter what. If Billy's not here, I'll kick the door in if I have to."

In the absence of light from any of the rooms, let alone the diner or the front office, Christina tried to recall which room Billy had entered when she dropped him off a thousand years ago this afternoon. She hadn't been paying attention of course, because at that time, she and reality still shared mutually agreed-upon parameters.

Christina and Morgan stopped in front of room 938.

"This is the one, I think," Christina said, trying the doorknob. It was locked, of course, and the room was dark as all the others. "Jesus *Christ!*" she shouted, kicking the door in frustration. Christina thought for a moment, then said, "Morgan, stay right here. I'm going to break into the office and get the spare key."

"Mom, no! Are you *kidding* me? I'm not waiting out here!"

"You're right. It was a stupid idea. Forget it. Come with me—but stay close, Morgan, I mean it."

The office, as it turned out, was not locked. It wasn't even closed. The office door banged in the wind. A cold cup of coffee sat atop the front desk and the floor was littered with shards of broken light bulb glass. Her foot slipped in a pool of something sticky and dark that she couldn't see, but which smelled like dirty pennies. She wondered what had happened to Darcy Morin, then decided that she couldn't bear the knowledge right now anyway.

"Morgan, step back please," Christina said, blocking the entrance to the office with her body. "Stay in the doorway here, but don't come in. But stay close enough for me to grab you, OK, honey?"

"Mom, what is it," she asked fearfully. "What's in there?"

"Nothing, honey, just looking for the key to Billy's room." Privately, she was grateful for the darkness—there was nothing she might stumble upon here in the office that she had any desire to see in the light. Under her breath she muttered, "935, 936 . . . aha! Got it!" She took the key to room 938 down off the peg and stepped outside, taking Morgan by the arm. "Come on, honey, let's get warm! Hurry-hurry-hurry!"

Outside, she slipped the key into the lock of room 938.

Blessedly, there was a click. She pushed the door open and stepped into the warmth of Billy's room, which smelled of leather and pipe tobacco and kindness, and when she switched on the light, it revealed nothing out of the ordinary.

Billy found them in his motel room an hour later with the doors barricaded from the inside, a chair wedged up against the handle.

He peered in through his window. Christina was sitting on the bed with her knees up. Morgan was in her arms, leaning with her head on her mother's breast. Morgan's eyes were closed, but Billy doubted she was sleeping. Christina's eyes were trained on the door, wide open and alert. In her hands was some sort of silver medal on a chain.

Billy could spot a St. Christopher's medal at thirty paces. All of the children at St. Rita's were given one and had been expected to wear it all the time.

Ironic, Billy thought. *For the first time in my life, it would have come in handy.*

He looked down at his clothes and wondered what sort of a picture he would present if he knocked on the door of his own motel room and asked Christina to let him in. Not a good one, he expected. He stank, and his clothes were covered with dirt and blood. He looked down at his hands, which were the colour of coal dust. *I could just leave them in there and not knock. They'd probably be safe.* Then he shook his head and sighed. *Of course they wouldn't be safe in there. They're completely unsafe in there.*

He knocked on the motel room door and called out, "Christina?"

From inside, Christina's muffled voice: "Billy, is that you?"

"Yeah, it's me," he said. "Let me in."

Christina opened the door and fell into Billy Lightning's arms. She hadn't intended to fall into his arms, or any man's arms, especially not in front of Morgan. But the momentum of her own relief propelled her.

Billy was solid and real and reassuring, and his presence was warm and strong. Christina was tired of being the strong one, and she was dead tired of being afraid.

"Billy, what's that smell?" She pulled away, wrinkling her nose in distaste. Her eyes widened as she took in his appearance. "Jesus, what happened? Were you in an accident? Are you all right?"

He stepped back, away from her. "Sorry. I should have warned you about that. Look," he said, pointing at her. "I've gotten you dirty." He reached out to brush the smear of dirt off her pale pink sweater. "Here, let me."

Christina's eyes darted to Morgan on the bed, who was watching their interaction with wide eyes, silently. Christina shook her head almost undetectably at Billy, who understood. "No, I've got it, thanks," she said, brushing the ash off the sweater herself.

"Of course," he said politely. "Yeah, that's it. There, you've got it." She smiled, grateful for his understanding.

"Billy. What happened to you? When you weren't here, we took the key from the front office. Mr. Marin wasn't there—no one was there. The whole place is empty."

"Marin is down at the old hockey arena," he said. "The one on Brandon Nixon Road. So are Elliot and Sergeant Thomson, and about thirty other . . . residents of Parr's Landing."

Christina was confused. "What do you mean, they're at the arena?" She shook her head. "The old arena? The *Takacs* one? Is that even still standing? Elliot and Jack used to play there. It burned down. It's a ruin."

"It's more than a ruin, Christina," Billy said. "It's a grave."

"Billy, what are you talking about?"

He glanced at Morgan, then back at Christina. "Maybe not here? Outside?"

From the bed, Morgan's voice was surprisingly strong and clear. "Dr. Lightning," she said. "Finn's dead. Uncle Jeremy's dead. I saw it happen with my very own eyes. Please tell my mom what you're talking about. I'm never going to forget the things I saw tonight, and *words* aren't going to scare me."

Billy sighed. "OK, fair enough. I found the place they were all . . . uh . . . sleeping. The . . . uh . . ." He faltered, looking helplessly to Christina for help, adult to adult.

"The vampires," Morgan finished impatiently. Her face was pale and hard, her mouth set in a steely line Christina had never seen before. "Finn said they were vampires. He knew what they were, but nobody believed him because we all thought he was just a dumb kid who read *Tomb of Dracula* comics. And now he's dead," she added flatly. "And it's our fault. And now we believe him. And now it's too late."

"OK, vampires," Billy said. "I found them there. It was everything Finn said it would be. Also, I found Richard Weal. I was right. He killed my father and stole his manuscript. Weal said he came here to wake someone up, someone who had been sleeping here in the caves. Those 'voices,' in 1952? He wasn't imagining them. They were real. Probably *all* the people who heard them were really hearing them."

"The priest," Christina said suddenly. "He looked like a priest. The one who carried Finn away."

"What priest? What are you talking about?"

Christina replied, "They killed Jeremy, him and Adeline. When we found him in Adeline's room, there was someone else there. An old man. I'd never seen him before. He was in a long black robe. I remember thinking he looked like a picture of one of the Jesuit martyrs in the church here. The ones who came here to settle. The ones who died here three hundred years ago."

Billy said, "Figures it would be a goddamn priest."

* * *

Morgan watched Billy carefully. She said nothing, but every nerve in her body was stretched as taut as wire. Something about him wasn't right. He was different. Maybe not *different* like Adeline was different . . . afterwards. Not quite, anyway. But she wished he wasn't standing so close to her mother.

"We need to get you two someplace safe," Billy said. "At least until dawn. Then you have to leave. You have to leave Parr's Landing. You have to drive to Toronto and you have to not look back. Never, ever come back here, Christina. I mean it."

"I don't think the car will survive the trip, Billy. Adeline's chauffeur has the keys to her car, and he and his wife are missing, too. And Jeremy said he found some money in Adeline's room, but he didn't give it to me before he . . . well, before what happened."

Billy fished in his pockets and handed Christina the keys to his truck. "Take the Ford," he said. "It's practically new. It'll get you home to Toronto. And there's about seven hundred dollars in the glove box. Take it. Just promise me you'll go. Get Morgan away from here."

"You mean 'we,' don't you? You don't mean *without you*, do you, Billy?"

Billy's expression was unreadable. "I can't leave," he said.

"What do you mean you can't leave? Are you kidding me?" Hysteria made Christina's voice shrill and jagged. "You *can* leave. You *have* to leave! There's nothing here for you! Nothing!"

"Weal came here because of my father," Billy said. "All these people are dead because of him. We brought Weal here in 1952 and put this all in motion. The arena was full of those things when I got there tonight. Who knows how many of them there are here, or what they'll do. I can't leave. I have to fix this. I have to find the one who did this and make it right. For my father's sake, at the very least. But I won't be able to do it unless I know that you and Morgan are safe, and a long way from here."

When she started to protest, Billy put up his hand. "No more talk," he said. "Get Morgan ready. I'll bring the truck right to the entrance here. I'm taking you to the church. When the sun comes up, leave. Don't look back."

"Dr. Lightning," Morgan said. "May I ask you a question?"

"What is it, honey?"

"You said that they were in the arena when you got there. How did you get away?"

"I burned them," Billy said. "I burned their bodies. Just like Finn said, fire hurts them."

Morgan sounded dubious. "You don't smell like smoke. And . . . they just *let* you?"

"They weren't awake yet," he said vaguely. "Not all of them, anyway. I guess the sun wasn't all the way down. Don't worry, I took care of it. Now," he said. "No more talking. We need to get you two to the church." He held up his hand again. "I mean it, no more questions," he said gruffly. "It's time to go, ladies."

He's lying, Morgan thought, but Christina was already pushing her out the door of the motel, and Billy had sprinted ahead and was standing by the door of the truck.

Billy drove the short distance between the Gold Nugget and the church in complete silence, looking neither left nor right. The beams of the truck's headlights carved a tunnel through the shadows and the snow, which had grown thick and heavy in the hours since they'd arrived at the motel. On either side of the road, houses like empty husks took momentary shape, then vanished back into the night and the falling snow.

Billy parked the truck in front St. Barthélemy and the Martyrs. The steps leading to the front door and the sanctuary were packed in wet snow. Gusts of it capered in the yellow light above the entrance to the church.

"End of the line," he joked. "This is where everyone gets off."

"Billy—?"

"Mom, come on," Morgan's voice was urgent. She didn't look at Billy. She opened the side door of the truck and jumped out. She grabbed at her mother's arm and practically pulled her out. "I want to be in the church. Right *now*. Please."

"Morgan, you go on inside," Christina said, shaking off Morgan's hand on her arm. "Wait for me. I want to talk to Billy for a minute."

"Mom, *no! Now!*" Morgan shouted. "I'm *not* going in without you! *Don't talk to him!* We don't have time!" Morgan stared defiantly at Billy. He looked back at her. Wordless communication passed between them. Then Billy looked away.

"She's right, Christina," Billy said finally. "Go inside where you'll be safe. It's open. Get some sleep. Then, tomorrow, take my truck and go."

Christina pleaded. "Stay with us. Come inside and wait until sunrise. Then leave with us in the morning. There's nothing for you here."

"Mom, *please!*"

"Goodbye, Christina," Billy said. "I have to go back." He stepped away from the church, out of the ring of light, and walked into the shadows beyond it.

A trick of the lamplight, Christina thought. *I can still see his eyes.* Then Billy Lightning was swallowed wholly by the darkness.

Morgan woke to the sound of rocks falling on the stained glass windows.

The sound startled her and she sat up. Then she remembered. *Oh yes,* she thought. *We're in the church. They can't get us here. That's why we're here.* She looked at her watch. It was four o'clock in the morning. Dawn was still three hours away.

Beside her, Christina moaned softly in her sleep and turned over. *She's dreaming,* Morgan realized. She reached out and gently touched Christina's blonde hair. Her mother's eyes were ringed with blue-black circles, and the skin on either side of her nose was dull red and raw in the dim overhead lights of the church. Christina looked exhausted. Morgan wondered why she hadn't noticed it before. Then she realized why—Christina hadn't *wanted* her to see it. Her mother had been trying to protect her in every possible way since they'd arrived in Parr's Landing. But in sleep, the lie failed and her face told the truth.

The scattershot of stones on glass came again.

Morgan reached over and shook her mother's arm. "Mom? Mom, wake up. There's someone outside. I'm scared."

But Christina slept on, oblivious. Morgan held the St. Christopher's medal tightly in her hands. The silver was warm, and comforting somehow.

The rocks came again, this time harder and more insistent. She ran to the window and tried to see outside, but it was impossible. This time the stones bounced off the glass directly in front of her.

"Go away!" she screamed. "Leave us alone!"

The voice that answered her was as clear as water. A soft voice. A boy's voice.

"Morgan. It's me, Finn. Come outside."

"Finn?" she cried joyously. "Is that you? Are you OK?"

"It's me, Morgan," he said. "I'm OK. Come outside."

"I can't, Finn," she said. "I'm not allowed."

Finn's voice was impatient. "Come to the front door of the church, anyway. I'll be on the front steps."

Morgan looked at Christina sleeping on the pew. "Mom," she whispered. "Mom, wake up. Can you hear me?" There was no answer. Christina slept on. "Finn's here. I'm going to go and see him. I'll be right back. Is it OK?" *She won't even know I was gone,* Morgan rationalized. *I'll be back before she wakes up. Finn's alive! Finn's alive!*

She walked the length of the nave and opened the church doors wide to welcome Finn back.

Finn stood on a small rise of accumulated snow on the lawn of the church.

His feet looked frail and blue in the light, and there was no disturbance in the snow leading in any direction to or from where stood. The wind whipped his dark hair about his face and the fabric of the pyjamas billowed ludicrously around his thin body.

Morgan stared. "Finn? Is that you? What are you doing there? It's *freezing*! Come in here where it's warm."

"Yeah, it's me," he said ruefully. "I'm always coming to you, aren't I? I wish I was older so I could have been your boyfriend, then I could have taken care of *you*."

"Finn, what are you talking about? You *did* take care of me. You saved my from my grandmother back at the house. You saved my life."

He went on as though he hadn't heard her. "You're really pretty, Morgan." He looked like he could be blushing, but in the light it was hard to tell. "Can I tell you something?" He sounded gently embarrassed, but didn't wait for her to answer. "I . . . I love you, Morgan. I guess I have, from the moment I saw you outside the school that day."

"Oh, Finn." Morgan's eyes filled with tears. "I'm so sorry I wasn't a better friend to you. I'm so sorry."

He paused. "You know, right? You know what happened to me?"

Morgan shook her head, but even as she did so, she realized she *did* know. She nodded, not trusting herself to speak. The tears that had been brimming in her eyes spilled down her cheeks.

"He took me away," Finn said darkly. "He took me to the caves up by Spirit Rock. He *changed* me. To punish me. You know. For, well, for what I did. You know, with the holy water." Finn shivered. "He did awful things to me up there," he said. "He's terrible, Morgan. He's so *old*. He's been waiting up there for hundreds of years. Waiting for someone to wake him up. Someone did. Some crazy person. That day I found his bag with all the knives in it— that was his. For waking *him* up."

Morgan glanced back towards the church doors, feeling a sudden stab of fear. She clapped her hands over her ears to block out the sound of Finn's voice.

This isn't Finn, dummy. It used to be, but it isn't, now. He's something . . . well, someone else. Like Grandmother Parr was.

But then, Grandmother was sort of like that even before, wasn't she?

Finn sighed. "I'm the same person, Morgan. I'm not going to hurt you. I promise. And you were hearing me in the church even though I was outside, so don't bother covering your ears."

Morgan's voice quivered. She pointed through the open doors, into the nave. "My mother is in there. She's sleeping."

"Your mom won't wake up till I want her to. She's just asleep, don't worry."

"You won't hurt her, either? You promise?"

"Your mom is a nice lady," Finn said, sounding wounded. "She was nice to me. I would never hurt her." He smiled, showing the small pearlescent fangs of a twelve-year-old boy on the edge of manhood, a state he would never attain. "She was nice to me. Of course I won't hurt her. I needed to see you before . . ."

"Before what?" she demanded.

He was silent, unmoving from his spot atop the mound of snow.

"It hurts," Finn said. His voice was small and hollow, even where it echoed inside her head. "It hurts something awful. It's not like I thought it would be. In my comics, the vampires forget about their lives and they stop feeling bad about it. Not me—I remember *everything*. And I still miss my dog. Sadie tried to protect me from this. She knew what was waiting up here."

Morgan was trembling. She wrapped her arms around her torso and rubbed them, trying to warm herself.

"You're cold," Finn said. "You should go inside."

"I don't need to go inside. But is it OK if I run inside quickly and get my sweater? Do you want to come inside and get warm?"

"I can't," Finn said. "I can't go in there."

"Why not?" Then she thought about it. "Oh, right," she said. "Sorry."

Morgan realized she should feel safer knowing Finn couldn't cross the threshold of the church, but instead it just made her feel sad. "I'll be right back," she promised. She knew he could probably stop her if he wanted to.

But he just said, "OK," and shrugged.

Morgan hurried up the nave to the place where Christina was still fast asleep—if anything, in a deeper sleep than before. The dark circles under Christina's eyes seemed to have faded by degrees, as though Finn were actually healing her mother from where he stood on top of the snow, outside the church.

I could stay in here and never come out. She picked up her sweater from where it lay on the back of the pew. *I could leave him out there in the cold and the snow and the night and never have to see him again. These things can't come into churches.*

But he's not a 'thing,' is he? He's Finn. He's my friend. He saved my life.

Morgan saw the St. Christopher's medal lying on the pew next to her mother. She picked it up and slipped it into her pocket.

"There's a house over there," Finn said, pointing across the snowy lawn after Morgan returned with her sweater. "Behind the manse. It's empty. Do you want to go in there?"

"What for?" Morgan said, suddenly fearful again.

"Because it's cold out here, dummy, obviously," Finn teased. "And even if I'm not cold, you are. I can tell. You're still shivering. I know you have that medal in your pocket. You could use it if you wanted. I wouldn't be able to stop you. Besides, I told you not to worry."

Morgan's voice was incredulous. "How do you *know* all this stuff?"

Finn shrugged again, but this time it was a self-conscious shrug. "Some of it from *The Tomb of Dracula,* some of it from *Dark Shadows.* Some of it from . . . from him. He steals people's memories, then he shares them with us. The rest of it I just know." He tapped his chest and his head. "I know it in here. I don't know how, I just do."

She thought about it for a moment, then said, "OK, let's go to the house. How do you know it's empty? Or that it's open?"

He glanced briefly at the dark window on the second floor. "Trust me. I've been inside already."

The living room was plain but clean. There was a photograph of Pope Paul VI on the wall above the television set, but no books anywhere.

The unmistakable odour of boiled cabbage clung to the cheap curtains, indeed had seeped into every porous surface in the living room. Morgan hated boiled cabbage, especially the way it smelled when it was cooking. At that moment, however, it reminded her of her neighbourhood in Toronto, and she just felt homesick.

Sitting next to her on the plastic-covered sofa, Finn said shyly, "Morgan, can I ask you a question?"

Her voice was gentle, but teasing "That's one question already, Finnegan."

"My mom called me that," he said.

"What was the question you wanted to ask me?"

He hesitated. "Have you ever . . . well, have you ever, you know . . . like, had a . . . a . . ."

"A boyfriend? Is that what you're asking? If I've ever had a boyfriend?" *If he could blush,* Morgan thought, *he'd be beet-red.*

Mutely, Finn nodded his head.

"Have you ever had a girlfriend, Finn?"

He shook his head. "Nope."

"Why not?" She took his hand lightly in hers, finding it ice cold. "Have you ever liked a girl before?"

"Only you," he said, looking down. "Never before. Nobody else."

She brought his hand up to her face and laid it there. He leaned forward clumsily to kiss her on the lips but missed, landing the kiss on her chin instead. Morgan inclined her head and kissed him tentatively on the lips.

Blood thundered in Morgan's ears and her face flamed. "Finn, just so you know, I never . . . well, I've never had a . . . a boyfriend, either."

Finn pulled away as though burned. "I'm sorry," he said. "I'm such a jerk. Why would a girl like you want to kiss somebody as ugly as me? I'm sorry," he said again. "I'm so stupid."

Morgan sat very still, as though considering. Then she unbuttoned the top button of her cardigan. Then the second. Finn watched, his eyes wide.

"Finn?" In the dark living room, Morgan's voice sounded alien, even to her—thicker, fuller, almost a woman's voice now.

Outside, the wind picked up, blowing thick fistfuls of snow at the windows. Morgan shrugged the sweater off her shoulders, letting it fall behind her on the sofa.

"What?" Finn breathed.

"You're not ugly. You were never ugly."

"I'm not?"

"No," Morgan said, reaching for him. "You're really not. You're really beautiful to me, Finnegan." She hesitated, then said, "Finn?"

"What?"

"Do you promise—*really promise*—that you won't hurt me?"

"I promise, Morgan," Finn said. "Cross my heart."

They held each other close, naked in the makeshift bed of ottoman cushions and crocheted afghan blankets on the floor of the immaculate, chaste house that smelled like boiled cabbage and carpet deodorizer, under the photograph of Pope Paul VI.

Morgan had asked Finn if he wanted to go upstairs, but he seemed to panic at the thought, insisting instead they stay in the living room. When she asked him why, he shook his head and said, "Here is good. Here is fine."

Later, in her arms, Finn's icy body didn't warm, but neither did Morgan's body catch the cold from Finn's and chill in sympathetic response. They tempered each other, explored each other's bodies with their hands and mouths, wondering at the bevy of sensations aroused as each touched the other in places they'd never been touched before.

"Morgan," Finn whispered in her ear when they were finished. "Would you stay with me?"

"We're leaving in the morning," she murmured. "I can't stay here."

"No," he said. His voice was ineffably sad. "I mean, just for a little bit longer. Just for tonight. I just don't want to be alone."

Morgan leaned up on her elbow and looked at him quizzically. "What do you mean? Of course I'll stay with you tonight. Why? I mean, what else would I do?"

"Just a bit longer," Finn said, gazing out the living room window at the lightening eastern sky.

Morgan realized she must have dozed off, because when she opened her eyes, Finn was kneeling at her side, shaking her arm with nearly violent desperation.

"Morgan," Finn said urgently. "Wake up. I need to ask you something."

"What?" she muttered, still mostly asleep. "What is it? Are you OK?"

"Morgan, would you do something for me if I asked you to?"

"Sure," Morgan said. "What?" Then her eyes opened wide and she focused. The scream caught in her throat, becoming a sharp gasp instead.

Finn was sweating blood—literally. It covered him like a delicate, dark red mist, a ruby dew that made his skin shimmer when he moved. He wasn't bleeding, exactly—instead, the blood was a fine, thin, glowing roseate spray that was becoming more opaque by the second.

"Finn, *oh my God*! What's *happening* to you?"

"It doesn't hurt, Morgan, I promise it doesn't. Not yet."

"Finn! What's happening to you?"

"Morgan, do you love me?"

"Yes! Yes! I love you! Now tell me what's happening!?"

"I need you to help me, Morgan," Finn said, his voice breaking. "I can't do this by myself. You have to help me. Please?" He looked towards the window where the sky was now bright enough for her to see everything in the room. Then back at Morgan with pleading eyes. "Do you understand?"

Morgan started to cry. "No, Finn, please. I can't," she sobbed. "Don't ask me to do *that*. I can't. Stay with me. We'll figure something out, I promise. Please, Finn, please. I just *can't*!"

"Listen to me," Finn said gently. "I want to find Sadie. I want to be with my dog again. I miss her. I want to be somewhere else—I want to be in the place I was in before all this happened. I want to go home. A lot of bad things happen in Parr's Landing, but it isn't all bad. Nothing is *all bad*. I was happy—I had my mom and my dad. I had my school, and my comics. And I had Sadie. I want to hug her. I want to go for a walk with her again, up on Spirit Rock. This morning—now. But I can't do it by myself. My body won't let me."

"What do I have to do?"

Morgan thought she had never seen a more loving or radiant smile in her life. Finn pointed to the door. "Just walk with me. Out there. Out into the sunlight. Where Sadie is. And if I can't do it, push me."

Mutely, she nodded, white-faced.

When they reached the door, Finn turned to her and hugged her. "I love you, Morgan," he whispered. "Thank you."

Then Morgan opened the front door and walked Finn into the dawn.

In the end, dying a second time proved different than anything Finn had ever imagined it might be.

For one thing, the pain that his small, shrieking body felt as the sunlight ignited a holocaust under his skin—an incandescence that boiled his blood and set alight his bones from the inside, charring them to ash in seconds—was surprisingly brief, even momentary. Such, it seemed, was the nature of the soul—even a soul like Finn's that had been severed from its natural life and forced into rebirth in an unnatural one.

Rising above his body as it writhed and burned on the ground, Finn saw, not without pain and shame, that Morgan was screaming, as well. He'd hurt her, after all—the one person whom he wanted most to spare any pain.

The bare skin of her arms, where she'd held him as he'd tried to duck back inside the house at the moment the sunlight first struck his undead flesh—exactly as he'd begged her to do—was scorched and seared and blistered from the fire—*his* fire.

Because there were no more secrets, because every truth of the world, past, present, and future, was laid bare to the dead—the true dead, as Finn now was—he knew that Morgan would bear livid scars on her arms for the rest of her life. They would fade a bit more every year, but he knew (as the dead know) that Morgan would think of him every day when she looked at them, and the thoughts would be tender ones, thoughts of love—and sadness.

The horror would eventually become a half-remembered nightmare, and he was glad for that. He knew she would never return to Parr's Landing, nor would her mother, and that neither of them would ever see Billy Lightning again.

Finn continued to rise.

The dead of Parr's Landing surged around him like transcendental tributaries to a larger sea of souls, and time itself spun like a great tumbler of history and memory. The dead opened their arms to Finn in love, pulled him close, carried him higher and higher.

His soul wept for the half-souls that remained, trapped.

As Finn was absorbed into the massive vortex of spiralling black light, he looked down one last time.

Below him, he saw the oak doors of St. Barthélemy and the Martyrs crash open. Christina Parr, screaming her daughter's name, ran with the speed only the mother of an injured child ever really attains to the place where Morgan knelt, weeping over the charred skeleton of the twelve-year-old boy Finn once was. Finn saw Christina tenderly wrap her daughter in blankets and carefully carry her to Billy Lightning's truck, depositing her gently in the passenger seat and starting it up.

The dead see all roads, spiritual and temporal alike, and Finn was well pleased with what he saw ahead on theirs.

And then, the part of Finn Miller that was eternal heard the sound of a red rubber ball striking his bedroom floor. His soul was suddenly engulfed in familiar fragrance—clover and lake water and sunlight on soft black fur, and he was awash in frantic movement, warmth, and love.

The sound of Finn's laughter fell like blue sparks and the sound of Sadie's triumphant, joyous barking fell like black ones, and together their essences became one with the souls around them, passing completely from the world of the living into a perfect, brilliant sunrise above Bradley Lake and the cliffs of Spirit Rock.

There was no pain in it this time, only sunlight that no longer burned.

PARR'S LANDING POLICE DEPARTMENT

75 Main Street E.
Parr's Landing, Ontario
P2T 1R2
807-731-1002

TO: Sergeant Gill Styles. Gyles Point Police Dept., Gyles Point, Ont.
FROM: Sergeant Dave Thomson, Parr's Landing

October 25, 1972

Dear Gill,

Following up on our telephone conversation of earlier this evening, a local boy, Finn Miller, found this hockey bag and its contents in the Spirit Rock area while looking for his dog. PC Elliot McKitrick came upon the young man over the course of doing rounds and brought the boy and the hockey bag back to the station where we took it into evidence.

The bag appears to contain archaeological tools. In light of the Carstairs disappearance on the night of October 22nd in Gyles Point, I recommend that you forward them to Bruce Benson at the RCMP in Sault St. Marie for forensic lab analysis of fingerprints and blood type.

Also found in the bag were several documents that have been identified by Dr. William Lightning, a visitor to Parr's Landing, as having belonged to his father, Dr. Phenius Osborne of Toronto, who was the victim of homicide early this year. Dr. Lightning believes they were taken from his father's house during the course of said homicide.

As an aside, he believes the perpetrator was Richard Weal, a former student of Dr. Osborne's, but according to the information we have from Metro Toronto Homicide, Weal is deceased.

We do not consider Dr. Lightning a suspect at this time, though we have asked him to remain in Parr's Landing for the next few days. Please call if we can be of any further help.

Dave Thomson, Sgt.
Parr's Landing

FROM THE NOTES OF PROFESSOR PHENIUS OSBORNE

~~Department of Anthropology, University of Toronto~~
Sidney Smith Hall, 100 St. George Street, Toronto
Fall Term, 1971

Note: The text that follows is my translation of an original document held by Professor Victor Kleinschmit of the Department of History at the University of Michigan at Ann Arbor. The document itself, written in French, dates from the seventeenth century and appears to be a letter from a Jesuit missionary on his deathbed, addressed to his superiors in Rome. I have cross-referenced both this document with every available edition of The Jesuit Relations, but have found no reference to it, nor to the priest mentioned (Fr. Nyon) in any available record pertaining to the history of the Jesuits in Canada.

Dr. Kleinschmit, upon hearing of my work on the St. Barthélemy dig in Parr's Landing in the summer of 1952, invited me to come to Michigan to read it and to translate, which I did.

It is worth noting that I did not share any of the specific events surrounding the excavation of the St. Barthélemy site during the summer of 1952 with Dr. Kleinschmit, so his delivery of this document into my hands was in no way intended to support any "fantastical" notions of what might have occurred there that summer. The story, as read here, presents a plausible theory of the origin of the Wendigo legend of St. Barthélemy by a writer obviously familiar with myths and legends of that period.

In 1968, I forwarded a copy of my translation to Fr. Pedro Arrupe, SJ, (the twenty-eighth and current) Superior General of the Society of Jesus in Rome to enquire as to why it had not been included among the official records of the Jesuit missions to New France.

On February 12th, I received a brief, very courteous reply (see later notes, attached) from the Superior General's secretary thanking me for my letter, assuring me that the Reverend Father had enjoyed reading the document I sent him and thanking me for my "assiduous scholarship" and my "interest in the glorious history of the Jesuit martyrs" but asserting that, owing to both its "fantastical and lurid" subject matter as well as its length, the document was clearly a forgery, though it had already been examined on both palaeographic and material grounds by Professor Kleinschmit, and found to be consistent, even if the subject matter itself was not. It's not surprising to me that the SG would find this embarrassing if fictional; and mortifying if it was proven to be an authentic record of the delusions of a Jesuit missionary likely driven mad by the isolation of northern Ontario in the seventeenth century. The Jesuit motto, "Ad Majorem Dei Gloriam"—to the greater glory of God—is repeated several times in this narrative, which struck me as unusual, since one can infer that both the writer and the recipient were already well familiar with its meaning. There is an earnestness to its use here that seems noteworthy, especially in context of the narrative, as becomes obvious.

NB: Must forward a copy to Billy. He will find this entertaining, esp. in light of our "adventures" with good Dick Weal that summer!

—P. K. O., Ph. D. 09/12/71

BEING THE LAST TRUE TESTAMENT
AND RELATION OF FATHER ALPHONSE NYON

Given at Montréal, Québec in the form of a Letter to the Very Reverend Father Vincenzo Caraffa, Superior General of the Society of Jesus, at Rome

Anno Domini 1650

Very Reverend Father in Christ,
Pax Christi

I send this last Relation in the hopes that it will reach Your Reverence by the ship returning to France before the ice in this bitter region renders entirely compromised the passage of our vessels across the ocean.

I fear that my time here in this land is short, as the pox that has plagued hundreds of the Savages, thankfully a goodly number of them baptized and brought to our Christian Faith and now resting in the arms of Our Lord Jesus Christ in Heaven, has taken me into its embrace as well.

I write with difficulty and have entrusted the care and delivery of this Relation to Your Reverence into the hands of my friend Father Charles Vimont. He has sworn to seal this document and not to cast his eyes upon its contents, which are for the eyes of Your Reverence alone, on the peril of his Immortal Soul.

For my part, my vain prayers that I should again see the shores of my homeland or the beautiful cathedral of Notre-Dame de Chartres where I first heard Our Lord's call as a young man, or indeed once again touch the face of my beloved mother, have been denied by Our Lord, and I submit myself joyfully to His will.

My one true regret during these many years of service to the Savages of New France is that I should have been spared the great honour of martyrdom, the great blessing enjoined upon so many of our fallen Fathers at the bloody hands of the Hiroquois—most lately Father de Brébeuf, Father Chabanel, and Father de Lalande, who died so horribly at Sainte-Marie among the Hurons last year, praising the name of Christ and giving absolution to their Barbarian tormentors with their last breath, even after their tongues were cut out, for they kept preaching till death released them.

I pray for Your Reverence's understanding, prayers, and meditation upon the reading of this, my last Relation and Testament, for it is with a heavy heart that I set down the strange and terrible events I witnessed at St. Barthélemy among the Ojibwa in the northern Lac Superiéur region of the country in the winter of the Year of Our Lord 1632.

These secrets I have kept to myself for nearly twenty years, confiding them not even in the Sacrament of Confession, though I regularly opened my heart to God and begged His forgiveness, not only for the blasphemies I have seen, but also for those I have wrought myself in my sad and pitiable effort to do His will as best as could be done by one so unworthy.

In the autumn of that dark year of which I write, word was received by Monsieur de Champlain at Trois-Rivières of the destruction of two of our settlements near Sault de Gaston, in Huronia, and the martyrdom of three of our Jesuit Fathers in what could only have been an attack by the Hiroquois, for their fiendish handiwork leaves a spoor as unmistakable as the handiwork of Satan himself.

In the first, the Mission of Sainte-Berthe, the martyrs were, by name, Father Renaud d'Olivier, Father Mathieu Glazier, and Father Nausson d'Uongue. The Fathers had travelled from

France together and, it was reported, had been as close as brothers. I pray they found comfort in their brotherhood at the end. The Indian trappers reported the hideous sight of the maimed and tortured bodies of d'Olivier, Glazier, and d'Uongue. Their scorched bodies still hung from the stakes to which they were tied and left for carrion. The Savages, it was reported, had poured boiling water over their heads in mockery of Baptism and cut out their eyes and tongues, placing live coals in the sockets.

Likewise, they reported the smoke still heavy and foul over the burned village, and many dead, including a number of baptized Savages. We wept at this news, even though we knew that our fallen Brothers had attained the heights of Heaven, having died in the greatest possible service to Our Lord Jesus Christ. Never have the words of our Jesuit motto, *Ad majorem Dei gloriam*, comforted me more than they did in the hours that followed the news of the Fathers' martyrdom.

In the second instance, the strange news was of the mission of St. Barthélemy deep in the Ojibwa region of that country, a region noted for the cruelty of the terrain itself and of the strangeness of its customs, superstitions and legends. So tight, it is said, is the Devil's hold upon these poor people that establishing a mission in this particular region had long been an ambition of the Crown in its support of our work here in New France.

In the case of the mission of St. Barthélemy, the trappers related that the mission seemed entirely abandoned.

Unlike the mission of Sainte-Berthe, which had clearly fallen to an attack by the Hiroquois, the mission at St. Barthélemy appeared deserted, as though the inhabitants, both Christian and Savage, had all departed freely and of their own volition.

The trappers observed this and more and related it to Monsieur de Champlain, who in turn related it to Father de Varennes, who was then the representative responsible for dispatching our Fathers on their missions upriver in the company of their Huron guides.

It was at this point that I was summoned to meet with Father de Varennes at Trois-Rivières. I was then still a very young man, all of twentyone, a year in New France since my departure from

Chartres, and foolish in the fearless way of all young men, but determined to serve the will of God with all of my body and soul. I knew even then that martyrdom for the greater glory of God would be the highest attainment, and yet my poor flesh dreaded it, dreaded the agony of the flames of the stake as it dreaded the butchery of blade and spear. I confess that fear with shame, but with the openhearted humility that my own unworthiness demands.

Father de Varennes wasted no time in asking me what I knew of the settlement of St. Barthélemy. Sadly, I told him, I had only heard of it in passing through the stories of the other young priests. I knew little of the region or of the mission itself.

"Do you, for instance," de Varennes asked me, "know anything of the Ojibwa people, Father Nyon? Do you know their language and customs?"

"I have studied their language, Father," I replied. "I am not fluent, but I have tried to prepare myself as best I could in the event that my service in New France led me there."

"You know by now, Father Nyon, of the recent destruction of our mission at Sainte-Berthe and the slaughter of our priests at the hands of the Hiroquois?"

I nodded, bowing my head. "Yes, Father. A great tragedy."

"Have you then also heard," he asked, "of the mystery of our settlement of St. Barthélemy near the shore of Lac Supérieur which has been reported as entirely deserted?"

"Yes, Father. But again, only in passing. Only in the form of rumour and conjecture. Stories from around the campfire in these last weeks. The gossip of trappers."

The old priest smiled at that. But again he grew serious. "Father Nyon," he said. "We have dispatched one of our priests, Father Lubéron, in the company of a party of Algonquians, to recover the bodies of our fallen Fathers at Sainte-Berthe and to give them a Christian burial. It is a gruesome assignation, but Father Lubéron has volunteered. We can only pray for his safe return, and that he does not meet the same fate that befell d'Olivier, Glazier, and d'Uongue."

"I too will pray for that, Father," I told him. "I would also have volunteered if I had known of the assignation."

Father de Varennes looked hard at me and said, "Is that what is truly in your heart, Father Nyon?"

I replied that it was, indeed.

"Father Nyon. I would like you to travel north to the region of Sault de Gaston and visit the site of the St. Barthélemy settlement and see if what the trappers reported is true. I would like you to find the priest, Father de Céligny. If the Savages murdered him, I would like you to bury him and perform the Last Rites. If he is alive, I would like you to bring him back with you to Trois-Rivières so he may give his own account of what transpired at the Mission."

"I accept joyfully, Father," I said, quite proud of myself for having been put in charge of such an undertaking. "What can you tell me of Father de Céligny, Father? I have not heard that name before. Has he been long in New France?"

"Father de Céligny arrived in New France in 1625 as one of the priests who answered the appeal of the Recollet friars in order to aid them in their work with the Indian missions," Father de Varennes explained. "The Recollets were insufficient in numbers to successfully cope with the nature and hardships of evangelizing the Savages."

"But what of the man?" I persisted. "Who is he?"

"The man?" Father de Varennes laughed. "Ah yes, the man. I know only the priest, but you ask me about the man. Let us see. Father de Céligny is descended from a noble family in the Nord-Pas-de-Calais, the most northerly region of France. He is kinsman to the Vicomte de Moriève of that region. He took his vows in Paris, at Montmartre. And, as I said, he came to us here in New France in 1625. By reports it was a long and terrible voyage from Dieppe to Québec. An unknown wasting sickness descended on crew and passengers alike. Many shrivelled and died, including some priests. Father de Céligny survived. He was dispatched to the Ojibwa that very year. He is a learned man. As I recall, he was also grave in manner and demeanour. In truth, I don't remember much of the man. And even now, it is the priest I am concerned with, not the man."

"Forgive my impertinence, Father," I said humbly. "But if he wasn't murdered by the Savages, might there have been another reason for his abandonment of his Mission?"

Father de Varennes sighed at that. "Sadly, I believe we must prepare ourselves for the worst, Father Nyon."

With courage I did not feel, I told Father de Varennes that I would do my duty and meet my fate joyfully, whatever it might be.

"Your journey will take you approximately five weeks," Father de Varennes said. "It will be an exceptionally difficult one, and fraught with hardship. You speak the Algonquian language, I'm told?"

"Not well, Father, but I can understand the language better than I can speak it."

"The Algonquians accompanying you will take you to the region of Sault de Gaston and will delivery you safely to the Mission of St. Barthélemy. They camp nearby and will wait to bring you back, either alone, or with Father de Céligny. Do you have any questions, Father?"

"No, Father," I said. "I understand everything. When will I be leaving?"

Father de Varennes hesitated, as though considering my youth. Then he drew himself up to his full height and said, not unkindly, "At dawn, Father Nyon. And may God be with you."

At that, we knelt together and prayed for some time in the chapel. Father de Varennes introduced me to my stoical Algonquian guide, Askuwheteau. He bade me spend the remainder of the afternoon in prayer and meditation, and then retire early for my departure from Trois-Rivières.

After the departure of Father de Varennes, I walked a bit about the post and then took myself down to the river, feeling the need to see it once, alone, before my departure at the dawn on the morrow.

As I approached the edge of the dark water, I noticed a man following me at a cautious distance. He was clearly French, one of those *hommes du nord*, or *hivernants* as the voyageurs who transport furs by canoe and overwinter in the regions beyond Montréal and Grand Portage are often called. Like so many of them, a crude and filthy-looking man who, through long exposure to the Savages and carnal knowledge of the vilest sort with Savage women, had begun to resemble the Indians more than he resembled a white man. By coincidence, I did know this man's name: he was called Dumont, and was known to be of low moral character, over fond of spirits, a dishonest dealer with the Savages and an unrepentant consort of their women.

I paused by the water and waited, my intention being to ask him what he wanted. I had no fear of him, for what Frenchman here in Trois-Rivières would harm a priest? But he spoke first, and most strangely.

He asked me, "You are the priest who will be going to St. Barthélemy with the Algonquians?"

I told him yes, and I asked him what business it was of his. He laughed and showed me a reeking mouthful of rotten teeth. The stench issuing from his open mouth was a horror in its own right.

"Do you know what awaits you at St. Barthélemy? Do you know what is there?"

"I expect to recover the body of Father de Céligny of that Mission," I said. "Though my heartiest prayers are that I will find him alive and well, and safely in the service of Our Lord."

At that, Dumont laughed again. But it was not a laugh of joy, or even one of malice. It was a forced laugh, one in which I thought I detected a trace of something akin to fear. And yet this man Dumont had already openly lived a rough and vile life. I could not fathom what could have made him afraid of speaking openly about the Mission.

"What do you know of the Mission at St. Barthélemy?" I asked him, with a boldness I did not feel. "What do you know of the fate of Father de Céligny? If you have something to share, share it now or keep your peace."

He shrugged again. "I know nothing," said he. "I speak of nothing."

"Not true, Dumont," I replied. "Tomorrow I am leaving for St. Barthélemy. If there is something you know, or have heard, I charge you to tell me—and indeed to tell me now and in all haste."

At that, Dumont leaned close to me and said, "The Indians of Lac Superiéur, they fear him."

"Who," I demanded. "Father de Céligny?"

"Yes, him." Dumont crossed himself. The reverent gesture, so earnestly performed, seemed so incongruous in that setting, and from that man, that I fear I laughed.

"Of course they fear him," I scoffed. "The Indians blame us for everything. These countries, and these poor, ignorant people, are in Lucifer's thrall. They blame us when there is an outbreak of the pox. They blame us when there is a famine. They blame us when there is a drought. They call the Rite of Baptism water-sorcery. They accuse us of performing witchcraft in our chapels. They call us demons in black robes."

"No," Dumont whispered. "They fear *de Céligny himself*." He looked all around as though to make sure no one was listening. "They call him *Weetigo*. An eater of human flesh and a drinker of blood. Human in form, but *mji-manidoo*, a demon."

"The Savages do not understand the Rite of Communion," I explained as patiently as I could, trying not to show my irritation. "They confuse it with their own barbarism, or the barbarism of the Hiroquois."

"No," Dumont insisted. "It is more than that. The Savages of which I speak have no quarrel with the Black Robes. But they give the mission of St. Barthélemy in Sault de Gaston a wide berth."

"Then perhaps those are the Savages who have killed Father de Céligny," I said in outrage. "If you have information about his fate, Dumont, you will come with me now to Father de Varennes, and you will tell him what you know, or what you have heard from the Savages."

"I know nothing," Dumont said. "I have heard nothing. And I will tell Father de Varennes nothing."

"If you know nothing, my son, then what is your purpose here? Why did you seek me out today?" I asked him in bafflement. "Do you have something to confess? Do you not wish to be granted absolution? I can absolve you, but before I do, you must confess to me."

Dumont again grew pale. Again, he crossed himself. This time, I did not laugh, for a mask of such dread and tragedy contorted his face that Melpomene herself would have recoiled from it. He seemed suddenly in the throes of a deep and profound spiritual terror. Were he not so clearly a man of a dissolute and profane reputation, I would have even said that he feared that his very soul was in peril from something he had done, or seen. So awful was Dumont's expression that I had but one thought: that he had, himself, witnessed the awful martyrdom of Father de Céligny at the hands of the Savages and that it had been a most fearsome and terrible death. In his eyes, I found every nightmare that had tormented me, as a young priest in Chartres, about the terrible and agonizing fate that might await me here in New France.

"I need no absolution, Father," Dumont said. "But perhaps God will grant you the strength and knowledge to conquer what awaits you in St. Barthélemy. We have brought terrible things to New France. There are worse things now walking in the forests at night than the Savages." He knelt and took my crucifix in his filthy hands, and kissed it. "I will pray for you, Father. Pray for me, also."

With that, Dumont rose to his feet. He looked around him, and then quickly took his leave from my company by a trail that I knew led to the other side of the post where some of the *hivernants* kept their canoes. He did not turn or look back as he hurried along his way before disappearing from view behind the trees.

The cold I felt in the wake of Dumont's leave-taking was due only in part to the sinking of the sun in the sky, or the freezing egress of the coming night. I looked all around me and saw anew the cruel beauty of this wild country of white rivers and black lakes and forests. I saw afresh the savagery here; in nature as in man. Truly, I thought, this is the Devil's own dominion. Even poor, mad Dumont, in all of his fear and confusion, knew it. *There are worse things now walking in the forests at night than the Savages, Father,* he'd said. I realized again that we soldiers of God were little more than pinpricks of His light in the vast darkness of this terrible place, and the only beacons by which the Indians might be guided, with Christ's help, away from Satan and into God's glorious light. I puzzled over his statement that we, meaning the French, had brought those things here, for surely the light we brought with us has been not only the light of God, but also the light of civilization and knowledge. But ultimately I ascribed the words to his confusion. Perhaps, ultimately, Dumont, after so many godless years among them, had become Savage himself. I swore to pray for him.

And pray I did, that night, though not only for Dumont, or Father de Céligny. Sleep was reluctant to claim me, but eventually it did. It seemed I had barely closed my eyes before Askuwheteau was shaking me awake with the utmost force and impatience to begin the journey upriver to the Mission of St. Barthélemy among the Ojibwa in Sault de Gaston.

We departed in two canoes into a dark grey dawn wreathed in heavy fog and a lowering sky threatening rain. The rains of that first autumn of mine in Trois-Rivières were unlike any I had known as a boy coming to maturity in Beauce. It was of a particular, piercing cold, as though the angels themselves were hurling frozen nails from a celestial height to pierce and humble the proud and unaccustomed. The rivers here also bore no resemblance to any of the three branches of the gentle Eure, near my family's home near Chartres. Instead, they were wild and serpentine, wending through the rocks and the forests to, it seemed, the very edge of the world.

The Indians are impermeable to hardship in a way that we Europeans cannot fathom. I had of course been made aware of the stoical inurement particular to these people before I left France, but hearing it described by returning priests was entirely different to seeing it in the flesh. The Savage women, too, paddle the canoes alongside their men, as well as carry their own heavy packs along the trails. Their hands are hard and calloused and would be unrecognizable, in France, as belonging to any but the hardest-working peasant.

I sat close behind Askuwheteau in the canoe and tried to match the force of his paddle-stroke. He bent his body to the task as though it were a Sisyphean machine, his back leaning into each stroke. Each time his paddle cut the black water, a perfect white-crested whirlpool spun away in its wake. Try as I might to imitate his movements, my own poor attempts were clumsy and ineffectual. In truth, I felt unmanned, and yet I set myself arduously to my own portion of the labour, remembering well the admonitions of Father de Varennes with regard to the Savages' measure of me. My life depended in no small part on their protection and goodwill.

Indeed, my position relative to theirs became more and more obvious. While I might be their intellectual and spiritual superior through the agency of my education and my role as Christ's humble representative in their world of godless ignorance, they were, in every practical sense, my superiors. I saw—and felt—this reality with every stroke of the paddle that took me farther and farther into the wilderness.

We camped that first night by the shore of a nameless lake—nameless to me, though I do not doubt the Savages had a name for it, as they have a name for everything in earthly nature, as well as names for their pantheon of pagan gods and spirits that, I had been told, dwelt not only in the heavens above, but shared the earth with them.

My hands were raw and bleeding from the repetitive friction of wet skin against wood after that first long day's paddle. Sitting about the campfire that night with the Indians, one of the older women, Hausisse, noticed my pain. From one of her packs, she withdrew a greasy poultice. She started to apply it to my wounds. When I pulled back and uttered some instinctive protest, she grasped my wrist as firmly as if I were an unruly child and rebuked me in Algonquian. Then she applied the poultice even more vigorously upon my wounds. In truth, the sting in my hands from the paddle began almost immediately to subside, a cooling sensation spreading across my palms, and indeed everywhere the poultice touched my skin.

"*Meegwetch,*" I said in awe, thanking Hausisse in my own crude Algonquian. I looked down at my hands in wonderment, for the pain had almost completely vanished, as though it had never been there.

She spoke again in Algonquian, calling me "stupid" or "foolish," but in no way unkindly. She smiled and put the poultice back inside her buckskin pack, then shuffled off to join her putative "husband" by the fire.

The Indians regarded me with amusement as I continued to stare at my hands, but then made room for me when I went myself to sit closer to the flames. I found the smell of them comforting—that curious mixture of buckskin, sweat, dried lake water and smoke from the fire. In truth, their very presence was a bulwark against the terrors of the unknown and the unknowable. The darkness surrounding the fire was of an opacity the likes of which I had never known in France, or perhaps it seemed darker because, in France, I knew reasonably well what it might conceal. Here, in this savage Devil's-land, God only knew what lay beneath night's cloak, hidden and in wait.

As we lay down and prepared to sleep, I looked about me uneasily, for, unbidden, Dumont's words had come back to me: *There are worse things now walking in the forests at night than the Savages.* I said a prayer for our safety and put myself in God's hands as we slept. This time, I slept soundly and without dreams, surrounded by my Indian protectors.

The next morning, upon waking, I washed in the lake before my morning prayers. The poultice on my hands that had dried and crusted while I slept was rinsed off in the lake water. Miraculously, my hands had almost completely healed while I was asleep. Examining them in the pink light of the early dawn, I saw that the wounds were dry and had already scabbed.

I went to find Hausisse, the old woman who had acted as my surgeon, to show her this miracle, but when I did, she seemed uninterested. Hausisse looked away, muttering words under her breath in Algonquian I could not understand. After taking our morning meal, we packed up our rudimentary camp, loaded the two canoes, and again we set out across the water in the direction of Sault de Gaston.

The first few weeks passed without incident. They evolved into a backbreaking cycle of repetitive days that began at dawn and ended at sunset. The air had grown decidedly colder as the days shortened in anticipation of the coming winter. The hills and mountains surrounding the lakes and rivers were dappled in scarlet and saffron yellow, breathtakingly beautiful in the wildness of their colour. One morning, we woke to a light dusting of snow around the camp, but it melted with the sun, almost before we were underway again. The men shot wild fowl that the women would then prepare as part of our supper, and they fished the dark water with a dexterity at which I marvelled.

Though the work of paddling and camping became no easier, and in fact the land grew more rugged and forbidding the closer we came to our destination, making the portaging of the canoes and packs more difficult, a *camaraderie* of sorts seemed to have grown between us. I am under no illusion that the Indians saw me as one of them, and indeed they often mocked my seeming inability to master the most rudimentary of their skills, from paddling to portaging, yet we had settled into a peaceable accord.

My proficiency with the bow and arrow, however, surprised them, especially the men. Unbeknownst to them, of course, my father had hunted often on our family's estate in Beauce, and he had drilled me throughout my boyhood in this one martial skill. Askuwheteau in particular took delight in my ability to shoot. On such occasions as we had time for recreation, which where precious few, he allowed me to practise with his own bow and arrow. While Askuwheteau was my unchallenged superior, I flatter myself that I won a measure of his respect in time.

I spoke my crude Algonquian with the other paddlers. With Askuwheteau, I spoke a mixture of Algonquian and French by which we both seemed to understand one another. We were not friends—the very idea seemed preposterous, especially then—but perhaps my utter dependence on him, coupled with my willingness to share a full portion of the work of our voyage and match the Indians effort for effort, had roused an answering kindness in him that made him more than merely my guide.

I came to find comfort in the sound of their voices, especially at night in the forest around the campfire. The sound had become a sort of lodestar of safety in the midst of the wilderness.

Blessedly there had been no sign of Hiroquois hunters along our route—in itself a miracle, for their appearance would have very likely signalled our doom. I realized that the Algonquians had been paid to protect me, and, as much as I might doubt their commitment to my safety, still I sensed that this group wished me no ill will, and indeed would safeguard me to the best of their ability and deliver me to the site of St. Barthélemy as promised, and wait there to return me to Trois-Rivières—either tragically alone, or in the company of Father de Céligny.

In the fourth week of our journey, we stopped in an Ojibwa village a week's paddle or more from Sault de Gaston. It was apparently a village where Askuwheteau was known and respected, for the chief received him. The Chief and some of the Savages took my measure gravely, and with what appeared to be suspicion. Askuwheteau turned his back to me and spoke to them in a low voice. Over his shoulder, the Chief and the men with him continued to regard me with something I took to be either anger or fear, or indeed some mixture of both. Anger I had seen before, during my year in New France, but their fear was something with which I was unfamiliar.

Clearly, at Trois-Rivières the Indians were used to us, and even farther afield than the settlement there, we Fathers were more likely to be met with contempt than fear. And yet there it was in the eyes of the chief and his men: fear, or so it appeared to me.

Finally Askuwheteau turned to me and spoke in French. "Black Robe," he said. "The Chief wants to speak with me alone. Go through the village, to the water's edge and wait for me."

I answered him in Algonquian, asking him what was wrong. I had a notion that the Chief might more kindly consider me if I spoke one of their languages.

Again, Askuwheteau spoke to me in French. "Go, Black Robe," he said gruffly. "Go wait by the water. Do not answer me in Algonquian. Do not speak my name. Do not answer me at all. Go, now."

Without a word, I turned and walked towards the village, which was not itself dissimilar to others I had seen: huts of birch-pole and tents, the whole place a seething, untidy coil of Savages, their filthy children, and their verminous dogs, all intermingling hither and thither in the mud, or squatting on their haunches, men and women both, in apparently earnest debate or parley. The acrid smoke from the wood cooking fires and the odour of the Savages themselves, combined with the noise of their squalling children and barking dogs, became almost overpowering. I was more eager than not to obey Askuwheteau, and so I went to the edge of the lake and waited for him there.

After a time, Askuwheteau came to where I was sitting. I had not heard him approach until he was standing behind me. I turned and looked up. The sun was behind him, so his face was hidden from my sight.

"Black Robe," he said. "We may stay here tonight, but only tonight. And we are told we must stand guard over you until the dawn. Also, you may not sleep in the village. You must sleep here, near the water, away from the people.

"Why?" I queried, rousing myself to a standing position. "For what reasons?"

"They fear you," Askuwheteau replied. He stared at me with no expression. It was as though the fact of the Indians fearing me was so entirely reasonable that it required no elucidation.

"What is there to fear?" I scoffed. "They know of us. They have seen Black Robes before. Surely we have more to fear from them than they have to fear from us."

"They have seen Black Robes before," Askuwheteau said, with that maddening, implacable stolidity of the Savages. "They are not afraid of Black Robes. They are afraid of you."

"Of me? Why?"

"They believe you are *Weetigo*. They believe you are like the other Black Robe. The one you go to." Askuwheteau was silent for a long moment. Then, he spoke again. "You will sleep here, Black Robe. I will guard you. I am not afraid of you. I do not believe you are *Weetigo*. If you go to the village tonight, they will kill you. And tomorrow, we leave."

"Why do they believe this?" I was again outraged. "This is nonsense. It is blasphemy."

"They speak of the other Black Robe. They say he eats flesh. They say he drinks blood."

"Askuwheteau," I said, trying to calm myself. I spoke slowly, enunciating carefully, in French, which Askuwheteau rudimentarily understood. "We have told you the meaning of the Eucharist. You know of the rituals of the Black Robes—how the bread and the wine become the body and blood of Jesus Christ through the miracle of transubstantiation. We do not eat the flesh of human beings, nor do we drink their blood. The very thought is an affront to God. The people of this village do not understand. You should have explained it to them better. You speak their language. Tell them they are mistaken."

"*Weetigo* eats the body and drinks the blood," he insisted stubbornly. He gestured to the village behind him. "There are many stories of *Weetigo* here. People have seen the *Weetigo* in the village where we go to your Black Robe. There are many dead." He gestured again, this time towards the lake. "Many dead in the water. They fell from the sky." He gestured overhead. "This *Weetigo* flies at night, like the owl. He runs like the wolf. He has killed many."

I was frustrated by Askuwheteau's dogged insistence that this gruesome Indian legend of a mythical demon (as I then understood it, an evil spirit that enters a human body and possesses it, turning the unlucky vessel into a cannibal monster) was true. I was horrified that it should be so blasphemously entangled with our own holy ritual of Communion. I was reminded again of Dumont's disquieting raving on the shore at Trois-Rivières about Father de Céligny being something other than human.

While it had been relatively easy to dismiss Dumont as mad, it was harder to be as sanguine in the face of Askuwheteau's declaration that he was all that was standing between me and a terrible death at the hands of an entire village of Ojibwa Savages who believed I was in league with a living demon.

Worse still was the ever more likely possibility that Father de

Céligny had been murdered by a group of terrified Savages who believed they were ridding their village of a monster.

I opened my mouth to protest again, but Askuwheteau silenced me with a sharp gesture. "Be quiet, Black Robe," he said. "You stay here. I will guard you. We leave in morning, when sun rises."

That night in the moonlight, at several separate intervals I was aware of the sly sound of moccasin-shod feet on dirt and stone as the Indians came to stare at me whilst I lay under my blanket, feigning sleep and listening to the sound of my heart in my chest.

Their gruesome legends, their tales of flesh-devouring, blooddrinking demons, and the spirits that walked their forests at night, were easier to dismiss in the daylight. But when, like at that moment, the dull moon was the only light able to pierce this infernal darkness at the edge of the world, the borders between our world of the living and their land of the dead seemed to shimmer and grow indistinct.

The Indians did not come too near. From their soft, fretful whispering, I came to believe that they were not keeping their distance simply because I was under the protection of Askuwheteau, but also because the Indians were afraid of *me*.

That morning, I again woke, shivering, to a light covering of snow upon the ground. The dark green trees were likewise wreathed and crested with white and stood out starkly against the deadened sky. The sun remained hidden behind lead-coloured clouds that seemed an advance guard of the deadly coming winter.

As I prayed that morning, I entreated God that we might find Father de Céligny alive and well, presiding over his Christianized congregation at St. Barthélemy, and that I might either return with him to Trois-Rivières or winter with him in Sault de Gaston if the route back became impassable because of the killing cold.

We again loaded the canoes in preparation for our departure. Askuwheteau and his paddlers were solemn that morning, entirely different in their demeanour than they had been every morning during the last month of our voyage inland. They whispered amongst themselves and, though I may have been imagining it, I caught them looking at me when they thought me unawares, glancing away quickly when I returned their gaze.

At one point, a near brawl appeared to break out between Askuwheteau and Chogan, one of the younger men in our party of paddlers, who had been glaring at me all through the morning. Askuwheteau struck him about the shoulders and rebuked him in Algonquian, though I was too far away to understand his words. When Chogan pointed at me, Askuwheteau seized the younger man's arm and forced it down to his side. Askuwheteau addressed him sharply, but in a low voice, and Chogan looked vindictively in my direction one more time, then dropped his eyes in submission to Askuwheteau, my protector.

Of course, I had seen the entire exchange, but still I pretended that I had not, as much for my own security as for Chogan's pride.

As we launched into the water, I saw that the entire village had arrayed itself on the shore, as though to assure themselves that we had indeed departed from their midst. They stared solemnly in our wake as the canoes glided into the morning fog, not speaking nor shouting, but entirely, raptly following the trajectory of our canoes with their eyes.

So general was the ghostly silence, that when one of the paddles rapped against the side of the boat, I cried out in shock. The Indians kept their heads down and paddled, showing no reaction to my outcry, no laughter this time, and none of the usual well-meant mockery. Instead, we paddled in silence until the mist enveloped us and the land behind us vanished from sight.

After five hard, uncomfortable days of mostly silent paddling, we made a gruesome discovery in the early evening of the fifth day as we crossed a particularly vast lake. Lulled and hypnotized by the repetitive motion of the paddle, I was suddenly jolted to consciousness by a sharp shout of warning from the bowsman of the other canoe.

I raised my head and squinted to see where he was pointing. There, floating face down on the surface of the black water was the body of a girl of perhaps no more than twelve or thirteen. I crossed myself and stifled my despair at the tragic sight. The girl's body must have floated on some sort of very strong underwater current, for we seemed several miles from either shore and there seemed no other earthly way for it to have found itself so far from land. The fantastical thought came to me that she had been dropped from the air, as though from the talons of some monstrous bird in mid-flight.

Too, there seemed to be no putrescence or other decay. She looked as though she had fallen asleep in the lake that very afternoon and simply drifted away on the waves.

"Pull her to us," I implored them. "Let us take her to shore, so that I may say a prayer for her and we can bury her."

The Indians, naturally, ignored me. But there had been no need for my exhortations in any case. The men were already carefully reaching for her, using their paddles almost as grappling hooks, pulling the girl's body towards them.

The combination of their paddles and the motion of the waves that had sprung up in the breeze caused the body to roll in the water. As it did, the full abomination of the tableau revealed itself to all of us, and I again had occasion to cross myself.

The girl's eyes had not rolled up in her head; rather they seemed to stare fixedly at us. The pupils were dilated so that they looked like two pieces of flat black glass. But O! the mute asseverations of dread in those eyes, the terror frozen eternally in violent death. Her mouth was stretched open in a silent scream of pain and terror. Worst of all, her throat had been all but torn out, as though by the jaws of a wolf, the flesh of the wound washed clean and pink by the lake water. Her poor fingers were fixed into claws, as though in her last moments she had been fighting to escape from whatever beast killed her.

The effect on the Indians was marvellous. With a collective cry of despair, they pushed the body away from them. They beat the water to a white froth with their paddles as they turned the canoes about, gaining distance between themselves and the poor dead girl's body in a trice.

"Stop! Stop!" I screamed. "Go back! We must bury her!"

But stop the Indians did not. They laid their backs into their paddling as though the spot was accursed. The lost child's body floating in that desolate lake shrank to a distant speck—a lonely sacrilege bobbing in the black waves as the sun sank behind the hills and the night came alive around us.

The next morning, Askuwheteau avowed to me that we were very near our destination. He said we would reach St. Barthélemy that night, and that we would portage inland from Lac Supérieur, then camp in the forest near a small lake, which, he told me, was hidden within a rocky region known to be treacherous.

It may have been the combined effect of the dramatic hibernal shift in the weather and the changing light, but the entire landscape appeared even more forbidding, remote and haunted than it ever had before. The water, dull pewter, violently wind-lashed and bitterly cold, smashed against the massive jutting islands of rock rising out of the oceanic vastness of Lac Supérieur. It froze my toughened hands, driving me almost mad with pain that I could not express in front of the Indians for fear of their reaction.

Their behaviour towards me had grown increasingly hostile, almost antagonistic. They now slept apart from me, and they built two fires, one for them and one for me, farther away. I ate separately from the Indians at their insistence, and never a word was passed between us now, except obligatorily, when Askuwheteau needed to communicate some detail of our voyage. Whatever the unfavourable sentence that had been passed upon me by the elders of the Ojibwa village where we had overnighted, it seemed that it had radically, unsympathetically, and permanently altered the Indians' view of me.

Finally, we landed on a beach of smooth rock in a horseshoe-shaped inlet just as the sun was beginning to lower in the sky. The strong, gelid wind that had raised such waves upon the surface of Lac Supérieur now whipped at our bodies and faces. My clothing was wet from rogue waves over the side of the canoe, and now, on that rocky beach as we prepared to portage, I had begun to shiver violently.

"When will we camp?" I asked Askuwheteau. "I am cold and wet. Perhaps we should make camp here, on the beach?"

Askuwheteau gestured with a wide swing of his arm. "There

is danger," he said. "It is too easy to find us here. We must go deeper into the forest."

"Who would find us?" I said. "The Hiroquois? Surely, we are in friendly country here? This is Ojibwa country. We are near the mission of St. Barthélemy, you said. The Ojibwa are not our enemies. From whom are we in danger?"

He stared at me, again that maddening Savage inscrutability. "Not the Hiroquois," he said. "Not the Ojibwa." Then he grew silent. He picked up his pack and began to carry it into the forest. All I could do was pick up my own pack and follow him.

As we portaged through the woods towards St. Barthélemy, my travelling companions grew more and more apprehensive in a way that was entirely out of character, for they had hitherto shown themselves to be fearless. It would not be incorrect to say that the Indians appeared to be at the ready, as taut as their own bow strings, the way they might be if hunting, or anticipating an attack by the Hiroquois, or some other enemy.

At last, in the growing gloom, we laid down our packs and made camp in the clearing of a coppice of trees and set about building temporary shelter. I began to gather wood for my own fire, as I had been forced to do throughout the last week of our voyage. When I had found several stout sticks, I made as though to arrange them apart from the larger fire being built by Askuwheteau and his men. The Indians regarded me strangely, though still with no hint of the amity I had known at the beginning of our voyage.

It was old Hausisse who spoke first—to Askuwheteau. Her Algonquian was so rapid that I was unable to follow it, though the urgency of her tone was unmistakable. Her hands flew in the air as she pointed to me, then gestured around her towards the trees, and the sunless sky above, then back to me. Whatever she said to him clearly gave him pause, because he told me to put my wood in the pile beside the fire that the Indians had already built, and which was already burning. Hausisse stared at me from where she sat, her regard almost approving. Askuwheteau told me that I would remain with the rest of them tonight. Too grateful to do anything but nod, I threw my wood into the pile.

The Indians reluctantly made room for me around the fire. When I say reluctantly, I mean that while they showed no overt malice or hostility, my apparent state of uncleanliness had not changed in their eyes, in spite of Askuwheteau's invitation.

My awareness of our complete isolation could not have been sharper than it was at that moment. Even the Ojibwa village where I'd received such a hostile reception seemed like an outpost of warmth and civilization compared to this wild, dark place.

I needed the Indians; they did not need me. This was their world, not mine, and I was lost in it without them. Indeed it was difficult to imagine anything human, Savage or Christian, existing here. Anything could happen to me here, indeed, to any of us, and none would be the wiser.

But still, Hausisse continued to stare at me, at the crucifix lying against my robe, as though it were a sorcerous talisman instead of a holy object, for I knew she had not accepted Christ.

What woke me from my sleep that night I could not say with any certainty.

I had been dreaming of my family's home in France, and of my mother. In the dream, I was still a young boy in her kitchen, by the fire. My mother was seated in a carved oak chair, and I on her lap, my body pressed against her soft breast as she ran her fingers through my hair. I smelled the lavender sachet from her black woollen dress beneath the starched white apron. From a massive pot on the hearth issued forth the magnificent odour of lamb stew with potatoes, vegetables, and red wine slowly cooking. The fragrance filled every corner of the room, making my mouth water. Never, I think, had I been as hungry as I was in that moment before waking.

At the very moment my eyes opened on the darkness, I was already fully awake, mouth still watering, every sense alert. All about me were the general sounds of the Indians snoring, and the crackle of the fire that had died to glowing embers. I smelled the smoke and the musky scent of the sleeping Savages.

I propped myself up on one elbow and glanced around. Nothing seemed amiss in the camp. The surrounding woods were silent as tombs, and I could see my breath in the air in front of me by firelight. I peered into the blackness, trying to ascertain what had roused me, for the sense was growing in me that I was being watched by something, or someone, beyond the tree line.

As my eyes grew accustomed to the darkness, I thought I saw a shadow moving slyly towards us. Terror leaped in my chest, for I could think of only two things: that it could be some deadly animal, a wolf, or some terrible bear, the stories of which I had heard even before boarding at Dieppe. That, or an armed, bloodthirsty Hiroquois scouting party.

As I stared, the shadow itself divided into two smaller shadows, forms human in shape and contour.

I rubbed my eyes, marvelling at what I saw before me, for standing at the edge of the coppice of trees were two Savage children, a girl of perhaps nine years, holding hands with a small boy who could not have been more than five. The girl wore a simple buckskin shift, and her arms and feet were bare in the bitter cold. The boy was completely naked, though the lower half of his face, his neck, and his upper chest appeared to be smeared with mud, or some other blackish substance.

I thought it a curious trick of the firelight, but even from my vantage point in the doorway, I could clearly see their eyes shining through the trees, even though their faces were deeply painted with shadow.

The two children stared fixedly at our assemblage. They could have been a brother and sister on a walk through the woods on a summer day but for the fact that, by the position of the moon in the sky, it was well past midnight, dawn hours away. And though their state of nakedness would have been tolerable in the heat of August, we were already in the mouth of winter and yet they seemed entirely insensible to the bitter cold. The wind whipped the girl's long black hair wildly about her face, but she made no move to push it back with her hands, or to cover her body against the deadly wind.

The thought came to me again that I might be dreaming, for it seemed impossible that they could survive, so lightly dressed in such cold, or that their appearance had not wakened Askuwheteau or his men, who could practically hear the day pass into night. But no, I pinched my own face and knew I was awake.

And lo! I realized that the children must be from the settlement at St. Barthélemy! If they were alive, then surely others must be also! But in this cold, I knew they would not survive, especially the naked little boy.

Carefully, so as not to wake the others, I pushed back my blanket and stood up. The cold struck me at once, and with terrible force. My teeth began to clatter and my body reacted with a violent spasm of shivering, but my only concern in that moment was for the two children. I stepped back inside and took up the blanket that had been covering me and wrapped it about me like a cloak. Carefully, I placed another log on the fire. It crackled, and then slowly caught the heat from the embers. Flames encircled it and a plume of smoke rose into the air. From one of the packs, I took another blanket, intending to swaddle the naked little boy with it before his poor little body froze.

I whispered to the children in my crude Ojibwa, indicating that they should come near the fire. I sensed, rather than saw, their response, for they stood as still as statues. And yet somehow I knew their bodies had tensed in anticipation. I beckoned with one arm, making sure to keep my own blanket wrapped about me for my own warmth. Still, they stood motionless.

Then, slowly, the girl raised her own arm and beckoned to me.

The gesture was a perfect facsimile of my own, an invitation to move away from the camp and come to where she was standing. Willingly, I took a step towards her. She and the boy took a reactive step backwards, farther into the trees. But at the same time, the girl beckoned me again. This time, her brother (for that is how I had come to think of him) gestured as well, as though imitating his sister's invitation to *me*.

Then they took two more steps backward until they were nearly invisible.

I called out to them again in Ojibwa as I walked into the forest. I stared hard, straining my eyes to see where they stood. And while I could barely make out the shape of them, I again thought I saw the strange crimson firelight glow of their eyes winking in the blackness like sputtering reddish candlelight. I felt my way through the trees, occasionally colliding painfully with hard branches and stinging needles of pine. I glanced backward and saw that I had walked a considerably farther distance away from the camp than I had first thought. The whole sequence of events had taken on the qualities of a nightmare. But still I pushed through the trees in search of the naked little boy and his sister.

I heard a sigh, and then soft breathing, and I looked down. The children were standing directly in front of me, silent and unmoving. I reached out my hand to touch the little boy's shoulder. His skin was unearthly cold, and it seemed a miracle to me that he could be alive, even given the legendary hardiness of these people.

Unfurling the blanket I carried under my arm, I draped it as best I could around the little boy's body and drew him to me. I felt his tiny hand on my leg, stroking it as though to assure himself that I was there. From the other side, I felt his sister's hands on my other leg, her fingers moving under the blanket, like spiders along the inside of my thigh through my robe. When the child's fingers caressed my manhood with an insinuating knowledge surely beyond her years, I pulled back in shock. I reached down roughly and pushed her fingers away.

What happened next must have occurred in a matter of seconds, but I remember it as though it was hours instead, and it still haunts my nightmares today.

My hand was seized in a vise-like grip. It was not the grip of a little girl, though the fingers grasping mine gave every appearance of belonging to a human child. I screamed in pain, for it felt as though the bones in my hand would surely crack under the pressure. At the same moment, the gentle caress of the little boy became a heavy, vicious clamp on my thigh. A row of dagger-sharp fingernails ripped into the flesh of my leg and dug deeper, securing the little boy's grip. I screamed again, and I heard a horrible serpentine hiss issue from the little boy's mouth. I pushed him away with all my might, but still he held fast. The little girl, too, refused to relinquish her excruciating grip on my hand.

I shrieked in pain, twisted my body every way in a vain attempt to shake them off. I lost my footing and tripped, falling to the ground with the children still on top of me. The little boy's teeth, impossibly long and sharp, sank into the meat of my thigh.

I screamed out to Askuwheteau, beseeching him to come to my aid. Behind me, I thought I heard faint shouts from the Indians, but it was impossible to be certain in the din. The little girl's fingers entwined in my hair, brutally pulling my head backwards. I felt her other hand on my chest. She ripped at the blanket, clawing it as though she sought to shred it in order to expose the naked flesh of my chest underneath. I lay contorted on the ground with the two child-demons writhing on top of me, trying to push them away and calling out to God and the Indians to help me, for in that moment the two seemed interchangeable.

And then her hand brushed against the crucifix I wore. A dazzling flash of blue light lit up the surrounding trees, and I smelled an awful foulness, like burning flesh.

The little Savage girl—for I could now clearly see her in the supernatural viridian glow—leaped back into a crouching position in front of me, snarling like some cornered, feral creature. Her mouth, ringed with the jagged teeth of a shark, was open in a perfect oval of agony. Peal after peal, she rent the night with her torment, flailing her charred and smoking hand in the air as though to put out a fire. At the sight of his sister's injury, the little boy also relinquished his grip and scuttled away from me in a sequence of crablike movements, taking up a cowering position behind her. His own cries of thwarted outrage blended with hers in an infernal cacophony such as I imagine must occur in the very bowels of deepest Hell. She lurched forward, baring her teeth at me and spitting like a cat, but again seemed to be stopped short by my crucifix, the effect of which upon her was not unlike that which might have occurred if she had hurled herself against a stone wall.

At once, I heard the thunder of many feet behind me. An arrow sang past my ear and embedded itself in a tree, just above where the children were crouched. The little girl glanced upwards at the arrow, then back at me, her face full of hate.

Before my eyes, as if by a miracle, the demon-child's body appeared to collapse upon itself, turning to smoke that blew away into the night. I saw that her brother, too, had similarly vanished, leaving in his wake that curious smoke which appeared to move of its own volition into the forest.

I stared at the spot where they had been crouching mere seconds before. For a moment, I again doubted whether or not I was dreaming, but I could feel the blood running down my leg where the little boy had bitten me, and I still felt the little girl's grip burn on my throbbing wrist. The arrow wobbled in the tree trunk as though stirred by a strong wind. The Indians stood behind me, their terrified faces recording that they had seen the entire hellish spectacle. This comforted me, as there was a part of my mind that refused to register what had just occurred. But the expression on the faces of the Savages was proof to me that I had in fact seen the demonic spectacle, and that it had been no nightmare.

But growing in me at that moment was the surety I now held the secret to the difference between faith and true knowledge. While the very existence of those two devils itself was a blasphemy, it could only be a warning from the Lord of the potent deviltry hidden in what I thought were the harmless pagan superstitions of these poor, lost people. Whatever witchcraft had been arrayed against me that night, I had defeated it with the power of Jesus Christ, through the medium of the symbol of His suffering. Triumphantly, I brandished my cross at the Indians, exhorting them to draw close and listen.

"Behold!" I cried. "You have now witnessed with your own eyes the miraculous banishment of demonic spirits from the forest, sent to torment us, but who fled at the sign of God! Can you doubt, any of you, the salvation that lies in accepting Jesus Christ and becoming one with Him? Askuwheteau? Can even you doubt? Your arrow could not hurt them, but the cross of Christ burned them. Will you now accept to be baptized before we forge ahead on the journey to St. Barthélemy? Shall we gird

ourselves in the armour of God and finish the task to which we
have set ourselves?"

To my shock, the Indians jumped back away from me and
averted their eyes, as though I myself were one of the very demons
of which I spoke. Two of them seized their bows and laid arrows in
the nock, pulling the string back and aiming them at me.

I threw up my arms in front of me, though I knew that if the
Indians chose to let their arrows fly, nothing I did by way of self-
preservation would save me.

And yet they did not: the arrows remained pointed in my
direction, but the intent seemed more to warn me not to come
closer than as the issuance of any sort of threat.

"Askuwheteau," I demanded, trying not to betray my terror,
yet at the same time striving not to unnerve the Savages whose
arrows were aimed at my heart. "What is the meaning of this?

Askuwheteau said nothing to me by way of reply, and the
Indians were silent. Then Chogan spat on the ground. He whispered something to Askuwheteau, then turned and stalked
determinedly away. The other Savages muttered amongst themselves and threw angry glances in my direction. Askuwheteau
said something to my two would-be murderers, who lowered
their bows, but did not look away from my face.

"What is wrong?" I asked Askuwheteau, gesturing towards
Chogan. "Where is he going? What did he say?"

"He said I should kill you and leave you here," Askuwheteau
said. "He says to leave you to find the other Black Robe by yourself." Askuwheteau pointed to my leg, where the little boy had
bitten me and the blood had soaked through my robe. "He says
your people brought demons with you to this place and that you
are cursed. He says he will not take you any farther and we must
not bring the other Black Robe, the *Weetigo*, to us."

"But you yourself saw, Askuwheteau, that the demons were
Indian in form and feature. They were spirits that sprang from
your own forests. They did not spring from the realm of Christianity. I did not summon them, they were here already. I sent
them away."

"Enough," said Askuwheteau. "Enough lies. You have brought

terrible things here with you, you and the other Black Robe. You
have cursed this land. You have brought death, and worse. They,"
he said, gesturing to the Indians, who were rapidly packing up
the camp and carrying their belongings back along the path
to the lake, "want me to leave you here, but I told the French I
would protect you. You can come with us now, Black Robe, or
you can stay. The choice is yours to make. But we will not go
farther. You choose."

I felt as though all the blood had drained from my body. Surely
I was not to be left here alone in this place to find the mission and
Father de Céligny without their guidance and protection?

I begged and pleaded with Askuwheteau to stay with me, but
even if he had been thusly inclined, he was outnumbered. There
were some who actually wished me dead and it had become clear
to me that he was the one person who was keeping me from that
fate. I told him that, with me, even the deviltry of his own people
was powerless before the power of Christ in the hands of one
anointed.

I threatened that the French would punish them for abandoning me, but even as I said it I knew that it rang hollow. The
Indians would say that I had drowned, or perished in some other
way due to my own carelessness or clumsiness.

Likewise, I could not force them to stay with me. I had no
leverage. We were not united in Faith, or by loyalty to our fellow
man. We did not even have the same sense of "fellow man." And
the Indians would do as they wished, or rather, in this instance,
as their terror of this place demanded. I did not count them as
evil for abandoning me. I forgave them, even in the midst of my
horror at the abandonment itself. I literally saw myself in the jaws
of Hell, at the mercy of its Infernal ambassadors, two of which I
had already met.

In the end, there was no choice, of course, though I wished
there were.

My duty as a Christian and as a priest was clear: I was to find
Father de Céligny and come to his aid, in whatever forms that
might take. Perhaps this was to be my own particular martyrdom—not death under torture at the hands of the Hiroquois, but

rather a slow death by starvation and freezing, looking for the Light of Christ in a dark forest on the very edge of the world. *Ad majorem Dei gloriam.*

Askuwheteau pointed me in the direction of St. Barthélemy and said he hoped my God would save me. I told him I prayed my God would save us both, but he and I knew that we were not saying the same thing to one another.

When the Indians abandoned me, I forced myself not to run after them, just as I'd forced myself not to weep in their presence. Now, I did weep. I knelt down in the dirt of the forest that had become my personal Garden of Gethsemane and wept from the deepest possible pit of my soul. I wept. I cursed God. I begged forgiveness, but cursed Him again, and asked for forgiveness again, and felt myself granted absolution. I did not weep blood as Our Lord is said to have done, but I have never felt closer to Christ's Passion than I did at that moment, for I felt truly alone. Throughout it all, I held tight to my crucifix, lest those two infernal devils return from the forest to taunt me.

When the first streaks of dawn lightened the eastern sky, I felt safe enough to release my hold on the crucifix. I was shivering. I spoke to myself as though I were my own friend, ordering myself to rise and collect some firewood in order to build up the fire and warm myself. There would be no one else to guide, help, protect, or support me in my aims unless, by some miracle, I found life and shelter at my destination.

Askuwheteau had told me that the Mission was half a day's walk from where we had camped. He told me to mark the trees and walk in a northerly direction until I found the inland lake that bordered the Mission. He said it would be unmistakable. He had told me to follow the perimeter of the lake until I came to the place where great cliffs rose behind it. Then, he said, I would be at St. Barthélemy. The Mission was adjacent to the lake, below the cliffs.

The Indians had left me a portion of dried meat, bread made from corn, and beans. Some of this I warmed up in the fire and ate. I wrapped the rest of it and placed it carefully in my pack on top of the blankets. Then, taking up a stout stick, which could as easily serve as a weapon as it did a staff, I began to walk north.

In spite of the general terror of my new, unkind station, I took both pleasure and comfort from the rising sun, which spoke to me not only of safety (for I felt that even in this place, the demons must likely absent themselves in the daylight, even if the Hiroquois did not) but of hope.

While I knew that it was entirely likely that I would reach St. Barthélemy and find it burned to the ground and all its inhabitants dead, there was also a possibility that I would, at the very least, find shelter there, if not companionship in my abandonment. When I did not return with news of Father de Céligny, the Indians would be interrogated and the Fathers might yet send rescue of some sort. Failing that, perhaps some passers-by, either friendly Savages or French, would find me and help.

I told myself these things over and over again, even if I did not believe most of them. At least they calmed me somewhat as I walked. I measured out the hours through the medium of an eternity of footsteps across the carpet of dead leaves on the forest floor. And yet, every sound of a tree branch cracking in the distance and every scream of a bird brought me to the very cusp of madness.

The cold hard sun followed me as I walked. By midday, the forest thinned out, and I felt the air grow cooler and damper. It was my fervent prayer that the unnamed lake was just beyond the next part of the forest, and that my prayer, unlike so many others of late, was answered.

In a very short time, there it was in the near distance, larger than I expected, the water calm and the colour of dull iron. The cliffs did indeed rise up behind it like great hulking shoulders, giving the region a pagan look, as though it were once the realm of ancient gods. I realized, even as I thought these things, that I was skirting the outer edge of blasphemy. But in the face of the terror of my abandonment here by the Indians, nothing in the world looked the same to me and, likely, never would again.

While I knew God was in His Heaven looking down on His earth, I truly felt in that moment that He must be looking elsewhere, for the silence of the place was both a temporal and spiritual vacuum. The wind did not blow, and no bird sang in the trees.

I hurried along the perimeter of the lake, always in sight of the water lest I somehow lose my way, even this close to my destination. I scanned the horizon in vain for some plume of smoke that might signal human habitation, but there was none.

And then, over the crest of one of those infernal mounds of rock that seemed to burst forth out of the ground everywhere like monstrous teeth, I saw it in the distance: the village wherein lay the Mission of St. Barthélemy.

I had arrived at my destination at long last.

My first impression of the humble Jesuit house in the village (the residence building itself, containing the chapel for Mass and the refectory, situated on a small hill) was that it seemed as fresh-built as the day upon which the construction was completed by the tribe. It rose up out of a clearing in the forest like some miraculous flower of civilization in the midst of a wasteland of rock and pine.

Around it was a scattering of crude huts of bent poplar and bark where the Indians of the village themselves obviously lived. What struck me immediately was the absence of the cacophony that accompanied life in their villages, the screaming children, the barking dogs, and the general tumult. The eerie silence persisted here as it had in the forest leading to it, but there was no smell of smoke in the air, and none of the buildings looked like any flame had scorched them.

My joy at this was boundless for, at the very least, this meant that I would have shelter tonight, barring any discovery of a gruesome nature inside the buildings themselves.

As I drew close to the Jesuit house, I was met with a distressing sight: the wooden cross that stood in front of the residence building housing the chapel had been torn down. That is to say, while the pine pole, which formed the primary pillar of the cross, was still firmly entrenched in the earth, the crossbeams had been broken off, or pulled down. I told myself that it had been caused by some storm of wind and rain, for surely if the intent had been desecration, the entire cross would have been demolished.

I climbed the small hill with trepidation and pushed open the door. In the dimness of the chapel, nothing seemed immediately awry, though dirt from the outside lay heavily on the floor, and even the altar. Here too, there was no evidence of the symbol of Our Lord's martyrdom, though neither was there anything suggesting destruction or other mischief, though again I was aware of that unnerving, tomb-like silence that lay over the chapel like a pall.

Instinctively I sniffed the air, at once terrified that I would catch the smell of death and relieved that I did not. The smell was one of general airlessness—lifelessness, even.

I walked slowly through the two "rooms" of the house, only to find more of the same.

In the section that obviously served as a kitchen, there was a crude table with cutlery and plates laid out as though for supper, but they too were covered with a dusting of dirt, as though those meant to dine had simply walked out and not returned. In the dead hearth, a black iron pot hung from a hook. In the pot, I observed, a spoon was encased in a dried mulch of some sort of grain stew that had petrified, but even from the pot there was no odour, for this meal had been cooked and abandoned a very long time ago.

The trappers who had reported back to Samuel de Champlain had not been wrong: St. Barthélemy was indeed entirely deserted. While there was ample evidence of the settlement having been inhabited, there was quite literally no trace of any living person in any part of it.

Feeling again that infernal chill, I stepped outside to retrieve some wood from the stack I'd noticed near the entrance. On a table, I found a tinder-box. I struck the steel and flint to some straw and built a fire in the hearth to warm myself. In the crude cupboards I found several bottle of wine, as well as stores of dry goods: beans, corn and the like.

I opened one of the bottles of wine and poured a healthy draught into one of the tankards on the table, caring little for its cleanliness after those many weeks on the water with the Indians. The taste of the wine on my tongue was wonderful. I had drunk nothing but lake water since we had left Trois-Rivières and my palette was starved for variance of flavour.

Before sunset, I hiked back to the lake and drew water, both for drinking and for cooking. It was a more arduous walk back carrying the water, but I made haste and imagine an hour or less passed between my departure and my return.

I boiled some of the beans on the hearth and ate plentifully for the first time in many days.

After I had eaten, I washed the plate and went back inside, where I found a crude bed made of a sheet of bark. Above it was a shelf. Clearly this had been the abode of Father de Céligny, for there I found some books and some clothes. His Bible and crucifix were not among the store. I dragged the bark-bed close enough to the hearth that I would be warm as I slept. I arranged the blankets on top of it and lay down, but not before bolting the door from the inside. Without thinking, I removed my own heavy crucifix for the sake of comfort.

The exhaustion of the past week on the water, coupled with my ordeal of abandonment by the Indians, had exhausted me beyond endurance and I fell deeply asleep before I could say any prayers for my own safety and protection during the night.

And then, there was a hand on my shoulder, shaking me gently awake. I opened my eyes. In the glow of the embers in the fireplace I beheld the figure of a pale old man bending over me, dressed entirely in the black robes of the Jesuit.

My eyes widened in disbelief and for a moment I wondered if I was beholding a ghost, merely one more in a long line of nightmarish sights in this godforsaken Land.

The figure lovingly caressed my face. His fingers felt cold, as though he had just come in from outside. He pulled back the blanket and lifted my robe, exposing my leg where the child had bitten me. This he touched, tracing the injury with his finger, gently, as though he were a surgeon inspecting an infected wound. Then he leaned down and kissed me on both cheeks, a chaste kiss of welcome.

"You have found us," he said in French—the first proper French I had heard since leaving Trois-Rivières. His voice was cultured, even aristocratic, a far cry from the coarse guttural peasant French of the *voyageurs* and *hivernants* in Trois-Rivières.

"Praise God. I had given up hope that anyone would. I have been waiting for so very long."

I struggled to sit up. Through eyes suddenly full of tears of joy and relief, I said, "Father de Céligny? Can it really be you?" I grasped his arms, finding them solid and real, not spectral. "I—we, all of us in TroisRivières—we feared you had been killed by the Hiroquois."

"Yes, Father," he replied. "I am de Céligny. I am not dead. Now, rest. We will speak tomorrow. All is well. You are safe, here, from harm. Sleep, now."

"But the Hiroquois . . ."

My eyelids were heavy. I heard Father de Céligny's voice as from a great distance, urging me to sleep. I tried to open my eyes, and with seemingly superhuman strength, I half-raised my lids to see him drawing away into blackness as he stepped from my bedside. I saw the glint of reflected firelight in his eyes, and then he was gone.

I closed my eyes and fell into a deep sleep. I dreamed of the young girl in the lake with the torn throat.

In my dream, her eyes were not opaque and lightless; they sparkled with bright black life. I looked to the Indians for succour, but found I was alone in the canoe, floating on an endless ocean of ash-coloured water with no land or horizon anywhere in sight. As I stared, trying desperately to scream and being unable to, her throat healed itself before my eyes until there was no mark or blemish anywhere on the wet bronze skin.

The dead girl swam up to the canoe, drifting snakelike through the water, her wet black hair plastered to her head and face. She reached up and grasped the gunwale of the canoe and began to rock it gently, and then with increasing violence. I believed she meant to swamp it and drown me, pulling me beneath the surface to live there with her there for a thousand years.

"You have brought terrible things here with you," she said in a voice full of cold dark water and rotted black pine needles. Her voice was the voice of Askuwheteau, my Judas-abandoner. "You have brought death, and worse." Then she opened her mouth to smile, and I saw her terrible teeth.

I woke myself with the sound of my own screams.

In the weak daylight that crept through the windows and under the doors of that haunted place, I wondered if I had only dreamed the appearance of Father de Céligny, for the door was still crudely barred from the inside, just as I had left it before falling asleep. Otherwise, the room was undisturbed. The windows were likewise barred and there were no tracks in any direction upon the floor other than my own. From outside came the sound of the trees shuddering with rain.

I touched the side of my face. I could still feel the imprint of the priest's cold fingers on my cheek. If that was a dream, I told myself, it had been a most vivid and realistic one. Were dreams even dreams in this evil place, where the legends spoke of the dead walking in the forest, going about as they had when they were living? Or were they auguries, visions, or portents? I thought of my dream of the smiling dead girl in the water and I shuddered.

After a Spartan breakfast and an hour of prayer, I set out to find Father de Céligny, if only to prove to myself that I hadn't been dreaming. While there was no evidence of him anywhere in the building, I believed in my heart that he was real and that I had not been dreaming. The puzzle of the door barred from the inside was one I would consider later, I told myself. So eager was I to believe I was not the only living soul in St. Barthélemy, I was prepared to overlook even the evidence of my own senses.

But if he were nowhere in the buildings, he must be nearby, perhaps in some secondary domicile, or perhaps dwelling among the Indians away from the village itself, however unlikely that seemed. I knew, for instance, that the Indians liked to visit our homes in the settlements, that they were attracted to objects of mystery to them, our crucifixes, our books, our writing instruments, and our clocks. But I had not seen them even in their own houses here, so why would they be elsewhere in the forest?

A cold rain was indeed falling outside, mining the ground with puddles. I covered my head with a shawl against the rain and set out to explore the area for some sign of where Father de Céligny might have taken shelter.

My intention had not been to wander too far from the village, for after inspecting every house I was able to ascertain that there was no human habitation at all within its confines and it did, indeed, appear to have been abandoned.

But my source of primary bafflement remained the lack of evidence of any kind of struggle or bloodshed. There were no bodies, obvious graves, no stains. As I have already written, nothing had been burned. I inspected every house, first tentatively and then with more boldness as I realized I was entirely alone. So the mystery remained, surely an entire village could not have simply vanished into thin air? Or, for that matter, migrated to some other part of this land, leaving behind their belongings, including weapons and cooking utensils?

Slowly and carefully I took my leave of the village and began walking towards the lake. The rain had not diminished. On the contrary, it fell in colder and more punishing sheets, seemingly with every step I took away from the settlement, into the forest and towards the lake.

I had been walking perhaps a half-hour and had almost reached the rocky hills above the lake when I heard a sound that chilled me to the very marrow of my bones. It came from behind one of the boulders in my path, and it froze me in my tracks with a terror so primeval that it must surely have descended from generation to generation from Adam in the Garden of Eden, after the fall from Grace, when all wild things had become his enemy.

A giant grey wolf had stepped into my path, its back low and arched in a menacing posture. Its black lips were pulled back from the cruel looking yellow fangs. Again, the wolf growled low in its throat. The murderous intent of this monster could not have been clearer.

To my horror, it was joined by another, and yet another, until there were five of the creatures blocking my path, each more fearsome than the last. I had seen wolves in France, shot by hunters. They had always struck me as fearsome, but these wolves were larger and more terrifying than any European variant. And in their eyes, I could see only the muddy hatred of the human species and a fierce hunger for human flesh.

The wolves advanced slowly, and in terrible unison, maintaining the half-circle around me with the precision of a military phalanx formation, driving me backwards. My eyes never left theirs, nor theirs mine, as they slowly forced me away from the caves.

Praying under my breath, I remembered what I had been told in Trois-Rivières about this exact danger, and the importance of neither showing fear, nor running quickly, lest those actions provoke an attack from the marauding animal in question.

The first wolf lowered its head even farther and from its throat again came a snarl of the purest menace. It moved aggressively forward. I looked around me for a stick that I might use as a weapon, but found none.

Even if I had, while a stick might have been of some use against one of these animals, there were five of them in total and any attempt to charge one of their number would have doubtless provoked an attack by the others in the pack.

I backed away slowly, my eyes on theirs, and theirs on mine. Edging myself onto the trail, I realized that the wolves were "herding" me back onto the path, the path that would obviously take me back to the village, or at the very least, to open ground. They kept advancing forward with every step backwards I took.

I stumbled towards the village, walking tortuously backward, my eyes on my pursuers. I flailed behind me with my arms, trying to anticipate the sharp branches behind me before they jabbed into my neck and back. When I failed, I tried to stifle my groans of pain.

They followed me at a hunting distance, but did not attack. In the one instance where I stopped, however, to get my bearings, they began to growl again. One darted forward and made a feinting snap at my hand. I cried out and jumped back, and when I again began to move, the wolf kept its distance.

Step by torturous step, always looking back over my shoulder, or walking backwards and glancing behind me to stay on the trail, occasionally stumbling painfully while the wolves moved like shadows and smoke among the boulders and low-growing trees and foliage as they stalked and herded me, I inched closer to what I hoped was the safety of the confines of St. Barthélemy. My terror was such that it felt as though it was hours before I saw the village, but obviously it could only have been a fraction of that time.

And still, they did not attack, though they had every opportunity to tear me limb from limb. They did not break their deadly silence, nor was there any lessening in the obvious malignity of their intentions, and yet it was as though they were somehow tethered and held back by some entity I could not see. I doubted that whatever providential force held them at bay was Heavenly—if it had been, the force would have sent them back to whatever sylvan hell they sprang from instead of allowing them to stalk me like wounded animal prey.

And then, finally yielding to my panic, I turned and broke into a run.

In the minutes during which I ran, I had every expectation of feeling the foul weight of their heavy bodies hurling me to the ground, and their foetid, hot breath on my exposed skin, and the death-bite agony of their teeth on my throat. But I felt nothing of the kind, and made my way to safety inside Father de Céligny's house without once turning my head.

Upon entering, I looked out the window to see if the fiends had returned to their wilderness. My heart sank when I saw that they had not. Instead, they sat, poised like living gargoyles in a semi-circle in front of the entrance. As I watched, they cocked their heads as though listening to some master's whistle, or to some command only they could hear. The entire tableau resembled a grisly sixteenth-century German woodcut depicting the fell horrors of werewolfery in some dark, forgotten forest.

As the day progressed, the beasts sat, or lay with their paws crossed in front of them. They must have known that I was vulnerable, and doubtless they could smell my terror as I knelt to pray, and yet they did not charge the entrance.

At one point in the late afternoon, I reached out with my hand to touch the door. As my fingers brushed it, a commotion erupted on the other side. A cacophony of howling and snarling greeted me.

Although I knew it was impossible, still it was as though the wolves had somehow known that I had touched the door from the inside, and that I might possibly be contemplating egress from the safety of the house. The fury in their bestial voices left no doubt whatsoever in my mind of the fate that would be mine if I dared step over the threshold.

I stepped backward towards the opposite wall and immediately they ceased their furor, again almost as though they knew my movements without seeing them. I realized that this must be more of the same deviltry that had plagued me since I left Trois-Rivières and it came to me then and there that I would very likely not survive that night. It came to me also that Father de Céligny had fallen to the same forces. If I had not dreamed his appearance by my bedside the previous night, whatever I saw could only have been his shade. I mourned Father de Céligny in that moment, and knelt to pray, for I didn't doubt that I would soon join him on the other side.

When I roused myself from my prayer, I looked out the window and saw that the sun had nearly set and the shadows were lengthening across the abandoned village. The wolves were no longer sitting or lying by the door. They paced nervously, sniffing the air as though they could smell the sun setting and the entrance of night.

As it grew darker, the wolves become more and more agitated. Two of them began to bark sharply and to whine nervously. Faster and faster the night came, more and more the wolves fretted and paced in circles. And then, in unison, they threw back their heads and began to howl. The plaintive sound, which I had heard before only in the distance, carried with it a quality of reverence, an aspect that was even somehow prayerful.

For several long minutes the wolves lamented. Then, to my amazement, they turned tail and ran, abandoning their guard posts in front of my door for the path that led back to the lake.

I stepped over the threshold in wonderment at what had just occurred. I looked left and right, but there was no trace of them anywhere.

Above the rise of the distant cliffs, a gibbous moon had begun its ascent, not full, but bright enough to illuminate, however dully, the deserted village and the surrounding forests, which I could hear coming alive. In the distance, the chorus of the wolves came again, this time louder, as though more of them had gathered to celebrate the awakening of the night.

Of a sudden, I imagined I saw movement among the huts—shadows flitting and darting. I rubbed my eyes, because the shadows were moving with inhuman, even preternatural, speed. They moved upright, and were human in shape, of medium height, and thin, or so they seemed—they vanished as quickly as the appeared, almost as if they were taunting me, for as soon as I was able to focus my eyes upon them they were gone.

I closed my eyes and said a prayer for my safety in the face of this wickedness and for strength to drive whatever evil had destroyed the village back to the Hell from whence it sprang. And I prayed for courage, for I fear I had none at that moment. I thought of the brave martyrs who had gone to their deaths praying for the souls of the Savages who were cutting their bodies and forcing them to eat their own flesh. If I was to meet my own death at more unearthly, numinous hands, I would strive to die with as much courage as they had shown, and with as blithe and open a heart.

"Come, demons!" I shouted, brandishing my crucifix aloft. "Do your worst! I have no fear of you, for the power of Christ makes my arm a hammer! You are powerless against His holy name, which commands you to be gone from this place!"

I swept the cross in front of me like a scythe. I imagined I felt the shadows leaping back in its advance, but again that could have been in my mind, for what I had seen before I did not see now—the blackness had become impenetrable.

And then, out of that same blackness, came the sound of slow and measured footsteps. My heart leaped in my chest, for the cadence of those footsteps was human. I squinted to see. Again, that flicker of firelike crimson in the gloom, but it vanished as quickly as it had appeared. As I stared, a figure materialized from the shadows. It was a man wearing a black cassock tied with a cincture. And—O! The joy! I saw that his head was crowned with the flat black hat of our Jesuit priests.

I called out, "Father de Céligny, is that you?" The figure stood motionless in the shadows, not speaking. I called out again,

"Father, show yourself. It is I, Father Nyon. You are safe, I mean you no harm!" They were odd phrases to have come to me, for why would Father de Céligny ever have reason to fear me? And yet the figure held back with an aspect that I can only describe as fearful. Again, I called out softly,

"Father?"

And then, he stepped towards me, and I saw that it was indeed the white-haired man I had seen the previous night, not a dream, not a revenant, but real as I was, made of flesh and blood. The joy I felt at that moment was the first joy I had felt in many, many months and the loneliness I felt in that desolate place left me at once. Finally, I thought, whatever fate I was to meet in that Land, I would not have to face it alone. And perhaps we would indeed escape together, Father de Céligny and I! Where yesterday there had been no possible hope for the future, there was now at the very least a glimmer of it.

In his face I saw the aristocratic lineage to which Father de Varennes had alluded in Trois-Rivières. It was the face of a descendant of nobility, the face of a refined man who belonged in the library of a fine country chateau, or presiding over Mass in one of the grand cathedrals of Europe. It was the face of a grand seigneur from an oil portrait of ancient riches. The nose was high-bridged and aquiline, the lips thin and red. His face held the pallor of long illness, and yet it was the face of a virile and healthy man. I opened my arms to embrace him with all the joy in my heart, but his voice stopped me where I stood.

"Father Nyon," he said. "Come no closer. There is no time to spare! We must quickly seek shelter. There is prodigious danger abroad tonight; we are not safe here in this village. Follow me."

With that, he began walking away towards the Jesuit house, beckoning me to follow him without turning back. I did follow him, struggling to keep up with him, for his own progress through the village was swift and sure, though the darkness was, to me, impenetrable.

As I think of it now, though I know Your Reverence will doubtless believe the fever guides my pen, he moved like smoke along the ground, appearing even to float. Which is to say, in one instant be appeared to be directly in front of me, then in another he was to the left of the path, then again, to the right of the path. I recalled the movements of the apparitions I had beheld earlier, flickering like wraiths throughout the village, but vanishing when my eyes strained to follow them. While Father de Céligny was plainly visible, the trajectory of his movements seemed likewise variable.

He stopped at the entrance to the Jesuit house and turned slowly towards me. Again, I was assailed by a sense of being on the edge of a precipice and looking abruptly down, for the tableau itself, Father de Céligny, the house, even the moonlight, seemed to sway before my eyes. I reached out by instinct to right myself, but my hands found no purchase and I stumbled and fell. He made no move to help me.

Though I would be hard pressed to explain how I knew, he appeared to take some private amusement from my discomfiture, but hiding it with the sort of slyness I would expect from the Savages, but not a white man, let alone a priest. But in his face, there was nothing to raise an alarum.

His voice was grave when he spoke. "Father Nyon, you must remove your crucifix. Hang it here," he said pointing to a spot over the window adjacent to the doorway. "I will reveal all to you once we are inside. But you must leave the crucifix outside, for your protection and mine. There are forces afoot tonight that are beyond our power to fight, but which may be kept at bay through the agency of the Blessed Virgin and her Son, Jesus Christ our Lord. The cross will protect us." Again, he pointed at the spot, looking away from it as he pointed. "Hang it there. It will secure our safety from what is afoot in this village."

Of course I obeyed immediately, for who was I to doubt the older priest?

I was a very young man, and it seemed clear that Father de Céligny had some greater knowledge of what had brought the mission to doom, and he had obviously survived the onslaught of those forces, whatever they might be. I very much feared I might not survive them without his help, guidance, and protection, for

I was lost in an ocean of unanswered questions and half-formed terrors.

Too, I was so enthralled by the notion of being no longer alone in this devilish place, where day and night held equal menace, I would have done anything to keep him close. I removed the crucifix and hung it where he indicated.

Father de Céligny smiled, but it was a vulpine smile, not a reverent one as might befit a gesture involving a holy object. Again I felt the vertigo, and this time a prickle of fear accompanied it, a primal instinct impelling flight, as one might feel upon discovering a snake. And then he slipped like smoke across the threshold into the house.

The building was cold and the fire had almost burned out. I shivered. I took a stick from the small pile I had assembled and stirred the embers. I placed the stick on the small heap of smouldering ash and watched the flickering tongues of flame shoot up from the ash to consume it. I added a few more dry sticks. The fire bloomed, beckoning shadows from all corners.

Across the room, Father de Céligny made no move to step towards the fire; rather, he stood against the farthest wall of the room, save for the whiteness of his face and hair, indistinct from the darkness of the room that wrapped him like a cloak. Again, I felt that haunting sense of dislocation and vertigo.

"Father," I said, for I could no longer abide my frenzy of terror and ignorance, "please tell me what has happened here. Where are the Indians? Why was the settlement abandoned? I was taught to look for Satan's work only after every other possibility had been exhausted, but I confess that all possibilities *have* been exhausted. I am at sea."

From the shadows, his voice came softly, more akin to a serpent's sibilant hiss than a sequence of words spoken by a human tongue, and it appeared to issue from nowhere, yet everywhere. My senses swam, and I staggered, righting myself in time not to fall. Again, he made no move towards me to come to my aid.

"Are you cold, Father Nyon?" he said gently. "This country is very cold, is it not? Very cold indeed. Cold and wild, and very dark in the winter. Do you not find it so? Winter approaches, even now, and the hours of daylight have grown so short. Do you see how dark it has become? Can you feel the night enter?"

And indeed I did see how dark it was becoming. The room itself was growing darker. The fire seemed very far away, and the only light in the room seemed to come from his voice. I cannot better describe it than to say that his words themselves seemed to me to shimmer in the growing dark. It was as though I had stared too long at the sun and had gone blind, and the sun had grown black, searing its image behind my eyes, blotting out all else except that burning shower of falling black stars. And yet, there *was* no sun. There *was* no light.

My knees buckled, and I fell to the dirt floor.

Father de Céligny's mocking laughter came as though from a great distance. "Poor little priest," he said. He sounded almost regretful. "You should never have come to St. Barthélemy. You should have believed the stories you were told about what happened in this place." I heard the rustle of his robes and the sound of his feet as he walked slowly to where I lay.

Even as I write these memories tonight, I am struck anew at how they appear to be the ravings of a madman, even to me. And yet: I write the truth of the events as they occurred; I swear it upon my soul.

I tried to rise to my feet but my limbs refused to obey the commands of my brain. I was powerless to move. Were it witchcraft or some other dark art, I was trapped in its spell, unable to move, as though I had found myself at the bottom of a vast dark sea, holding my breath and struggling desperately to swim to the surface before my chest exploded and I took in all that cold, black water.

"Can you hear me, little priest?" de Céligny said, leaning close to my face.

I tried to answer, but found that, though my wits were still my own, I could not even speak—though I knew that if he commanded me to speak, the words would come, even if they were not my own words, but his. But I was able to move my eyes. I saw his face with a hellish clarity that had heretofore eluded me, and with that awful sight came another surety: that I had, God help me, found the author of the malefaction that had proved the undoing of the settlement.

O, how can I describe what I saw as I gazed upon the visage of Father de Céligny, the murderer of St. Barthélemy?

Shall I say that his eyes glared with a reddened light unlike any fire of God's earth, the same burning crimson that I had seen in the eyes of the Savage children two nights ago? That they stood out like beacons in the waxen pallor of his face?

Where I thought I had seen aristocracy I now saw the visage of a devil—a degenerate, ravenous archfiend wearing a well-tailored mask of human flesh. His foul mouth was open, and I could see the dull gleam where his teeth lay against his lower lip, and the smell of rotted meat, and worse, issued from his mouth.

"Do you see?" the beast said. "Do you understand?"

"Monster," I whispered, my voice suddenly my own again. "Monster. Monster. Monster. What have you wrought here?"

"I carried the seed inside me," he said. "The gift was in my blood, as it was in the blood of my ancestors. It is my inheritance, an inheritance I have brought with me to this new, unspoiled world. I have shared its light generously with these poor, lost people, to whom I have given a new catechism: mine. And now, they will have two priests. You will stay here with me and we will minister to our new congregation." He cocked his head mockingly. "Does that please you, little Jesuit?" he said. "That we bring the true light of our darkness to this unspoiled place?"

"I will stop you," I said. "I will save these people. And I will kill you, and I will do it in God's name, and to His glory, devil."

"No," Father de Céligny said. His voice sounded almost pitying. "You will not."

Then, by the grace of God, three things happened in quick succession. A slumbering log on the fire exploded behind us, sending up a shower of sparks, the retort as sharp as the crack of a cannon. Father de Céligny hissed, startled by the noise of the fire. And in the moment he turned away from me, the spell was broken. I found I could again move my limbs.

I pushed my body away from where I lay, leaping to my feet. My hands instinctively went to my chest, where the crucifix usually lay. With horror, I remembered that devious creature had tricked me into hanging it outside the hut. I was defenceless, as I had always been intended to be.

De Céligny turned slowly towards me. His smile was one of pure, hellish triumph, for we both knew it was my time to die. I closed my eyes and made the sign of the cross in the air in front of me.

There was a terrible snap, like a lightning strike, and de Céligny screamed. I opened my eyes to see him flinching away, as though from a terrible, searing heat. I made the sign of the cross again, and again he screamed. As I stared, he fell forward as though to collapse on the ground.

But before his hands even struck the ground, yet another wonderment occurred, though this one was as malign as the other was divine. In the first second, I had beheld the falling human form of Father de Céligny, but what landed on the ground instead was the shape of a colossal, towering black wolf with blazing red eyes and the jagged teeth of a stone-carved gargoyle.

I cried out in shock and stumbled backwards away from this new incarnation of the monster. From its gullet came a roar of rage such as I have never heard from any animal. The wolf crouched before me, as though poised to strike, but instead it turned and leaped easily over my prone body and ran out through the doorway into the night.

I reached for the remaining pile of sticks by the fire, and seized two slender ones. These I crossed, one over the other, in the shape of a makeshift crucifix. Thus armed, I held it in front of me and pursued the creature through the doorway.

In the unearthly brightness of the full moon, I beheld the entire village. But tonight, the village was not empty, not deserted.

Twenty, perhaps thirty Savages, men, women, children, young and old, stood ranked in a motionless perimeter like statues, eyes fixed upon me, fixed upon the makeshift cross I held in front of me, neither moving towards me nor backing away.

In the centre of the crowd stood Father de Céligny. Our eyes met. He stared at me with deep hatred. When finally he spoke, his words echoed only in my mind, for his lips did not move.

We will come for you tomorrow night, little priest, when the sun is down. We will come for you then, and nothing—neither your crosses, nor your prayers—will keep us from you.

A cutting wind sprang up suddenly from the north, carrying with it the knife-edge of winter. One by one, the shapes of the Savages and Father de Céligny shimmered, becoming misty and indistinct, then vanishing entirely as though carried away into the darkness beyond the trees and the rock cliffs by the sudden blast of frigid air.

I stood there till the first fingers of dawn coaxed the tentative morning from the night's entombment. Some vestiges of my courage returned with the daylight. I let my aching body fall stiffly to my knees in a prayer of thanks, and an invocation for the strength I would need for what would—what *must*—come next.

I ate the remainder of the dried meat and corn mush that had been left to me by Askuwheteau's band before deserting me, and I drank some of the water I had drawn the previous day, for my thirst was fierce. Had it only been two days ago that I arrived at the godforsaken ruins of St. Barthélemy? It seemed as though I had been there for an eternity, for time had begun to turn inwards on itself with the progression of this waking nightmare.

Despite my febrile, sleepless state, I remembered as a boy growing up in Beauce, I had heard the legends and tales of these revenant creatures, the *morts-vivants* who slumbered in their coffins beneath the earth in churchyards and sepulchres and rose from their graves at sundown to nourish themselves on the blood of the living. In the legends I recalled, these creatures would never die unless a shaft of wood was driven through their heart and, afterwards, the head stricken from the body. Even as a child, I had dismissed these stories as peasant folk-tales or, at worst, the blasphemous heresy that the Lord would allow the dead to leave their tombs in order to walk about among the living before the great Day of Judgement. And yet, here was that very abomination in the flesh, and I had seen it with my own eyes.

I knew then as I had not known before what my true, God-ordained mission was to be. I would have to kill this creature that had devilishly disguised itself as a priest, and consign it to whatever Hell its soul was destined.

As well, I was duty-bound to free the souls of the Savages who had died to slake this monster's unholy thirst. I owed it not only to these poor people, but also to the honour of the Society of Jesus, for we were the ones that provided its blasphemous disguise.

If the stories were true, and if Father de Céligny had brought his plague with him from the Old World to the New, then he and the Savages would have had to find a place to rest during the daylight hours. There were no obvious graves (nor would there have been, in light of the Savages animosity towards the interment of their dead, preferring, as I understood the custom, to raise the departed one's body on a sort of platform above ground).

A thought came to me then, as a blessing from God. I remembered the diabolical wolves that had stalked me without attacking when I came too close to the cliffs outside the village yesterday morning. The very same wolves that had proved such ruthlessly efficient jailers, which had kept me inside the house until sunset when these creatures would once again walk unencumbered through the night. If control of the wolves through supernatural agency was within de Céligny's power, than it could only mean that they were protecting him while he slept.

Which meant, simply, that the place where he—where they—slept could only be the place where the cliffs rose up. Perhaps there were caves. Dark places where the light would not reach, wild places where they could sleep undisturbed.

I searched the huts in the village and was in despair of finding what I needed until I came to the last one, which seemed to be a storehouse of some sort. In that hut, beneath a pungent heap of dried animal hides, I found a bundle wrapped tightly beneath the skins. Eagerly, I pulled it open and found a smallish bow and two crude arrows. Even to my untrained eye it seemed old and warped, and more like a child's toy than an actual weapon. But I took it gladly, adding it to my poor arsenal, along with a candle, and a tinderbox.

I turned my eyes towards the sky. Though it was still morning, there was a silver-grey quality to the light that hinted of shortening days and early dusk. I struck out across the village towards the cliffs with the bow and my faith. My fate was now entirely in God's hands. If I were to fail in my mission this time, it would be into His hands that I would consign my martyrdom.

By the position of the sun, I reckoned that I had spent three hours, perhaps four, exploring the cliffs that ringed St. Barthélemy. The upward climb had been difficult, but the rock face was dry enough that my feet could find purchase.

It seems strange to think of it tonight, but as I remember the early hours of that bloody day so many years ago, the immediate recollection I have of that long walk to the caves is not only a memory of terror, but also of great beauty.

They say that in the hours before his execution, a condemned man experiences a fatal sort of calmness, one that allows for deep meditation, prayer, and reflection. Since my arrival in New France, I had not allowed myself to see anything but the perilous danger of the unknown, be it the inclemency of the seasons, the barbarous inhospitality of the Savages, and the dangers that seemed to lurk behind every distant, jutting island in every impossible lake. While I had grown accustomed to the foul smells and the casual barbarism that infected even the most mundane interaction in New France, from the crudeness of the filthy voyageurs who came to resemble the Indians in appearance and bearing, to the awful customs of the Savages themselves, I had never been able to see any beauty anywhere, except in my memories of home.

Today, facing certain death, I saw beauty. Wild, cruel, implacable beauty, to be sure, but beauty nonetheless. The world was gold and blue, the trees aflame with fiery colours the likes of which I had never seen. Against them, the sky was an indescribably exquisite lapis. All around me was a sense of silent vastness, as though this land was its own world, a world whose borders were so distant as to be irrelevant. I could easily picture the sun rising on one end of this country whilst simultaneously setting on the other.

And then, I felt yet another chill, this one coming from my soul. For I remembered that to all this beauty had come Father de Céligny, carrying his secret like a plague bacillus from the old world into the new. Did the monster wonder at his good fortune at finding such an exquisite expanse of unspoiled innocence upon which to stake his claim? Had this been his plan, perhaps? Had he intuited that, in France and elsewhere in Europe, there would be those who knew what he was, and, ignorant peasants though they would most likely be, they would also know the means of dispatching him?

Here in New France, the creature would find only innocence upon which to prey. He would only find the childlike, trusting Savages whose own superstitions did not encompass European superstitions that might correctly show him for what he was.

Did de Céligny dream of outwardly spiralling concentric circles of cannibalistic creation—of feeding on these people and making them like him, then sending them to prey on other Savages, first ten, then a hundred, then a thousand, then a million, until the entirety of New France was his personal Tartarus, with de Céligny crowned its Lord of Chaos?

Did this demon delight in mocking by his very existence our sworn mission, as Jesuits sworn to bring the light of Christ to the Savages by bringing them darkness? By taking from these poor people their lives and eternal souls instead of saving them? By disguising himself as one of us, turning our priest's robes into the cerements of the grave, wreaking fiendish machinations while calling himself a holy Father?

The very thought filled me with revulsion and outrage. Ahead, through the trees, loomed the cliffs. I was awed yet again at the uncanny silence all around me, as I had on the first day I'd arrived at St. Barthélemy. No birds sang, nor even wind in the treetops. The only noise was the sound of my feet on the leaves and the fallen twigs on the ground.

The wolf attacked without warning. There was no stalking, nor growling, no herding this time. It was almost as though they had read my mind and understood that my intentions this time were not exploratory, but rather carried a purpose that was deadly to their master. Into the silence came a sudden sound, like thunder or galloping horses. I felt it before I heard it, and then the daylight was momentarily blotted out by a massive, hurtling form that appeared to spring at me from everywhere and nowhere all at once. I was knocked into the air. I fell backwards, my body smashing to the earth.

Pain sang through every joint and fibre of my being, and the bow secured around my shoulder cut into my back like a knife blade.

I barely had time to raise myself on one elbow when the beast launched itself at me again. But I was ready for it this time. I raised my leg at the same moment it leaped and kicked the filthy animal as hard as I could. I heard the sickening sound of the wolf's ribs cracking against my boot and its own scream of agony. It landed in a heap a short distance away and lay there, writhing in pain.

Scrambling to my feet, I ran for a thick pine tree with low-hanging branches and began to climb it. Like a madman, I strove crazily to remember if a wolf could climb a tree or not. Normal wolves could do no such thing, of course, but in that moment, my imagination was flooded with images of werewolves and sorcery, unsure as I was of the limits of the powers of the creatures that commanded the wolves. Or even whether what had attacked me was a wolf, or merely something in the shape of a wolf.

From the vantage point of the higher branches of the trees, I watched the wolf struggle to raise itself to its feet and limp over to the trunk of the tree. In any other circumstance, I would have felt pity, for it has always distressed me to see an animal in pain. But this creature wanted—nay, *needed*—my death. It glared upwards balefully, then threw back its head and howled.

The cry was clearly a summons, for another of its kind soon joined the beast. The second wolf was larger and obviously older, though no less powerful for its age. Its muzzle was white, and its coat was flecked with the same. But if anything, its age had merely added layers of strength and cunning and malignity, for it circled the tree with a hellish determination, its jaws snapping when it looked up to where I was perched.

I reached around for the bow tied to my back. It was not

broken, thank God. I could only guess my distance in relation to the creature on the ground, no longer pacing, but standing stock-still, waiting for me to fall out of the tree.

Carefully I fitted an arrow into the bow and took aim, remembering Askuwheteau's lessons from what seemed like an eternity ago. I squinted my eyes and willed the death of my prey. Then I pulled the string back as steadily as I could, and let the arrow fly.

The arrow struck the second wolf in the flank. It fell, lurching to the ground in stunned shock, yelped once, and kicked its legs as though it were running. Then there was silence as the wolf lay on its side, tongue lolling out of its maw.

The first wolf, the injured one, whined pitifully and licked its fellow as though trying to wake it. Ruthlessly, I forced down my pity. Climbing partway down, I took aim at the first wolf with my bow and the one remaining arrow. Snarling defiantly in spite of its broken ribs, it began to back away from the body of the second wolf as though to take shelter, its hate-filled yellow eyes not leaving mine for an instant. In the same moment it turned to run, I pulled back on the string and sent the arrow home.

The arrow transfixed the wolf through the thick of its neck. Its body went rigid and from its throat came a wet, choking sound, as though it were trying to bark, or scream, but could not. Blood gushed from its mouth. Its eyes rolled to one side and it collapsed on the ground near the body of the second wolf.

I exhaled audibly, surprising myself with the sound. I did not even realize I had been holding my breath. What I felt in that moment was more than the sin of pride or vanity, though it encompassed both of those things. I felt as though God Himself was guiding my hand, moving me ever closer to my goal. My robe was soaked with sweat, and it felt cold and damp against my back and chest in the chilling afternoon light.

I cast one last glance at the bodies of the two dead wolves, as though to assure myself that they were truly dead. There was no time to tarry. Squinting, my eyes explored the rock face, searching desperately for some clue.

And then, my heart suddenly felt as though it had ceased beating, and my breath caught again. My eye had been drawn to a patch of recessed shadow between two jutting promontories of rock a short distance above where I now stood. It appeared, even from the distance at which I stood, to be a sort of opening, or cave mouth.

Upon reaching it, I used the tinderbox to light the candle I had brought with me. Shielding the flame with my hand I squeezed myself through the portal of natural rock outcropping and found myself inside a space tall enough for me to stand without encumbrance.

By candlelight, the cavern seemed enormous, though that might have merely been an illusion caused by the twisting shadows. I felt along the cave walls, walking carefully in the near-darkness, for I knew that if I fell here, or was otherwise injured, one of two things would happen: I would either die of some combination of hunger, thirst, or my wounds, or worse still, I would become helpless to defend myself against the devils' depredations.

And then I made the discovery that has haunted both my nightmares and my waking hours for nearly twenty years. Even writing it now, tonight, I am overcome with the horror of my memory of it.

I cannot have gone any great distance into the cave, though it seemed like I must have, so smothering was the blackness, when I felt something move in the darkness. I say felt rather than heard, for there was no sound, but rather some displacement of the air above me. I raised the candle and looked up.

Hanging upside down, toes bent slightly for impossible purchase on the rock ledge, were the brother and sister I had met in the forest on the last night before my arrival at St. Barthélemy. Their arms folded against their bodies like wings.

The little boy was still naked. His legs wrapped around his sister's middle-section in a grotesque parody of vile, incestuous carnality. Hers were likewise entwined around his middle-section. Her dress had fallen downwards, and her maidenhead was plainly visible through her brother's spindly bronze legs.

And then I lowered the candle and looked down.

Strewn all around me lay the bodies of the Indians of St.

Barthélemy in similar positions of repose, or death. Their eyes were closed, their arms crossed against their bodies as though for warmth, or comfort. Their chests neither rose nor fell, nor did any sound of breathing issue from their mouths. I put the candle very near the face of one, a woman. Her face was calm, and oddly beautiful. The candle's light sculpted her high cheekbones with shadow. Her lips were full and voluptuous, and yet there protruded from those lips the sharp points of two white teeth, human in shape but somehow resembling the fangs of an animal.

I counted five, ten, fifteen of them in the immediate vicinity where I stood. There were doubtless more of them beyond the circle of my candlelight.

Holding my crucifix tightly in my hand, I nudged the woman's body with the tip of my boot. I braced for her to awaken, but again there was nothing. No sound, no movement, nothing to indicate that I was anywhere other than an ordinary tomb, surrounded by the natural dead.

Without thinking, I placed my hands under the woman's armpits, and tugged. Her body seemed very nearly weightless, certainly unlike any human body I had ever touched. It was as though, along with their souls, the curse that had been visited upon them had taken their physical heft. I glanced upwards at the two obscene children hanging by their toes from the ledge and wondered if this condition was what enabled them to suspend themselves in that manner.

The woman did not stir as I dragged her towards the opening of the cave. I was not sure what I would do with her once I brought her outside, but I had some vague memory of stories about these monsters' abomination of sunlight and was hoping that there might be some truth to it.

As I approached the entrance with my burden, the darkness of the cavern brightened until I could see the actual rock opening. I felt a shudder move through the woman's body, though she retained her sleeping posture and made no sound.

And then, as I stepped through the entrance to the cave, into the light, she awoke.

Her eyes flew open and she shrieked as though prodded with redhot iron tongs. Her mouth yawned open, exposing her full arsenal of sharp white teeth. The woman pulled away from me and began clawing at the ground as though to bury herself in the stone. Her screams rent the afternoon air, recalling to me the stories of the terrible witch burnings, and how the condemned women shrieked in the flames to which they had been sentenced.

For indeed, this Savage woman appeared to be burning alive in the sunlight.

In one second, her skin was clear and unblemished; in the next, it was festooned with enormous blisters that blossomed all over her body, seemingly all at once. The air was suddenly full of the smell of burning meat and something darker and fouler. White smoke poured from her body, rising from her limbs, her face, her hair, from any part of her that was exposed to the light. Still screaming, she looked at me with pleading, tortured eyes, and reached for me as though to beg my help, or at least my pity. In the instant our eyes met, I believe I saw her human soul, trapped in that terrible state between life and death and I knew that these creatures were not beyond the grace of God after all.

I crossed myself and gave her absolution, speaking the words "*Ego te absolvo a peccatis tuis in nomine Patris et Filii et Spiritus Sancti. Amen.*" Then I stepped back, for the air around her suddenly shimmered and began to burn. And in the next instant, her body exploded into flame. Boiling blood poured from her nose and throat, thick steam rising from it, the stench beyond foul.

The heat of fire that consumed the Savage woman's earthly flesh was not of this earth. In less than a minute, the flames had reduced the woman's body to ash, leaving no fragment of bone unconsumed, and the charnel house stink was everywhere.

This gruesome exercise I repeated twenty times or more, dragging each of these creatures to meet their second death, the final death, in the waning sunlight outside the cave. I blessed each one in its final moments as a soul to be saved and sent to its eternal rest in the arms of God. I absolved each one, for whatever their sins in life, this terrible end to which they came was not of their own choosing.

The two children, the brother and sister, I took last.

I carried them into the sunlight together, and they died together there. In their last moments, they seemed to again become children, innocent and trusting and terrified, and something in my soul died as they lay screaming in agony as the sun reduced their small, frail bodies to dust. It was children I saw being burned alive before my eyes, not monsters. The memory of it seared itself into my soul forever. Was I now a murderer of children? Was this the final curse that had been laid upon my head by the monster still inside the caves? Would God forgive me for this, even if I could never forgive myself?

All around me were smoking heaps of ash. My clothing was nearly white with it, and I knew it was in my hair and it burned in my eyes as well. I was grateful not to be able to see myself in a mirror at that moment, for I fear I would have seen a monster in my shape staring back at me through the glass.

The sun was dangerously low in the sky, and a cold wind had sprung up, scattering the smoking ash across the rock face and into the forest in spiralling whirlwinds. Around me, the shadows were beginning to lengthen in the forest, and I still had not found the author of all this grief. Resolutely, I turned back towards the cave, praying it would be for the last time.

I found the monster much farther back from the place where I'd found his flock, in a natural anteroom of sorts formed where the walls of the cave split off from the main section of the cavern. He lay upon a natural rising of rock, his arms folded across his chest in an aspect not unlike that of a stone-carved knight atop a sepulchre. His own noble ancestors in France, centuries dead, might have been buried inside a sarcophagus of that exact kind.

His face, by the light of the guttering candle, was beautiful. I cannot claim otherwise. It was the face of a handsome man in the latter prime of his life, with high cheekbones and well-formed features: a proud brow, and strong nose. It was the face of an aristocrat. Pale as death, he was, save for the redness of his lips. His mouth was half open and I shuddered at the length and sharpness of his terrible teeth.

But whereas the eyes of the others had been closed, his were open, fixed and staring into the darkness above his head.

I started in shock, but realized in an instant that he was no less immobilized by the sunlight than the others had been. I passed my hand in front of his eyes. He neither blinked nor gave any other sign that he was aware of my presence. Like the others, his chest neither rose nor fell, nor did breath issue from his mouth.

I yearned to drag him by his white hair along the cruel rocks of the cavern floor, but I feared, doubtless irrationally, that it might somehow wake him. Instead, I wedged the candle in a crevice, then placed my hands under him as I had the others, and half pulled, half carried him. Like the others, he was very nearly weightless.

The cave mouth was darker than it had been even a few minutes before. With a sinking heart, I realized the reason: the sun was setting. If it had not already set, it would set within minutes. I cried out to God and pulled harder, moving even more quickly through the gloom.

And then I felt a bony hand grasp my ankle, and sharp nails digging into the soft flesh there. It was too late, I thought. The sun had set, and the creature was awake.

I screamed and dropped Father de Céligny's body, backing away from it until my back was parallel with the cave wall next to the entrance. As I watched, he rose to his feet with a dreadful, majestic, malefic grace. For a moment, he stared at me, his eyes full of hate, then he lunged towards me, arms outstretched, his teeth bared like an animal. I ducked through the opening of the cave into the dark red setting sunlight.

"Come and get me, demon!" I shouted, looking into the cave. "I have killed your congregation and undone your work here. Look at the ashes of your children! If it is your plan to punish me for killing them, I am here, you coward! Do not hide in your hole like a snake! If you were once a man, show it now! Night has fallen; come fight me on your own terms!" It was a gamble, for there were still some streaks of redness in the sky, but I counted on the fact that traces of the monster's human vanity might have survived into its current state of existence.

De Céligny stepped through the entrance of the cave, into what was left of the sunset. There was a flash of light and the familiar abattoir smell of seared flesh. He shrieked and covered his face with his hands, stumbling backwards into the cave. When he removed his hands from his face, I could see that the skin was charred and blackened and smoking, as though he had fallen into an open fire. I held up my cross and stepped towards him. "Tonight you die, monster!" I cried out. "Tonight, one way or another, you will die! And if not tonight, then I will find you tomorrow wherever you hide and burn you in the sunlight like the beast you are!"

As I watched, from inside the shadows of the cave mouth, de Céligny lowered his head and closed his eyes. I saw his lips move, as though he recited a prayer, or an incantation of some sort. The sound of his voice carried across the space between us, though the words he whispered were unclear.

He opened his hands in the aspect of an invocation, extending his arms towards me, encompassing me, the forest behind me, even the night itself in his blessing.

Then he raised his head and began to laugh, a foul, cruel laugh entirely bereft of warmth, or joy, or indeed any human emotion, and stepped out of the cave into the new-fallen night. His eyes shone like rubies in the charred skull of his face, his teeth even longer and sharper than they had seemed mere moments before.

"We are coming for you, little priest," the creature said. "We are coming for you *now*."

Before I could reply, I heard the familiar hiss of an arrow in flight and felt the wind of it pass by my ear. The arrow struck Father de Céligny full in the chest. His eyes flew open in shock and pain. De Céligny grasped the arrow in his hands at the base in a vain attempt to pull it out of his body. He roared in fresh agony as a second arrow sang through the air, striking him just above the place where the first arrow had found purchase. Black blood streamed from the wound, drenching the front of his robe. His screams had risen in pitch to the point where he sounded more like an animal than something that had once been human.

Behind me I beheld a miracle the likes of which I had never dreamed I would see. It was an angel, or so it seemed, for Asku-wheteau stood there in the darkness with his bow and arrow, taking a third from his quiver and aiming it at the monster who writhed in its death throes in front of the cave that had lately been its living grave.

"Askuwheteau!" I cried, running to him. "You came back! My friend, you came back to me! How can I thank you? Praise God!"

I fell into his arms and embraced him, holding more tightly to him than I had ever held to my father, or my brother, or indeed any friend. In that moment, the love I felt for my friend was even more encompassing, I confess, than any other love, including my love of God.

My noble Savage friend gazed at me with something I dared to imagine was pride, and put his arm around my shoulders. He guided me to the place where the creature that had called itself Father de Céligny lay dying. Its body was crumbling before my eyes, passing into some sort of malodorous, smoking foulness.

Askuwheteau drew back his head and spit. The spittle landed on the creature's face. Askuwheteau said something in Algon-quian that sounded like a curse, then averted his face.

But as I stared at the dying creature, a curious thought came to me. Its last words had been, *We are coming for you, little priest. We are coming.*

And then, all around me, I saw the glimmer of what seemed like hundreds of yellow eyes, and I heard the sound of panting. The wolves were perched on the rocks above us; they circled us at the base of the rock face, and even more of them lay in wait beyond the tree line.

I felt, rather than saw, Father de Céligny die. His—or *its* spirit surely passed me in the blackness, leaving a trail of hate in its wake. And as if the trail of hate were a signal to the wolves, they sprang as one, it seemed, and surged up the hill to where Asku-wheteau, the *de facto* murderer of their master, stood.

In the face of my Savage friend I saw bafflement, and then, wonder of wonders, I saw terror. At that, my heart sank, for I knew that if brave Askuwheteau was in terror of his life, we were doomed. He backed away slowly from the deadly advance of the wolves.

He reached out with his arm as though to touch me, but I realized he was not seeking out my camaraderie. He was not seeking to die with me. He was seeking, even then, to save my worthless life.

Wordlessly, lest he hasten the inevitable coming assault from the wolves, he was frantically trying to communicate to me that I should run, that I should save myself.

And to my eternal shame, run I did, back to the mouth of the cave where I crouched behind the stinking, smouldering ashes of the monster whose power to ordain our bloody murder seemed to survive even its own apparent death. I knew somehow that the wolves would not dare approach the remains of their master.

My saviour Askuwheteau stood proud before the advancing horde of wolves. Even as he recognized the inevitability of his own horrible, coming death, his face was impassive.

And then he began to sing.

After a short time, the only sound was the ripping of flesh and gristle, and the terrible crunching of Askuwheteau's bones in the gore-clotted maws of the wolves. They peeled the skin off his face with their teeth and tore his limbs from their sockets the way kitchen dogs might fight over a soup bone. When they had finished their awful work, there was nothing identifiably human in Askuwheteau's remains.

They licked the bits of flesh still clinging to his bones with a horrible delicateness, as though it were a special treat being passed to them under the table by an indulgent master.

By then, night had fallen to such a degree that Askuwheteau's blood soaking the ground was black in the rising moonlight, and the wolves themselves looked like ghouls squatting over an open grave devouring a freshly dead corpse.

They raised their heads then, and looked at me, growling low in their throats.

I closed my eyes and fell to my knees, hands clasped in front of me. I prayed to the Blessed Virgin that my death would be pleasing in God's sight, and that it would be over quickly, and with as little pain as possible. Or, if that were not God's will, that I be granted as much strength to endure it as He had granted Askuwheteau.

But the wolves did not attack. Instead, they loped over to where the arrow-pierced skeleton of Father de Céligny lay on a bed of rocky soil and fallen leaves. They circled it, tentatively sniffing the pile of smoking bones, but giving it a wide enough berth to suggest they feared that the ossified remains might yet be something alive, something hellishly vivid that could hurt them as no bullet or arrow could.

Then, as though it had burned them, they leaped back from the pile of bones, cowering like mangy curs before a master's whip. As one, they threw back their heads and howled. My poor words here cannot do justice to the effect of that unearthly, haunting sound as it rose into the night and fell down upon the tableau in which I knelt. Then the wolves turned and bounded into the forest without looking back, not aimlessly, but as if they were being pursued by a hunter and were in search of safety.

Again, I was alone—truly and utterly alone. I mourned my Indian friend Askuwheteau, this man whom I had dismissed as a Judas and a Savage, but who had shown the courage and faithfulness to come back to a place he feared in order to secure my safety. In all truth, he had saved my life, and he had died in my place. The tears I wept that night for Askuwheteau were the bitterest of my life, and none I've shed in the long years since that night have been harsher or more absinthial.

I drew the sign of the cross over what remained of his poor mauled face, and bowed my head. "Eternal rest grant unto thy servant Askuwheteau, O Lord," I prayed. "And let perpetual light shine upon him. Grant him absolution, O Lord. May he rest in peace. Amen."

Feeling my way through the darkness, I walked back to the village. I knew that there were perhaps more of these demons hiding in the forest watching me, but I cared little of it, so heavy was I with the weight of grief and guilt. If the Devil and his minions had been so able to use a priest as a vessel to serve his will as he had with Father de Céligny, then my life, and my immortal soul, were in God's hands, as they always had been. But my work that night was far from over.

Inside the Jesuit house, I found a torch of cedar and pitch. I lit the torch, then put a second torch in my bag. There was a shovel leaning against one wall. The heft of it gave me comfort, for I believed I could make a decent weapon of it if it came to that.

The path back to the caves through the trees was easier this time because of the light of the torch. Easier in one sense, for the path was well-lit and I made good progress. Harder in another, for I now knew, beyond any measure of a doubt, what monsters, earthly and unearthly, could hide outside that ring of torch-light.

Upon arriving at the caves, I saw that the two piles of bones were as I had left them. The first pile, the remains of my poor Askuwheteau, I would bury. Though it was against the customs of his people to lay them beneath the earth, Askuwheteau had fought and died as bravely as any Christian, and it was only natural that he be buried as one. I lamented the fact that I had not had the chance to baptize him before he died so horribly. After I had completed my most pressing task, I swore to him that I would attend to his burial with due reverence.

The second pile of bones, the bones of de Céligny, I approached with dread. I pushed the torch close to the charred skeleton. At first I doubted the proof of my own eyes, for it surely seemed as though the creature whose body I had watched crumble and dissolve once pierced by the arrow would have found some way to render itself vivid once again.

And yet, as I said, it was where I'd left it, and as I left it. I wedged the base of the torch between two boulders and, by its guttering light, I surveyed the grotesque thing.

I raised the shovel over my head and brought it down squarely across the neck, severing the skull from the body with a single blow.

In my hubris and vanity, I half-expected to hear a sound, perhaps a scream from beyond the shadow of the Valley, or the trumpets of angels and the beating of their wings as they celebrated my triumph over the forces of Darkness. But there was nothing save the sound of the wind high in the trees that danced in the moonlight.

Using the shovel, I scooped the dreadful mix of bones and ash into my bag. I lit the second torch by the fire of the one wedged between the boulders and by its light I made my way to the mouth of that abhorrent place, carrying my ghastly burden in my other hand. To say that the blackness of the cave was forbidding by daylight is to render the description of it at night, by torchlight, almost beyond possibility.

Deeper and deeper into the cavern's depths I went, the aureole of torchlight illuminating only the area immediately around it. The silence was the silence of the grave. No sound broke that silence; no sounds save for that of my feet on the rock and, from far away in its recesses, the steady drip of water on stone. The weight of the bag seemed to grow heavier with every step I took into that obsidian blackness.

And then, suddenly, there was a sound. I stopped in my tracks, straining to identify what I heard, or what I only thought I'd heard. My torch sputtered and for one terrible moment, the fire burned low as though some wind had blown it out.

In that moment, as the darkness swam towards me, I heard the sound again. It was the sound of breathing—not my own, but coming from somewhere in the lightless recesses of the cave. And then I felt the horrible dead heft of the bag twitch against my leg as though there were something inside it, trapped, but still alive.

I screamed and dropped the bag on the floor of the cavern. Wildly I swung the dying torch in front of me. The low-burning flame revealed only the walls of the cave, appearing and vanishing like a chimera with every sweep of the torch. And the sound of breathing was no more, if indeed it had ever been.

I brought the torch, which again blazed to life, close to the bag containing the bones of Father de Céligny and bent down to examine it. The sweat soaked my hair and ran down into my eyes, but when I wiped it away with the back of my hand, and squinted to see, the bag was where I had dropped it, and it was still, unmoving.

Had I imagined it? Had the nightmare sensation of carrying a trapped animal that had been merely stunned, but was waking, been nothing more than a phantasm born of my terror? I had no answer but this: that the bag was not moving and my torch would not burn forever. I had to do what I had to do; I had to hide the remains of this monster where they would never be found, where no human hands would soil themselves with the contagion it represented. I crossed myself and pushed farther into the cave.

I have only a blind man's reckoning of how much farther and deeper into the cave, and then underground, I went before I found what I was looking for—a natural recession in the rock, oblong and shaped like an sarcophagus, surely carved by centuries of natural erosion, a natural coffin for my most unnatural and unwholesome freight. Surely here, in the wildest, darkest part of this wild, dark wilderness, the bones of this monster would remain unmolested till the end of time.

I placed the bag into the recession and covered it with the weight of some of the large stones and boulders I found scattered about. The work was arduous and the rocks were heavy, and by the time I placed the last one on top of the makeshift grave, my hands were bleeding with my exertion. I wiped my hands on the robe, leaving the traces of my stigmata on the coarse fabric.

Then, taking up the torch again, I turned and began to retrace my steps through the blackness. After an eternity, I came to the mouth of the cave. I wept joy when I saw the glimmer of the first torch, the one I'd left outside the cave, wedged between the rocks.

From the position of the moon in the sky, I ascertained that I had been about my mission for the better part of the night, though dawn was still a few hours away. I took up the shovel and began to dig. By the time I had dug a grave deep enough to bury Askuwheteau, the sky had begun to lighten in the distance, pale violet streaks, and dark blue lifting from the blackness like celestial foam on a wave.

I laid his body reverently into the grave. I was surprised to find that I still had tears in me left to shed, but I did, and I shed them there as I covered his body with the dark, flinty soil upon which he had so bravely died. I bowed my head and prayed for the progression of his immortal soul on its journey towards the Light of God.

And then, from overhead, came a sound like the flapping of giant sails in a strong wind.

In the light of the torch, the creature dropped from some unknown height. As it landed, crouching like an animal about to spring, I had a brief, vivid impression of giant, unfolded wings, but the wings seemed to melt away, leaving in their place a pair of thick, muscled arms. Its head was bowed, and long dark hair streamed from its scalp like a black halo.

When it stood, I saw that it was of vast height, taller than any Savage I had encountered, but Savage it was—or, rather, Savage it had been in its original, God-ordained life. Now, reborn, its eyes burned with that familiar crimson fire and its teeth were deadly and terrible. From that mouth issued a high, shrill whistle that was human in neither pitch nor form, but somehow communicated a fierce, inhuman hunger that would, I realized, brook no denial.

Instinctively, I lifted my torch in my own defence as it leaped. The effect upon the creature was instantaneous. To my wonder, the thing retreated, as though terrified by the fire. Emboldened, I advanced on it with the torch. It screamed in rage and continued to recoil. I expected any moment for it to shift its shape, as I had seen these things do. I knew that if it did transform itself, it would effect an escape.

The thought filled me with terrible, righteous rage. In that moment, I saw it as the incarnation of all the pain and fear I had encountered since arriving in that Godforsaken spot. Now, worse still, it had even profaned the site of Askuwheteau's grave. With an oath, I shoved my torch in the creature's face.

Its hair exploded into flame. Shrieking in agony, the thing clawed at its face and hair attempting to put out the fire. Alas, for the creature, the fire only burned brighter and hotter, spreading to its face and arms by some supernatural providence.

The demon flung out its arms in an aspect of crucifixion, and before my eyes its body appeared to shimmer, dwindling and yet appearing to stretch, but becoming smaller. The arms elongated, becoming as the wings of a bird, or an enormous bat, beating furiously as it rose into the night, still burning, still transforming as it took flight into the darkness like a fireball streaking towards the village of St. Barthélemy. My eyes followed its upward trajectory for a few seconds, and then watched in awe as it crashed to the earth. Its screams as it fell to its death—or what I prayed was its death—were the pitiable lamentations of a damned thing.

But by then, my only emotion was joy, and I delighted in the foul creature's death, a death I prayed had been agonizing beyond endurance.

And then, like a benediction, the air was full of snow, falling in heavy flakes as pure white as the wings of any angel, and in the red light of dawn's advance in the east, winter was upon me with a hunter's killing stealth.

On the edge of the village, the spectral shapes formed themselves out of the falling snow, moving wraithlike towards me. Exhausted, starving, blind with sweat, drenched in dried blood, I fell to my knees and accepted my death, for I was beyond fighting further, beyond the ability to endure any more of these horrors. When they reached for me, I closed my eyes and commended my spirit into the hands of Almighty God, and waited for the end.

And then I heard the sound of human voices speaking in a language I did not understand. Warm hands touched my face and my own hands. Strong arms lifted me and bore me aloft, carrying me through the deserted village. The snow continued to fall in a heavy sheet of cold, cleansing white. My eyelids fluttered and the light swam.

Before I lost consciousness and yielded to the tide of new darkness rushing towards me, I smelled the awful stink of burning flesh, and something worse. I looked down and saw the smouldering remains of the monster I had burned with my torch.

It had not survived the fire. Perhaps it had died attempting to cast off its shape, attempting to return to its human aspect. Its body was manlike in shape, but where its arms would have been were the webbed wings of a giant bat, ending in human hands with nails that were like the claws of a great Oriental tiger. Its face was a half-human, half-basilisk nightmare.

I turned my head away from the abomination lying on the ground, already beginning to be covered by the falling snow. Around me, I saw that some of the men were setting fire to the village. I heard the crackle of wood and smelled new smoke.

A wave of heat came to me, and my first thought was to stretch towards it. I cannot tell with any certainty as I write this if my impulse was to throw myself on the growing pyre, or merely to warm myself by it. And then, my eyes closed and I yielded to the mercy of complete insensibility.

When I awoke, though I had no bearings, I sensed that I was very far from that haunted place. I was on a sort of sledge, wrapped in furs. Above me the trees were heavy with snow, and we were moving silently through the endless, damnable forest that binds this Godforsaken country like a slave's chain.

The Indians cared for me with a mercy and a tenderness that put Christian charity to shame. I travelled with them to their winter hunting grounds and lived as their guest and under their protection for the long months of ice and snow. In time, I came to understand that they regarded me as some sort of deliverer, and in exchange for that delivery, they were prepared to extend to me an acceptance that I would, as a Black Robe, never otherwise experience.

I heard the word "Weetigo" many times. It was a word I knew well, though I knew none of the others they spoke. It was the word I had first heard in Trois-Rivières from the drunkard Dumont, and then later from my saviour Askuwheteau, who died that I might live. I understand the word now, as an old man who has spent his life among these people, in a way I could not have understood it as a young man.

To my shame, I believe that the Savages who rescued me believed I had defeated just such a monster in St. Barthélemy, for they saw the remains of the demon creature that had fallen from the sky wreathed in fire. In it, they had seen the incarnation of their most terrifying legend; in a sense, I had made their word flesh.

At that time, I had not the words to explain to them that what they had seen was not what they called a "Weetigo," but rather something that we ourselves had brought from the Old

World to the New. I suspect that the scarcity of those words likely saved my life, for I could not have answered for their rage if they had known the truth of what Father de Céligny, or whatever the monster's real name was, had wrought there.

That they saw me as a saviour instead of merely an extension of the same corruption that destroyed an entire village of souls— a village of innocent men, women, and children, who died without the blessing of baptism and God's mercy, suited my cowardly purposes, though I wept with shame and grief and guilt that winter when I was alone.

In my nightmares that winter, I revisited that terrible day when I dragged the sleeping bodies of those poor creatures into the sunlight and listened to their agonized screaming as the sunlight turned them to ash, especially the children. It haunts me that I never discovered if they could have been saved, or returned to their natural state, and if my actions had been a mercy, or merely an extension of the blasphemy.

In the spring, the Indians passed me on to a brigade of *voyageurs* who, by some miracle, knew of me and my mission to rescue Father de Céligny and return him to Trois-Rivières. Perhaps in anticipation of a reward, or perhaps only out of charity and a sense of fellowship with another white man, the voyageurs returned me to Trois-Rivières and the embrace of our Jesuit headquarters there.

Father de Varennes wept with joy, for he had counted me as dead. Together we praised God and the tender mercies of the Blessed Virgin for my safe return from the perils of the wilderness and the incivility of the Savages. We said a Mass for Father de Céligny, our most recent blessed martyr to the barbarous cruelty of the Savages.

As we said that Mass, Askuwheteau's face rose up in my mind like an unquiet, reproachful ghost. I added a silent prayer for his forgiveness for all the lies I was about to tell.

I told Father de Varennes that the Indians had left me near the site of St. Barthélemy. I told him that I had made my way to the mission and had found it burned to the ground.

I told him I had a sense that a rival tribe, perhaps even the Hiroquois, had slaughtered everyone in the village and left the carrion for the wild animals. I told him that I had found bodies and that I had buried them. I told him I had not found the body of Father de Céligny. I told him that I had thrown myself at the mercy of the Savages who found me, and that I had paid them with gold I had found buried beneath the remains of the Jesuit house.

Even as I told those lies, I realized that the winter snow and ice would have obliterated any possible evidentiary challenge to my account, even if it were doubted, which it was not. Who would doubt the word of a priest, especially one who had survived such an ordeal?

I covered myself in shame by blaming the Savages for the massacre of the settlement of St. Barthélemy when I knew that what happened to all of those poor people was something that we, the French had brought into their midst, something that corrupted and afflicted them, and eventually killed them.

More than anything, I told the lies to prevent anyone from ever returning to the site of the Mission of St. Barthélemy and discovering the secret that I buried in those caves eighteen years ago.

I am dying now, Your Reverence. I have asked for Father Vimont, who comes shortly to collect this document for your perusal, but also to give me Last Rites and absolve me for my sins, which have been many.

My body burns with fever from the pox. I fear that the very effort of writing to you this last Relation has hastened my inevitable commendation of my soul to Christ. This Relation is my confession of the things I did, but it is also as I said my true Testament of the things I saw with my own eyes, and I swear to it on peril of my Immortal Soul.

I know that some who read it will think it the ravings of a madman in the last deliria of fever. I pray that Your Reverence will not number among them, and that you will be able to see into my heart and know that I speak the truth in this Relation.

Reverend Father, I have lived as a Jesuit, and I die a faithful one. Our way is not the way of ignorance and superstition, but rather of wisdom and learning. And yet, I realize now how much

I had yet to learn, and how dangerous was the arrogance I had brought with me from France to this New World. I do not doubt the glory of our work among the Savages, and yet in these final hours of my life, I am plagued by questions and doubts. I realize it is not my place to question.

But I ponder, Reverend Father, and I pray for wisdom. And I pray for your forgiveness, and for God's, for the burden of these doubts.

I have watched these poor people shrivel and die from mysterious illnesses they have blamed on what they call our sorcery. They claim we brought the pox to them. They claim that it did not exist in their world before we arrived. We have wrapped them in our blankets to comfort them, and watched them die, praying for a conversion before death claimed them, a baptism before they breathed their last. We have given them Christian names, and we have buried them under those names. We teach them to reject their customs and beliefs. We teach them to believe they are ignorant and lost for believing in their world of spirits and oracle, while we hold the belief that the Devil has them in his thrall.

And yet, Reverend Father, may God forgive me, I believe I have seen the Devil walking in the forests of New France. But— O, blasphemy of blasphemies! He wore the same robe I wear, and his mission and legacy was a most wicked one. While I pray that I was somehow, through my sad efforts, able to halt the spread of that ungodly contagion, I am haunted by the words of the drunkard Dumont, words I have heard in my nightmares for eighteen years.

Dumont said: *There are worse things now walking in the forests at night than the Savages.*

In light of what I have witnessed, I have searched my poor ignorant soul to know, beyond a doubt, that we do God's work here. Yea, and that we have brought these people Light and not more darkness. But my soul is silent. Around me, the Indians die, either at our hand, or at least beyond our ability to save them.

If I have committed blasphemy here, I beg for God's mercy

and forgiveness, and for Your Reverence's prayers after I am gone. But the account contained in this Relation is true, and I die as I have lived, as Christ's most humble servant, and Your Reverence's.

Ad majorem Dei gloriam.
Fr. Alphonse Nyon of the Society of Jesus
Montréal, Québec, 1650

ACKNOWLEDGMENTS

First and foremost, my deepest thanks for Brett Savory and Sandra Kasturi of ChiZine publications, the original publisher of *Enter, Night*.

Special thanks to my supremely patient and nurturing agent, Sam Hiyate of The Rights Factory, for his belief in my work, and his unflagging support of it.

I'm grateful to my great friend, former teacher, and former St. John's headmaster, Fred Parr, who inculcated in me a fascination for Canadian history in the classroom when I was a teenager, and later shared with me what it was like to grow up in northern Ontario in the early '70s, as well as some of the folklore of the region. He also read through part of this manuscript, pronounced it worth pursuing, and allowed me to name a town full of vampires after him—not a bad endorsement, all told.

Thanks to my friend, Elliot Shermet, who let me borrow his first name and physical appearance to create Elliot McKitrick (but not his character or personality, which is infinitely admirable, certainly more so than his fictive counterpart).

I was very fortunate to have had an extraordinary young writer named Stephen Michell as a research assistant on this project. I am even more fortunate that we became friends over the course of working together on *Enter, Night*. I look forward to reading Mr. Michell's own novels in the future, and so will you. Remember his name—you heard it here first, which is my great honour and privilege.

My friend, author and screenwriter Robert Thomson, generously read through the manuscript of *Enter, Night* at every point in its evolution and offered his usual superb editorial insights, as well as talking me down from the ledge more than once. My gratitude to him for his kindness is beyond measure, as is my admiration.

I'd like to thank the powerhouse women of my writer's group, the Bellefire Club—Sandra Kasturi, Helen Marshall, Sephera Giron, Nancy Baker, Halli Villegas, and Gemma Files, accomplished authors, all—who read part of the seventeenth-century section of the novel, offering insightful advice and encouragement.

On a purely personal note, Christopher Wirth and Barney EllisPerry are my two oldest friends, and they've been agitating for this book since I was using an electric typewriter, as has Werner Warga.

And Ron Oliver, my constant partner in crime—he's the one who knows where all the bodies are buried.

Thanks to Steward Noack for always making New York feel like home to me; Thane MacPherson for his constancy; Chuck Gyles for getting the ball rolling that day in the car on the way home from Kitchener; Michael Thomas Ford and Sephera Giron always picked up the phone; and my dear friend Eliezenai Galvao kept the home fires burning during the writing of it; Mark Wheaton remains a personal hero as well as one of my most precious friends; Helen Marshall kept vigil and wielded a dexterous editorial scalpel; and Helen Oliver— my "second mum"—always seemed to know just when to call with encouragement and love. So did Tabatha Southey, who came bearing cocktails and *divertissements*.

Likewise, immeasurable thanks to my great friend, J. Marc Côté, for too many reasons to list here.

I'd like to acknowledge my father, Alan Rowe, and my stepmother, Sarah Doughty, a very great lady who came late into my life, but who has left an indelible impression on my heart.

I would also like to acknowledge my late mother, Helen Hardt Rowe, who bought me a paperback copy of *Dracula* at ten, and my first typewriter at eleven, but never told me what I could or couldn't write on it. I think she would have been proud of *Enter, Night,* vampires or not.

Lastly, to Brian McDermid, my husband, who makes all things possible, and to Shaw Madson, the heart of our family—this book belongs to you, offered with my love and thanks.

ABOUT THE AUTHOR

Michael Rowe was born in Ottawa, and has lived in Beirut, Havana, Geneva, and Paris. He is the author of the novels *Enter, Night*; *Wild Fell*; and *October*; and created and edited the anthologies *Queer Fear* and *Queer Fear 2*. An award-winning journalist and essayist, Rowe is also the author of the nonfiction books *Writing Below the Belt*, *Looking for Brothers*, and *Other Men's Sons*. He has won the Lambda Literary Award, the New Millennium Writing Award, and the Publishing Triangle Award; and was a finalist for the National Magazine Award, the International Horror Guild Award, the Sunburst Award, and the Shirley Jackson Award. Rowe lives in Toronto and welcomes readers at www.michaelrowe.com.